One Little Word

T. A. Peters

Text Copyright © 2015 by T. A. Peters
Cover by The Cover Collection
TheCoverCollection.com

Published by Greenefisher Publications™
Sarasota, Florida USA
GreenefisherPublications.com

One Little Word simultaneously
published in e-book format.
First print edition: January 2016
First e-book edition: January 2016

Contact the author:
E-mail: TAPeters@GreenefisherPublications.com
Twitter handle: @TAPetersAuthor

ISBN-13: 978-0-692-59601-2

ISBN-10: 0-692-59601-1

For Susan. Always in spirit.

One Little Word

'This it is, that was in the kirk in wildirnes, with the angele
that spak to him in the mont Syna, and with our fadris;
quhilk tuke wordis of lijf to geue to vs.'
-The Actes of The Apostles, chaptur vii: verse xxxviii
From *The New Testament in Scots* (translated in 1520)

Saturday, 18 April 1896

Hunger formed like squares in her stomach.

Since her earliest memories, the round things of life brought the peace she so sought. She knew so little, but she knew her shapes. Circles and rounded edges were good, and squares and sharp angles were bad. Soft lines were the way of nature; only man forced things into boxes.

'We're going to church,' her Mama had said.

She didn't understand what that meant, but then Mama supplied: 'A church in the wilderness.'

There were only so many words she knew, and though she couldn't form them with her mouth, she recognised the few she had learned within the silence of her mind when she heard them. The words strung together, one after another, like the pearls on Mama's necklace. Wilderness was followed in line by trees, and then came nature, and so the place they were going must be soft, and therefore good.

They rode in a wagon for the longest time, bumping along beneath a thick canopy of branches and leaves. Then the vehicle stopped and Mama rose, carrying her down a wooded path with just enough width between the trunks for a single person to walk down.

She reached up and clutched the strand of pearls around Mama's neck with her little fingers as in the light of the newly risen sun her mother carried her further into the trees, into the wilderness, and everything was good until she saw the building. This 'church' was nothing but one great square made by men.

Once inside, for a time she buried her face in her mother's bosom, for there she found comfort, and peace, the very fount of her belief in the sanctity of round things. But then they took her away.

Pulled apart from her mother, she could only see eyes in every corner of the square staring at her. And then, surrounded by a rainbow of colours, came a woman in white. They called her an angel. She had the feathered wings of a bird and wore strands of gold and glittering jewels about her neck.

The tension made sharp angles in the air, and she wanted to cry, yet the roundness of the angel's eyes calmed her. Then there were these words, spoken gently by the woman in white:

'This child needs no healing, for Almighty God has made her perfect already.'

Then there was trouble.

She didn't understand. She only knew that Mama was upset.

There was discord in the square. She felt the distress of those around her the same as pain within her very bones. They were yelling, and fighting. In the confusion she simply walked unsteadily away.

She set out through the trees and would have been happy to be among the natural. Only now it wasn't a question of location, for the square was within her making her stomach hurt like the time she ate a round, yellow flower, thinking its shape made it all right to consume.

For a time she wandered unsteadily and alone, the squares growing within her. And then two people came. She was scared of the tall, straight one in brown, but the woman in green reminded her of Mama. The woman let the child put her face to her bosom, and there she was the same. Soft and round and warm.

The sharp angles seemed to flee from her then, and for a time, peace reigned. So comforted was she by the natural roundness that she didn't even realise they were taking her directly back to the big square in the wilderness.

2 September 1936

My dearest daughter-
　　After three weeks of isolation, cruived up in my wee room without so much as one human countenance to look upon with my eyes, The Doctor returned yestreen to report to me the results of the Games of the XI Olympiad held at Berlin. Apparently it was quite the propagandistic success since it effectively demonstrated, at least to the goose-steppers' satisfaction, how superior the Nordics are in sporting events. I stifled a yawn as The Doctor recited the medal count for the third *Deutsches Reich*, and he returned my impertinence by pointedly changing the subject when I speired after the American Jesse Owens' showing during the Grecian festival. This exchange probably set a poor precedent for the next week's worth of our socialising, for after making a brief, taciturn review of my auto-biographical writings scribbled out during his absence, The Doctor abruptly left the room and I have not seen him since. Thus I continue on alone, picking up right where I left off, contemplating all of the days of my youth so as to set down my works, both good and evil. My only distraction in my task is when the lift of the dumb waiter sets down with my tray of food twice a day. I often ignore it, and in an hour's time I hear it being drawn back up again for my unseen Captors to dispose of.
　　In light of the present political climate here in Europe which threatens to consume entire nations of people, I am reminded of the many times in my life that I have known the masses to be led astray by only a few persons claiming to have their best interests at heart. The

circumstances I am about to consign to paper relating to the small village of Bela, which, forty years ago, sat hidden among the palms, oaks and pines of Florida, is exemplary of how the many, no matter what their backgrounds or where they came from, can justify to themselves the need to simply fall in line and ignore the evil surrounding them for the sake of not making waves in an otherwise tranquil ocean. I can count myself among them, for in my younger days I was just the same in my desire for smooth sailing at any cost. It was only when I once glimpsed the terrible price paid by the innocent that I knew I could never live with myself unless I intervened. The auto-biographical account I now begin to write is the story of my taking another step forward in becoming a woman-grown as I continued my maturation from frightened bairn to steadfast adult, only to finally be surpassed by whatever it is I have now become.

Throughout my seventeenth year, though I had made the decision of which side of the worldly fence I wanted to stand on, many of my actions were still ruled by fear, and as was often the case, this timidity was rooted in the dread of learning something more about myself, for both my eldritch ways and altogether queer nature were still a source of worry for me. Although I had consciously made the choice to allow Abigail to lead me into the grooves for which the particular notches of my soul were made, as yet I was unable to stay on track at all times. I was still learning to accept myself then, and truth be told, am still gaining in daily self-knowledge even now, four decades later.

In her younger days, Abigail was the sort of person who thought a lass was only to be tested once within a lifetime, and that having passed that test, all would be smooth sailing from there on out. Having only unfurled our sails that very morning as we escaped the town of Loggerhead, even I expected troubles to keep at bay for a time. Unfortunately, we wouldn't even come close to being safe from the storm until we made port at the peaceful harbour of Greenhaven. In Loggerhead, together we had been shown the fire once, but as we were about to discover, though our purification would still be far from complete, we were about to be scorched again.

  As for my current situation, in remaining a model inmate in the present day, giving no real trouble of any kind to my Captors, I have stayed true to my word, and presuming that They keep Their half of the agreement, then I hope this letter will find you, sooner or later, in the best of health. I trust in you to follow my commandment not to leave safety, and not to attempt to intervene on my behalf. I have a little time left in my lifespan, and if I work swiftly I should complete the writing of those queer, younger years of my life prior to your birth which I remained silent on for so long a spell. You are a woman-grown now, and can not only handle the whole truth, but deserve to know it.

Your loving Ma

I

Sunday, 19 April 1896, 4:05 PM

We were in the back of a horse-drawn cart, sharing the shyte-covered straw with a massive sow and her litter. I was sitting up in the corner, facing towards the rear, with our single piece of luggage, an old carpetbag, crammed behind my back to provide some cushion against the birsing of my spine produced by the rocking and swaying of two rickety axles, four unbalanced wheels, and a muddy roadway alternately baked hard by the sun and flooded by the recent tropical rains which are so common to Florida in the springtime.

My lass was sitting between my legs, and for the first few moments of our journey near dawn, she had remained awake to make comment on how delightful she thought the piglets were, though I reasoned that was only so long as I kept her physically separated from them with my long legs.

As Abigail began to dover on account of her exhaustion at having been kept up all night, I considered the advisability of pointing out that the cute beasties, seemingly already mud-stained black on the bottom half of their bellies and trotters, were the progenitors of the pork products she so often enjoyed for breakfast. I never have gloried in making light of such issues since, despite being a life-long vegetarian, I felt it somewhat sanctimonious of myself to try to reconcile for the meat-eaters the fact that such living creatures were one and the same with what appeared on their supper plates. It is a quirk of my character that opening my mouth on the subject has always felt to my own lugs to present myself as overly self-righteous, and so I prefer to lead by example. Only I have to admit that rarely seems to work very well.

Such thoughts swirled about in my ken as the sun beat down upon us, our only consistent shade being supplied by the wide brim of my cocoanut leaf hat. Trees occasionally provided relief, but we oftentimes passed through wide stretches without their cover, and as the sun began to bake us through, I started to nod off myself. It was somewhere within the realm of dreams that the lower consciousness of my mind suggested it was time for us to step out of the cart.

When my eyes opened as the result of a particularly rough jarring, I turned to look over my shoulder at the driver, Mr Cartwright, who sat on the box behind me facing away towards the front. Knowing little of the man, it occurred to me that we might not want to let him know precisely where my lass and I were getting off to since we preferred to keep our terminal destination of Greenhaven a secret.

This secrecy was, of course, naturally part of the charm of living in a hidden town where the people bide by their own rules. But there was more to it than just that. Recent events, in fact so recent as just that morning, had brought us lassies to the attention of the local sheriff, and while I felt secure in the righteousness of our actions, I didn't wish to be speired the sort of questions that had no answers good enough for the lugs of the law. An unfortunate circumstance of being a resident of Greenhaven was that, with rare exception, the townspeople tend to have no legal standing according to the citizenship laws of the mainland, and for that reason, one of the unwritten rules attendant to our privacy was that one never drew unnecessary attention to the town.

In my mind, made somewhat feverish by the overwhelming radiance of the sun, I saw our recent actions to form a chain of which, link by link, we should wish to separate ourselves from where we had just been, which was in a small coastal town called Loggerhead, and where we wished to be, which was Abigail's hometown of Greenhaven, situated just off the coast on its own isle. We had broken the first, most obvious link by quietly escaping from beneath our friends' noses in the dark to quietly ride out of town in the back of a cart full of swine, and now something deep within my subconscious mind told me we had reached the next length to be severed. Based on earlier statements of Mr Cartwright as to how long and how far we had to travel, I had been estimating at what point we should make our exit from his cart so as to have the least distance to cover by foot while still maintaining some amount of discretion as to our destination. I reasonably decided that we had reached that point in our journey together, more or less, and decided to act appropriately.

For a few ticks I considered how to quietly get us out of the vehicle so that we might simply disappear into the trees and then make our own way the rest of the distance by walking, only an obvious circumstance presented in which we could easily make our exit with the least fuss. From what little I knew of Mr Cartwright, he was so taciturn and set in his ways that suggesting any alteration in his agenda was likely to be met with a rebuff. We had already experienced that attitude upon first boarding the cart when I speired if Abigail might ride on the box next to the driver himself instead of laying in the bed with a pile of piglets. This question had been incomprehensible to Mr Cartwright. Clearly his bearded sheepdog always rode next to him on the box, and I might as well have speired him to extinguish the sun until noon in consideration of the delicacy of my lassie's porcelain skin for all the sense I made to him.

I looked up just in time to see that there was a turnoff to our left, which as we were heading south would effectively lead out to the east. I said over my shoulder, 'Mr Cartwricht, we need to gae on that turnaff a ways if ye dinna mind dreeving us.'

His head whipped around and he glared at me as he said, 'I'm headin' south to Venice, Mr Fisher. I've got pigs to deliver.'

I reasonably replied, 'That is weel, sir. If ye could stop the cart, then, my wife and I will get oot here and walk the rest of the way.'

This request irked him nearly so much as the notion of turning off his normal route, but after looking to his dog and apparently finding the correct answer within a pair of agreeable canine eyes, he sighed and drew up on the reins.

When the horse halted, and the cart suddenly came to a stop, Abigail jolted awake in my arms and sleepily speired, 'Are we there already?'

'Na, na, lass. This is as close as we are gang to get.'

We spent a moment getting up and out of the cart, deftly making our way among the squealing piglets, while Mr Cartwright watched our actions with impatience. I stepped down, then helped Abigail out, and upon her new derby shoes safely hitting the sand, I went to dig a dollar out of my coat to hand over to Mr Cartwright for the favour of allowing us the ride, only he instantly whipped up the horse and pulled away from us so fast I didn't even have time to drop the bill over the splashboard to land in and among the swine.

Abigail looked at the receding wagon and quietly said of the driver, 'Well, there was no need to be rude,' then turned to regard me with her tired eyes verdantly glowing green in the afternoon sun.

My lass didn't have to say a word to me. I already knew it was time to play the part of the gentleman who knows what he is about and where he is going. Reasoning that I had only a few ticks of the clock before her disgruntlement would rightfully set in, I quickly pocketed the single dollar, then took up the carpetbag in my left hand, and gently took Abigail's fingers in the other.

Mr Cartwright had wasted no time in making his way down the sandy roadway, and I didn't expect him to look back for an instant in consideration of his former passengers, so I immediately began walking my lass along the same southern route he had taken.

'Mm, how far do we have to walk, Mary?'

I looked back once to see that Abigail had closed her eyes. She was walking along blindly, letting me lead her by hand.

I said, 'Nae muir than a few miles, I'm certain, based on what Mr Cartwricht said earlier.'

Abigail's eyes opened at that and that disapproving look crossed her countenance immediately. 'A couple of miles? Are you in earnest?'

I turned my gaze ahead and said, 'Aye, lass. I'm sorry, but I didna want that man to ken waur we are gang. After the mess we left ahint in Loggerhead, the sheriff's gang to be aboot speiring questions for a while, and I dinna want Mr Cartwricht to be able to tell exactly waur we got aff to when he returns to toun. So far as he kens, we're heading aff to the east, into the mainland, the noo.'

'Well, how prudent, Mary,' she coolly said. I didn't reply.

A moment later when I turned to look over my shoulder at her, she had again closed her eyes and appeared to be walking in her sleep as I drug her along behind me.

* * *

There was a general clearing of the trees at the turnoff. To the east we could see distant farmlands, cotton on the high lands, small rice fields, with the attendant winnowing barns on stilts, in the low lying areas where it tended to flood, and orderly orchards of citrus trees surrounding houses and outbuildings. To the west we could see the Gulf, a nearly flat plane of water stretching to infinity for all the eye could see. Then as we walked further south, the palms and pines began to edge in towards the road. After about half a mile of walking, the trees were so dense that their vine-covered trunks effectively concealed the views both east and west, while their thick spring foliage blocked out the sun above us, for which I was personally thankful.

Not a word had passed between Abigail and myself since that first brief exchange and a near perfect silence prevailed for a spell only to be broken after fifteen minutes of walking when Abigail's stomach growled ferociously.

'Are ye hungry, Abigail?' I casually speired.

'Mary, my waist is so sunken I can feel my empty stomach squishing between my rib bones,' she replied exhaustedly.

'Ach, weel, give me a moment to figure something oot,' I said as I came to a stop.

Abigail opened her eyes and scanned the dense copse of trees which surrounded us before speiring, 'How are you going to find food out here?'

'Juist wait, lass.'

Before closing my eyes, my final sight was of a sceptical, yet trusting countenance. I loved that Abigail had confidence in me and my abilities, yet it also concerned me, for I always worried at what sort of danger I might lead her in to.

But I had to let my worries go, and moreover, I had to shut out most of the world until all that remained was what I sought. With my eyelids closed, I focused on the air passing in and out at the tip of my nose, and let my mind empty. Reality seemed to flee from me, and for a time, there was nothing. Then, beginning with Abigail, I let my sense of the living energy of nearby bodies come

13

back to me, and in a few moments' time I was aware of two additional bodies not far distant. I began trying to feel them out when the sharp eruption of my lassie's hunger pangs again filled the air and I felt myself drawn back to the real world.

Abigail had sat down with her back against the smooth, ringed trunk of a palm tree. Her eyes were shut, she had a pained look on her face, and her hand was pressed against the flat of her stomach where she was beginning to look a little wasted. Her immediate hunger may have been the result of our having eaten nothing in twenty-four hours, but multiplying that exponentially was the fact that in the previous month she had generally consumed food so sparingly that her entire body was beginning to take on the look of one suffering from consumption. This had occurred during those four weeks that she was recovering from her loss, what she placidly referred to as her 'accident' which had resulted in the amputation of her right hand. In only barely coming to grips with the new reality of her life, and finding herself isolated far from her family and home, she had for some time lost much of her will to live, and, despite my best efforts to combat her despond, she had allowed herself to fall ill with stress and malnourishment. Now that she had regained her composure, and her hope for a future in which she would return to her home in Greenhaven, she found herself paying for her lack of self-concern, and so was I. Looking down upon her I felt myself to be the worst sort of lover and the most terrible kind of friend, for I should have never allowed her to fall so low.

After forcing such thoughts from my mind, I said, 'Let me help ye move aff of the roadway into the trees. Then I'll gae and see aboot getting us something to eat.'

Abigail looked up to me for a few silent ticks, then when I offered her my hand, she gave me hers. I helped her to conceal herself in case someone should come along the road while I was away. Then, before going, I dug an old pair of ill-fitting, brown trousers out of the carpetbag and changed into them on account of my new pair having a large split in an unfortunate location. The brown of the old trousers clashed somewhat with the autumnal colours of the tartan pattern on my greatcoat, but they were the only pair I had that weren't in dire need of stitching.

Once newly girded, I left my cocoanut leaf hat and the carpetbag behind with a dovering Abigail and set off into the trees in the direction I had felt the bodies a few moments ago. As I carefully made my way between the pines and palms, warily avoiding stepping anywhere that I might suddenly sink to my knee, I dug through my coat pockets to take stock of how much money I had. I expected to have roughly thirty dollars in various denominations, only imagine my surprise when one of the bills bore the portrait of General Joseph Mansfield. It was a U. S. Note for five-hundred dollars.

For a few ticks I simply stared at it in disbelief. Then I realised where it had come from. In Loggerhead, having recovered the take from a bank heist and inspecting what had been stolen, I had held one of the five-hundred notes in the loof of my hand for just a tick when there was a sudden distraction. Without consciously thinking about it, I must have put the bill in my coat pocket. To this day

I uphold it was an accident for I have never in my life had an issue with sticky fingers.

After making a financial inventory, I put all of the bills in one coat pocket save a single one dollar note which I put in my trouser pocket.

I continued walking through the trees for about ten minutes. They grew so densely and had such intricate systems of thick vines with flat, heart-shaped leaves growing between their trunks that I could neither see nor easily navigate between them. For the most part, it seemed my best move was to simply step over the shorter fantail palms with my long legs while using the larger trees for hand grips. On the rare occasion that I looked down to notice a gap between the trunks, it invariably was nothing but a mud hole which, like much of Florida during the rainy season, meant I was essentially traversing one great swamp. For this reason I did my best to keep my boots on the roots of the trees, using the thatching of palms and occasional cypress knees as footholds. As I slowly proceeded, the canopy of palm fronds over my head effectively blocked much of the afternoon sun, and then, suddenly, there was a light ahead of me.

The trees opened up onto orderly rows of corn grown to full height and ready for threshing. I hovered on the edge of the field for a few ticks thinking that I could just pluck a few of the ripe, silk-sheathed ears, but a wee voice told me that was wrong, not only because it would be stealing, but because I knew I could do better for my lass than a cold cob of corn. As was common for me in those days, I was reluctant to get involved with people if I could possibly avoid them, but the thought of my starving lass was enough to prod me on.

I began walking through the corn rows with no idea of how far the field stretched, for though I was the longest lass ever, the stalks rose to my full height effectively blocking my forward view. As it turned out, it was a slim planting, feed for either the farmer or his beasts, on the back side of a small farm house which was otherwise surrounded by acres of young cotton shrubs.

When I came to the end of the corn field I paused again, finding myself only about twenty yards from the rear of a cracker style house. There on the raised back porch sat a hatless, long-haired man with skin burned lobster-red by the sun, his feet up on the railing as he looked at something in his lap. I observed him just long enough to realise he was reading a book.

I hesitated, worried at how the man might perceive my appearance on his property and imagining within my ken how many ways this endeavour could turn out. Based upon previous experiences, I didn't doubt the possibility of firearms being involved, for it was often the case that my queer countenance was enough to warrant some sort of violent reaction in the locals when I suddenly presented myself before them. It seemed that nearly every man in Florida had a gun of some sort, but the only weapon I had was a clip-point Bowie Knife that was sheathed and shoved in my tall left boot. Not that I would have wanted to use a weapon against a man on his own farm anyway, rather my first inclination if faced with actual violence in that situation would have been to retreat.

The more I thought about things, the more my nerves swithered as I considered again that I might ought to simply go back and pluck some corn. Finally, my shame at being so hesitant overcame my fear, and I made the firm decision to go through with it. Not knowing exactly how best to approach the subject of food with the man, I decided to simply let my feet carry me forward so as to present myself before him, thus forcing me into a position that I would have to act. I had already realised in my young life that, for all my fear of getting involved with people, once I found myself inescapably faced with a situation I did all right. So, taking a deep breath, I emerged from the corn and began to close the distance between us.

As my big clog-feet carried me forward I put my hands to my head to comb the part that hung over my forehead. The rest of my black hair was so short it required no attention. Having finished this duty in a few ticks of the clock, my hands again fell to my sides and rather restlessly plucked at the seams on my tartan greatcoat as I could think of nothing else to do which would improve my presentability.

It felt like a long trek through the open, and the man being absorbed in his book never once looked up. I was rather surprised to make it all the way to the railing of the porch without him becoming aware of me. Lining the porch was a sad looking bed of wilted red tulips, their fate apparently consigned to the will of God so far as their watering was concerned for they appeared to be dying of thirst. I carefully set my two big feet among the tulips and finally, as I stood still before the man, I hesitated one last tick before saying, 'Excuse me.'

The man made a single, surprised motion of several parts, in which he jumped up from his chair, flung the book aside onto a table, and withdrew a revolver from the waistband of his trousers all in the time it took me to raise my open hands and make clear that I was unarmed. Just as I had expected, I suddenly found myself staring at the business end of a gun. I didn't panic, rather much like usual when faced with such situations, I remained cool and, if anything, under-reactive. Besides, I felt that the man holding the gun was more than warm enough for both of us.

A few ticks passed in silence as we faced each other. I cast my eyes aside briefly to see he had been reading a battered old edition of the Bible, which seemed appropriate for a Sunday afternoon. After noting that its worn leather cover was pulling apart from the sheaves of the text, I turned my attention back to the man.

I felt an urge to break the silence, but reasoned it was better to let the man holding the gun do so. I decided to allow him a moment to regain his composure during which time he inspected me. His reaction to my features, which under normal circumstances might be considered either too sharp or too blunt to be appealing depending on who is looking at me, would have been somewhat jarring if I wasn't used to it. Since my earliest days I had been aware that my countenance held little appeal in the classical sense, and on this particular day, my cheek was just beginning to turn green where it had been birsed early that morning by the fist of a large Russian gentleman with whom I had a political disagreement. Add that to the fact that my nose had been slightly misshapen when a big bitch smashed my face into the ground a month earlier and I was certainly not a pretty sight.

After a spell of inspection, the man slowly began to lower the gun from where he had it pointed at my bosom. Then he speired, 'What the fuck do you think you're doing?'

My mouth had gone dry, and after working my tongue about some I spoke as kindly as I could. 'Please, sir, I wonder if ye could spare me a bit of food?'

His eyes narrowed at that and he said, 'The fuck you say?'

I made a clear effort to speak unaffectedly without accent as I said again, 'Please, sir, I am travelling out on the main road, and I wonder if you could spare me some food, for I have not eaten today.'

The gun was beginning to rise again, and I felt that the next words out of his mouth were essentially going to be to 'get the fuck off of his property,' so I let my eyes slide towards the Bible and rather meekly said, 'For I was an hungered, and ye gave me meat... Inasmuch as ye have done it unto one of the least of these my brethren, ye have done it to me.'

The truth was that I felt somewhat disingenuous in making that statement, though it did have my intended effect.

The man cast his eyes aside at the book, then after allowing his face to twist into a rueful smile, he said: 'Dammit!'

The look the man had given the old Bible implied that he was less fearful of this moment being reviewed before our Creator at some distant time in the future than of the book itself jumping off the table and kicking him in the airse. At the time I didn't fully understand it, but I would come to see that if there was anything on Earth a large portion of the local population actually revered as being holy, it was the scriptures themselves. Bishops and beads and crucifixes held no sway with these people, but show them an even slightly suggestive Bible verse and you might convince them of anything.

The man slowly lowered the revolver to his side, and went stalking in the back door of his house, from within which I could feel another body I supposed to be the farmwife. If God loves a cheerful giver, then this man was probably not high on The Lord's list just then, for when he returned a moment later, he handed over a sizeable loaf and a chunk of cheese, both bearing only a few spots of mould, with such an air of reluctance that I nearly felt guilty in taking it. He set the foodstuffs on the railing, taking care to choose a spot none too overcrowded with white and grey streaks of bird shyte, then stepped back and crossed his arms over his chest, the revolver still clutched in one hand with the barrel pointing up. After giving one angry look to the book still laying placidly on the table-top, he turned his attention back to me with a sneer.

Once I had the cheese in my hand and the loaf under my arm and shoved up in my oxter, I reached in my trouser pocket for the single dollar only to have the man nervously drop the gun level with my bosom again. I gently withdrew the note, and laid it out on the railing. Only then did the man seem to relax, and as I turned to leave him, I almost thought he looked ashamed of himself.

I wasted no time in returning to the corn, and finding my feet on high, level ground, I ran all the way back to the tree-line at which time I was necessarily slowed, although thanks to the clear path I had earlier delineated with broken vines, I was able to make better time going than coming.

I had been gone no more than twenty-five minutes total, and when I returned to Abigail I expected to find her asleep. Instead, she was wide-awake and visibly relieved to see me return. I showed her what I had found and said, 'Beggars canna be choosers.'

She said nothing, simply smiled weakly up at me. After scraping a furry patch of fungus off of the crust with my finger-nail, I broke the bread and handed her a chunk and watched as she began to eat it. Her hand shook a little bit as she put the first bit to her mouth, but twenty minutes later, after she had slowly consumed a good amount of bread and all of the cheese (for dairy of any kind would only make me ill), she appeared strong and steady again.

We ate half of the loaf between us and then I wrapped up the remainder in an old paper sack in the carpetbag. After taking that piece of luggage in one hand, and my lassie's fingers in the other, we set off again on the roadway towards the south.

* * *

The path we were following was little more than a heap of mud, sand and dead pine needles raised a few feet above the common level. It was just wide enough to admit a single vehicle, and I wondered what should happen if two carts were to meet going in opposite directions, for there was rarely a turnoff, and no space available to pull to the side.

At long intervals, the rustic road was bordered on either edge by a deep, mossy sludge which might have been bottomless for all I could tell. A careful inspection of its depths revealed tadpoles, thousands of mosquito larvae, and occasionally small, trapped fish. It was preternaturally quiet, and in the gloom of the densely packed trees it felt as though we were in a cave. At times the only sign of wildlife to be seen was in the white Great Egrets fishing in the green sludge, their beak-yellow eyes warily observing the passing of our two bodies before being turned back to the still waters. Other than that, once we observed a family of long-tailed weasels who warily returned our curious stares from the other side of the water. Then for a time, there was nothing.

For the longest spell I could feel no sense of humanity outside of the immediate presence of my lass who had revived somewhat since our brief repast. It was a curious thing, but the farther south we walked, and so far as I knew, the closer we came to the town of Venice, the deeper into nowhere we seemed to find ourselves. Fruit canning was the main industry of the small town in those days and I kept expecting to come upon cleared fields of citrus trees, denuded of their winter fruits, at any moment. Instead, we felt ever more isolated as the woods grew more dense by the moment. This did not greatly concern me for some hours, only as the gloom among the trees deepened, and I realised the sun was beginning to dip, I started to worry.

Finally, we received a literal sign of mankind's presence. From a distance, I could see a wooden placard nailed to the trunk of an oak tree with a single word upon it, painted in red. When we came close enough to it, Abigail read it aloud. 'Repent,' she announced with distinction.

We stopped at the base of the tree for a few ticks and simply stared up at the word. Then I looked down to my lass and she shrugged before we set off again, foot for foot.

About twenty yards down the way, there was another sign with the same hand-painted word. We didn't bother to stop and we passed it by without comment. At another twenty yards, there was the same.

After about the sixth such sign, Abigail archly stated: 'I wish he would find another subject to paint signs about.'

Then came the seventh sign, and from a distance I could see that it contained three words. As we approached it, I kept trying to feel out the presence of who might have nailed up the signs, but it seemed that so far as humanity was concerned, we were in a desert.

When we came within range, I read the sign aloud. 'Repent. Final warning.'

Abigail made a small sound of derision, and I thought that likely to be the end of things, only something began to needle at the corner of my ken as we passed the sign. A few steps farther on, I stopped and brought Abigail to a halt with my hand.

'What is it, Mary?' she speired.

I began looking to our left on the east side of the road around the base of the oak with the final warning nailed to it. Beyond the edge of the path there was nothing significantly out of the ordinary, except that there was a lack of the green sludge that had effectively boxed in the rest of the roadway for the past few miles. Looking up and down the length of the dry area, I realised that there were two piles of stones on that side of the road, one at each end of the dryness, effectively damming the sludgy waters. Casting my gaze out into the woods, I noticed that there was a slight clearing among the trees and vines towards the east, nearly so much that a body could squeeze herself through without too much trouble.

We stood quietly looking that way for a spell before Abigail tugged at my arm. 'What is it? Do you think someone is out there?'

I was quiet for a few ticks more, then I shut my eyes. I felt something throbbing in the trees, like a tiny heart pumping blood in a wee body. So long as my eyes were closed, I maintained a connection with the thrumming mass. It was something that felt nearly tangible and so proximate that it was as if I could reach out and brush it with the tips of my fingers. I very nearly walked away then, leading my lass back down the road to the south, except that I was struck with the distinct, though barely perceptible, impression that the blood pump was failing. I opened my eyes again and looked in to the trees and said, 'Aye. There's a bairn oot there. I feel her. A wee lassie.'

When I turned to look down into Abigail's green eyes, I saw the slightest flicker of disbelief. Yet she trusted me so thoroughly.

Without another word between us, we stepped off the wide, beaten path which led to the south and entered in among the trees together.

II

Sunday, 19 April 1896, 7:15 PM

Not one of us is perfect, and Abigail, eternal angel that she is to me, was not without her faults though her good qualities far outweighed her negatives. If there was one virtue particular to her that stands forever in the forefront of my ken it was her willingness to volunteer herself on behalf of any random waif we might encounter during our travels who was in want of succour. Maybe at the outset this doesn't sound like much of a surprise for a young woman of nineteen years who frequently felt the biologic pull of her body's natural desire to produce offspring, but keep in mind that she maintained her insistence to assist the bairnies even after having been mauled so terribly that her hand had to be amputated from her body in a previous, quite recent encounter involving a lassie in need of our help. I had already learned in such situations that when Abigail set her mind to something I might as well go along with her from the get-go. There was nothing I, or anyone for that matter, could do to dissuade her, and in the event that she needed my support I wanted to be readily available.

It was a queer thing, but only fifteen feet from the road we had been traversing, we found a path open up just wide enough for a lass to walk down without trees and vines and such grabbing a hold of her at every step. I looked once over my shoulder when we were about thirty feet in and found that the main roadway was already fully obscured behind us.

We were silent as Abigail proceeded forward with me following directly behind. After a full minute of quiet, she stopped and I ran right into her airse. After tilting her head back to look upside-down at me, she said, 'I am surprised to see this clearly marked path, but where is the girl you thought you saw?'

I laid my hands upon her golden brown hair, pushed at her head to properly re-orient it in the forward-looking position, and then shut my eyes. Immediately I said, 'She's near.' By the time I opened my eyes, I found that Abigail had already run ahead a good fifteen feet.

I was sprinting to catch up with her when she shouted, 'Mary!' Then she went to her knees at the base of a palm tree with a wickedly thatched trunk.

As I arrived behind my lass I looked down to see who she had found. After putting her right arm and its stump behind her back for fear that the cicatrix might frighten the child, Abigail gently offered her open left hand forward to a lassie-wean who upon first inspection I could not guess to be more than three years old. The very fact that she stood upright against the sharp thatch of the palm's trunk surprised me for her legs appeared far too under-developed to support her short yet stout body which was made altogether unsteady by the wobbling of her large head, which would have been nearly perfectly round if not for the oddly flat, nearly bald crown. For a few ticks, the lassie hesitated and looked upon Abigail's outstretched hand fearfully. Then the lassie's eyes roved past the proffered fingers to Abigail's bosom, and she seemed to be contemplating something.

'It is all right, dear!' Abigail was saying sweetly to the bairn.

She made no motion towards her, but kept smiling and speaking encouragingly to her, and after a minute or so she had her reward. The lassie decided to release her hold on the palm and took two tottering steps towards Abigail before collapsing forward on her arm. The bairn naturally allowed herself to curl up onto Abigail, and laid her face on her bosom directly above her heart.

'Oh! Are not you sweet!' Abigail said as she gently brought her right arm around to help support her charge. 'What is your name, dear?'

As the bairn gurgled out a few unintelligible sounds, I hooked my hands beneath Abigail's oxters to help bring her back to her feet. For a moment, my lass was utterly absorbed in her new friend and I might as well have not existed. Then she speired, 'Where do you think she came from?'

I had been looking about in the wooded area that surrounded us, trying to feel out the presence of anyone nearby, but there was nothing, no one. The small path we had followed out from the roadway continued on in the same direction towards the east, so I thought it possible there was some sort of habitation in that direction. Looking to either side of us, there was little to see among the densely packed trees due to the increasing dark, so it seemed we had only two options.

'It would seem prudent to suppose she came from farther alang this path,' I said.

'Yes, well, where else could she have come from?' Abigail speired. Then, gently addressing her friend, she said, 'Where did you come from, dear? Can you show me?'

As the bairn made no reply except to nuzzle her face against Abigail's bosom, I said, 'It's possible she micht have come frae the roadway. She could have been on a wagon and fallen aff the back, then wandered oot here. Maybe she was riding with her family doun to Venice and they got all the way there afore they realised she was gane.'

Abigail frowned a little at the thought then said, 'I allow that as a possibility, but somehow it does not seem right. Besides, how many other vehicles did you see on that road while I was asleep?'

'It does seem rarely traversed,' I admitted.

I looked farther down the path to the east and felt a certain dread. It wasn't from anything I feared finding there, rather it was an internal worry that I had been foolish to have us step out of the cart without knowing for sure how much farther we had to go on foot. Now we really had no idea where we were, or where we should go, and what was worse, the sun was clearly on his way to bed.

Abigail was gently swinging about on her happy hips so as to daundle the lassie a bit as she smilingly said, 'What is your name, dear? Can you tell me your name?'

The bairn made no response.

In making my decision as to what we should do, I finally settled upon the idea that it would be better to do something, anything as opposed to nothing. I speired my lass, 'Do ye want me to take her?'

Without looking at me, Abigail replied, 'No, I am fine. She is incredibly light.'

'Aye, weel, come alang. We'd best see what's at the end of this path, I suppose.'

I started walking and Abigail immediately fell in line behind me.

As we proceeded, over my shoulder I speired, 'Hoo auld do ye think she is? Three?'

Abigail didn't reply right away. She seemed to be contemplating the question for a spell. Then she said, 'It is difficult to tell, Mary. I think maybe four or five, but...' she hesitated. 'It is hard to be certain with her. She might be some years older.'

'Weel, at that age I sud think she could tell us waur she came from, or her name, at least.'

'Maybe,' was Abigail's only response.

We were silent a while longer and then a sliver of direct sunlight struck us from behind. We stopped and turned to see a break in the trees at just the right angle to admit the light from the sun which had turned a deep red as if preparing to sink over an unseen horizon. The thought of its approaching disappearance again filled me with dread, for I feared what would become of us if we were lost so deeply in the woods all night.

Abigail, on the other hand, did not seem to share my immediate concern. Instead she held the lassie so that the light fell directly on her face so as to get a good look at her. 'Oh, Mary!' she exclaimed. 'Look at her eyes.'

Upon looking down upon her, the first thing I noted about her eyes were how incredibly heavy and thick their lids appeared. I wondered at how the lassie was able to keep her eyes so widely opened given their weight. But then Abigail said, 'Do you see the soft lines in her eyes? They are like little brushstrokes,' and I looked more closely.

Surely enough, the lassie's bonnie grey irises bore what looked like a pattern of swipes made hastily with a paintbrush radiating out from the pupil. A further inspection revealed that her two eyes were unable to focus on the same object at the same time, though I doubt Abigail noticed that at the time.

The lassie was looking at me with one eye, attempting to make a studied decision of my friendliness, I supposed. While she made her inspection of me, I said, 'She's a bonnie thing, Abigail. I hope we can find waur she belongs.'

My lass smiled gently and quietly said, 'Me too,' at which the short hairs of my head stood on end, a sure sign of deception. I didn't give it much thought at the time, rather I pulled my hat off just long enough to give my scalp a scratching.

As I started walking forward again, Abigail fell in line behind me without another word.

* * *

It was like stepping through a thick curtain behind which stood an incredible heat source. We were making our way down the path, and though there was no visible difference in our surroundings from one footfall to the next, upon taking one casual step forward I found myself suddenly infused with the heated, though somewhat diffuse feeling that some dozens of bodies were present within a small area about fifty yards ahead.

I stopped and Abigail speired from behind me, 'Do you see something?'

I replied: 'There are bodies ahead. A lot of them, I think.'

'Then that must be where she came from.' With only the slightest hesitation she said, 'I suppose we should go and see if we can find her family.'

That sounded simple and prudent enough, but I was worried. I turned to look upon Abigail and her friend while I considered what to do. The wee lass still had her face pressed tightly to Abigail's bosom, but her feet were kicking about freely, almost rhythmically, as if she were performing a sort of dance. She wore no shoes, rather her legs and feet were encased in thick, white stockings, which had turned a grey towards the bottom and altogether black beneath the soles of her feet. Her white, cotton-cambric dress had turned dingy and while I thought things over, I casually pulled a few pines needles and other items of debris that had stuck to it and deposited them on the ground.

'What worries you, Mary?' Abigail gently speired. 'I am certain we left our troubles behind in Loggerhead this morning,' she said before returning her attention to the lassie.

'Aye, I hope sae.'

'Well, we must do something. It is getting dark.' She looked back up to me, and her hazel eyes were losing their green lustre and beginning to turn brown in the gloaming. 'I trust you, Mary. We shall do whatever you think is the right thing.'

We smiled at each other, then I turned back around and began to lead the way east again.

Sometimes when I can't sleep at night, I think back and wonder at how these situations could have turned out so very differently for so many people if I had only made a different decision. Months and years in the future, Abigail would at times become frustrated with me when I could not make up my mind on something so simple as what I wanted for supper, but that was only because she would come to forget that I was the one who had to make decisions like this that were of actual consequence, though it didn't seem that way at the time. In this case which seemed perfectly innocuous, it was a simple matter of east or west, and to this day I still don't know whether I chose right or wrong.

* * *

I could see flames ahead in the distance. At first they appeared no larger than two candles, but by the time we reached the end of the path where a large area had been cleared of trees, I could see that they were actually two flaming braziers set out in front of a long building with a single-gable roof. We stopped when we reached the open area and looked about. It was a huge tract where nearly every tree had been culled, I would come to realise that it was in total some hundred acres or more though we couldn't tell that at first in the dark. From that particular location we could only see the one structure and were as yet unaware of what lay behind it.

After a spell of inspection, upon witnessing several people entering a set of double-doors open at the end of the building facing us, we began to proceed forward. Finding ourselves with ample room to manoeuvre, Abigail had fallen in step alongside of me, though after only a few feet I silently motioned her back with my arm. There was a line of widely spaced oak trees between us and the building, and I could feel someone on the other side of one of them. I walked forward on my own, purposefully making a good deal of noise so as to announce myself, and when I was only a few feet away, a lad on the far side of one of the tree trunks stepped around to block my path.

We were still a good fifty or sixty feet from the flaming braziers, and because they were behind the lad I couldn't get a good look at him, but I estimated that he was probably about fifteen years old upon first meeting him. Without further preamble than a curt, high-pitched, 'Hello,' he speired: 'Were you invited?'

I honestly answered, 'Nae, sir, we were no' invited.'

Abigail came up alongside of me then as the lad seemed to consider his options. Apparently unannounced visitors were a rarity in this place, wherever we had gotten ourselves off to.

After a few ticks he hesitantly said, 'Well, you can't stay if you ain't invited. We don't have extra room.'

My hair stood up at the casual lie, but I ignored it. Looking past the lad at the building I could barely discern a wooden cross attached to the forward point of the gable and speired, 'Is that no' a church? Perhaps we could axe for some charity from the parson, seeing as hoo it's dark and we're sae far in the middle of nae-waur.'

While he considered this for a few ticks, I could feel my lass getting impatient. When the lad hesitantly began to speak again, she spoke over him saying, 'Look, we found this child which surely belongs to someone here out in the woods. On her behalf, I think we could consider ourselves invited. Do not you agree?'

The lad looked to her and even in the dark I could see he had a queer look on his face. He kept staring at her and it seemed that he was unable to even process what she had said.

I could feel Abigail's annoyance growing, so before she had a chance to vent her spleen I said to the lad, 'Take a look at the cheeld. Does she or does she no' belong here?'

He seemed to think this was a good idea, and though there wasn't much light to see and the wean still had her face pressed against Abigail's bosom, he leaned in to look and simply said, 'Oh.' Clearly he recognised her.

Another few ticks of silence passed and Abigail said, 'Well?'

The lad took a few steps back then said, 'Stay right here. I'd better go get somebody.'

He turned on his heel and hurried off towards the building.

I was content to wait; Abigail was not. She allowed the lad just enough time to enter the double-doors, and then began stalking after him. I would have fain remained patiently waiting but I immediately jumped beside my lass and kept with her foot for foot.

As we approached the structure we saw perhaps another dozen bodies enter. They all walked from somewhere behind the long length of the building and entered the double-doors which remained open. Most of them were young girls, though there were a couple of boys, and a few older lassies approaching womanhood. All of the girls were attired in the same long, white gown, and the two boys both wore identical sarks and trousers cut off at the knees. Noticing our approach, some of them looked curiously at us with their dark eyes, but none seemed particularly concerned. They proceeded on their way and calmly entered the building which bore a long sign above its entry similar to the 'Repent' notices we had seen on the main roadway. As we got closer, I saw that it read *Holiness Assembly Church in the Palms.*

Other than those entering the doors, the only other body to be seen was in the form of a man on his knees only a few feet from one of the braziers. In understanding that this was a church we were approaching, I at first thought him to be praying, which seemed a queer thing to do on the outside of the building. Only as we came nearer I realised he was carefully weeding a small flower bed filled with begonias, which seemed even queerer than praying since it was now fully dark with the exception of the light of the flaming braziers.

So far since stepping off of the narrow path into this clearing, this was the only person I had seen that I could truly call an adult, so I decided it might be wise to address our concerns with him. When we stepped up behind the man I got a good look at him and noticed that his thick, white hair provided a stark contrast to the dark of his skin. He was gently humming some curious tune as his hands deftly wandered through the flowers in search of weeds which he plucked in sharp, staccato motions and then flung randomly into the scrub grass behind him.

Not wishing to further irk Abigail, I didn't hesitate in addressing the man. 'Excuse me, sir,' I gently said.

The man's hands stopped moving, and then he slowly rotated his head on his shoulder to look in our general direction. I realised then why it made as much sense for him to weed a flower garden at night as in the day, for his eyes were both covered with milk so thick that I presumed him to be perfectly blind.

'Who's that?' he speired with a reasonably friendly tone.

'My name is Fisher, sir,' I replied. Then, picking up with our Loggerhead *charade* in which my lass and I played a couple of foreign-born honeymooners, I introduced Abigail. 'And this is my wife.'

The old man's eyes moved about for a few ticks and based on the fact that he actually looked at us I realised that he could still see at least basic shapes. After focusing on Abigail, he speired, 'Is that you baby?'

Abigail stepped forward and said, 'No, sir, she is not. We found her on the path that runs between here and the main roadway.'

'We were hoping to find that she belongs here,' I supplied.

The old man was squinting up at the bairn as he speired, 'That you, Ellie?'

The lassie gave no response except to kick her feet about some more.

The old man grunted and began to manoeuvre himself into a position to get off the ground. I held out my hand and said, 'Micht I help ye up, sir?'

He considered my offer for just a tick before accepting. His hand didn't go directly to mine, rather once he put it in the general area of my own I grasped it and pulled him to his feet. The loofs of his hand felt rough, but his finger-ends were surprisingly soft.

Once he was upright I speired, 'Is Ellie's mither aboot? We really only came to see her safely returned to her hame, but it's getting late the noo and I was hoping we micht find some-waur suitable to stay the nicht.'

'Mm-hm,' he said. 'Her mother around here somewheres. But...'

Just then a woman stepped out of the double-doors and entered the light of the braziers. She sharply said, 'Moses!' and the old man stopped talking. Once she saw he was silent, she spoke with a somewhat friendlier, though authoritative tone, and said, 'Moses, it is almost time to begin. Why don't you go ahead inside?'

The old man regarded us for one tick before stepping away. He seemed reticent to leave, and I sensed that he had a host of thoughts pent up in his old head, but felt himself stifled in his ability to share them. As he hobbled in the door, he simply said, 'Nice to meet you Fishers,' with the slightest air of regret.

As he entered, a couple of young girls holding hands who had come from around the building stepped in beside him. One of them happily said, 'Hi, Moses!'

Without looking at the girls he said, 'Hi there, Janie, Alice,' as if he could sense who they were without having to actually visually identify them. For one tick he hovered in his walk, appearing nearly ready to turn back to us, but then the two lassies went one on each side of the old man and took his hands in theirs to lead him away. Then they disappeared together into the relative dark inside.

Although more bodies would shortly come up to enter the building while we spoke, this left us alone with the woman for a few ticks. Since she was standing directly in the light of the braziers I had a good look at her. I figured her to be somewhere around fifty years of age with long grey hair pulled back severely from her sharp face. Her whole body looked sharp in fact, for she had the appearance of one who had never truly enjoyed a meal once in her life. There was no excess of flesh to be seen anywhere upon her, rather her thin skin adhered so perfectly to her skeleton that she could have done well to provide her living body to an anatomy class for osteological study.

Her gaze was as sharp as the rest of her, and though she spoke politely, even somewhat warmly, her eyes betrayed her dislike of us. Not that she seemed to bare us any particular ill-will, rather from the very beginning she gave the impression that we were as unwelcome a burden as two houseguests who had overstayed their welcome.

By way of introduction the woman simply said, 'I am Esther. I see you have found something that we lost.'

As the woman turned her attention to Ellie, Abigail seemed to reflexively pull away a bit. I said, 'Aye, ma'am, we found her on the path leading oot to the main roadway to the west. It wisnae oor intention to intrude, only we wanted to be sure she was safe for the nicht.'

Esther regarded me directly for a few ticks then said, 'That was a very charitable, very Christian action on your part, especially at this time of the night.'

'It seemed the only choice at the time. Is her mither aboot?'

The woman hesitated for a tick then said, 'Yes. But she has taken ill.'

My hair stood on end at that and I found myself wondering what had really happened to Ellie's mother, though I didn't say anything. Instead I speired, 'Is it possible my wife and I could stay the nicht? We have oor oun food,' I said, thinking of the half loaf of bread in the carpetbag. 'And we would leave at first licht in the morning.'

There was only the slightest hesitation on Esther's part before she said, 'Of course you and your wife may stay. Only understand, that normally guests are allowed by invitation only, and then with the understanding that there are rules here, and rules are meant to be obeyed. A visitor disobeys our rules, which are meant for the safety of everyone, at their own peril.'

Her discourse seemed clear enough to me, so I nodded and said, 'Aye, of course. We wouldna wish to be any trouble.'

Esther flicked her eyes over to Abigail and said, 'The child's mother is unavailable, so why don't you let me have her now.'

The woman stretched out her arms in an unnatural manner as if expecting to be laded with firewood. Abigail hesitated in handing over her charge, but after exchanging glances with me, she stepped forward and began to affect the transfer, only Ellie wouldn't have any part of it.

Upon having her face separated half an inch from Abigail's bosom, the bairn began howling at the top of her little lungs. Esther's eyes grew large at that and she stepped back with a fearful look upon her face. Abigail let Ellie fall against the bodice of her dress and she immediately quieted again.

My lass said, 'I do not wish to incommode you, but maybe if you took me to her mother it would be best if I could hand her over personally.'

Esther still looked aghast as she replied, 'I am afraid that's not possible.' Then she turned silent. Given her actions, I wondered if she had ever had direct dealings with children in her life.

As the three of us stood there staring at each other, the tinny sound of a piano playing some slow hymn emanated from somewhere deep within the building. Some several seconds of silence on our parts passed, then Abigail brusquely said, 'Well, if there is no one to take Ellie, then maybe I will just hold on to her.'

Ignoring my lassie's tone of voice, Esther nodded at this then turned her attention back to me. After making a visual inspection of me from head to toe, she said, 'You were not invited to church, so I shall show you to your rooms now. We eat *after* the services. When supper is ready we will come and retrieve you.'

Abigail had often said that she didn't hold with church services, and having never been a kirker myself in my bairnhood I was content to hear that we would not be attending. Then something suddenly caught my eye. In the first instant of my seeing her as she entered the light of the braziers, I thought my mind was playing a trick on me, trying to resolve a fuzzy, dimly-lit human shape into something recognisable. But as she came closer to the flame and her image refined itself, I realised that I knew one of the people entering the church building. She was clothed in a rich looking blue dress festooned with ribbons and embroidery and her long, blonde hair was pinned up in a rather elegant, braided mass on the back of her head. She wore a small straw hat adorned with pink silk flowers on the brim, the sort of thing that was designed for style instead of keeping the sun off of you. It was an opulent look, which seemed queerly uncharacteristic of the lass, and though at that time I could hardly claim her to be more than an acquaintance, I knew her appearance to be a false presentation.

Although she passed within ten feet of me, she didn't look in my direction, and it almost seemed that she purposefully ignored me, though I thought then she might not have been aware of my presence. Silence prevailed as I watched her trim, short figure proceed towards the double-doors with another much taller and darker young woman in a plain, brown serge uniform-looking dress walking by her side.

I thought that was to be the end of the encounter, simply the random chance of two ships passing in the night, but then she made a curious motion. She still didn't look at me, yet as she made the gesture, I knew it was performed for my benefit. She lifted one ring-covered hand ever so slightly, and behind Esther's back rubbed her first two fingers and thumb together in that classic pantomime indicating *money.* Then she dropped her hand to her side, and she and her companion walked in the doors and silently disappeared inside.

Esther was looking directly at me when she said, 'Well? Shall we go to your quarters?'

My wonder at what sort of strange place this was had been sparked, for it seemed utterly queer to see anyone I knew in such a remote location. And then having had her make that motion at me I felt my curiosity not only piqued but prodded.

Esther appeared somewhat impatient to move us along as I said, 'Ma'am, my wife and I have been travelling the day and missed oor common morning service. Is there nae way that we could attend yer church?'

Esther frowned and vehemently voiced: 'Absolutely not.'

She nearly continued with her negations when I reached in my trouser pocket and removed the wad of money it held, then deftly peeled free the five-hundred dollar note. I held it up between us and said, 'I'd gladly make a donation. If the service were to oor liking, I'd certainly give muir.'

The woman's eyes widened ever so slightly as she looked at the denomination of the bill hovering before her.

Then she gently reached out and took it in her bony fingers and said, 'Certainly you may attend... Mr Wisher, was it?'

'Mr and Mrs Fisher,' I corrected with a smile.

The woman looked from the note to my face and gently returned the friendly gesture with an air of bony pain as if even the slightest of grins was a rare occurrence for her. Then, for the first time, she set her stony gaze upon my lass, and it seemed she was sizing Abigail up. It was little more than a brief flick of her eyes over my lassie's form, but it unsettled me somewhat. Then the woman suddenly turned toward the open doors behind her and said, 'Follow.'

Esther wore the same plain white cotton gown that nearly every other female in the building was wearing, there being only five exceptions with myself included. Those of us out of uniform, as it were, all sat in the very back, as we found that most of the fourteen rows of pews in front of us had already been filled. Upon entering the building, I marvelled at the fact that there were so many bodies about, for as yet we had seen nothing to indicate that there was any sort of town nearby.

The pews were separated by an aisle and there were only a few pews on the left at the very back that were empty, and one on the right. The young woman in blue I had recognised and her companion filed in the rear-most pew on the left and Abigail followed after them with Ellie still clutched to her bosom. I naturally began to follow along as there was enough room to sit six people in each pew, but Esther disavowed me of that notion before I could take my seat.

The woman was standing in the middle of the aisle staring at us as she imperiously intoned: 'A rule never to be broken is that the men always sit to the right, and the ladies to the left.'

Several heads in the nearby pews turned to look at us as I lied, 'Madam, we are married.'

'Nevertheless,' she replied, 'you must take your seat on the right. Here,' she pointed, 'you may sit directly across the way from your wife.'

I made a short bow of my head and then took my place. Once seated, Esther leaned in towards me and said, 'Since the establishment of the church, men and women have sat separately and in this assembly we hold fast to the traditions which the apostles taught us.' Without awaiting a response from me, the woman quickly turned away and took to her feet.

After Esther started walking up the aisle, Abigail slid to the end of her pew and we were only separated by a few feet. She said to me, 'Mr Fisher, would you go in your bag and pull out some of the soft centre of that bread for me? I should like to see if Ellie might eat a bite or two since it will be a while until supper.'

'Aye, of course, Mrs Fisher,' I said as I began to dig around.

When I came back up with the bread and handed it across the aisle, I took my opportunity to look past Abigail and confirm that the young woman sitting next to her was who I thought her to be. She was a braw creature so long as you didn't mind a woman somewhat short in stature and slim in body. She sat primly staring straight ahead at nothing in particular, as if she were in a trance of concentration, which afforded me some several ticks to study her. There was a pile of candles up near the front of the church, but even in the relatively dim ambience at the back where we were seated, my eyes told me there was no doubt. By some twist of fate, I had been brought into contact with this lass whom I had only first met a few weeks earlier and had no expectation of seeing again in the near future. Her name was Hannah, and the queerest thing about the situation, even odder than the very fact of finding her in this place, was that although I recognised her by sight, I couldn't feel her energy. In our previous encounter, she had felt to me like a barely contained bundle of excited nerves. Now there was nothing there. It was as if she were a blank, which surprised me about as much as if I were to crack an egg shell and have nothing but air come fizzing forcefully out.

Hannah, as she had told me upon our previous meeting, was then twenty-one years of age. While I was inspecting her, I got a look at the other young woman who appeared to be accompanying her and thought her likely to be about the same age, or perhaps slightly younger or older, I never was particularly good with ages unless someone volunteered the number of their years to me. She was much taller than Hannah and wore an altogether dissimilar, plain, brown dress, the colour making an interesting contrast to the shade of her skin, which was a deep, rich coffee with only the slightest hint of cream. She kept speaking to Hannah, and at one time leaned forward far enough to look around the front of Hannah's face and fixed her gaze directly upon me. She was already beautiful before she smiled, but when our eyes met, her mouth opened so warmly to reveal the white of her teeth that I couldn't help but return the gesture. Then she looked down to see Abigail feeding Ellie bits of bread and her smile grew even larger.

Throughout all of this, Hannah continued to look ahead. Only once did I hear her make a remark, a single syllable, in reply to something her companion had said in her lug. She didn't look at her, or me, or even to Abigail and Ellie who were sitting next to her. She seemed to be concentrating on something at the far end of the room.

As Abigail continued feeding Ellie bits of bread, I began to look about the building. There was nothing remarkable about it and if it hadn't contained rows of light, oaken pews all facing the same direction it could have been used for just about any function: dance hall, beer hall, dining hall, whatever. The winnocks lining both of the long sides of the building were all clear and appeared to have been recently cleaned with vinegar. They all had thick curtains held open with golden cords and through them there was little to be seen outside except for the dim shapes of multiple, small buildings in the distance. There was no apparent movement outside as it seemed that everyone in the vicinity had gathered for the Sunday evening service in the kirk. Nearly everyone, anyway.

I began to cast my eyes about inside to see what kind of people these were. As stated by Esther, all of the females not including myself were on the left side of the room and all of the males on the right, with one exception. Sitting in an otherwise empty pew directly in front of Abigail was a woman in a rich looking cream corsage and matching skirt holding a child cross-wise in her lap. She might have been thirty years old, if that, and the one thing that immediately grabbed a hold of my attention were the earrings she was wearing. They appeared to be sizeable pearls, and they gave her a somewhat opulent appearance.

She stood out as being the fifth female in the room not wearing the plain white uniform gown. She seemed somewhat tense, and I observed her for a minute or so until I got the opportunity to lean forward and see her bairn. He was a lad of about five years, well dressed in a little grey suit of matching trousers and coat. There was nothing remarkable about him with the exception of his feet. Contained in highly polished black boots, they were both twisted inward at such a horrific angle that I cringed to see them. The lad didn't seem to be pained by them, however, and I reasoned that this was no injury, but rather he had been born that way.

I leaned back in my seat and looked ahead to the rest of the parishioners. Every male wore the same plain sark and trousers, although the younger lads up to about age thirteen had theirs cut off at the knees. The white-gowned girls all seemed to be in high spirits and happily chattered away at each other as they sat patiently in their pews. Peppered throughout were only a few older lassies, some in their teenage years and one I supposed to be about twenty. I recall thinking it odd at the time that there was such a large number of young lassies, mostly all under the age of ten, when there was a greater number of males of all ages perhaps approaching as old as thirty, but I didn't dwell on the subject long. Just as odd was the fact, made obvious by the separation of the sexes, that there were so many more males present. Even taking into account the fact that each individual male on average took up more space than each female, I easily estimated there were far more within the church. They filled in every pew on our side of the aisle up to the one directly in front of me, whereas there was a great deal of empty space on the opposite side of the building.

As the bairns went about their conversations and turned their heads this way and that, I took my chance to inspect them. It didn't take me long to notice that they all bore a strikingly similar appearance, as if they all belonged to one grand family. Most of them were quite trig and sharp, and if not for the fact that Esther seemed so distanced from the very notion of childrearing I might have supposed her to be their matriarch. Only I reasonably supposed then that the woman would have had to have herself produced a number of children in order for there to be so many young about. At the time, that didn't seem correct.

Throughout my visual tour of the room the piano had continued producing its slow melodies. The tunes being played were none too familiar to me then, although in the upcoming years I would come to recognise them as being quite common. I recall several of the slower hymns of Charles Wesley being played in particular. In straining my eyes all the way to the front of the building I found that it was the old man named Moses playing the piano.

I tried to relax somewhat then and turned my attention back to Abigail whose charge had apparently had her fill of bread. She had re-positioned Ellie in her lap so that the lassie could look up at her and she kept leaning in to give her wee kisses on the head. Hannah still sat next to her staring straight ahead while her companion leaned around her to observe Ellie with a small smile on her face.

Everything seemed pleasant enough, yet I found myself filling with a certain anxiety in sitting there. I wasn't accustomed to sitting in a kirk, and queer as it may sound it bothered me that the room was filled with bairns who were so acquainted with such things that they didn't think anything more of it than sitting down to luncheon.

At the time, the entire notion of what took place within such a building still felt like a mystery to me, and it felt odd that it should be so. At that point in my life, I had attended a total of one kirk service following my kirstening, and nearly the entirety of my religious training had been through the reading of a Bible (aided in interpretation in those days neither by man nor Spirit), and that only after I had first come to Florida during the previous year. In Greenhaven, the local priest had provided me with a copy of the scriptures, and I spent several months reading and studying them for the simple reason that it was the one book I had in front of me that my older sister wouldn't fash me for reading. As a bairn, I had read my mother's old Psalter repeatedly, but that was only the psalms and proverbs and so I had never even gotten so far as the Good News until I was sixteen.

With the ending of a particular tune from the piano, a young man of about five and twenty years, wearing the same sark and trousers outfit as the rest of the males, stood up at the front of the building in front of a great, flat wooden table, behind which hung a thick curtain which matched those adorning the winnocks. Neglecting any overture, he simply called out: 'Number thirty-six!'

As everyone else in the room immediately stood, I joined in. I quickly realised he was referring to the number in a hymnal which I found in a wee shelf on the back of the pew in front of me. I opened up to *A Mighty Fortress is Our God* and listened as Moses played through the tune once before everyone began singing as the young man led with the waving of his arm.

Not trusting my voice, I silently mouthed the words of the first stanza until I caught a sight of Abigail from the corner of my eye, then spent the rest of the verse studying her. For as long as we had been acquainted, I had never known her to attend a kirk service and she commonly told me that she did not hold with such things. Hannah, who was still silently looking as far towards the front as she could, had stood next to her and was holding the hymnal where Abigail could see it, but my lass had no need of it. I was somewhat surprised when her clear, angelic voice strongly sang out the lyrics as if the tune had been sealed up in her heart and the words imprinted upon her mind by Martin Luther himself. I listened as she sang the lyrical musings of the reformer:

> 'A mighty fortress is our God,
> A bulwark never failing;
> Our helper he amid the flood
> Of mortal ills prevailing.
> For still our ancient foe
> Doth seek to work us woe;
> His craft and power are great,
> And armed with cruel hate,
> On Earth is not his equal.'

When she had stood, she brought Ellie with her in her arms, and as the bairn had again put her face against the upper region of her keeper's bosom, Abigail gently laid her head sideways and rested her cheek on the flat part of the lassie's head as she sang. Ellie seemed to be immediately lulled by this action, and was quickly beginning to dover with her heavy-lidded eyes shut tightly.

When we began the second verse, I returned my attention to the hymnal and followed along somewhat, though I kept occasionally looking aside to my lass across the aisle. In paying attention to her, I missed most of the song only picking it up again with the foretold doom of the Prince of Darkness at the end of the third verse: 'One little word shall fell him.' Ultimately, we made it through all four verses, and Abigail knew every word.

Once the song was ended, the books were returned to their wee shelves in the back of the pews and everyone sat down. I hastily took my seat for fear of sticking out like a sore thumb and gave the young man at the front my rapt attention. At that point, I presumed that he was the priest, or pastor or parson, or whoever was in charge of this kirk.

He spoke kind words of welcome for a few moments. Though his speech was loud enough for my big lugs to hear, I wondered how others in the back were faring and began to doubt that he was the one who regularly gave the sermon. Looking over to my lass, I saw that she herself appeared to be dovering with her arms wrapped up around the sleeping Ellie. They made a beautiful pair and I found myself smiling at them until there was movement up front.

Two men of about five and twenty years of age began moving up the aisle then, each carrying a large basket which they supervised the passing of. I watched as everyone present threw something in the wicker bowls. Even the most wee lassies dropped what appeared to be pennies onto the pile with glee.

I felt somewhat apprehensive in seeing this, for although there was no one behind me or even next to me in my pew, I thought I might feel guilty in not putting something in the basket under the gaze of the man working his way up the aisle. I had already given up my one big bill to Esther, so after digging around in my coat pocket I extracted a one dollar note which I held at the ready in the loof of my hand. As the man with the basket on the women's side approached, I noticed that he was paying close attention to what was deposited. I watched as the woman in the cream corsage with the clubfooted laddie placed a single bill in the basket. She had pulled it from the inside of the laddie's coat. From my vantage point in the dimness I couldn't see what denomination it was, but I saw that it had three digits which struck me as being an extravagant offering. Then without giving it any apparent thought, she reached up to her lugs and snatched the two pearl earrings from their perch upon her lobes and cast them in the basket with the siller.

In consideration of the five-hundred dollar note I had already donated, I should have thought this little kirk in the wilderness was having the best night of charity in its existence, and yet it didn't feel that way. Looking about the room, there was nothing particularly ornate, no gold, no stained glass, no grand, vaulted ceilings, not even any cushions on the pews. Yet a feeling within told me that these sorts of grand donations were not unusual, despite the fact that the local oeconomy had been in a slump since 1893, and we were yet to enter into the prosperous years known locally as the 'Gay Nineties'.

The man seemed to take careful note of the woman's offerings before passing the basket to the final pew where Abigail and her wee friend were sleeping. The man paused for one tick with the basket hovering before my lass as if he didn't know if he should wake her, and then Hannah reached over and took the basket from him with one hand, then withdrew a massive wad of bills from her handbag and threw them in. She handed the man back the basket and his big eyes looked into its depths for an instant before he turned and walked back down the aisle.

I couldn't see any numbers, but I could reliably estimate that it was more than thirty notes that Hannah had casually thrown in. Throughout the entire event she never seemed to pay any great attention to what she was doing and acted as casually as if it were an every day occurrence for her to cast heaps of filthy lucre in the offering basket. Her friend added nothing but barely looked aside to witness as if altogether disinterested in the proceedings. Abigail and Ellie appeared to sleep through the whole thing.

The man on my side approached then and though I felt oddly inadequate in doing so, I threw my note in. Upon seeing what I had donated, the man smiled sharply at me, then turned and walked back up the aisle.

I have to say, I rather detest the fact that most kirks speir the offering before the service. This was a perfect case in point, when they wanted you to pay up front though as yet you had no idea what you were laying out money for. After all, there was no guarantee that their doctrine wasn't going to clash with your own.

Still, I had an open mind as I awaited the continuation of the service. No one seemed to have any great anticipation over its beginning with the exception of the woman in the cream corsage. She still held her laddie in her lap and was leaning out into the aisle so as to have an unobstructed view of the front.

I leaned out a little myself to see what came next, and I have to say it surprised me somewhat. The lad who had led the song had stepped forward to take a seat in a pew at the front. And then the great curtain which hung behind the table before which he had stood parted just far enough to allow entrance of a man rather phantastically dressed as I supposed him to be a hybrid between a crusading Christian knight and a Mussulman. The most of his outfit, which appeared as a long robe in shape, was patched together like a quilt with various patterns making up the individual parts, but a giant, red St George's Cross, as it appears on the flag of England, made up the greatest portion across his chest. Upon his chin was a great white beard, and upon his head he wore a white turban. There was a great corded, golden belt around his waist, and from it hung what looked like the curved blade of a scimitar, with a rounded jewel in its hilt, winking devilishly in the light of the candles like a devilish, red eye. He stepped up even with the table, and the entire congregation immediately grew still and quiet, with their complete attention focussed upon the man, excepting my lass and her wee friend who were still dovering in the pew across the aisle from me.

A few ticks of the clock passed in perfect silence, and then the man began his discourse, speaking with such volume that he might as well have been sitting next to me in the pew.

'When the Hebrews, the once chosen people of God came to the place called Marah, they had only just been delivered from the hand of Pharaoh at the Red Sea. In joyous thanksgiving Moses and the children of Israel had only just sang a great song to the Lord, but in three days' time they would lose their faith and murmur against God for the waters of Marah were bitter. But the Lord reproved them with a miracle, for He directed Moses to cast a tree into the waters, and they were made sweet. In Exodus 15, God then says to the Hebrews: "If thou wilt diligently hearken to the voice of the Lord thy God, and wilt do that which is right in his sight, and wilt give ear to his commandments, and keep all his statutes, I will put none of these diseases upon thee, which I have brought upon the Egyptians: for I am the Lord that healeth thee."'

The man spoke these words perfectly from memory, with no need to actually read from the Book itself, then hovered for a tick in his speech before proceeding.

'During his Earthly ministry, our Lord said that among the signs that will prove the church are to cast out devils, to speak in new tongues, and to lay hands on the sick, so that they may recover. Here among us tonight is one in need of such healing, and we know, we true followers of God in fact are given to verify, to prove the faith of this one, for through faith anything can be accomplished, if it is prayed for in the name of our Lord.'

This necessarily had my attention, though I had no idea where it was going, as yet. I looked across the aisle once more to see Abigail soundly sleeping with Ellie in her lap. The lassie had balled up her wee fist and thrust a thumb in her mouth. Next to them, Hannah was staring intently at the robed man.

I forget the exact nature of his discourse, but faith seemed to be the chief point, with the understanding that perfect faith led to miracles, and to healing, and to intercession by angels. I was only vaguely acquainted with the practices of faith healing that had recently become so popular in America, and had no idea what was to come next. In looking upon my dovering lassie, I found myself desiring to nod off somewhat, only I wouldn't get the chance. Not only was a great deal of attention about to be paid to the rear pews in our vicinity, but throughout the whole building all hell was going to break loose.

As the preaching man continued his sermon, his voice began to reach a certain crescendo as he quoted all manner of verses regarding the apostles and the day of Pentecost. Though I cannot bring to mind every one, I recall the following being voiced loudly: 'And when the day of Pentecost was fully come... suddenly there came a sound from heaven as of a rushing mighty wind, and it filled all the house where they were sitting. And there appeared unto them cloven tongues like as of fire, and it sat upon each of them. And they were all filled with the Holy Ghost and began to speak with other tongues, as the Spirit gave them utterance.'

It seemed then that there was no delaying a certain inevitability, for no sooner had these verses from the Acts of the Apostles been spoken, than a great, unintelligible ejaculation spewed forth from the man's mouth with the force of a cannon. What he pronounced I could not say, only it resounded with such force that no one, including Abigail and Ellie, could ignore it.

My lass and her wee friend jumped at the sudden advent of noise, and no sooner had the echo of the man's voice finished its reverberating search of every nook and cranny of the building than the various bairns of the congregation in their short trousers and white cotton gowns took up the call and began screaming what seemed to me at the time to be random syllables at the top of their lungs. They flooded the aisles only to be followed by every other body in the pews, including the older lassies and Esther herself, whose sharp face instantly became the visage of a howling madwoman.

There was such a cacophony of noise, and such utter pandemonium throughout, that I found myself fearing what could possibly come next, since for all I knew given the queerness of this whole enterprise, we were about to be offered up as a sacrifice to Baal and murdered in our pews. Seeing that all propriety in keeping the genders segregated had been lost anyway, I jumped across the aisle next to my lass. Abigail's eyes were wide and surprisingly green in the dim light. I caught sight of Ellie's face and saw that the bairn was alert but not overly concerned. Leaning in close enough to Abigail so as to be heard over the racket, I said, 'Maybe we sud gae the noo.'

She looked to me and nodded, only we were arrested in our movement when Hannah reached around Abigail's shoulders to grasp my arm. She loudly, but steadily said, 'You won't want to miss this.'

She released my arm and I barely had time to regard her when the attention of the entire congregation turned in our direction. A dozen screeching bairns of both sexes came running up the aisle and I seriously thought they were coming for us, only they stopped one pew short. The woman in the cream corsage still sat clutching her lad in her lap, but she surprised me then in turning her head to look somewhat fearfully over her shoulder at Hannah, and in the silent communication of their eyes, I realised that they knew each other. Hannah smiled reassuringly at the woman as the bairns came for her.

The children clung to the woman, pulled her to her feet, and beckoned her forward. During their transit to the front of the kirk, she appeared somewhat fearful yet altogether resolute to proceed. As she carried her lad to the front, the congregants in the aisle parted to allow her passage. She approached the table, with its great, flat, empty space, and stood opposite of the robed man. There was still so much wild screaming, mostly random and unintelligible but occasionally peppered with Hallelujahs and Amens, that I had no idea what the man was saying. Clearly he indicated to the woman that she was to place her child upon the table, which once having been accomplished, she knelt on the floor and bowed her head over her folded hands.

At that point, Hannah and her friend stood and made their way to the aisle. Before leaving us she leaned in towards my lug and said, 'You bought a ticket, you might as well enjoy the show.' Then she turned away from me and started walking forward towards the table with the kneeling woman and her clubfooted lad.

Looking to Abigail I said, 'Is this normal for a kirk service?'

She made no reply except to shake her head as she looked upon me with wide, surprised eyes. Then she stood, and with Ellie reclining against her bosom again, she stepped around me into the aisle. I got to my feet and took my place next to her, and we cautiously advanced to see what was to happen next.

There was a mass of bodies in the aisle, but carefully wending our way through we were able to get within about fifteen feet of the table. Then, as if the wild ululations had not been queer enough, every hair on my body stood on end as man, woman and bairn alike began to fall to the floor and thrash about wildly as if one and all were suddenly suffering from a severe case of *delirium tremens*. The only bodies to remain standing were the preacher, Hannah, her companion and Abigail and myself. The woman in the cream corsage continued to kneel with her head laid down upon her clasped hands. Her lad remained on the table, looking about curiously, but strangely rather calm given the situation.

Again I felt as though I should be leading my lass away, but again Hannah was there to stop me. As I began to pull Abigail towards the back of the building, Hannah put her hand on my arm and when I looked to her face, she shook her head. Then she held up a finger as if to indicate that I should wait a moment.

The robed man held up his hands, and everyone quieted immediately. After all the terrific noise that had echoed within my lugs for the past several minutes, the sudden silence felt nearly unbearable. In the quiet he said to the kneeling woman, 'Is your faith great enough?'

She tearfully responded, 'Yes, yes it is!' without looking at him.

The man looked up above him, to where there was a great opening in the ceiling directly above the table. From where I was standing it was difficult to see at the correct angle, but it appeared to open directly to the night sky. The man turned his eyes upward as if looking all the way to heaven for confirmation before saying: 'O woman, great is thy faith: be it unto thee even as thou wilt. Behold, the Angel of the Lord!'

All were silent. Then a curious thing happened. Wee, wispy clouds began to pour into the room through the opening in the ceiling, only to evaporate within a few seconds of making contact with all of the pent up hot air inside the building. Upon seeing this minor sign, everyone again went wild and began screaming praises as they wildly gesticulated, waving their arms about, dancing, and in some cases falling to the floor and rolling around. If any of the regular members of this group retained their composure, it was the robed man himself and Moses, who still sat up front at the piano with his back turned to us. I didn't realise it until later when I reviewed the entire episode in my mind, but as the events proceeded, Moses had begun to play a queer, tinkling tune on the piano as if in accompaniment to what was about to occur.

At this, the first sign of the angel's coming, Abigail stepped back and I put my arms around both her and Ellie. Throughout the entire appearance of this angelic apparition, I held my lass and her wee friend tightly as if fearful that this winged visitor should recognise them as those of her own kind and whisk them away to heaven with her.

Certainly the sudden entry of clouds from the aperture in the ceiling was curious, but that was nothing compared to what happened next. The most magnificent light suddenly filled the room, only it wasn't a white light, rather it was the complete colour of the rainbow filling the building from the night time darkness above. And then we saw feet.

Slim, delicate, stocking feet with the crudest of sandals adorning them appeared, and then slowly, as the form of the trig body was further revealed, the long skirt of a shimmering, white gown was displayed. A womanly form came into view, but this was no common earth-bound female, for the creature we saw descend before us bore the most magnificent wings covered in white feathers, which spread from behind her back and flapped ever so gently until she set foot upon the table. Upon her head was a golden crown, about her neck was a great chain of gold, and upon her fingers were rings bearing jewels of many colours. She was a splendid sight. Looking upon her, I could think to call her nothing other than an angel.

She came down to one knee next to the lad with the thrawn ankles, and after looking upon him with a beautiful, calming smile, she brought her gaze up to the woman who still knelt with her head bowed before him.

The angel softly laid her long, delicate fingers on the woman's cheek, and gently caressed her skin until she dared to look up. As tears streamed from the woman's greeting eyes, the angel said: 'Be it unto ye, according to your faith.' Then she turned her eyes back upon the lad, and with a sudden tremor in her right hand, the angel grasped the lad's leg and sharply drew her hand over his calf and ankle. Like some sort of magic trick, some kind of simple sleight of hand, as the angel's bejewelled fingers passed over the joint above his right foot, his leg suddenly became straight. My whole body shivered as I witnessed this, and as a storm of Hallelujahs erupted from all quarters, I looked to Abigail to see her emerald eyes were huge with wonder at the sight.

I turned again to the table to see the miracle repeated as the angel again put her right hand to the lad's left leg. As he was again healed, glorious shouting filled the building. I looked to the laddie's face to see that he exhibited no pain in this procedure, rather he looked up to the angel with a wondrous curiosity. Then without further ado, there was a great flapping of condor wings as the angel rose into the air, and quickly moved to make her egress by way of the opening in the ceiling. Only before she did, she cast her gaze upon one more person within that building filled with bodies. As if magnetically attracted to my countenance, her deep, blue eyes shot directly to me. Since first making her appearance, this angelic being had appeared tractable and benevolent, desiring only to spread joy and hope, and then she looked upon me. She transmitted nothing pernicious with her eyes, rather her study of me bore an air of neutrality, so lacking in feeling that it felt utterly ambivalent. Yet that is what unsettled me so about that simple look. It felt as though she recognised me for what I am, and earnestly set me apart from every other body in that building. And then her eyes were gone.

I watched as the sandaled feet disappeared, then observed as the prostrate woman physically took possession of her laddie again. She scooped him up in her arms and began to wail tears. As for the lad himself, as yet he appeared to not even know exactly what had happened to him.

I was still holding Abigail close, and as I turned my eyes upon her again I saw that Ellie was sitting up in her arms, somewhat alert. She seemed to be curious as to what all the noise was that had interrupted her nap, but held no greater concern in the matter than that.

There was a great deal of casual talk among the bairns then, as if this entire event was of no great import, and I realised that the service was suddenly at an end. As I watched Esther walk up to the turbaned priest and begin whispering in his lug, from next to me Hannah said, 'I told you that you would not want to miss out. I had to really pay up for the angel to put in an appearance. I doubt even Mrs Kibblewhit's hefty donation was enough to reach the threshold.'

I looked down to her. Her gaze was still up front, focussed upon the kneeling woman, whom I correctly presumed to be Mrs Kibblewhit, and her bairn. I speired, 'What threshold?'

Hannah turned her light blue eyes up to mine and said, 'There is a minimum, collective donation required in order for the angel to appear.' She shrugged somewhat sceptically and continued, 'If the money isn't there, it doesn't matter how much faith you have, the angel won't even show.'

I turned my attention forward again and speired, 'Why are ye here? I never expected to see ye here of all places.'

As I said this, I noted that the priest was looking in our general direction, although I was able to see that he was quite specifically staring at my lass. For a tick, I thought he was looking at Ellie, perhaps in some way concerned about her, but then I noted the movement of his eyes. There was a hard, up and down motion, as if he was studying Abigail.

Hannah said, 'We came to see the angel, of course. The Network sent Rodríguez and I,' she said as she indicated the young woman standing next to her with a flick of her thumb, 'to observe and write up a report on what we found.' She was looking at the priest as she quietly said, 'You seem to be attracting a lot of attention. That's usually bad news, Fisher.'

I shook my head and said, 'Na, he's no' looking at me, raither he's looking at Abigail.'

Just then, the priest turned and walked through the curtain behind him, leaving Esther alone next to the table.

Somewhat more loudly, Hannah said, 'Yup, but it looked like the angel had eyes quite specifically for you.'

The young woman identified to me as Rodríguez turned and looked up to me over Hannah's head and said, 'I noticed that myself.' She spoke fluidly with a pleasant accent that suggested her origin as being somewhere south of the border. After stepping back to remove the obstacle of Hannah's body between us and flashing her brilliant, wry white smile at me, she said, 'Mr Fisher es it?' She daintily held her hand in my direction with the wrist bent and said, 'My name es Ana-María de la Paz Rodríguez y Morataya.'

I looked briefly into her expressive, dark eyes before gently taking the finger-ends of her right hand in my left and said, '*Mucho gusto, Señora Ana-María de la Paz Rodríguez y Morataya.*'

Her braw countenance fell somewhat at that, though she didn't remove her fingers from mine. Realising my mistake, I simply corrected myself with, '*Señorita Ana-María de la Paz Rodríguez y Morataya.*'

Ana's smile returned just in time for a sharp clearing of the throat to be heard next to us. I dropped the offered hand, and immediately put my arm around Abigail and said, 'And this is Abigail.'

As Hannah turned back to look at us, my lass intoned, 'Mrs Gail Fisher.' She was holding Ellie still and had a proper excuse to not offer her one hand to either of the other two lassies. Ana smiled pleasantly at her. Hannah smiled queerly at me. Abigail graced us all with the general beauty of her visage and Ellie kicked her stocking feet and gurgled until we were interrupted.

As the building was beginning to be cleared of its occupants, Esther had walked up and now said, 'Supper is served in the dining hall. All of you, of course, are invited.'

I looked past her to see that Mrs Kibblewhit and her son were being slowly walked up the aisle with a couple of the older girls on either side of her. She still carried her lad in her arms, possibly fearful of putting his newly corrected ankles to the test. Or perhaps out of force of habit. Only once did she look aside to Hannah as she passed us in the aisle, and after smiling widely at her, Hannah gave a curt nod of her head.

Esther was looking at us all rather sharply, and I could nearly hear the little wheels in her skull turning as she tried to ascertain whether or not we knew each other prior to our appearance at the evening service. She was so thin that the veins on the side of her head were clearly visible, and even in the candlelight I could see them pulsing quickly as if her brain needed an extra dose of oxygen in order to properly flesh out the possibilities of our story.

We all stood quietly together for a silent tick, and then I realised that in the standard social sense of humanity, the five of us with Ellie included, had made of ourselves a little grouping, and as the supposed male, it was up to me to lead the interaction and agree to our hostess's summons.

'Thank ye, Esther,' I said. 'Of course we are ready to eat.'

I held out my hand with my fingers splayed as I politely inclined my head to indicate that all of the ladies ought to precede me. Esther led the way out of the kirk building with Ana and Hannah behind her. My lass stayed at my side and I speired, 'Do ye want me to take Ellie for ye?'

Abigail replied, 'No, thank you, dear. I think I like her right where she is at.' Then she put her lips to the flat top of the lassie-wean's head and kissed her.

As we walked out into the darkness, I gently put my arm about them both and smiled to myself.

III

At first, she didn't like the tall, straight one in brown, but this woman in green, who already felt as safe and familiar as Mama, had given her recommendation, and so she had made peace with the presence of the brown one with the dark hair and eyes. It seemed that while she was in the arms of the green woman she could handle any adversity, and the only time the sharp angles formed within her on their trip back to the church was when the grey-haired woman had tried to touch her. She had seen squares before her in that moment as she cried out in distress. Even when inside again, when all the noise and commotion started up, she could feel the arms of love about her, and was able to simply observe.

Outside the church she had seen the nice man with the flowers. Inside she had seen the angel with the blue eyes and the feathery wings. Then she had seen the gruff man in the turban. There were plenty of strange things to contemplate within the silence of her head, but the one thing that remained clearly in her mind, the single image that she seemed to constantly see, was that red jewel at the end of his big sword. So far as she could tell from a distance, it was a soft, natural, beautiful object, and ever *since she had first seen it that same morning, she had wanted to touch it. Even after the man went away, she kept thinking on it, willing it to come to her, so that she might put her little fingers about it for study.*

Sunday, 19 April 1896, 8:55 PM

As I recall, even if we had been able to see the moon at that time, it would have been only the slightest sliver of a crescent. What little light it might have provided was fully blocked, however, as a thick covering of low clouds had flown in during the brief evening service to oppress us with stagnant, humid air. The braziers were still lit in front of the kirk building, but they did little to illuminate the nearby structures to the south. They stood as various, poorly-defined wooden and canvas cubes, with the exception of one grand building which was filled both with light and people.

We followed Esther and entered to find ourselves within what was clearly the dining hall. Easily, sixty bodies filled it and we found ourselves surrounded primarily with the same lads and lassies of the kirk service. Every last one of them was chattering away again, only the noise was much less debilitating here as the wooden walls of the structure only rose to a height of about four feet. Above that, and terminating at the eaves of the wooden roof above, was an opening normally covered by great sheets of canvas, but which had been rolled up allowing for the ingress of fresh air and the egress of some of the excesses of conversation. Mosquito netting covered most of those apertures and seemed effective at keeping the majority of the insects out.

Esther found us an empty table flanked with a single, crudely knotted oak bench on one side and the lassies sat. I noticed that Ana made a point of taking her place just next to Abigail, and no sooner had they found themselves seated than a pleasant conversation regarding Ellie began. I turned to launch some speirings at our hostess regarding the angel, and the kirk, and the situation of this queer place in general, but she was already walking away.

I watched for a moment as her long grey hair went wagging side to side while she quickly made her way outside and then I turned back to the table. Ana and Abigail were both playing with Ellie, gushing over her pretty eyes in the sweet manner some lassies like to carry on over every positive they can associate with bairns. I looked past them to see Hannah sitting some several feet apart from them. She looked to me and then raised her hand, crooked a finger as if to say *come here* and then pointed next to her at a knot in the rustic bench on the side farthest away from Abigail. Looking to my lass again, she seemed to be thoroughly occupied with Ellie, and already making friends with Ana, so seeing that she did not need me just then I made my way to Hannah and obeyed her command to sit after setting my carpetbag on the floor next to her own handbag beneath the bench.

'Do you mind telling me how you came to be here?' she speired.

I flicked my eyes down the length of the table towards Ellie and said, 'That lassie-wean, richt there. We were simply making oor way south doun the roadway atween here and the Gulf, and then there is this lass oot in the trees. We couldna leave her there.'

'No, I suppose not,' Hannah said and looked at Ellie for a few ticks. Then she turned her attention back to me and said, 'Whose is she?'

I shook my head. 'I kenna. We've been trying to find oot waur her mither is syne we arrived, but nane will tell us. Esther juist said her mither was ill, but she was lying to me.'

'How do you know she was lying?'

'Anytime a body lies to me my hair stands on end,' I succinctly replied.

Hannah nodded and, without a shred of doubt in her voice, simply said, 'Interesting.'

I swallowed and speired, 'Is it no' queer that ye and I sud meet up like this? I mean, we only made oor first acquaintance a few weeks ago.'

Hannah shrugged and said, 'Not really. It's a question of proximity. I happened to be in the same general area and, frequently, those of our kind get drawn to the same oddities like moths to a flame. One way or another.'

'And what sort of oddity, as ye say, are ye particularly speaking of in this instance?'

She smiled a bit and said, 'The angel, of course.'

The bench we were sitting on had us looking across the table at a blank wall, which meant we had a full room behind us with all of the eyes of those facing us upon our backs at one time or another. Hannah turned her head and looked briefly over her shoulder at something behind us then said, 'What did you think of the performance?'

I thought for a few ticks and said, 'Was that real? It looked real. At least the healing part. I'm no' sae certain about the wings and clouds and lichts and sic.'

'A prudent observation. I believe, for the most part, the clouds and rainbows and the getup she was wearing were all part of the show. But that healing was the real deal.'

'I thocht sae as weel, but hoo can ye be certain?'

Hannah turned her whole body about on the bench and pointed across the room. There, atop a table, stood Mrs Kibblewhit's son, his mother holding him by one hand, and a lass in a white cotton gown of about twenty years I recognised from the kirk holding the other. They were helping him to balance as he slowly, tentatively tried out his new feet. The lad's face presented an ongoing range of emotions from cautious to pleased, but they were all happy, positive feelings that he put on display, and they were only overshadowed in power by the exultant pleasure of Mrs Kibblewhit herself.

As we watched, Hannah said, 'I've spent the last few weeks since you and I met out at Doctor Lamb's carefully positioning myself to be invited out here to this church, greasing palms with thousands of dollars and pretending to be someone of society, and, moreover, to ingratiate myself with Mrs Kibblewhit and her son, Percy. We thoroughly checked out both of their stories. This was no false, emotion induced faith healing, tonight. It wasn't a scam of any kind. That boy was really born with twisted up feet, and as you can see, he's all better now.'

I observed as the lad carefully reached the end of the table, and then with the help of his mother and the other attendant lass, Percy turned about with a smile on his face and began marching in the opposite direction.

When I turned my attention back to Hannah, her face bore a mask of disgruntlement. 'What?' I speired.

'All that work, acting like an ass for weeks and giving hand-outs just so Rodríguez and I could be allowed here, and then you show up, uninvited, and they simply open up and let you in on the spot. To say the very least, it annoys me.' She hovered a blink before adding: 'More than that, it makes me wonder...'

'Ach. Hoo much did ye pay into the basket the nicht?'

She shrugged. 'About twenty-five hundred, I think. I peeled over twice that much out of the slush fund and pretended to be Mrs Kibblewhit's best friend ever just to be offered an invite to this place. There have been rumours among certain circles about it for years, but everyone's so hush-hush about it we never would have found it, otherwise. They try to keep this place quiet, but although since the beginning they've pushed the need for us to be discreet should we see a miracle, I can see how it would be impossible to fully keep the lid on things.'

I was trying to calculate within my ken what the total bill for the night's performance was, then speired Hannah, 'Ye said there was a particular threshold. What is the minimum cost for the angel to appear?'

She made a shaky so-so motion of her hand as she said, 'Ten-thousand in total between the amount paid just to be invited and the amount collected at the service itself. More or less.'

'And ye pretended to be Mrs Kibblewhit's friend?'

'She's rich, she was already in the loop with this local cattle farm heiress, Mrs Oglethorpe, so I got in good with her because it's generally a long process to get to the point of actually being invited.' Hannah turned to look across the room at Mrs Kibblewhit again and continued, 'She's a rich, lonely young widow, and none too bright. If I needed money I could probably have soaked her for everything she has by pretending to be some distant relation of her husband's. The long-lost niece or cousin who's fallen on hard times or needs an expensive surgical operation, or whatever. Instead I pretended to be another rich young woman looking for some hole to throw my money in and we got to be friends in a manner of weeks.'

'Weel, with that jewellery and yer clothes ye look the part. Nice dress, by the way.'

Hannah sighed. 'It's a *Charvet* from Paris altered to fit me. It's rich, but I don't like it. It doesn't show off any of the subtleties of the few good parts I have.'

'Ach. Sae ye used Mrs Kibblewhit to get here?'

'Don't make it sound cruel. I just borrowed her affections for a few weeks in order to get an introduction, then I started paying out to Mrs Oglethorpe who acts as a *liaison* between the church and the real world. I made clear to her that the cash flow would come to a quick halt if I didn't get to come up here with my dear friend Edna Kibblewhit and see the supposed miracle myself.'

'So Mrs Oglethorpe, the cattle heiress, is a kirk member?'

Hannah shook her head. 'Not exactly. She's rarely ever here, apparently. It's another question how she first got involved with this place and I don't wonder that geography had something to do with it. I haven't seen it, but my understanding is that the Oglethorpe ranch isn't too far to the east of here. For the most part, she goes about in society in the cities and gets invited to parties where she solicits donations for charities. Foreign missionaries and starving children in Africa and what not. We haven't looked too far into where the money is really going, but it appears that at least a sizeable amount of it is ending up where she says, out of the country.'

'And she was yer connection to get here?'

Hannah nodded. 'Yup. Apparently, that's how it always works. Most of the time she just asks for charity, but occasionally she finds someone who meets certain criteria.' She looked again to Mrs Kibblewhit and her son. They were both enjoying a bit of celebrity status as a mob of lassies surrounded them and made a sort of pet of Percy. Hannah continued: 'Rich, mostly unconnected to any friends or family, but with some relation in need of healing. And I think it helps if they are a little dull, too. Edna and Percy Kibblewhit were already well on their way when Rodríguez and I were able to insert ourselves, and I think we nearly ruined things. I had to convince Mrs Oglethorpe that I was rich and could be discreet. That helped, but I almost feel like our being allowed here involved more than that.'

'Hoo so?'

'Well, it may sound odd, but Mrs Oglethorpe isn't just some rich rancher's wife, she actually worked in the business of husbandry and breeding for years. I got the feeling that I was being sized up by her the same way as a cow might be for his meat. Me and Rodríguez both, to be honest.'

That seemed a queer statement but I didn't know what to make of it. Ellie suddenly ejected a sharp laugh, and I looked past Hannah towards the two lassies playing with the wean and speired, 'And wha is Ana Rodríguez, exactly?'

'Just another member of the Network. In relation to our act with Mrs Oglethorpe and Mrs Kibblewhit, she played the part of my lady's maid. Back in our world, the real world, she's being trained as a shooter. Jackson sent her along with me simply because she was available.'

'Shooter?' I laughed a little under my breath as I said, 'I hope ye're no' expecting gunplay.'

'Nope. This is a total no fuss situation. Find a way in, observe, and get out and report on it. We're already done, except for the report.'

Hannah's eyes flicked up to mine and we stared at each other for a few ticks. I said, 'And is that all? Like when we met afore, ye came and listened to oor story aboot hoo Doctor Lamb and I fell in a sink-hole and found that trapped Highland Lassie with her arm and legs cut aff and were attacked by Shell Indians and wound-up automatons? Ye did naething to help, didna even say a thing aboot oor experience, and ye were gane ten minutes later.'

Hannah maintained her chilly gaze, and without blinking she nodded and said: 'Yup. That's the Network, Fisher. Sorry if that disappoints you.'

'But what aboot everything else? All the money, and hoo Mrs Oglethorpe got involved and the way she sized ye up, as ye said. And what aboot the angel herself? Ye saw what she did, but wha is she really?'

Hannah looked away and shrugged. 'More mysteries, but nothing to do with why we are here. We came to see if the so-called angel really performs miracles, and we saw it. First light tomorrow, we'll disappear and go find some other questionable event to gather intelligence on. If our higher-ups at the Network think they should act on it, then that's up to them.'

'When micht they do that?'

Hannah looked back at me and earnestly said, 'Never would be my guess.'

I shook my head. 'Ach. What's the use?'

'Well, knowledge, for what it's worth. We learn a little more about the oddities of the world every year, and someday, maybe, we'll have answers.'

'To what?'

'To why a supposed angel has the ability to physically heal the crippled. To why your hair stands on end every time someone lies to you. To why I can so often feel the very emotion and intention of people through brick walls. Only little things like that.'

We were quiet again and the only nearby sound was that of Ana and Abigail talking and Ellie laughing as they played with her. Then there was an eruption of clapping from the bairns behind us as supper was produced. A massive side of beef skewered on a long wooden stake was brought in from outside, carried aloft on the shoulders of two young men. This was followed immediately by steaming pots and loaves of bread. The beef was suspended in air by placing the ends of the stake atop two tables and the pots were set out with great ladles while the loaves were dispersed all over to individual tables.

When the clapping began, Abigail and Ana neatly worked together to each take one of Ellie's hands and help her to join in the approbation. The wean smiled. Ana leaned in and said to her, 'Are you hungry?'

Ellie stuck her tongue out and chewed at it some.

As bread and cutlery was being spread about the dining hall, Hannah calmly stated, 'She's quite striking.'

It surprised me to hear her say anything about Ellie since so far she seemed to have fairly well ignored the wean. But, as if reading my thoughts, Hannah turned to me and said, 'Not the child, I mean "Mrs Gail Fisher."'

'Hoo do ye mean?'

One side of Hannah's mouth pulled up rather wryly as she said, 'When we met before, and she was sleeping behind that closed door out at Dr Lamb's, I just assumed she was some sort of hideous hag of a woman.'

'Ach.'

She leaned towards me and quietly said, 'You surprised me, Mary Fisher. Like I said, there often seems to be some kind of unseen attraction to oddities like we witnessed tonight by our kind, and so I should have expected to see *you* here. But her?' she said as she looked back towards Abigail. 'Nice.'

Again I said: 'Ach.'

Two lassies came along then and set various pieces of silverware, a pile of roughly cut, badly stained napkins, and a loaf of bread on our table. Across the room behind us, two lads were hacking off pieces of the dripping beef carcass and throwing the cutlets on plates while more lassies were ladling out what looked like stew into big bowls which were then passed hand to hand to the far corners of the dining hall.

'Does it no' strike ye as queer hoo all these bairns look alike?'

Hannah was watching the various foodstuffs making their way about the room as she said to me, 'The result of isolation, I'm certain. No concern of mine.'

'What *does* actually concern ye?'

Without bothering to look at me, she said, 'Right now: supper.'

I was still facing across the table, effectively looking the opposite direction from Hannah when I saw something roll beneath my bench. Instinctively, I pushed my two boots together to stop the object and looked to see that it was a lumpy ball of perhaps a few inches of circumference, and though my first thought was that it was made of leather, upon further consideration it appeared to be made of some form of latex. No sooner had I made a close inspection of it than a thin, wee lass of about five years, wearing the uniform white cotton shift, came scooting along after it on her knees. She stopped and stared at the ball where it was trapped between my boots for a few ticks, then slowly lifted her dark eyes to look at my face. As she did so, I noted the unco bumpiness of her head. It was so extreme that even though her scalp was covered with a wild mop of mousey-brown hair, I could clearly see numerous crests and troughs where it appeared that her very skull was undulating with the force of an ocean current.

It was obvious to me that the lassie had been chasing the rubbery ball, and so I pulled my feet apart so that she could retrieve it, only she continued to gaze into my eyes with a tentative look of ambivalence. In those few ticks of the clock in which we stared at each other, I felt as though her opinion of me could easily have gone in either direction, and to be perfectly honest I very nearly ruined our introduction through my casual style of inaction. But then a queer thing happened. I smiled at her.

For most people, it wouldn't be particularly unusual to pleasantly bare the teeth at a bairn upon first encountering them, but the truth is that at that time I was still such a social blockhead that I bore a natural fear of weans and generally went out of my way to avoid them. When it came to the befriending and aiding and abetting of the bairnies, Abigail was definitely their best bet at promoting themselves into an uplifted situation, and while I was beginning to change my ways, at that time I was still too inexperienced to usually take any initiative with them. But then this lassie came along and stared up at me from beneath the table, and without even thinking about it, I did my best to make nice with her. If there was any immediate pleasure to be taken, it was in receiving a smile in return from her.

From the other side of Hannah, I could still hear Ana and Abigail laughing and fussing with Ellie. Hannah herself was saying something about being ready to divest herself of this present project in favour of something more interesting as the wee lass reached between my boots and took the ball in her tiny fingers. For just a tick, she held it up between us where I could better see it in the light, and I thought it to look like vulcanized rubber. The lass gave me one final smile then scooted out of sight.

Hannah had fallen silent for a moment as she continued to watch the food being dispersed throughout the room, but no sooner had the lassie-wean departed than she said, 'Making friends under the table, Fisher?'

I looked to the side of her face and she pulled her lips into something resembling a smile, but said nothing else. I held my wheesht.

I heard Abigail saying to Ellie: 'Oh look, dear, here comes supper! Are you hungry, Ellie?'

I looked past Hannah and smiled a bit at my lass. She was so thoroughly enjoying herself that every trace of her fatigue temporarily fled her. Instead she looked vibrant and healthy, and Ellie sitting upon her lap with two braw lassies beaming smiles upon her seemed to be responding nicely. Abigail happened to look up to me then and, after catching my gaze, said, 'I certainly hope supper is worth the amount you paid, Mr Fisher.'

I nodded to her but said nothing in response.

She turned her attention back to Ellie and said, 'Of course, that was quite a show we were made privy to, as well.'

'Aye, lass. I kenna what to make of it myself.'

I felt a slight judgement had been made upon me, communicated by my lassie's eyes, but then a lad brought a pitcher of water to the table and Ana began to conduct some level of pre-supper toilette upon Ellie with a wet napkin and Abigail's attention was taken away from me.

I didn't always have access to someone in the know like Hannah, and I was thinking to speir her some more questions when hands baring plates and bowls were thrust over my shoulders. Like manna from heaven, a generous spread was suddenly laid before us. In receiving this gift, I thought to turn to our benefactors and give thanks, only in looking over my shoulder I found the one older lass near to about twenty years staring at me with unco concern. I locked eyes with her and expected her to simply run off. Instead she stepped right up to me, and at our relative heights with me sitting and her standing we found ourselves nearly on the level. Staring hard at me she said, 'I'd pray real hard afore I et if I was you.' Then she glanced down the length of the bench and took Hannah, Abigail and Ana in with her eyes before turning and stalking off with an uneven gait suggesting that one leg was some inches longer than the other.

There was silence at our table for a tick, then, out of the corner of her mouth, Hannah quietly said to me, 'It almost feels like this is our last meal.'

She turned about on the bench to face the table and I said, 'Aye?'

'Yup.' She began pulling the rings off of her fingers as she said, 'It is almost as if somewhere an electric chair is waiting for us. Believe me, I've been there, once,' she earnestly said. Then she reached down and threw the rings in her handbag before turning her attention to the repast.

Abigail and Ana had already retreated into their little world where their fancy revolved around Ellie and nothing and no one else. Abigail was saying sweet things to the lass as she positioned her to eat and Ana was laying out dishes and silverware for them.

Hannah hooked a finger over a big steaming bowl and pulled it in front of us. It appeared to be some sort of thick meat stew with assorted vegetables. As she began spooning some into a bowl she unconcernedly said, 'Usually executions come at dawn. I think we might ought to be out of here by then.'

'What if trouble comes early?'

She smiled and said, 'We're always ready for it, though I sincerely doubt anything of the sort is brewing. These are just odd people.' She pushed a bowl of stew at me saying, 'Best eat up.'

I immediately pushed it away with a sharp, 'Ach.'

'Problem?'

'Nae meat for me.'

'Odd.'

'Juist hoo it is.'

There was a bowl of snap beans at the other end of the table which, after removing a few of the best specimens in order to present to her wee friend, Abigail pushed in front of Hannah. Hannah then passed it in front of me and said, 'Mmm-mm, eat up,' before tasting her stew.

I would have preferred some salt on my beans, but finding no cellar among the dishes I proceeded to eat them plain from the bowl with my fingers. I looked down the table to see no one else speiring a blessing before the meal except for Ana. She quietly bowed her head then genuflected a cross upon herself before returning her attention to Ellie. Hannah tasted her food without preamble. She said nothing for a few ticks as she ate and stared through the mosquito netting before us into the darksome night.

I could hear Abigail tempting Ellie with the various foodstuffs available and turned my attention to her for a time. Over Hannah's head I saw that she had made a wee dish of samples for Ellie where she had separated the various vegetables of the stew as well as some snap beans,

85

bread and beef and was proceeding to have the wean taste each in turn. 'Do you like the potato, dear? Can you tell me if you like it?'

Ellie had yet to say an actual word in our presence, though even I could see it wasn't a complete lack of physical ability, rather a difficulty she had that originated somewhere within her mind. Or maybe her heart.

Abigail was looking at her ward's face as she said, 'Can you tell me if it is good or bad? Good? Bad?'

Ellie spent a great deal of time working the potato about in her mouth then smiled up at Abigail.

Ana was mashing a stewed carrot on a plate as she said, 'She should try the *zanahorias*. Very soft.'

Abigail held Ellie upright as Ana proceeded to feed her. The wean had a gurgling fit over the carrot which seemed the most positive response she could make and the two lassies went to laughing about it. I continued eating my beans. Hannah ate her stew. The noise of a hall full of people continued behind us. Which began to bother me.

'Hoo come I can only barely feel oot all of these bodies?' I quietly speired Hannah.

She shrugged. 'Someone's putting a damper on things. To keep things hidden from folks like us on the outside. Probably that angel.'

She spoke casually and went back to eating her stew. I said, 'Why are ye so unconcerned aboot this? This whole place, this whole situation is queer.'

'So? There's queer things, as you say, all over. It's nothing to me. We came to see the angel, we saw the angel, and now we go. That's our job. *Veni, Vidi*, but no need for *Vici*.'

'But there is something wrong here. I swear, all these young bairns. It is juist like with Ellie's mither wha is nae-waur to be found. Waur are their parents?'

Hannah threw her spoon in her stew and looked disgustedly up at me. 'Who cares?' When I stared without waver at her she rolled her eyes then continued: 'Like I said, what you see here is born of isolation. These people for whatever reason are religious, like plenty of people naturally are, and it just so happens that they have someone on hand who has a natural talent for straightening people out, example being Percy Kibblewhit. So they make a business out of it, out of putting on a show, and take in plenty of money doing it.'

'And waur does the money gae? It seems the performance has a vera expensive ticket but there's little to show for it.'

Hannah shrugged and reached for some bread. 'Who knows? Who cares? There's money everywhere for the taking. People put on shows all the time, and other people buy tickets.' She broke off a big chunk of bread and handed it to me, then threw a second piece in her bowl and began rolling it about in the dregs of her stew. 'If you want to moralise over the situation, simply realise that in exchange for money good things are happening here. Ten-thousand to get a boy's feet straightened out is a good deal. People commit mass-murder for ten-thousand. Hell, some'd kill for ten cents.'

Hannah began eating her bread while I weighed my own in my hand. It felt unnaturally heavy to me, like a stone. I looked down the table to see Abigail leaning over

Ellie saying, 'Good or bad? Can you tell me? If it is bad, you do not have to eat any more.'

Ellie was working something around in her mouth and then finally ejected her wee tongue with what looked like a masticated mass of onion on its tip. The lassies laughed a bit as Ana delicately removed the offending vegetable.

I sighed and said, 'All richt, I winna worry aboot it. Juist seems queer, is all.'

As I began to nibble at my bread, Hannah said, 'It is *queer*, but it's none of our business. Rodríguez and I are going early, and as soon as I report on the angel I'll forget the whole thing and hopefully move on to something more interesting, preferably somewhere out of Florida. This tropical heat is awful.'

I was beginning to let my concerns go and focus on eating when I felt a definite shift in the ambience of the dining hall. Apparently, Hannah sensed it as well, since she sat up straight and closed her eyes. Then she opened them and we both turned about on the bench in unison to see the priest, still dressed in his half-European, half-Arabian, turban-crowned glory, coming directly for us. Or, more specifically, it seemed he was coming straight at me.

As if we had made some sort of silent agreement, Hannah and I both stood up, side by side, to face the man as he strode to us with the great scimitar and its jewelled hilt still hanging at his side. The two lassies and Ellie continued on as they had as if oblivious to our movement.

The man came to a sudden halt with a space of only a few feet between us and stared up into my eyes as if searching for my very soul. His eyes were dark like most everyone else's I had as yet encountered who were associated with the church. Most everyone except the angel.

'I am Reverend Adoniram Lotson,' he intoned so deeply that he instantly had the attention of Abigail and Ana.

I gave the most curt incline of my head before simply stating, 'I am Mr Fisher.'

He looked at me quietly for a few ticks before taking in the other four souls. Then he speired, 'Are these your women?'

That sounded queer to my lugs, but I decided introductions were in order regardless of his crusty manners, so turning to my left I said, 'This is my friend Miss Hannah Beardsley, doun at the end is her personal maid, Miss Ana Rodríguez, and this is my wife. Mrs Abigail Fisher. Upon her lap is Miss Ellie, wha I am led to believe is a resident of this area.'

The man scanned the three lassies, his eyes making a cross on each of them as he ran his gaze across their bosoms and up and down their length. He appeared to thoroughly ignore Ellie.

I looked aside to Hannah and noted that her face was rather harsh as she stared up at the man. She seemed to be concentrating on him, as if she were trying to discern what his intentions were by boring two holes in his head with her eyes.

When he turned his attention back on me I said, 'That was quite the show earlier the nicht. I'm glad we were here to witness that.'

Lotson's face turned down only slightly before he said, 'We were not expecting you. Usually, such matters of the Holy Spirit are private in nature.'

'We didna mean to impose oorselves, only we found Ellie and thocht she maun belong oot here.'

Lotson shook his head as he gave me a studious look. From the corner of my eye, I saw that Ellie had taken a great interest in the jewel at the end of the man's scimitar, and Abigail was leaning so far with her in her arms that the wean was able to grasp it with her little fingers.

Initially, the man didn't notice as he intoned: 'That child does not belong here. Her mother will take possession of her again soon.'

Ellie was still grasping the jewel. She seemed to be concentrating on it.

'Can ye tell me when soon is? We plan to leave at first licht, and it would be guid to hand her back over afore then.'

Lotson considered this a tick, then nodded and said, 'That is when she will be retrieved.' Then he looked down to see what Ellie was doing and suddenly, sharply said, 'Don't touch!'

He pulled away from a bewildered Ellie as Abigail stared dirks and daggers up at the man and then turned back around on the bench. She began to ply her charge with more food, again speiring loudly, 'Good or *bad?*'

Lotson observed her for a few ticks, his eyes narrowing only ever so slightly as they settled upon the stump of her right arm, then he started to walk away without saying another word to any of us. I decided to follow him.

Hannah stayed behind at the table and I caught up with Lotson halfway across the dining hall. I said, 'Sir, could we speak for juist a moment?'

He stopped and looked at me again and contemptuously said, 'What is it?'

'I perceive that ye are upset at oor unannounced arrival, and I am sorry for that. I can assure ye that we will no' speak of what we have seen to any one else.'

He didn't seem to care. He casually said, 'Good,' then began to turn away from me.

I had not enjoyed the man's brusque manner, so I remonstratively said, 'Of all things, it seems ye could be kinder to a wee bairn like that Ellie. She meant nae harm. She simply found that jewel to be raither braw.'

Lotson looked at me again and said, 'I don't know half of what you are saying, but as to that cretin, she needs to learn early not to touch what isn't hers. Children must learn obedience and fear from an early age, lest they fall sway to the charms of the devil.'

Our dark eyes were tightly locked as I speired, 'Fear? Why maun ye make the cheeldren frichted of ye?'

'Fear is the beginning of all wisdom.' He continued to glare at me as if he thought his eyes might cow me. I simply stood firm as he said, 'And I can see you are a fool. Goodbye.'

I watched as he walked out the door, then looked about me at the masses of chattering, happy bairns, all of who seemed oblivious to the conversation that had just taken place between Lotson and myself, and wondered at what the relation was between them and the gruff man.

Another mystery, another oddity, I thought, then walked back to the table.

When I returned, I found that Hannah was cleaning the last bits out of her bowl. I sat next to her and she said, 'What a charmer.'

'Aye. A real airse. Hoo did he get to be in charge of a church?'

Hannah shrugged and said nothing.

Just then I heard Ana exclaim, 'Oh, *señorito* Percy! Look at you!'

I turned to see that Mrs Kibblewhit had brought her son over. Ana had turned about on the bench to address him with a glorious smile upon her face. Little Percy was standing with his mother's assistance and gazing pleasantly up at Ana's face. He strained forward at her, and it was clear that they had made good friends over the past few weeks of Ana posing as Hannah's maid.

After Ana took charge of Percy, Mrs Kibblewhit turned to Hannah and said, 'Did you see that in the church? Wasn't it miraculous? I... I never dreamed that it could be so perfect!'

Hannah barely screwed her head around and calmly said over her shoulder, 'Yes, Edna, it was quite a sight. I'm glad you got what you paid for,' she said somewhat disingenuously.

Mrs Kibblewhit was looking up towards the ceiling where it appeared some wasps had started a nest in a wooden joist as she said, 'Oh, thank you, God! Oh, Jesus, thank you!'

Hannah returned her attention to her bowl and after attacking the soggy bread it contained with her spoon, she continued eating.

I observed Mrs Kibblewhit for a few ticks, and when her eyes cast back down from heaven, she set her gaze upon me. For a spell she simply studied me as if trying to figure out what I might be with a pained looked on her face. I took no offence, I was perfectly accustomed to people having some difficulty in dealing with my queer countenance upon first setting their sights upon me, but when seconds began to drag on towards a full minute, I slapped Hannah in the arm with the back of my hand.

After uttering a wee ejaculation of pain, she looked angrily to me, then as she followed my eyes her face relaxed and she said, 'Edna, these are some friends of mine.' Indicating both myself and Abigail with her hand, Hannah said, 'This is Mr and Mrs Fisher. And that's, ah...' she said as she flapped her fingers at Ellie.

'Ellie,' I supplied.

'Ellie,' Hannah repeated then spooned some more mush into her mouth and began chewing with the grace of a heifer contemplating her cud.

Mrs Kibblewhit said, 'Oh, I am so pleased to make your acquaintance.' She was looking at Ellie when she caught sight of Abigail's stump of a right arm. Her eyes grew large and she speired my lass, 'Are you here for the angel as well?'

Abigail's eyes grew suspicious at that and she said, 'Pardon?'

Mrs Kibblewhit pointed at the cicatrix where my lass lacked both wrist and hand and said, 'I mean, for that. You know... a miracle!'

Apparently Abigail had heard some of our earlier conversation because she said, 'I can assure you that I am not in possession of such funds as to buy myself a miracle.'

The woman began vehemently shaking her head as she said, 'No no! Money has nothing to do with it. It is only a matter of faith.'

Abigail smiled pleasantly at her and plainly said, 'Then let us say I do not have enough faith.'

'But Mrs Fisher,' the woman earnestly continued with beatific hope written all over her visage. 'Surely you must be faithful?'

With a measure of honesty, Abigail said, 'Madam, I can assure you I have a great deal of faith. Only, perhaps, not in precisely the same things as you.'

My lass returned her attention to Ellie then. Behind her, Ana was up walking Percy about. She held the lad's hands in her own and was helping him to toddle up and down between the benches. Scores of eyes of the other diners were upon them. Percy's head was tilted back and his adoring eyes were upon Ana's braw face and her white smile.

Mrs Kibblewhit seemed confused as she looked down upon Abigail who was calmly feeding Ellie more toothfuls of food. I studied her for a few ticks, examining the vacuousness of her countenance, a look not improved by the seeming excess of skin about her weak chin, as well as taking in the richness of her attire. She had thrown her pearl earrings in the collection basket, but she still wore a wedding band coupled with a diamond ring on her finger, a reminder of the now deceased man she had once betrothed. Beneath her long cream coloured skirt she wore silk stockings and her shoes were suede. Finally, the woman said, 'Is that your baby?'

Abigail didn't bother to look up or even turn back in Mrs Kibblewhit's direction. She hesitantly, somewhat ruefully said, 'No, madam, she is not. I am only caring for her.' Then she reluctantly continued: 'For a while.'

'Oh, well, she is a beauty.'

I saw Abigail smile a bit. She earnestly replied: 'That she is.'

Esther came along then still looking as trig and sharp as ever. She eyed both Ellie and Percy suspiciously, then announced to the air for all of us to hear: 'Your rooms are ready. It seems that this has been a big day for everyone, a big day of travel and, for some,' she said looking down to Percy, 'a day of change. Since I am certain you are all tired, I am equally certain you are ready for bed. If you will all come with me.'

The woman held her bony arm at length and I started to stand. 'What aboot the dishes?' I speired.

'Leave them. They will be attended to. No need for guests to do the dishes,' she said dismissively. 'That is what all of these children are for.'

Mrs Kibblewhit took possession of her son again and I picked up my carpetbag and handed Hannah her handbag. Then I helped Abigail to her feet and we walked foot for foot out of the dining hall into the dark, leaving the building full of people behind us.

Outside, two lads with kerosene lamps led the way forward through a maze of tent-houses. They were small cubes with wooden frames covered by canvas. I assumed that we would be lodging in similar dwellings, but instead discovered we were to spend the night in sturdy-looking, more permanent structures.

After its dimensions were slowly revealed in the light of the lamps, we stopped at one long building fully constructed of wood. Esther announced, 'Ladies and children sleep here.'

I immediately speired, 'Will my wife no' be lodging with me?'

'No, Mr Fisher. As I said, there are rules here, and rules are meant to be obeyed.'

The two lads carrying the lanterns looked at me somewhat sharply and I said, 'Aye, but I sud think a man and his wife could share the same bed.'

Esther stepped forward a bit and looked up into my face. 'They could. Perhaps. If we were certain that they were in fact married. But you see, we have no proof that you have been properly bonded in the sight of God, and so we might be allowing some sort of sin in letting you lie together.'

I looked past her to my lassie's eyes and saw the tired concern there. Like Hannah had said, everything about this place seemed relatively benign, yet if I had my druthers, I knew it best to not be separated from my lass. So I lied and said: 'I can assure ye that we are married.'

Esther replied, 'It is a matter of policy. We might, or might not, believe any individual who comes along, but any one of them might be lying, and so we must simply say that everyone must be separated for our own protection against the evils of the flesh. You will be leaving tomorrow, and it is only one night.'

'But hoo are we to be fruitful and multiply if we canna be thegither?'

Esther seemed to nearly smile, but then she scoffingly said, 'One night!'

Abigail gently said to me, 'It is all right, Mr Fisher. I will be fine for one night without you.'

I looked to her and she silently mouthed three syllables to me. Even in the dark I knew that her lips had formed the word *for-ev-er*.

I relaxed a little then as Esther said, 'Ben, would you show Mr Fisher to his room?'

One of the lads motioned with his free hand and, as if acting the part of an obsequious waiter showing a rich patron to the best table, said, 'This way, sir.'

As I began to walk away in front of him, I heard Esther ushering Hannah, Ana, the Kibblewhits and Abigail and Ellie inside the building. I looked one last time over my shoulder for my lass, but the last glimpse I had of her was only the green of her dress disappearing into the dark interior.

It was a short walk to a similar building where a heavy door stood open to reveal darkness within. When it came to the many errors I committed that night, I truthfully was extremely fatigued, but more problematic than that was the fact that I was still so young, still so trusting and naïve, still so unobservant in my daily doings. I kept thinking that there was some sort of mystery about this place and its inhabitants, something hidden and unexplained, yet at any time I could have looked to see what was in plain sight, the facts presenting themselves to me directly before my big nose, and drawn some particularly alarming conclusions. If nothing else, the fact that I was being led into a closed structure, with nothing but long, thin winnocks running the length of the building just beneath the eaves, should have concerned me. Add to that the fact that there were numerous metal clasps on the outer frame of the doorway dimly reflecting in the lamplight and I should have become overly suspicious of what was about to happen to me. Instead, my concern upon setting my foot on the door-sole, the one speiring that I voiced aloud, was, 'Waur's the watterie? Ye know, the oothouse?'

The young man, Ben, whom I suspected to be about five and twenty, calmly said, 'There's a pot inside. And a jug. And a cot. We'll be back for you first thing in the morning.'

I turned to look down at him. He was somewhat non-descript, bearing the same basic features of face that most everyone else in the area possessed. Of all things, I remember noting that his trousers seemed somewhat ill-fitting. A bit tight in the crotch.

'Please, sir, go in and have a restful slumber,' he said with an air of placation. 'Morning will be here soon, and then you have your whole life ahead of you.' He paused before oddly adding: 'You and your wife.'

I continued to look back down at him for a few ticks of the clock, then I stepped back. As he began to swing the door shut, evil thoughts shot through my weary mind in an instant, and I didn't wonder too hard that I could have trounced the lad, either a sudden danging of my fists about his face, or swinging my carpetbag at his head, or sharply kicking the lamp he was holding awkwardly so that it broke against him, the resulting fire providing enough of a distraction to run, find my lass and Ellie, and make our escape into the woods. But then I still had no particular reason to think evil was coming despite feeling a certain uneasiness at the situation. Only in the last instant before the door shut did I notice something else in the light of the lamp. Within those tight trousers, Ben possessed in the usual area a bulge as his gender commonly did, only it didn't bear the proper organic shape or standard dimension. As the heavy, oaken door shut, my tired mind registered the truth that it was a gun concealed by his trousers.

For one further second, this realisation was of no concern to me as I reasoned that it seemed that nearly every man in Florida had at least one firearm at the ready at all times. And then I heard the sound of a metal bolt being slid into place.

I felt of the inside of the door, and finding no handle, I pushed against the wood. As I heard further scraping, I called out, 'Am I being locked in?'

No answer.

'Ben?' I said a bit sharply.

'Sir, we have to lock you in,' I heard as another bolt was thrown into place.

'Why?'

'So there's no question of you getting out. Getting out and finding a woman. And.' That was all.

Of course I understood what he was saying, but it seemed a queer way to say it. I decided to try to make nice to the young man in hopes that we could further converse and maybe work out some better circumstances to my sleeping arrangements, so I speired, 'Ben, are ye married?'

There was a hesitation. My natural ability at feeling out the presence of other bodies had been greatly dampered ever since we came to this place, yet I was still barely aware of his presence due to his proximity. Finally he plainly said, 'No.'

'Ben, ye micht no' understand, but my wife sometimes gets frichted when left by her lane. I do wish ye would let her stay the nicht with me.'

Again a hesitation. Then Ben said, 'It is only one night. She has the other women with her.' I nearly spoke again when he said, 'You don't know how lucky you are. How blessed.'

I gently put all of my weight against the inside of the door and found that it didn't so much as creak. I could feel Ben still waiting outside, and sensing that he wanted to know if I was going to make trouble, I said, 'Okay, Ben, I understand. Ye've been vera hospitable, ye and all the bodies of yer church, and I'm grateful. My wife and I baith are grateful. We'll be gang first thing in the morning. Guid nicht.'

Again Ben hovered a blink before saying, 'You should pray before bed, Mr Fisher. Pray and be grateful for everything you had and ask God's blessings for your future. Good night.'

I stood quietly at the door and listened. For a full minute, Ben didn't move. Then he slowly began to walk away. The last bit of ambience from his lamp disappeared from the high winnocks, and I was left in utter darkness.

'No' sae much as a candlestick,' I said aloud as I began to feel about me.

I spent a few minutes taking stock of my surroundings in the dark. I found a cot with a thin mattress, topped with a pillow bearing the potential comfort of a sheet-covered brick and a thin blanket which seemed appropriate in the heat of the night. There was a jug on the floor and a couple of tin cups next to it. Moving towards the far end of the room I found the piss-pot beyond two more cots. Apparently the kirkers had multiple visitors on occasion.

I sat on a cot and pulled my boots off. Within one was concealed my clip-point Bowie Knife. I set it on the bed next to me and thought about things for a bit. *Maybe Hannah's richt,* I thought. *Maybe I sud no' worry and juist gae with the flow.* That sounded easy enough. For a young, still malleable lass, that was the way. Just do what they tell you. No worries. Hannah knew best. I wanted to believe that then because it was convenient, only in hindsight I can clearly say that despite being three and a half years older than me, Hannah was scarcely experienced enough in the great range of oddities inherent to this life to always know what she was doing, either.

I was exhausted after being awake for the previous night followed by a long day of riding in a cart that had been actively shaking itself to pieces and then doing a good deal of walking, so, after setting aside my coat and hat and laying my long body out on the cot with my feet dangling off the end, I immediately fell asleep, my earlier concerns about locks and guns and my sweet, trusting lass concealing themselves behind a weary curtain of fatigue.

IV

She didn't like the woman with the grey hair. Everything about her felt sharp, and her very voice projected angles into the air.

'I'm certain you'll be most comfortable here,' the woman said as she studied the faces of the others in turn.

Then the sharp woman left a single candle burning and went out and shut the door behind her.

The woman in green had her on her lap. She began to kick her feet in worry.

'It is all right, Ellie. We will just get comfortable and have a little sleep. Then I am certain we shall find your mother in the morning...'

She laid her head against the woman's bosom. She wanted to let the peace reign within her again, but now she was worried.

As the woman in green began to ready her for sleep, she wanted to think nothing but, 'Good, good,' only her mind kept settling again and again on, 'Bad, bad.' There were bad things in this place, and she could not understand why only the straight one in brown was worried.

Sunday, 19 April 1896, 11:25 PM

I might have slept for an hour. Then the shrieking began.

She was just outside my private dwelling, and about every thirty seconds or so, she would let out the most horrific shriek. Most people associate owls with hooting, but I can accurately report that the Florida Screech Owl, so distinguished from other Screech Owls of the continent by its brown plumage, frequently engages in shrieking. I say they *shriek* because I have read plenty of ornithologists' statements attesting to the fact that they do not in fact *screech*. Whatever the sound is, it is quite disturbing, especially when a person is trying to sleep through it, and so I will at least refer to it as shrieking.

Later observation of Florida's flying fauna would reveal that while the male goes hunting, it is the female who sits up in a tree awaiting her meal, all the while nagging at the male to hurry things up with her incessant shriek. This continues throughout the springtime and sometimes into the summer and is then replaced with the far more pleasant hoot-hoot-hooting as the birds begin to audibly define their territories.

I was so tired that night that I believe I may have slept through the first several shrieks, but slowly began to become aware and awaken as the performance continued. For a time, the single-second long call would barely bring me to my senses, and then I would go back to dovering again, but each time this happened, I became slightly more roused, until finally I thought I could no longer stand it.

103

And then a miracle: sudden silence followed by the flapping of wings.

I fell into repose again, and tried to relax only to feel the gentle pattering of about a hundred pairs of legs upon the back of my hand. It was too dark to clearly see what creeping thing had found his way to me, but I already knew from the feel that it was a millipede. Despite the name indicating that the creatures had a thousand feet, I've never yet seen one coming even close. Believe me, I've gone to the trouble to count their legs myself.

For a while, I didn't think too hard on anything, and even while the millipede was making his way about my hand, I thought I was likely to simply fall back asleep and awaken to the sight of the sunlight streaming in the open winnocks.

Only I couldn't sleep.

That millipede kept going about in circles on the back of my hand, and as he did so, thoughts kept swirling about in my ken. I laid and stared into the darkness. The creature seemed trapped within a few square inches of flesh just as I felt trapped within the few square feet of that building. The millipede didn't like it and neither did I.

I decided then that my wee companion needed to find his way to a more natural setting, and in order to help him achieve this, I decided to attempt escaping my own prison.

The appearance of my ill-put together body may be off-putting to many people, but being the longest lass ever certainly has its advantages. Other than my arguably fat head, the stoutest parts of my body are my fingers and my fairly flat clog-feet, yet my legs, arms, wrists and ankles are all quite thin.

While treating the millipede tenderly so as not to harm him, I carefully, quietly brought my cot over to the door and stood atop it. Thanks to my extreme length, I was able to see out the thin winnock. Looking into the distance, I could see tiny flames at the farthest stretches of my vision, what appeared to be the flaming braziers in front of the kirk building, again lit and burning bright. Other than that, the dark silhouettes of various buildings could be seen, but nothing else.

I've always had the habit of worrying things with my finger-ends, and while I held the insect in the loof of one hand, with my free fingers I began to pick at the mosquito screen covering the winnock with the notion that I could deposit the insect outside. But then a thought occurred to me. Why simply drop the millipede into the sand below when I could find some proper undergrowth nearby?

After picking a hole in the netting, I decided to put my hand out, and discovered that my wrist and arm were just thin enough to be able to pass through. And then something else occurred to me.

If I were to give an honest estimation, I probably spent half an hour, at least, in squeezing and stretching and manoeuvring myself into the particular position required to reach the bolts on the outside of the door and open them. The first one came quickly, I could easily reach it. The second, below the first, was a little more difficult. I couldn't quite reach the metal tab, but rather I had to inch it out with the tips of my finger-ends. Then there was the third. I stretched, but there was no chance of my reaching it.

I stepped back down to the floor and found my boots. When I had laid down, I replaced my Bowie knife in my left boot, and now withdrew it. Reaching back out the winnock with it, I was able to pry the lowest bolt open with its tip and suddenly found myself free.

Before my egress, I put my boots back on but left my coat, hat and the carpetbag behind. After pushing the door open with my hand, I took a cautious look about, then feeling myself unobserved, I warily stepped out and shut the door behind me. Looking about in the dark, I could scarcely tell where I was in relation to the wooded areas I presumed ultimately surrounded me in all directions, so I senselessly began walking with one hand in front of me in search of some form of foliage. I walked in a straight line, and after about twenty paces, I felt the points of a fan-tail palm and also discovered that I was beneath the sheltering arms of a pine tree. Going to my knees, I felt the ground to find that the sand was covered in a layer of decomposing leaves, the perfect environment for the herbivorous millipede I carried. I gently put my hand down and he calmly stepped off.

Coming back to my full height, I turned on my heel and walked back in a straight line until I found my building. Then I considered my options. Certainly I could return to bed and try to sleep, but something told me that my mind wasn't likely to allow me rest. No more than a few ticks of the clock passed and I decided to walk to those distant flames and see if I could discover what, precisely, was what.

On the way, I passed close to several other buildings. So far as I could tell, all of the wee, canvas-enclosed, wooden-framed dwellings contained occupants in some state of repose. Then I came near to the heavier structure in which my lass and the others slept. I looked to the door and could barely make out in the ambient light that a series of bolts had been closed, locking every one inside. I considered this for a moment, and thought to maybe go in and rouse my lass, thinking even that I could secretly return to my own lodging with her to sleep in my arms until Esther discovered us in the morning. But then I waited and attempted to feel her out, and sensing that she was slumbering peacefully, and not hearing another sound from anyone else within, I decided to walk on. Only before I did, I quietly, silently unlatched the bolts, then continued on my way.

A few times during my journey, I thought that I became sensible of other bodies moving about in the dark. It was difficult to be certain, but anytime I suspected some one was nearby, I stopped and did my best to conceal myself in the shadows, of which there were plenty. Ultimately, my trip to the kirk building was uneventful, as the only life I directly saw was a family of raccoons who were attempting to gain access to the darkened dining hall. Upon seeing me, they quickly fled from my sight.

As I came closer to the lit braziers, I skirted around the building and approached the winnocks from the darkest side. I could feel bodies within the kirk, and was naturally curious as to what they were up to so late at night, but I found that the curtains on all of the winnocks had been pulled shut, and I was unable to see anything.

Thinking back to the main double-door ingoing, I recalled that there were two small winnocks, one in each door, that while above the level of most bodies, I ought to have been able to strain myself into a position to see through them.

I walked along the dark side of the building, then hesitated at the corner and looked and listened. I neither saw nor heard anything, so I took a few steps into the light of the braziers, and walked up to the shut doors. First, I gently tried the handles, but discovered they were locked. So then I went up onto the tips of my toes at which time I was happy to find that there were no curtains on the wee winnocks. Then I let my eyes focus on what was inside, and instantly let myself fall back onto the flats of my feet.

'What the fuck?' I quietly speired aloud before realising that some body was nearby, just behind me.

'Please, Mr Fisher, there can be no swearing here.'

It was Ben. He was speaking as plainly and as solicitously as before, but I made no mistake now in his intentions, as I could feel a bit of metal, cold and hard even through the fabric of my sark, pushed gently into my back.

For one tick, I thought to fight him, for I had already learned that being in such close proximity with a single person holding a gun actually tended to work to my advantage so long as I could manage to negotiate his allowing me to turn and face him. At a distance of two to twenty feet, a man pointing a revolver at you has a great tactical combination of being just out of your reach yet close enough to easily shoot you if he had any ability in aiming his weapon. If, however, he is within your reach and hasn't pre-emptively blown a hole in you, you're actually given quite an advantage so long as he is putting any great faith in the weapon to scare you into submission. But then I sensed the presence of others with him. Too many others which I reasonably supposed to be armed. So, I slowly raised my hands into the air.

Ben stepped back first and then said, 'Turn around, Mr Fisher.'

I revolved on my heel to see several more lads, anywhere from about twelve years of age up to Ben's five and twenty or so. I suddenly had half a dozen firearms pointed in my direction and no method of escape immediately occurred to me.

As if comprehending that my mind was trying to think up some form of violence in order for me to remove myself from this situation, Ben gently said, 'Think of the women, Mr Fisher. You are a man, and men care about women, for one reason or another. You've disobeyed the rules and gone and seen something you shouldn't have. That's your problem, but why make things tough on them? They're still sleeping, unaware of any trouble. Why not come peacefully with us and spare their feelings? We only want to talk right now.'

I stood with my hands up for a few ticks then silently nodded. Ben made a motion with his revolver and I began walking away from the light of the braziers and into the dark of the night.

V

    In the back of her mind, she began to think about Mama, only beginning to truly worry about her as she found her own bodily concerns so readily attended to. Like some miniature monarch she had her own ladies-in-waiting to see her washed and fed and put on the pot. One thing she had been good at, that Mama always made her feel proud about, was her own self-control in such matters. And then, in the dark, the woman in green laid with her, and placing her cheek against her bosom she felt the beating of her heart. It was lulling, a physical comfort in the blindness brought on by the all-encompassing night after the candle went out, but it wasn't enough to dispel her concern over Mama. She fussed about some, liking the feel of the woman in green as she gently touched her in an attempt at producing calm, but finally within the silence of her mind, she had to focus on something else in order to cast off the sharp angles that threatened her. The one thing that she kept seeing, and that she finally allowed herself to contemplate, was the red jewel on the end of the gruff man's sword. All was dark, yet in her mind she could still see it winking at her like a red eye floating within the nothingness. And then she thought on its feel, as she had briefly put her little fingers upon it, and in wondering over it a bit, she started to become drowsy and the whole world finally fled from her.

Monday, 20 April 1896, 1:30 AM

It was beginning to become a bad sort of habit of mine to attract the pointing of firearms in my general direction.

Originally coming from a land where guns other than the occasional fowling piece are a rare sight, in my first years in Florida it seemed odd that revolvers and rifles were about as commonly seen as herons and alligators. Odder still was the propensity of people to point them at you in order to politely move you along. To my foreign-born mind, at first this seemed unconscionably rude, but I would come to understand that there was a great difference between being inconsiderate of the feelings of others and the actual intent of doing great bodily harm. Technically speaking, depending upon which jury is doing the interpretation, simply pointing a loaded weapon at a person wasn't in absolute terms necessarily illegal so long as you had no intention of pulling the trigger, and given that I hadn't been immediately plugged full of holes, I was willing to wager that the intent wasn't there. At least not just then, not yet. Setting legal arguments aside, however, I still didn't feel too grand at my prospects as they led me away.

Normally, I tended to have a pretty good sense of direction, but things weren't working to my favour that night. As I had noted all along, there seemed to be a certain dampening of my skills of feeling out the unseen people in the area, and this coupled with my general fatigue had me feeling oddly lonely despite the fact that I knew some dozens of people, including my lass, were in the vicinity. Added to that was the fact that the sky was covered in an exceptionally low trough of thick clouds that blocked out the stars and crescent moon so I had no fixed point of heavenly reference. Furthermore, the only lightsource to be seen on the ground was from the braziers in front of the kirk building, and having never seen the lay of the local land in a light greater than that cast off by a couple of kerosene lamps, I was becoming increasingly disoriented as they moved me.

Most of the buildings, those constructed primarily of canvas, had a feeling of transience, as if like the tepees of the natives of the American Plains they could simply be folded up and carted away. But then there were our two dwellings in which it had been intended that we spend the night, and which were necessarily far more sturdy structures since I was beginning to understand that we were quite specifically expected to remain locked within. Also, the kirk building itself seemed fairly permanent, but it was nothing compared to where I was led.

At first I couldn't tell what I was looking at. It appeared to be a cement foundation rising to a level of a few feet above the sandy ground. Then they herded me towards wooden stairs that descended on its outside to a doorway, which upon being opened revealed an electric brightness from within. Ben gently motioned me forward with his revolver and I entered to find that the cement I had seen above was in fact the roof of a building sunk almost fully beneath the level of the ground.

The other armed laddies stayed outside and shut the door on Ben and myself. We were standing in a long hallan strung with a wire bearing several incandescent bulbs. The walls were nothing but rough concrete of which the bottom foot or so was covered in moss and mould in places where the damp underground air condensed into a constant drip pulled by gravity into a long, metal grate that ran along the length of the floor.

I turned to look at Ben and nearly opened my mouth to address him when a door at the end of the hall opened. Ben said, 'Someone wants to speak to you, Mr Fisher.' He motioned with his hand towards the door which stood open at a distance of about twenty feet down the corridor.

For one tick before moving, I looked down into Ben's eyes. I studied their darkness as if they might reveal something to me, but, sadly, their toom, vacuous depths told me nothing. So I began to move towards the open door, and was somewhat surprised to find that he didn't follow me.

The door itself was made of metal and having already made the mistake of missing the obvious signs of my coming incarceration earlier in the night, I was reticent to volunteer myself for further imprisonment. So as the distance between myself and Ben increased, and not sensing the nearby presence of anyone else, I began to consider my options. The door in question stood open in the corner of the hallway which then curved away to the left, and it wasn't beyond my comprehension to reason that it might be prudent of me to take my chances and discover what else lay down the line. But then I saw her as she stepped into the open doorway, and she instantly had my full attention.

She was still wearing her white gown, her jewellery, her stockings, and her sandals. But she had no wings. Her big blue eyes looked just as lustrous in the glare of electric bulbs as they had in the light of the candles. As she gazed upon me, all thought of walking past that open door to test my fates elsewhere fled, for her eyes were too intense, too horrible and too beautiful all at once to ignore. I stopped at a pace of a few feet from her and she finally looked away before saying, 'Please, Mr Fisher, come in.' She motioned with her hand and stepped back. As I walked into the room, I was aware that Ben was coming up behind me, and that another lad was walking from around the corner in the hallway to meet up with him at the door. It seemed as though I was in a bad position, but there was something so disarming in the eyes of the woman before me that I felt as though I could trust her. Or, at least, I felt that I wanted to trust her.

The room she ushered me into was pleasant, to say the least. After the damp, harsh, unadorned concrete slab of the hallway outside, this room had the feel of home-sweet-home. The walls were papered, the floor was carpeted, and there was a false fireplace with a mantelpiece holding a few trinkets. Before the perfectly clean, ash-free hearth, two comfortable looking wingback chairs sat atop a small rug. There was a cherry-wood table next to them with a large oil lamp emitting a warm glow.

Casting my eyes about, I noted two things. Firstly, there was no exit other than the door through which I had entered, including a lack of winnocks which seemed reasonable since we were below ground level. And, secondly, despite the use of the oil lamp, there was a large, unlit light bulb suspended from the ceiling. A line of wire was running from it and tacked to the underside of the uneven cement ceiling.

Standing next to the angel, I found that I towered above her. I looked down into her face and her blue eyes locked with mine. 'Please, Mr Fisher, have a seat. I would like to take this opportunity to speak with you.'

She motioned to a chair, and being naturally quite interested to hear what she might have to say for herself, I sat.

I was facing towards the door then, and as the angel sat down opposite of me, I saw Ben and the second, younger lad of about thirteen who still wore his trousers cut off at the knee standing and looking at us. Ben said, 'Do you need anything, Alexandra?'

The angel didn't look to him, she simply said, 'No, thank you, Ben. Please shut the door and let us speak privately.'

For a tick, Ben didn't move. He and the other lad were both gazing at us with curious looks on their faces. Ben was still holding his revolver loosely clutched in his hand, and as he backed away into the hallway, I again noticed how tight his trousers were. Far be it from me to normally look at such things, but in the absence of his revolver being concealed within as it had been earlier, I noted that he seemed to be particularly lacking in a defining feature of his gender. Then he gently shut the door and I was alone with the angel.

My eyes shifted to hers, and I found that she was smiling at me wryly, as if intuiting what I had just been looking at, what I had been thinking. Then she relaxed a little before gently parting her lips in a smile and saying, 'So, what brings you here, Mr Fisher?'

I studied her for a few ticks, not just her blue eyes, but her long brown hair, the slender length of her arms so delicately displayed in their alabaster smoothness by her sleeveless gown, the golden bracelets upon her wrists, the jewel-encrusted rings on her fingers and the strands of gold about her neck. Taken altogether, she had a braw look, and I admit I enjoyed looking upon her. In recompense for my open investigation of her physical form, the angel simply gazed into my eyes as if thirstily drinking up my interest in her as I visually absorbed her bodily presentation.

Finally, I said, 'That wee lass we found oot in the trees is what brocht me here. Us here. My wife and I,' I hastily added, already feeling the need to make my status clear.

The angel smiled gently at this, and looked ever so slightly away with a downward tilt of her head. A stray lock of hair went falling forward, and she delicately, affectedly ran it back behind her lug with the tips of her finger-ends. Then she looked back to me as her eyes seemed to glow and she said, 'Yes, I know who you are referring to. Little Ellie was brought to the morning service today, in hope that I might be able to do something for her.'

'And ye couldna do it or wouldna do it?'

The angel gave me a somewhat self-deprecatory smile as she said, 'I am only an instrument of The Lord, a conduit, as it were. I make no choices of my own in these matters.' For a few ticks she looked away and considered her words before saying, 'Besides, you can't improve upon perfection.'

'So that's juist hoo Ellie is.'

The Angel looked back to me and nodded with a pleasant smile.

'But ye fixed that laddie's thrawn ankles. Why was he no' perfect?'

The angel gave a slight, theatrical shrug of her petite shoulders and said, 'It is a matter of perception. As I said, I do not get to choose these matters. Some need healing, others don't, even if some think they do. As I said, that decision is up to God, not me.'

We were looking at each other again for a spell before I said, 'But ye're no' really an angel, are ye?'

The angel looked down the length of my body and took in my dimensions. I had my hands laid casually upon my lap, and she inspected their size with her eyes and smiled. I felt queer in sitting there with her in that unusual space designed to look pleasantly domestic, but the real discord within me was being brought about by her physical interest in me. At the time, I tried hard to convince myself that I was imagining things, for occasionally I had thought in the past that someone had taken an unco liking to me only to reason later that I had misinterpreted their feelings. But not this time. This angel had eyes for me, and at the very notion I felt myself twisted in a hundred different ways at once, for something within both my heart and my mind warned me that I should do everything within my power to escape this unco woman, and yet my body, somehow reacting to her very gaze, had turned to stone and I could not so much as shift my position within my seat. Yet already I was aware that while I could not seem to motivate myself into movement, I would be fully malleable within the hands of this angel if she were to take me to task. If she so desired, it seemed she could have sculpted my rough shape into whatever form she thought fit, and at least I had presence enough of mind to realise then what sort of danger that might potentially put me in.

She had silently studied my length, then looking back to my face, with another wry smile she said, 'But you saw me in the church. You saw me fly down from heaven and heal that boy of his infirmities.'

'I saw ye do something, perform some sort of miraculous feat because a ton of money was laid oot for yer performance, but I've seen that sort of thing afore and it had naething to do with churches or God. Or money.'

We were silent, and she again looked to my hands. Then without speiring my favour, she leaned forward and reached out to take my right hand in both of her own. 'Such big hands you have, Mr Fisher.' I felt electricity surge through my fingers, my knuckles and my wrist, fluidly running the length of my arm and into my bosom where my heart quickened its beating as she inspected me. Then I felt doubly queer as she shut her eyes and said, 'I can feel you already.'

I looked at her as she opened her eyes and turned them back up from my hand to look me in the face. 'Even in the church, before I put on my performance tonight, I was aware of you. You said you have seen such miracles before, and I know it to be true.' She patted my right hand before replacing it in my lap. 'You have performed them yourself, of course, because you are just like me. Perhaps

119

in many ways, but in no manner more than in the ability to heal.'

I was feeling a bit worked up over nothing more than a simple touch and the longing gaze of her blue eyes, so I hovered a blink as I let my breathing and heart resume their normal courses and brought to mind the fact that I had a lass who so purely loved me. For one tick of the clock, I shut my eyes and saw Abigail's image within my mind and felt steadied as I saw the glow of her expressive green eyes. This queer angel sitting before me could make me temporarily dizzy with her studied, sultry looks, but I felt steadied by the very thought of my lassie's spirit. It was as if I could look directly through the angel who, to my thinking just then, was nearly so opaque as a well-washed piece of glass, and see my lass standing solidly on the other side of her. I think I smiled a little to myself to think on Abigail as I had seen her that night, the bonniest lass in the world, with her wee friend Ellie cradled in her arms.

'What's her name?'

I was brought back from my reverie by this simple speiring, and without consciously moving my mouth, my lips dreamily produced her name: 'Abigail.'

'A very beautiful girl. Your wife, you say?' she speired again with that wry smile.

'Aye.'

The angel licked her lips and said, 'I know her name, and you heard mine earlier.'

'Aye. Alexandra,' I said as I resumed my study of her with a more critical eye.

She nodded and said, 'And yet I don't know yours, other than Fisher. If that is even your real surname.'

Ever since Abigail and I had begun this *charade* in which I played the part of the gentleman, we had successfully evaded any need for me to have a first name, and I wasn't about to alter that trend just then. Nonetheless, Alexandra insisted, and though I wasn't game, she announced her intention to guess it.

'Na, na, ye'll never guess,' I stoutly said.

'Oh? Is it something uncommon?'

'Actually, it's vera common, but still ye'll never guess.'

She cocked one eyebrow and said, 'Are the same names where you come from as common as they are here?'

'Maistly,' I said. 'So far as I ken that is the case, despite this land being so vera much muir diverse than waur I was born.'

'Then I can surely guess what name you were given at birth,' she said. She smiled at me again, and I presumed that she was about to let loose a strand of Tom, Dick and Harrys, but she surprised me as she said, 'Margaret, Helen, Florence, Anna, Elizabeth or Beth, Ruth, Emma, Ethel... stop me when I get there,' she said as her teeth shined at me.

I felt chilled as I speired, 'What? What are ye saying?'

She laughed a little and said, 'Did you think you could hide the truth from *me?* Believe me, you are quite convincing, and I can see how no one in the regular world would ever doubt how you're presenting yourself. But I know. I knew who you were the instant I laid eyes on you, Mary Fisher.'

I felt my blood go cold within me as she laughed gently. 'Is that it? It's Mary, isn't it? That was the name you were born with.'

My breath felt like ice as I exhaled: 'Aye.'

'But things are different now,' she plainly stated. 'I understand.'

I was looking at her again, contemplating Alexandra and her claim that we were the same. And then I speired, 'And what was yer given name at birth? Alexander?'

She closed her eyes and gave a curt nod. 'And now, as I have been these past several years, I am Alexandra. And you?'

I thought for a few ticks, then said, 'When ye get richt doun to it, I am still Mary. Abigail and I are happy with waur we are at, so that is hoo it is.'

Again she gently nodded and said, 'Well, Mary, now that we have been properly acquainted, I feel that we can share our stories.' Again a lock of her hair had fallen forward and she gently swept it back into place with her finger-ends and a dainty curl of her wrist. It was a studied sort of feminine elegance, and the effect was precisely what she intended.

* * *

'First, let me assure you that as we talk tonight, your wife, as you call her, and your friends are quite all right, Mary. They are safe. No one is going to molest them while they sleep.'

I felt the honesty of this statement, and so I was more than willing to continue on with our pleasant *tête-à-tête* for the time being. In fact, I was feeling somewhat

122

glorious in conducting this interview, as it seemed triumphant of me to have achieved it over Hannah's intention to simply view the angel at work. As she had said, all of those weeks of work and all of that money paid just to get invited to the church so that she could see Percy's ankles straightened out, and yet here I was, after only a few hours of casual effort with direct access to the truth. As we spoke, I felt myself glowing somewhat, not only with my success, but at the very attention of the angel herself.

'So you saw me at work earlier, Mary. Now tell me about yourself. You've done the same?'

'Aye, weel, a few times. And it is like ye said earlier. I dinna get to choose wha gets healed, raither I juist have to happen to be there when someone needs it.'

She wrinkled her nose at me like some mischievous elf and said, 'Tell me about your first time.'

I cleared my throat then began: 'Weel, actually I was having a wee disagreement with Abigail when it happened. It was juist after we first met, and I didna ken myself or what her intentions towards me were vera weel, so there were some ups and douns atween us. We were up in the second floor of the Toun Hall back hame, standing on a balcony when a storm came alang. From there, we saw lichtning strike ahead of the storm, one of those blots from the blue that shoot oot front betimes, and it scared a horse dragging a cart and he flipped it. There was a lass riding in the back, and her melon-heid got smashed on the roadway and the cart turned on top of her.' I shook my head as I thought back on those moments from the previous year, then said, 'I kenna what came over me.' I lifted my right hand and looked upon it as I said, 'I simply ran for her as if my hand was attracted to that one spot waur her heid had split on the ground. Then I put my hand there and she was healed.'

'Did anyone see you?'

'Oh, aye, many a body. Everyone already thocht me to be quite queer, but then that happened and they didna ken what to make of it. The toun doctors saw it as weel and tried to play it aff in various ways, and soon after, every body simply pretended naething special happened. Probably I helped with that by adding muir queer doings to my *repertoire* as a distraction against that odd episode.'

'Have you had any other such experiences?'

I looked upon her for a few ticks and considered whether I should speak of my left hand. My right hand's desire to heal made for pleasant enough conversation in the company of an angel, but my left hand's desire to deal out death seemed an unnecessary detour just then, so I continued on in the same vein. 'Aye, no' sae lang ago, I was oot with a veterinary surgeon to see a horse with a broken leg. Usually, sic a beast is in an unfortunate position of likely being shot, but I felt my richt hand start to swell and... weel...'

'Really? A horse?' Alexandra said with earnest surprise.

'Aye, it juist sort of happened.'

She smiled and said, 'Often that is how the best things in life are discovered. They just sort of happen.'

In taking in her appearance as I sat there, I realised she was referring to more than just the horse. 'Aye, it was the same for me,' I slowly said. Seeing her agree with a nod of her head, I continued, 'I didna gae looking to

124

become Mr Fisher. It juist happened naturally, of its oon accord. Is that hoo ye came to be an angel?'

She nodded and replied, 'Like you say, it just happened.'

'Ye never set oot to play this role of pretending to be heavenly?'

Alexandra gave a single shake of her head. 'Most certainly not. And was it the same with your relationship with Abigail?'

'Aye. She pursued me, and for the langest time I didna understand. Finally, we baith juist had to let it naturally happen.' I was quiet for a few seconds then speired, 'What can ye tell me aboot this place?'

'Well, I don't know, it is pretty much exactly what it appears.'

'Please tell me. Everything aboot it is so queer.'

'Well, clearly you have questions, so ask.'

I thought for a tick then speired, 'Firstly, why are ye here of all places?'

Alexandra gently put one long finger to her chin as she contemplated. Then she said, 'I think you might already understand this to some extent, but you have to follow the spirit in this life, you know? Sometimes I have wondered myself why I am here, performing the occasional healing when someone in need is brought before me, when I could go out in the world and find some public place to have masses of the infirm brought to me.' She held up her right hand and said, 'But as we have already established, you just have to be in the right place at the right time, and I feel, spiritually speaking, that occurs for me right here in the church.' She laid her hand back down and said, 'Besides, here I have protection.'

'What kind of protection? From what?'

'From the outside. The world's a dangerous place, and I don't need to tell you that some people would commit all kinds of sin to get a hold of me and use me for their own purposes.'

As she said this, I thought of the gruff Reverend Lotson and how much his church seemed to be charging to allow access to her in her guise as an angel. That seemed sinful to me, but not wanting to interrupt Alexandra's narrative, I held my wheesht just then.

'Here I have the protection of people who care for me, although that caring is somewhat on account of the fact that I provide for them in turn. But I also have a great deal of discretion. Rarely do I have to even let my face be seen.'

'Hoo often do ye appear as the angel?'

'At most one Sunday a month, usually, although at times it is only once or twice a year. Candidates have to be carefully selected, not only for their need, but for their ability to be quiet after their miracle.'

And for their ability to pay, I thought to myself.

'Yesterday was somewhat unusual. They wanted me to put in two appearances, one in the morning and one in the evening. I hadn't expected there to be trouble, but things didn't go as planned in the morning.'

'Ellie,' I simply said.

She nodded and said, 'Before they even began to winch me down into the church, I knew it wasn't going to turn out the way her mother wanted. She had paid good money, I am sure, to be allowed to bring Ellie to me, but there was nothing I could do.' She sighed and said, 'I played my part to the best of my ability, but after all the time spent hoping for a miracle, to be told it wasn't going to happen didn't sit well with her.'

'What did ye do?'

'I told her that Ellie was already perfect, that there was nothing I could do for her, and that she should feel herself fortunate to be blessed with her. But she didn't want to hear that. Then there was trouble. As they winched me back up, a fight was starting below. If I had known that Ellie was going to be neglected during the hullabaloo and wander off outside, I would have taken her with me.' With a smile she said, 'Right back to heaven.'

I nodded and said, 'All richt, I suppose that explains yer present situation. But what aboot that Reverend Lotson? And Esther? And all those cheeldren? It all seems quite queer to me.'

'Mary, considering how we go about, do we two, you and I, really have the right to question how other people live their lives?'

'Aye,' I said decisively.

Alexandra thought on this for a few ticks then said, 'You say that because of the children.'

'Aye. Something is vera wrong here. I saw somewhat in the kirk earlier after I escaped being locked in my room, something I was of course no' meant to see, and it certainly appeared vera, vera wrong. Still, if ye and Lotson and wha-ever else wish to carry on in whatever way, that is fine, but I worry aboot the cheeldren.'

Alexandra looked away from me and seemed to be contemplating something at a distance, something far beyond the papered, concrete walls of that room. Finally she said, 'You may as well know the whole truth.'

'I would like to. If only some one would tell me.'

She looked back to me and said, 'Esther is Lotson's daughter. He has another daughter named Edith that I have scarcely seen in years, though she's somewhere not far off, I reckon. Esther is a winemaker. Blueberry wine. In most ways, Lotson was a normal man, following a spiritual path that many others have before him. Then, after his wife died, the strange things started happening. I was just a child then, but I remember when this whole business of the Assembly in the Palms and Bela began.'

'What is Bela?'

'That is what they call this little town with all of the children.'

'What was yer relation to this place?'

'My father ran a ranch nearby.'

'Oglethorpe,' I said aloud.

She smiled and said, 'That's right. We're a branch of the family that originally settled Georgia. My ancestors moved south to Florida after the charm of the gold rush up in the Blue Mountains wore off back in the 30's. Growing up on the ranch, I was the youngest of six brothers, and I never quite fit in with the rest of the boys, if you know what I mean.' I nodded. 'Pa always had a mind of beating the girl out of me.' She looked down in her lap and her brow furrowed ever so slightly when she said, 'He used to tell me that if I wasn't going to act like a man, he'd take away my man parts the same way he castrated calves.' Then she laughed gently and said, 'Imagine saying that to a ten year-old boy.' She seemed to brush the notion away with a batting of her eyelashes. 'As you can see, he failed, miserably, I'm still just as much a girl as ever. I wasn't sorry when he dropped dead when I was about twelve years old. Anyway, as for Lotson and his daughters, like I said, the strange things started after the reverend's wife died. Mrs Lotson was running from a bull out at the ranch one day and made the mistake of looking over her shoulder and slowing her pace some. I saw the whole thing from the fence when she got run down and gored in the kidney and died months later due to her chronic hypernatremia. I'm not sure if this is really how it began, things between the old man and his daughters, I mean, but I don't doubt that Esther got her father drunk. You know, just like those Old Testament stories, going all the way back to the time of Noah. Fermented fruit always seems to lead to trouble.'

It took a few ticks for the realisation of exactly what she was saying to dawn upon me. She saw the comprehension in my eyes and smiled at me. She said, 'And no, it wasn't just her. Not to be outdone by her sister, Edith got in on the action as well.'

Alexandra was speaking somewhat glibly, but I found myself feeling ill. In a wee voice I speired, 'Hoo lang has this gane on?'

'Twenty-five years? Since I was young.'

I thought back to what I had just barely glimpsed through the winnocks of the double-doors of the kirk. That table, which sat like an altar at the front of the building with all of the pews facing it, was being used in a most unceremonious manner. I saw two pairs of flailing legs, one hairy set belonging to Lotson, the other pair, creamy and smooth, belonging to someone in a white, cotton dress, as the reverend thrusted away, his scimitar still at his side where it was dangling from the golden cord which was wrapped around his wrinkled old airse, with the red jewel on its hilt winking at me in the light of lanterns held high by Esther and another woman who were grimly observing the spectacle from a distance of only a few feet.

My mouth was dry and I had to work my tongue around in order to speir, 'And these bairns? All the little lassies in the kirk and the dining hall? And the lads? And Ben?'

Alexandra nodded. 'Daughters and sons, and daughters and sons of daughters and sons.'

The room suddenly felt to tilt and I felt ill with weariness. I made a conscious effort to steady myself and speired, 'Hoo far does it gae? Do they keep on, generation after generation... ye ken?'

Alexandra shook her head, 'Oh, no. They geld the boys at age thirteen to make certain nothing like that happens. The family line is continued by Lotson alone.' She lightly said: 'I've always wondered if he didn't get the idea for castration from my father all those years ago.'

I thought then to Ben and his queer statement at how lucky I was to have what I have. How men always seem to care for women for some reason or another, as if it was something he didn't fully understand, and how in looking upon him, his physical form, it seemed he was missing something definitively masculine.

I looked back to Alexandra's face but she no longer bore the visage of an angel. She smiled ruefully as she said, 'Has this been something of a trip down a rabbit hole for you, Mary?'

I gently nodded. 'Aye. Queerer and queerer.'

Alexandra laughed harshly again and with an air of cruel irony said, 'Now consider this: I'm more man than any of the boys here.'

'Stop!' I said sharply, and her smile faded as she realised that I was not amused. Then: 'Why are ye telling me this? Are ye no' afraid of what I'll do with this information?'

Her face became serene as she said, 'Mary, you can do nothing with it. They'll explain nothing to you, right up until the very end, but I feel it is only fair that you know the truth before you go to meet your fate. You can do nothing with the information because it is already over for you. Don't you see?'

'Nae.'

'The moment you showed up at the church tonight, they knew they had to do something with you. You had already seen too much. You'll be given a chance, one chance to see if they can trust you, and then...'

I wondered *and then, what?* but held my wheesht.

'The same can be said of Abigail and the other two women who were with you. First, I'd reckon, my mother would have taken stock of the blonde and the dark one up in Tampa. Then, down here, Esther considered them for their potential merits, mostly physical attributes, and I'm sure Lotson will give them a try. They'll have one chance as well, and so long as they give no trouble they'll get to breed. And when they produce offspring, in their way, they'll get to live forever,' she said flippantly. 'It's like a little game between Esther and Edith, to see who can bring the best prizes home to Daddy. Over the years there have been some good ones, and they help keep things *diverse*, as you like to say.'

I thought then on how Hannah stated that she felt as though she were being sized up by Mrs Oglethorpe like a piece of meat and didn't wonder that was why they had been allowed to come. It was probably decided, based on their bonnie appearance if nothing else, that they would make nice additions to Lotson's harem. But then I thought about the receivers of the miracles themselves and speired, 'What aboot Mrs Kibblewhit and her son?'

'Assuming they don't inadvertently discover any of the other secrets around here, they'll go back to where they came from with the expectation of silence on their parts regarding the exact nature of the miracle, and when she gets the chance, my mother will keep after them for more donations. They are the true benefactors of this situation, as they will be allowed to go on with their lives as before, only with the young man having a steady gait, now. No one directly related to a healing is allowed here as a witness unless it has already been proven that they can keep their mouth shut unless asked to testify before others with money in order to garner more donations.'

'And what aboot me? If they think I'm a man, hoo can they allow me to gae aboot with all these women?'

'Of course they intend to geld you as well.'

And then another of Ben's statements skirled through my ken: *be thankful for what you had.* Of course he knew what I had was effectively at an end. Apparently for him it had never even been at a start.

Alexandra smiled and said, 'Of course they're going to be in for a big surprise when they disrobe you.'

I swallowed hard then said, 'Ye said the women would be safe the nicht?'

'Yes, until first light. Then they will get to discover how things are. That was how things were to be for you, as well, if you hadn't escaped.'

'Aye, execution's at dawn,' I quietly said.

'Don't act like it's a funeral. It's more of a re-birth, of sorts.' She leaned forward and gently took my left hand in hers, squeezing my fingers as if trying to be comforting. A few ticks passed, and while she looked up at me with her big blue eyes, she gently laid her other hand on my leg. I glared at her until she said, 'Of course, if this coming transformation that they erroneously wish to inflict upon you sounds frightening, and having the equipment myself I can understand even better than you why it would, then perhaps something could be worked out.'

There was silence in that room as her hand rested on my thigh, though inside my head there seemed to be a storm of thrushing blood as my heart beat heavily in my bosom. Then she said, 'As you can imagine, I hold a great deal of sway with these people.'

Things had changed between us. At first I had found myself liking this so-called angel, but that was long past. Her touch, her gaze, they only annoyed me now whereas they had at first enticed and, dare I say, roused my spirits. Now Alexandra was nothing to me if not repulsive in her easy acceptance of these queer happenings she so casually reported on, yet I felt the honest truth of her statement that she had some level of influence with these people. And so I was willing to listen to her for a moment more, because it occurred to me that my best general course of action at that point would be to locate Abigail and Ellie, and get the hell out of there with them in tow.

It was a measured, gentle motion the angel was making as she touched me. Her finger-ends were delicate as they brushed their way further up my thigh. Then she said, 'Of course, if I were to convince your captors that I wanted you to visit my private dwelling, and if while there,' she tentatively said as she danced her fingers ever-higher up my leg, 'you were to escape...'

I was trying hard to control myself, yet on account of my fatigue and the utter queerness of the situation, I found my heart thrumming ever harder in my chest, and my lungs began to gasp at the air again as if I had just surfaced from an extended underwater swim. There was something so beguiling and gentle in those eyes, something within them that presented her soul as being so needful and desirous of a masterful man to set her straight that I very nearly allowed myself to make a terrible mistake born of my queer sentimentalities, one that would have come to fruition only through my own negligence if I didn't take action to wilfully combat it. So, doing my best to forget where I was, I forced myself to think on my lass, to remember how much danger Abigail and Ellie both were presently in, and then without any direct willing of the appendage on my part, my left hand shot to Alexandra's digital probes which had nearly made the journey so high as the intimate junction of my hochs, and after grasping a hold of her, twisted her fingers so sharply that she gasped out in pain.

'No' like that, bitch,' I growled.

I was so forceful that Alexandra fell out of her chair, and from the floor where she knelt, she looked up at me with genuine fear tinged with surprise. Apparently, so secure was she in her own abilities to charm that she had not expected this sudden turn in events. But then, in speaking to her, I was beginning to realise she was too shallow to understand exactly what there was between Abigail and myself, and as I comprehended that fact, I felt pity for her above all else, and so my right hand went to prying my left away from her before permanent damage was done.

For a few ticks she remained on her knees, her hands shaking as she breathed heavily, her slight bosom rising and falling violently as she tried to catch her breath. And then she forced herself to regain her composure and stood again before me.

At her full height, Alexandra's face was barely at the level of my chest, but she tilted her head back to address me, looking me in the eyes again.

Finally, she said, 'Well, Mr Fisher, you may judge me if you like. Just remember, even angels get lonely sometimes. It has been a long while since I had someone to be physically close to.'

'I'm flattered that ye'd consider me,' I said sarcastically.

She ignored my statement, and after taking the oil lamp in hand, she turned and began to move away from me, and it suddenly occurred to me that I was letting a golden opportunity walk right out the door since she did after all clearly have monetary value so far as my captors were concerned. As if someone in the hall had read my mind, the door suddenly opened and I saw Ben and a few of the other lads standing about with their guns at the ready. I remained rooted in place, and the last I saw of Alexandra just then was as she turned to say, 'It is a shame you didn't accept my offer. At the very least, things would have been very... interesting. And, I believe, in the end, quite satisfactory for all parties involved. Now I shall leave you to your fate.'

'Dinna fash yerself aboot me.'

She smiled gently and said, 'You are only one... man. What can you do?'

'Ye have nae idea wha I am, bitch. Yer best chance is to never set yer eyes upon me again in this lifetime.'

'Threats do not become you, Mr Fisher. When the end comes, remember that you had your chance and chose not to take advantage of the divine mercy offered to you.'

Worry over Abigail was beginning to take over my mind, so having nothing else constructive to say, I held my wheesht. Then she was gone, and the door was clashed shut and the sound of bolts could be heard sliding home through the metal.

VI

Something was happening. She wasn't sure who, but someone was moving about in the dark of the room.

The woman in green was so tired that she slept peacefully throughout the movement. She thought to wake the woman, but when she used her little fingers to pinch at her, the woman only murmured in her sleep and pulled her in closer to her bosom. Then the door quietly opened. Two left the little room. Then the door shut.

In the quiet, she heard the woman in green's words from earlier that night. 'Good or bad,' she had patiently said again and again. As she lay and listened to the lulling beat of the woman's heart, she thought to herself: 'Good.' For a while she simply enjoyed the comfort of her love and thought some more on the red jewel on the angry man's sword. Finally, slumber found her again. She began to dream of someone who was neither her mother nor the woman in green. Somehow, she was both. And she had wings.

Monday, 20 April 1896, 3:10 AM

When Alexandra walked out with the lamp and the door was suddenly shut, I found myself shrouded in darkness for a few ticks. Then the electric bulb over my head snapped on to reveal to me the same room, with the same wallpaper and the same carpet again, only in a less pleasant glow.

The wingback chairs in my wee concrete gaol were surprisingly comfortable, and given my fatigue, I would have fain done my best to lay out across the two of them with my airse in one and my feet in the other and simply go to sleep.

Of course, the circumstances of the situation forbade my doing so, though in hindsight, I see it would have served me well to get some rest instead of utterly wasting the next several minutes in a futile attempt to find a way out.

I was coatless and hatless, but I had my boots, and more importantly, I had my knife concealed therein. Not that I expected it to do me much good as a weapon considering the number of firearms about, but as a possible lever to escape my cell, I was glad to have it.

First I stuck my head in the fireplace and looked to verify that it did in fact go nowhere. What should have been a chimney stretching up towards the night sky instead terminated in cement directly behind the mantle.

I withdrew myself and turned my attention to the door. It was a plain piece of metal without so much as a door knob on my side. There were no visible hinges, they were on the outside. I put my face right against the jamb and strained to see, but the door was tightly wedged into its metal frame. I dropped to my knee and found that the bottom of the door appeared to be flush against the ground. Using my fingernails I was able to yank out and pull back the thin carpet and found that it was somewhat worn where it ran beneath the door. Even with it removed, there wasn't enough room for me to see beneath the door, even with my cheek smashed against the ground. I slid the tip of my knife beneath it, but found that I could only push it about two inches forward until the width of the blade was too great.

When I stood back up, I looked around and found myself feeling oddly faint at the notion that there was no source of air in this room. Ultimately, if one were to remove the carpet and paper and false fireplace, all that would remain would be a small, concrete cube, with only a tightly fitting metal door to allow oxygen in or out, and it occurred to me that if they left me in there long enough I would likely asphyxiate. I decided then to return to the chairs and try to reserve my energies and my breath, but before I did, I gently pushed at the door with increasing pressure. Even with putting all of my force against it, the door didn't budge within its frame. I sat down and contemplated the possibility of kicking it, but of course, that would make an enormous amount of racket and seemed likely to gain me nothing other than a stubbed toe.

I did my best then to consider my options. I grasped my knife by the hilt with my left hand and looked down upon it wondering if there was any way I could fight my way out when they came for me. Occasionally my left hand seemed to have a mind of its own when it came to violence, but I got nothing from it then. I sadly shook my head, resigned to the hopelessness of a physical solution to my problem. As poor thoughts began to crowd in on my weary soul, my mind began to unleash on me, and with each passing tick of the clock, I descended deeper into self-loathing as it seemed that I could do nothing but reproach myself for allowing this situation to come about.

Ye had yer chance at a 'physical solution' to this problem, I was thinking. *Ye could have gane with Alexandra and then been free to find Abigail and Ellie and escape with them from this horrid place. But, nae, ye didna. Ye chose to stay here. That was yer choice, and everyone's gang to pay for it, the noo.*

'Shut the fuck up,' I said aloud to myself.

What were ye so frichted of, anyway? She only wanted a wee bit of love...

'Ach.'

Disnae every body deserve that from time to time? Did ye no' see her eyes? Did ye no' see the soul within that wanted to experience ye? Did ye no' see the way she looked at ye, the way she tiched ye, the way she wanted ye? Did ye no' wish to experience her as weel?

I began to beat upon my head with the knuckles of my right hand then. 'Stop thinking aboot her...' I said aloud, but her appallingly braw blue eyes kept coming back to me.

Hoo lang would it have taken with her? An hour? An hour of tiching and caressing and kissing and feeling her wee body wrapped up around ye in the night. And then when all of that sweetness was over ye could have tied her up and run aff to find Abigail. And then what? The lass would have slept through the whole thing, and it could have been oor wee secret to keep from her...

'Rrrrrrgh!'

Oor wee secret to contemplate forever when things are slow, when ye need something to tide ye over until it's time for action again. It could have been richt there in yer oon ken to savour whenever ye wanted: the memories of the time ye laid with an angel, felt an angel trembling with need in yer arms, felt an angel moving richt there inside of ye...

I was shaking then. My hands trembled so hard that I dropped my knife. Then I whispered to myself, 'Aye, it is true.' I shut my eyes and said, 'I was tempted and curious, but dear God, I didna gae through with it.'

And yet nothing I could do or say as I was locked in that wee room seemed to dispel those eyes. I looked across from me to the chair she had so recently occupied, and felt her presence again, as if she had left something of herself behind.

I drew up my knees and held them against my bosom. As I was still shaking like a frightened bairn, I contemplated Alexandra, reasoning within myself that I should want nothing to do with her. I wanted to be only forever repulsed by her because our little interview had revealed to me that she held a corrupt view of the world and how it should be run, yet her exotic physicality, her eyes, her hair, her skin, had easily overridden what should have been my good sense in the matter to eternally distance myself from her.

This wasn't the first time that I had looked upon a braw creature and felt that innate tug, that internal yearning for physical contact that so often either brought two bodies together in love, or ultimately, utterly destroyed one or the other. Yet it was the first time that this had happened that I felt such a pull from someone that I knew, without doubt, was no good for me. It took only a bit of contemplation to arrive at the obvious conclusion that her actions, her very desires, were evil.

For whatever reason that I did not yet know, Alexandra had allowed herself to be put in a position to be misused by that deranged man Lotson, and I knew as surely as the sun would rise the morrow that if I had fallen sway to her charms, I would have consigned myself, and Abigail, to a similar fate. I think, on some level, even Alexandra would have understood my feeling in the matter, my need to stay away from her, since as she had said herself *sometimes in this life you have to follow the spirit.*

Clearly, she and I had very different spirits leading us.

It seemed that if there was any spirit to follow just then, as I found myself locked in that room, it was telling me quite plainly that giving in to my desires with someone like Alexandra would only lead to a fate worse than death. Out of a sense of fealty to my devoted lass, I had not partaken of that cup when it was offered, but now I was beginning to reason out the why, not only of how it was an immediate sin against my trusting lass who had unreservedly given to me her very soul, but how it ultimately might very well have led to my own downfall.

Yet this did little to calm my conscience as thoughts of her blue eyes, and her gentle touch, continued to swirl within my ken.

'I dinna deserve ye, Abigail,' I whispered quietly to the still air as a few tears ran down my cheeks.

But then I remembered. I had spoken those words previously.

It had happened before, subsequent to the joining of myself to Abigail, that I had met someone in whose very presence I felt my body to tingle as if warmed by nothing more than a pair of eyes being laid upon me. I said nothing to Abigail, but of course she knew. And amazingly, she understood.

Poor thoughts often assaulted my mind when I was by my lane, but sometimes I suffered the same even when Abigail was by my side. My self-disgust at not being able to control my emotions often presented physically in the form of an audible groan, and once hearing me so detest myself, Abigail said: *Are you having poor thoughts again, Mary? Never think that some passing fancy or errant thought can derail us. Do not forget that we are forever. All of this, this beautiful physicality we share is not the end result of our love, rather, it is only the beginning. I will allow that there are distractions in life, Mary, but never waver in your belief in us. Do you understand what I am saying?*

When she had said those words to me, I was only just beginning to understand. And now, in contemplating them again, I thought I understood even more so. I had been presented with a physical temptation, but it was only the weakness of my own flesh that had permitted my mind to even consider the wicked possibility. I knew the ultimate

143

truth, however, and that was that my spirit and soul belonged to Abigail.

I continued to think on my lass and recalled her statement: *If you choose me, and I choose you, and we have faith in each other, then we are forever. It is as simple as that.*

I smiled at the thought of how tenderly she had treated me when she spoke those loving words to me. And then I contemplated the one thing above all others that had so filled me with wonder when it came to my lass. It wasn't her physical beauty, it wasn't her ability to so easily befriend the bairns, it wasn't even her ease in loving a queer wight like myself. It was, simply put, her decisiveness. She had decided on me, and that was that. It was an eternal surety on her part, and meditating upon it, I realised just how powerful a force it was.

A moment passed in which I earnestly felt the value of what I possessed in my relationship with Abigail. And then a queer realisation crossed my ken. In thinking on the virtues of my lass, Alexandra's false blue eyes had been replaced with the green eyes of a true, earth-bound angel. I saw Abigail again on the stage of my mind, standing in all of her green glory, cradling Ellie in her arms, kissing the lassie-wean atop her flattened head. Despond fled from me then. Suddenly, once again, I had faith.

* * *

I barely had time to set my feet flat on the rug, wipe the tears from my cheeks, and pick up my knife before I had the vague sense that bodies were approaching the door. I put my knife beneath my hoch with only the hilt exposed and sat patiently awaiting what was coming next.

As far as I could reason, it was still some hours until sunup, and if what I had been told was true, this wasn't the time in which they were going to try to remove that which I didn't possess. Nonetheless, not knowing what was about to happen, my hand went to the hilt of my knife as I prepared to fight, if the proper situation presented itself.

The door opened out into the hall, and from my position I couldn't see anything except for the sheer metal face of its backside. Then I heard a somewhat shuffling step, and the old man named Moses appeared on the door-sole. The natural darkness of his skin made a wild contrast to the lightness of his hair and the near perfect whiteness of his milky eyes. For a tick he simply stood and cast his gaze randomly about the room, trying to make out the dim shapes presented, and then he said, 'Mr Fisher?'

'Aye. I'm here.'

His eyes cast towards me and he took one step inside. 'May I come in, suh?'

'Aye. It is a free kintra.'

He moved further into the room, and as he stretched out his hand to feel the back of the chair facing me, the door shut again.

I released the hilt of my knife and stood, leaving the blade behind in the seat of my wingback. Then I put out my hand and the man grasped it, and I led him around to the front of his chair and he sat heavily with a little grunt. I resumed my own seat.

Without preamble I began, 'Moses, do ye no' realise hoo un-Christian and altogether wrong this is?'

The old man turned his face up towards mine. The milky whites of his eyes provided the thinnest of veils between us, for it seemed as though I could still see straight to his soul through them.

'Mr Fisher,' he began, 'this has gone on year after year, and even a young'un like you will understand when I say that in time you can get used to anything. If you honest with youself, suh, you can admit that sometime in you life this has already happened where something seemed out of place, and then you got used to it, either fuh good or fuh not so good. When it fust happened, of course I thought it wrong. But you get used to it.'

He turned his blank gaze down towards his hands which he held together in his lap and continued: 'You can probably guess from my skin and my age, I was born a slave. Perfect case in point. When I was young, no one ever said, "Hey, Mo, not every negro is a slave, you don't got to be one." I had to find that out myself, and it was a shock at the time when I learned how the rest of the world off the farm was, you'd think the biggest of my life, but I got used to it. Used to freedom, or at least what some white man thinks freedom should be. No one ever asked us Negros.'

He hovered a blink in his speech then started again: 'Maybe it was because we was all the way down here in Flor'da that we never even knew there was a war goin' on. You young'uns today think we all knew better, like every day of our lives we said, "Hey, let's see if we can run off and git to the North." No, suh, we didn't. We didn't know any better 'cause no body ever told us any diff'rent. The white men all disappeared one day, but no body said it was to fight in a war, or that the big issue at hand was what they goin' do with us. We didn't know. We didn't even think 'nough of ourselves to think any body'd be fightin' over us. We thought if you was born a slave, that's just how it was. God set it up that way, and I remember thinkin' that if I ever got freed or bought my way out, first thing I'd do is buy me up some men myself. Move right on up in this world if I had me my own men. Head north? Didn't know nothin' 'bout that. Might as well rode a chariot of fire all the way back to Africa.'

He shook his head then continued, 'Now let me tell you somethin' else, when I did find out I was free, when old Mrs Conerby told me that the war was over 'cause some soldiers shot each other and burned Atlanta to the ground, I had no idea what to think. I never seen nothin' but one house where the Conerbys lived and a bunch of fields and shacks. Atlanta may's well been New Jerusalem that got burned up, for all I knew.'

He sat back in his chair and said, 'Master Conerby and his boy went off and got killed, I don't care, whatever, and that fat ol' bitch of his was the one to tell us how things turned out. Never in all my years did I hear her talk like white trash, and never did I hear her use our word. But when I asked her what was to become of us, 'cause I'd never done nothin' but what they always told me to do, she says to me, "That's your problem, nigger. Now git!"' His brow creased deeply as he said, 'I was all the way off her land 'fur I realised she'd pulled my coat, shirt and shoes off me, 'cause those were hers, belonged to her slave Mo, not the free Mo that was on the road.'

He paused another few ticks and relaxed before continuing, 'Those were strange days, and when that fust happened, I thought it was wrong. Everything I ever knew

147

was upset. God had set things up in his way, and I thought, that is how they had always been and should always be. It was strange and scary at fust, but I got used to it. Even learned the value of my freedom. But it took a little time, and then one day I forgot that there was anything out of the ordinary 'bout bein' free. Just like this church. It seemed as though there were strange happenings here at fust, but now it is the same day in and day out. And so what? What's the diff'rence? Hang 'round and you'll get used to it, too.'

I had remained silent throughout this discourse because I always felt it proper to afford my elders a certain level of respect, even when I knew them ultimately to be in the wrong.

After taking a deep breath I said, 'The diff'rence is, sir, that while ye were born into slavery the first time, this time ye've chosen to bring it upon yerself of yer oon free will by allowing yerself to be used by this so-called reverend and his so-called angel in this so-called church. Why would ye do that? Do ye no' see that they've got ye chained with moral sin?'

His eyes roved about a bit, then he said, ''Cause just like my slavery befur, this is normal to me now. This is a church, after all, and God's set it up just like he does. Just like in the Old Testament, in fact. Besides, what's a blind old Negro goin' do in this world with no one to take care of him? I ain't had no family since my wife got sold off by Mr Conerby 'round 'bout the start of the fightin'. Used to after the war I worked the ranch fur old Mr Oglethorpe and played the piano on Sundays. Then my eyes go. Now what? I should make trouble fur these nice folks takin' care of me?'

'Aye, ye sud,' I said with certainty. 'But I see ye winna do it because ye're nae aulder the noo than ye were when ye were a cheeld and all ye knew was hoo to be a slave.'

He made a sound of derision at that, but before he could speak I said, 'Ye say that nane ever told ye as a cheeld that ye didna have to be a slave. Would ye have no' liked some one to tell ye?'

He shook his head, 'I don't know I would have even understood, then. I always thought the end of my days of work pickin' and plantin' would come the day I died.'

'But would ye no' have liked to have had the information? The choice? The knowledge that this world is much bigger than what ye saw on one farm? What aboot all these cheeldren being kept here and never knowing aboot the rest of the world? Ye ken this isna richt, and if people on the ootside were to find oot, this would be over in a heartbeat, because decent people would never let this stand. And so I'm certain these cheeldren dinna know hoo the rest of the world really is, otherwise they wouldna be so content to live in this backward place.'

Moses worked his mouth around some then said, 'Mr Fisher, you may not agree with how they come to be, but these children are well cared for here, and then as many as possible are adopted out. Every month. Sometimes, dozens a year. They parents, Lotson and Esther and Edith, and the others, they tell these children they going to be adopted someday by families that want them. They go to what you seem to think a regular family is. And you know what Lotson tells the children while they wait? He tells them they going to heaven, and he believes it. A bit of heaven on Earth where they'll have a mom and pop to love 'em.'

It was a queer sounding statement, the notion of where they went when they left this place, and the thought occurred to me that perhaps the reverend, or someone else in his employ for that matter, was simply killing them, sending them to heaven, as it were. After all, for someone with a twisted mind, the Book of Judges might provide justification to that notion in the story of Jephthah's sacrifice.

Moses shook his head. 'I know what you thinking. No, not like that. The church and our little village of Bela are hidden, but the ranch runs up on a public road, and out next to it they built a little house for folks to come stay in and meet they new children. Happens all the time.'

'I suppose they have to pay for the cheeldren.'

Moses nodded. 'Small donation, what they can afford, and then that money goes to make things nice for the rest of 'em still here.'

'That and the money from the angel's services.'

'That, too. It's a good deal for everyone. If you can only get past how all these children get to be here in the first place. When you get right down to it, Lotson's only doin' what he supposed to. Bein' fruitful and multiplyin'.'

He was silent for a few ticks and I unconsciously ran my finger-ends through my short, dark hair, searching for some prickling of my scalp. It seemed that this man was telling me the truth, at least so far as he knew and from his point of view, for I could sense no deception in him. Yet I still felt ill over the entire thing.

Moses sat and calmly waited. Finally, I speired, 'Why are ye here? Why did ye come to see me? Certainly no' to clear yer conscience.'

He shook his head and said, 'No. I came to see if I could maybe talk some sense into you, suh. To be truthful, you kind of caught us by surprise. There was a bit of a ruckus this morning when Ellie escaped the church. Still don't know how she made it out, almost as if everyone went as blind as me, but even more than that, we had folks all over these woods looking fur her fur hours, and no one could find her. She small, but she ain't that small. Surely we shoulda found her. Anyway, when you showed up with her and you wife tonight, we were taken by surprise. Don't think Esther knew what to do with you. She never should have let you in the church service, but I guess you flashed some money at her and she lost her mind.' He sadly shook his head as he said, 'Lovin' that money is the root of all evil. Best thing would have been they sent you to bed with you supper and then on you go in the morning. Now you seen the angel and they 'fraid you might talk, see?'

'Aye. There is much to talk aboot.'

He nodded first, then sadly shook his head and said, 'See, that's the wrong attitude, Mr Fisher. You want to say: "No, suh, I'll keep my mouth shut. Me and my wife, both."' He sighed and said, 'But you won't, will you?'

In the back of my mind there was a dawning perception that told me this man was not privy to every detail of what went on in this place. Certainly he knew

151

about the convoluted, unimaginably gnarled branches of the Lotson family tree, but as to the rest, I wasn't certain. For a tick I thought about apprising the man of the complete horror of the situation, of the gelding of men and raping of women reported by Alexandra, but then I thought of his own story. Moses didn't know, and he didn't want to know. He had made peace with the sins of the situation as he knew it, but that was fine with him so long as they treated him nicely, and supposedly did right by the bairns. He even went so far as to convince himself that Lotson was a decent man sending his descendants to live peaceably in 'heaven.' I didn't believe that for a tick, and I wanted to present to him what the so-called angel had said to me, but then I reasoned that if I tried to tell him these things, he would simply shake his head and tell me I was misinformed.

Reading the none-too-small print between the lines, I realised that Moses was presenting me with an opportunity here. Despite his denial that his visit had anything to do with his conscience, in his own mind he seemed to be justifying not only his actions but his own moral turpitude in the matter by finding in me someone who would concur with his estimations. I didn't agree, not by a long shot, but I saw that if there was anything altruistic in this man it was in the fact that he was presenting me with an earnest opportunity to get out. And so I decided to hold my wheesht when it came to the more serious allegations, and instead cultivate my false complicity in the matter in hope that the old man would come through for me.

A few quiet seconds passed as I thought on these things, then I said, 'I can keep my mouth shut. For myself, for my wife.'

Moses didn't move. His eyes were staring, unblinking, in the general area of my face. His whole body was tense, and he looked to be uncomfortably awaiting some physical relief as if he felt tortured from within by the nature of his very own soul. I could tell he was awaiting my approval, so I said, 'And ye're richt. I've travelled all over, and in the grand scheme of things, what is happening here is no' so terrible. I'm sorry that we came uninvited, and if we can only gae, return to oor hame as we had intended, then we'll have naething to say aboot it. I uphold it is nae business of oors.'

The old man visibly relaxed some and let out a deep breath.

'All right,' he said. 'We all do what's best for everyone, including ourselves. You and your wife go on and have a lot of happy years together.' His eyes shifted away and he smiled a little as he said, 'I may be old, and maybe I cain't see so well, but I can tell she a beauty.'

I smiled somewhat earnestly as I said, 'Aye, that she is, sir.'

Moses started to get to his feet, and I jumped to mine and helped him up with my hand. After he was standing, he held my right hand in his for a few ticks as if weighing it, then hesitantly withdrew his grasp. He slowly shuffled around the chair and said, 'It 'bout three now, or there'bouts. Couple hours you be going. I hold a lot of sway with the children, and they goin' to step aside, look the other way, for you to go. For now, rest easy, Mr Fisher.'

'Aye, sir. Thank ye.'

His eyes cast to me one last time, and then he turned to the door and started walking with his hand stretched before him. When he reached it, he rapped his knuckles against the smooth metal, and then it opened. After he exited, the door quickly shut and I could hear the sound of the metal bolts slowly sliding home again. I sat back down in my chair to wait.

* * *

Time passed. In an effort to calm myself, to reserve my energy, I gently shut my eyes and focussed on the air moving in and out at the tip of my nose. In time the physical world seemed to leave me as I gently fell away from the weight of my tired body, made weary both by every day fatigue and the worry of this situation in which I found myself and my lass. A sort of guilt had frothed up within me in regards to Abigail, always churning and rising to the top of my spirit like cream, and I wanted so badly to skim it away with a few moments of peace. When I opened my eyes again, I felt some respite. The first thought that came to my mind was Abigail. The first concept, the first feeling, one of faith, despite my earlier wayward thoughts.

The light bulb above me had begun to dim somewhat. I tried to imagine within my ken what time it might be, but to be honest I wasn't sure at what hour we had eaten supper the night before, or exactly when we had been lead to our rooms, or for that matter how long I had slept, so by the time I made my way back to the kirk and was subsequently led to this place I was already hopelessly disordered, chronologically speaking.

Although it didn't seem exactly accurate to me, Moses had said it was about three when he left me, and I would have estimated about ninety minutes had passed when I felt a disturbance in the hallway outside. I still had no idea what to expect, so I stood at the ready with my knife's blade up the left sleeve of my sark and its hilt resting in the loof of my hand. I casually placed my right arm across the back of my wingback and stood looking at the door.

A few ticks passed and, still feeling my senses dulled the way they had been ever since I came to this place, I couldn't discern the particulars of what was taking place in the hallan, but I was aware of some bodies going and some coming. I thought, perhaps, this had nothing to do with me, that maybe it was only a sort of changing of the guard of the lads. But then my whole body tensed up again when I heard the bolts on the door slowly being retracted. I waited in a swither, not knowing what to expect. Then a friendly face adorning the long body of a bonnie lass appeared and I couldn't help but smile.

'*Buenas, Señor* Fisher,' Ana pleasantly said and flashed her teeth at me.

After quickly sheathing my knife in my boot, I made my way around the chair and she stepped in the room and looked about. '*Muy interesante*,' she said as she took in the décor.

I walked up to her and said, 'Ana, I am vera, vera glad to see ye.'

Then from the hallan I heard, 'Enough fooling around. Come on, Fisher.'

155

I stepped out to find Hannah waiting for me. She was still wearing her fancy blue dress and held her frilly handbag by its strap, but she had dispossessed herself of the wee hat with the ridiculous flowers as well as her jewellery.

Looking past her down both lengths of the hall, I saw that we were completely alone. I quickly took in the dimensions of this underground building, and noted the presence of a few other doors, all shut, leading to unknown rooms.

As we began to walk I speired, 'Hoo did ye manage this?'

'We were invited. That old man took care of it. We were going to get out of town before sunrise anyway, and once we got out towards the tree line, the old man was waiting for us out in the dark and he said we were free to take you with us. To be honest, I was going to leave you to your own fate because you seem like more trouble than you're worth...'

'Ach.'

'...but of course I know you were the one who unlocked our door making so easy our escape, so I figured we could be kind enough to escort you out of this place. The old man made sure everyone would make themselves scarce in here for a few minutes so we could just walk on out.'

We were at the door leading up to the outside darkness, and the air felt unusually still and thick. We paused for a few ticks before exposing ourselves and Hannah said to me, 'This would be a convenient trap for all of us, but it occurs to me that they'd have already made the effort to do us in if they simply wanted us dead. Still, it pays to be cautious. Anyone out there?' she speired me.

I shut my eyes and again briefly let the world fall away from me. Everything felt so thick and my senses were so dull that it was difficult to feel the bodies that I knew must be nearby. But then a curious thing happened. Hannah laid her hand upon mine and I felt everything magnified twice over as a sudden surge of energy seemed to course through my veins.

I took a deep shuddering breath as she pulled her hand away from mine and opened my eyes. 'What was that?'

'Just my way of helping. I'm a lot more rested than you. Now, what did you see?'

I said, 'There's nane directly ootside, but I feel like there's fifty people nearby all cruived up thegither in one spot, which seems somehoo queer. And then there are a few scattered aboot, all of them raither wakeful for this time of morning.'

Hannah nodded then looked to Ana and gave a motion of her head to indicate that she should precede us. Ana crouched, and after allowing her body to repose into a graceful, feline form, she stealthily slunk her way up the steps towards the ground above and looked about with only the crown of her head and her eyes exposed. The electric lights of the hallan behind had further dimmed, but in their ambience I was still able to see that she carried a revolver in her hand. Hannah had only her bag at hand and my knife was in my boot.

Hannah speired me, 'Can you find our room where we were sleeping again from here?'

'In time, aye. I could find it by sensing oot waur Abigail is. Otherwise, I have nae feel for the layoot of this place. It's rare that I become so confused.'

'All right, I paid attention as we came this way and I can find it again. This place is a maze in the dark, but we'll go back together before we get out of here.'

Ana made a motion with her free hand and began to move up onto the ground. 'Come on,' Hannah said. 'We're going.'

In her plain brown serge dress, Ana fairly well disappeared from view as soon as she left the electric light behind, but having her so close I could easily sense her presence. I followed just behind her hinder and grabbed a hold of Hannah's arm so as not to lose her. We stopped only a few times in order for Hannah to redirect us and, without directly encountering another body, soon found ourselves at the ladies' dwelling. However, before I so much as went to the door, I felt my heart turning to ice in my bosom for I was already well aware that the structure was toom.

'She's no' here,' I dismally said.

I walked up to find the door standing wide open. I stepped into the complete interior darkness followed by Hannah and we made certain with our hands what our senses had already revealed to us. Empty. No Abigail, no Ellie, no Edna or Percy Kibblewhit. I began to shiver.

From the dark, Hannah casually said, 'Well, I'm sure she's around here somewhere.'

I took a deep, shuddering breath, then decisively said, 'Aye, we'll find her.'

Without hesitation, Hannah said, 'No, *we* won't. Miss Rodríguez and I are leaving.' Before I knew what was happening she was already making her way out the door.

I quickly followed and whispered, 'Ye said ye'd take me to her.'

'I said we would take you back to our room, and we did, and she's not here. You helped us, we helped you. But now we're going. We got what we came for, but we're done. I told you, executions always come at dawn, which is rapidly approaching, and I'll be glad to miss mine.'

I was so distraught at the notion of being abandoned that a sudden, forceful insanity took hold of me then, and I felt utterly dangerous as I roughly grabbed a hold of Hannah and said, 'Listen to me, ye wee bitch! Ye're gang to...' but then I stopped speaking when through my sark I felt a cold piece of metal stuck in between the ribs at the exact crease at the bottom of my wee, left tit, pointing straight up at my heart.

'Oh, no, Señor Fisher, a banging would wake everyone up now, no?' Ana calmly said. 'You could try and fight me for the weapon in the dark, but we want to be quiet and not make a noise, no?'

For a few ticks I maintained my rough hold on Hannah and felt out the emotions in the air. Ana had the intention and ability, if I truly made it necessary, to pull the trigger, yet she hesitated for the sake of discretion. There was something honest and straightforward about that young woman that made me feel no doubt that she would do what she felt was right in the moment. So, I gently released Hannah and felt the metal pull back from me.

I had balled up the fabric of Hannah's dress when I grabbed her and I could hear her running her hand over it to straighten it out somewhat as she said, 'I'd love to stay, Fisher, really I would. But in this case, firstly, it isn't my job, and secondly, we're not outfitted for this sort of thing. You have no idea what sort of hardware there is laying about here, and all I have is Rodríguez for support. Usually if we were going in to deal with something big like this we would have a full crew and several strategic plans in place before we even made contact with anyone involved.'

Ana said: 'I look around some yesterday in the light for the report. I do not know why these *puritanos* think they need so many guns. They even have *una ametralladora* up in the tower of the school. Very bad.'

I had no idea what *una ametralladora* was but it didn't concern me just then. My lassie's whereabouts, and getting some help in locating her, were first and foremost in my mind.

Hannah continued: 'I only came here to see if that angel was really healing people or if it was just nonsense, a dupe-show like most of them are, and I've seen all I needed to see. Now we're going. I'll report and let someone else decide what happens next.'

I didn't like to beg, but I heard my own most pleading tone emit from my mouth as I said, 'Hannah, please. I ken ye have a heart in there somewaur else ye never would have gane oot of yer way to be nice to me back at Doctor Lamb's. Obviously I need help here. If ye dinna care for me, or Abigail, surely ye maun care aboot these cheeldren. What aboot wee Ellie? Remember her?'

Hannah scoffed, 'I don't like children,' she said as I scratched at my head. 'But that's beside the point. I have orders, and I cannot fulfil them by staying here and risking myself and Rodríguez. One thing was made perfectly, painfully clear before I was sent out on this matter: I wasn't to lose her.' She paused for a tick before saying, 'I've lost a few before, unfortunately, and I don't intend on going back to the office without her no matter what the consequence.'

In a certain sense I could appreciate Hannah's straightforward desire to get out of that place. After all, I only had to find Abigail and Ellie and I would gladly do the same myself.

Without saying another word, Hannah began to walk away and Ana regretfully said, '*Adios, Señor.*'

I supposed she was there to watch out for Hannah, and she did her job, only with the slightest hint of reluctance when it came to the need to pull a gun on me. Feeling her recede from me I again took to begging, 'Ana, *por favor*, please, ye have seen hoo things are around here, and remember Ellie, sweet little Ellie, wha ye were feeding last nicht and wha smiled so sweetly at ye. And what aboot Percy? Wha knows what they micht be doing with him. He was yer little friend as weel, I could see.'

Silence. I could barely make out her elegant form, long in the body as she was, as a silhouette. Hannah seemed to be speaking from somewhere below us when she said, 'Come on, Rodríguez. Now.'

Ana's final viscous words carried to me slowly in the thick air. '*Lo siento.*' And then they were both gone.

Rage threatened to consume me then as I felt myself cast off by the very people who were in the best position to help me, but I calmed down and did what I could to pull myself together. It seemed there wasn't much I could do to change their minds, and I wasted the next minute in grinding my teeth about as I felt evil thoughts of self-hatred constellating within my ken in regards to my failure in convincing them.

'Na, na, na, na!' I quietly, decisively said to myself. I couldn't allow myself to descend into bairnish pity again. Things looked dark, but in thinking on Abigail, I felt the faith her purity inspired in me, and resolved to do everything I could to find my lass. Only, it seemed, I had no idea where to start.

VII

Good or bad. Bad or good.

She had woken up again and was thinking peacefully on those two words for a while, but then she began to worry. Two people had left, and where had they gone?

She gently rolled herself out of the cot, leaving the pleasure of the woman in green behind. She carefully made her way to the door and pushed it open. Outside, all was still.

She thought on Mama. Then she heard her own name sweetly called out.

'Ellie?'

It was the woman in green, somewhere behind her.

'Oh, Ellie, where are you?'

She felt the angles in the air, the sharp points in the worried woman's voice. It would have been so easy to turn back, return to her arms and lay her cheek against her bosom and sleep again. But Mama was out there somewhere. And she reasoned that it would be good to go to her.

163

She walked out into the darkness, not certain of where she was going, but happy to be in nature again. The woman had taken her stockings off of her, and now the grass and sand tickled at her bare feet.

'Ellie?'

She stopped after taking several steps. She let the woman briefly see her white dress before moving forward again.

In her earlier dream, the woman in green and Mama were together, they were one. Now the woman was coming for her, following her, and she thought maybe that she could bring them together. It was a good thought.

Monday, 20 April 1896, 6:30 AM

In troubled times, when my mind becomes overworked and altogether febrile with worry, I generally resort to my experience and training when a particular opportunity fails to present itself. While in years to come I would in fact receive plenty of both training and experience, at that young age I was still rather lacking in the knowledge that would allow for me to make proper use of my skills. Yet this was hardly the first time that I had found myself embroiled in such queer circumstances, and so I already had a few life lessons on which to call upon.

Firstly, I made a more thorough search of the dwelling to make certain there was nothing useful to be found. I was conscientious in my search, although I didn't waste any great amount of time. The only thing of note I discovered was a pair of lady's derby shoes. They were Abigail's Gibsons, and I felt chilled in finding them since it seemed to me some terrible, sudden circumstance must have prompted her departure from the dwelling if she didn't even have time to put her shoes on.

I started to leave the structure after that, but then I brought to mind my earlier experiences with meditation and reasoned that perhaps I could locate my lass if I made the effort. I sat on one of the cots, closed my eyes, and focussed on the air moving in and out of the tip of my nose until the world fell away from me save one feeling. In one of my darkest moments, Abigail, my sweet loving lass, had taken me in her arms and wordlessly sang out the aria of an opera recording we had once heard on an Ediphone.

165

The fact that she didn't know the Italian and had to create her own syllables to sing only made the experience the more heavenly and ethereal. There was a feeling associated with that moment, one of relief, and tender love, and in thinking of Abigail, that aria, and the emotions I associated with it, often came to mind. As the physical world fell away from my senses, that was the one thing, the one sense, that I allowed to remain. I opened my eyes then, and became aware of the journey she had undertaken in the none too distant past.

Before my feet, stretching out through the door, was a green path that within my inner eye appeared to glow faintly with the luminescence that algae sometimes displays when churned up within the local waterways at night. This queer sight was something nearly undetectable, yet it was certainly there if I looked directly for it.

I stood and began to follow it outside, only to discover that the faintest glow of the risen sun was now visible as the thick, low clouds dispersed a grey light upon the earth, revealing more of the so-called township than I had yet seen.

It seemed that the ladies' dwelling was somewhat near to one side of the densest clustering of the canvas-covered structures, so in an effort to conceal myself from what I thought to potentially be the greater number of eyes, I knelt and flattened myself against one of its walls where there were only a few buildings behind me, and then keeked around the corner for the purpose of getting a feel for my surroundings.

Somewhere behind the nephological sheet of strati which blanketed the sky over me, the sun was rising and doubtlessly performing his usual efforts at dawning a beautiful morning upon the earth, if seen from above. Unfortunately, from below, it was a nasty, grey, overcast morning, and the clouds felt to be so heavy that the air was horribly dense with humidity even before the drizzle began. The light, but steady downpour would shortly saturate my clothes, and moreover, I would find it ever more difficult to draw in my breaths as my lungs fought to inhale air so thick with moisture I might as well have been underwater.

For a few ticks, I remained at the corner and cast my eyes about, making out what shapes I could in the dim light. I couldn't see much before the area of the human habitations terminated in a thick line of vine-covered palms, pines and oaks, the twisted trunks of which were interspersed with undergrowth so abundantly overgrown that the wooded areas essentially formed an impassable, natural wall. Canvas-covered cubes, the long kirk building, and one other larger, gabled structure with a tower standing at one end were visible. I remembered that Ana had said there was a school house with a tower. And *una ametralladora*. As yet I had not encountered that word in my time in Florida and even after straining my eyes to look at the mist-shrouded tower had no idea what she was talking about.

That building looked none too inviting. It was wooden and appeared to be lined with winnocks, much the same as the kirk, but they were all heavily shuttered. In gazing upon the structure, and thinking of my earlier feeling that a number of people, perhaps fifty or so, were all together in one place, I didn't wonder that was where they were all cruived. With the shutters all closed up the building looked ready to weather a storm.

I could see no movement anywhere, although I was aware that at least a few people remained outside of the shuttered building. Casting my eyes back down to the ground, I picked up on the path that my lass had walked and did my best to follow it visually as it wound erratically about the various buildings until it became hidden from my line of sight. Then seeing no further advantage to staying put, and not detecting any obvious danger in setting forward, I ran the rear length of the building and set off on a course running roughly east, with the green of Abigail's earlier passage running parallel to me on the left, where in the dim light of the dawn I felt I would be too visible to any eyes that might happen to be watching from the north.

I moved quickly, running in between the canvas dwellings and then stopping to look about from behind them again. In seeing the advances made by my lass, I observed that she had taken a rather ponderous route, looping about buildings and occasionally side-stepping for no apparent reason, and I even thought she seemed to have made her journey in fits and starts, something like a drunken tourist haltingly making the rounds in an inebriated attempt at sight-seeing in an unfamiliar city.

Normally this would have worried me, but I didn't stop to think too hard upon it, and then another concern was to come to the forefront of my mind, anyway.

I followed the haphazard path from the rear of about nine or ten dwellings, occasionally following her precise footsteps, and sometimes watching as the verdant track wended away from me. All the while I was making progress, I became increasingly concerned as the sight seemingly began to evaporate before my very eyes. At first, I thought I was simply imagining this, and then I thought it was the growing brightness of the grey light that was obscuring the sight. But I had already learned the truth that what I thought to see laid out as a path on the ground was really nothing but my imagination creating a physical reflection of what my deeper consciousness had discovered, and quickly disavowed myself of the notion of the sun's interference as it rose to prominence behind the clouds. The reality was, the further along I followed, the more obscure the image truly was becoming. I continued either directly upon it or with it in my eyesight until there was nothing left. And then I looked up to see someone standing before me.

When I had first met her, I knew she was small, but then she had been beneath me, under a table, on her hands and knees staring up at me, and from that perspective it was difficult to properly determine her length. We had traded smiles. Now she stood before me in the grey, morning light, and the top of her extremely bumpy head didn't even come to my waist.

The lassie was wearing her white cotton gown but stood barefoot in between two of the canvas-covered cubes. She had her misshapen ball of rubber and was gently tossing it back and forth between her wee hands. When I first set my eyes upon her that morning, she gave me another tentative look, as if awaiting the possibility that our encounter could go in one of two very opposite directions. I was worried sick at my circumstances, and over the whereabouts of Abigail, but that didn't obscure my comprehension that I should presently act pleasantly towards this lass who seemed oddly alone. I did my best to relax, and without specifically thinking to do so, I felt the corner of my lips pull up into a genuine smile.

The lass returned the favour, and I was pleased to see that it was not an automatic gesture, rather her whole face, not just her mouth, smiled up at me as evidenced by her twinkling, dark eyes.

We regarded each other for just a tick, and I was about to speak when she suddenly speired, 'Wanna play?'

She held the ball of rubber up and I understood that she wished to toss it about some. My first response, what my mouth nearly pronounced without any consideration, was that this was no time for games. But before I replied, I reasoned that this bairn likely possessed a great deal of information that could assist in my endeavour if I could only extract it from her.

My first impulse was to demand that she tell me everything she knew, but of course that would have been wrong in every possible way. In a flash, I thought back to every interaction Abigail had ever had in my presence with an unco bairn, three recent cases in particular coming to light in an instant, not least of which was her meeting of Ellie the previous evening. As Abigail had demonstrated, slow and steady was the way, and you had to meet them on their own terms. Every bairn was different, unique, and while the mode in which you would achieve the result might not be identical, the goal was, ultimately, to show that you were a friend to them.

Curiously enough, in the case of this particular lassie, I had already made a great leap forward in simply smiling at her when we first met in the dining hall. I was such a blockhead when it came to human interactions in my younger years that I never understood how a simple smile in social situations could draw two bodies together. It is the queerest thing to me still that so much can be communicated between two particular souls with the baring of teeth, and yet at the same time, if one were to simply go about smiling at strangers all day every day she would likely be considered at best to be giddy and at worst a mental in need of being locked up.

In the case of myself and this lass, something had been wordlessly communicated between us in that dental flash, and thus the door had already been opened. Now it was time to play ball.

I held up my right hand and she tossed the uneven wad of rubber up to me. I thought it an odd sight to see such a latex in this isolated place in the woods, and my first thought was to speir her as to where she got it, but she spoke first.

'Your name is Mr Fisher, right?'

I realised that she was of course correct. Introductions were to come first.

'Aye. What is yer name?' I said and tossed the ball back.

'Zoara,' she said.

'That's a vera braw name. Vera beautiful.'

'Thanks. But no one calls me that. I'm just called Teeny because I came out so small,' she said as she returned the ball.

'Hoo auld are ye, Teeny?'

'Seven. How old are you?'

I smiled and said, 'Seventeen.' Then I threw the ball to her.

She held on to it and furrowed her brow. Then she said, 'I really thought you were much older than that. Hard to believe but my sister Rebekah's seventeen years old.' Then she threw the ball back to me.

I reasoned that it might be to my advantage to speak to this older lass if I could negotiate an introduction through Teeny. 'Do ye live with her? Is she around?'

'Yeah, we live right over there,' she said as she pointed at the structure behind me.

I tossed the rubber to Teeny and said, 'Any one else live with ye in that tent-house?'

'Nuh-uh,' she said with a shake of her head.

'I suppose she takes care of ye.'

'Nuh-uh,' she said with another shake of her head. 'I take care of her, mostly. I came out small with a ripply head, but I'm not stupid. Bekah's head got smushed when she came out.'

I swallowed and seriously said, 'I'm sorry to hear that.'

Teeny shrugged and gripped the ball tightly as she contemplated my dimensions. Then she speired, 'Did your head get stuck when you came out?'

'Why do ye axe that?'

'Well, you have kind of a big head, and you're so tall, and I thought maybe your head got stuck when you were coming out of the mommy-hole and they were pulling you by the feet and you got stretched.'

'Ach.'

'It's okay. Everyone's a little different. We just have to make sure and take care of each other.'

I nodded and said, 'Ye're smart for a seven year auld.'

She smiled to reveal several missing teeth, and said, 'Thanks.'

'Teeny, can ye tell me waur every body is? All the other cheeldren?'

From where we were standing between two cubes, the school and its tower weren't visible. Teeny pointed in its general direction and said, 'They're all in the school.'

'It seems they have all been in the schuil since weel afore sunup. Is that no' early for their lessons?'

She tossed the ball back at me and said, 'For learning, yeah, it's early, but they're not in there for that. Someone was ringing the bell earlier and everyone has to go inside and be shut up for safety. That's the rule.'

I hadn't heard the bell, but reasoned it may have been rung while I was cruived in the wee, concrete room. I returned the ball and speired, 'Why are ye no' in there as weel?'

She shrugged, 'Mostly I don't like being stuck in there. It's so hot and boring and you don't know when they'll let you out, and I need space so I can roam around. Bekah and me just hide on our own until they shut up the school. Some of the others do so sometimes, too.'

'Do ye no' get in trouble?'

She nodded and threw the ball. 'Oh, yeah. If we don't do right all the time, we don't get to go to heaven.'

'Teeny, I wonder if ye could tell me something. Do ye know my wife?'

173

The lass held up her hand and I threw the ball at her. Then she speired, 'Is she the lady in green who was carrying Ellie around?'

'Aye. Ye know Ellie?'

Teeny nodded and threw the ball. 'She and her mother came in Saturday afternoon. They ate supper with us and then they were at church Sunday morning.'

'To see the angel?' I threw the ball back.

'Uh-huh. Her mother thought Ellie was going to get fixed but nothin' happened. Then she got mad and started a fight. They had to carry her out of church.' She threw the ball to me.

'What did she want fixed on Ellie?'

'Maybe she thought she should talk, you know? She's as old as me but never says a thing.'

I felt somewhat astonished at that, yet I felt it was the truth. I honestly had thought Ellie to be about three years old when I first met her due to her size. She was even smaller than Teeny, and in addition to her hair being so thin and short that she looked nearly as bald as a newborn, she also bore an unseen air of infancy about her. But in some way the truth occurred to me as I spoke to Teeny that Ellie would, in some respects, forever be a bairn. She was a sweet little thing and I understood why Abigail loved her so, and to my simple mind I couldn't want a thing changed about her. But I wasn't her mother, and neither was Abigail, and I could also understand how a person might wish to do something, anything they could to improve their child's life. Based on what I had heard, Ellie's mother had likely paid more than just one pretty penny to get so far as being invited to the kirk. But more than that, a great deal of emotion, and prayer, had probably preceded the Sunday morning service, and to not receive the intended result was probably devastating, no matter how gently Alexandra had tried to let her down. It wasn't beyond the contemplations inherent to my queer sentimentalities to see how the woman might almost feel it as an insult from God Himself if she truly thought all of this angel business was divine in origin.

These thoughts formed in my mind within the time it took me to toss the ball to Teeny's wee hand, and they began to swage within my grey matter by the time she threw it back to me. Teeny started to say something else when I became aware of another body behind me.

I was still holding the ball when I turned to look and see a bonnie young lass of what I would have thought to be no more than fourteen years old based upon her overall size and appearance. She was very trig and had the most basic features visible within the confines of her white, cotton dress to suggest the fact that she would grow into a woman. When I first saw her, she was looking somewhat blankly ahead of her, perpendicular to my own gaze, and so I only saw the left half of her face in profile. She had a braw look to the curve of cheek and nose and the corner of her mouth curled up pleasantly. Unlike most of the other bairns I had seen, she had light red hair that appeared untameable as even in the heavy air that morning it fanned out about her in wild wisps.

There seemed to be nothing particularly remarkable about the lass, and then Teeny said, 'Over here, Bekah.' The lass turned her attention in our direction, and I observed what her younger sister had

175

earlier reported. The left side of her face was perfect, and in fact, much of the right side was intact, but her head itself, just about her right temple, looked hopelessly crushed, not in the sense of some recent injury, but appeared to be an inherent part of her makeup. A careful inspection of her right lug showed that it, too, had suffered somewhat in being malformed. Teeny said her sister was 'smushed' when she came out, but this appeared to me to be a direct product of the womb.

Rebekah turned her gaze in our general direction and barely seemed to focus on Teeny before vacantly saying, 'Hullo.' Then she turned towards me and again said, 'Hullo.'

I nodded my head and said, 'Hello,' back to her. Then I remembered to smile, but the lass seemed not to notice.

Rebekah said, 'Are you playin'?' She held up her hands with them somewhat widely spaced and said, 'Can I play, too?'

Something about the way Rebekah stood and looked at me made me wary that her natural reflexes might not be exactly appropriate to this game, but then it was only a bit of rubber and no harm if she dropped it, and unlikely to do her any harm unless someone purposefully threw it in her face. Still, I looked to Teeny first and saw that she had effectively read my mind. She smiled up at me and made a gentle underhanded motion with her empty hand. I gently tossed the ball towards Rebekah and it went through her hands, hitting the skirt of her dress and then rolling to the sand. She said, 'Oh!' with a lopsided smile and went down to her knees to retrieve it.

There had been a sort of easy exchange of conversation between Teeny and myself that was effectively mirrored in our tossing of the ball of rubber. With the addition of her sister, things became somewhat more difficult, but I pressed on with the specific intention of seeing if Teeny could tell me either directly where Abigail had gotten off to, or if she had not seen her, possibly give me some ideas of where she might be.

It was difficult to remain cool given the circumstances because I wanted to proceed forward on my search, not stand about playing ball like a school-bairn. My feet wanted to run all over so that I could keek in every last hidie-hole until I had my lass and I had to force them to stay put. But again, following the spirit, as it were, I felt it was right to make nice and talk with these two lassies. Something, some unseen communication, like a fairy whispering secrets in my lug, informed me that my lass was at present safe and that if there were any danger to be guarded against, it was in relation to these two lassies I was presently playing ball with, and not Abigail and Ellie.

While we had been tossing the ball about, I had occasionally looked back over my shoulder to see that the green path I had earlier followed still remained, growing thicker the farther back towards the ladies' dwelling that it stretched. In the same manner, it grew lighter and finally dispersed near to where we were standing, yet I was under no illusion that Abigail had brought an end to her journey at this location.

The three of us stood as points on a triangle, and always the ball was thrown from Teeny to me, and from myself to Rebekah, and from Rebekah back to Teeny.

The older sister threw so wildly that there was no telling where the ball might go in relation to the younger sister, but so patient was Teeny in dealing with Rebekah that she never once fussed over her poor aim, even when the ball was bounced off of her bumpy head.

We got to talking again and I speired, 'Waur did ye get this rubber from?'

Teeny said, 'Over in the meat factory.' She threw the ball to me and pointed towards the east where another thick wooded area obscured our view from anything that might be beyond.

I gently tossed the ball to Rebekah and speired, 'Is that to do with the Oglethorpe Ranch?'

'Yeah, they have lots of cows over there in big open fields a ways on the other side of those trees.'

Rebekah held the ball, squeezing it with her fingers, and said, 'You're not supposed to go there, Teeny. I wish you wouldn't say that you have. It makes my stomach hurt to hear it.'

I speired, 'Why are ye no' supposed to gae there?'

Teeny shrugged and said, 'We're not supposed to go anywhere, really. Go to church, go to school, pick beans, eat and go to bed. That's all. I like to get out and roam around. I've gotten out on the roads before and waved at people riding by, but there's nothing really around here. I get out to that farm sometimes and just watch. I like the cows. And then I got in the factory where it's really cold and icy, and then I found where they have all these machines. Some of 'em have rubber coming off of 'em and I like the way it squishes.'

Rebekah was still squeezing the ball hard between both hands as she said, 'Teeny, please don't say that! You know if they find out you were over there where you don't belong you'll never go to heaven!'

Teeny replied, 'So what, Bekah? I've seen heaven. It ain't that great anyway. I don't like all that pink and gold. I don't want to go there.'

'*Don't say that!*' Bekah shrieked and then wildly threw the rubber clear over her sister and far out of her reach.

Teeny's dark eyes watched the ball sail over her head as well as the canvas covering of the structure next to her as she tilted her whole body back to take in its trajectory. She shouted, 'I'll get it!' and went running around the corner of the dwelling towards the north.

The wee lass was still just barely within my line of sight when something occurred to shatter the utter still of the viscid, early morning atmosphere. The rubber ball had bumpily rolled along and then came to a stop perhaps twenty feet beyond the corner of the dwelling in a patch of sand where it sat surrounded by scrub grass and a few red and yellow Indian Blanket wildflowers. Teeny was running for it when the ground suddenly seemed to explode upwards, one-two-three, in tiny plumes of sand. So cloyingly thick and still was the air that the sound seemed to take an eternity to reach my lugs, an eternity in which without even thinking things through I went running for the lass without thought to my safety. When the report did reach me, I thought the gunshots, fired in rapid succession, to simply be emitted from the muzzles of three separate long-arms but was soon to discover otherwise.

At first it made no sense to me whatsoever. Wee Teeny was the most harmless of creatures and for what purpose someone was unleashing a fusillade upon her I could not imagine, for being as yet inexperienced with the level of depravity some souls can sink to, it felt altogether anathema to natural law, to reality itself, that a firearm could even be fired in the direction of one so innocent. In hindsight I understand that an itchy trigger finger belonging to some unknown person desiring to find my long body in his sights had committed this terrible act of firing down upon the lass, who was supposed to be safely hidden away in the locked school, when she suddenly emerged from the fog. I am only thankful that she was not struck in that first instance of open hunting season.

But as for me: *One-two-three* and still having no idea what was really happening, I mindlessly ran like a horse unleashed from the gate at Churchill Downs, beating my hooves against the sandy ground to find Teeny standing frozen in place only a foot away from the ball with the sand so recently ejected into the air yet to settle back into place. Without thinking, before my feet even began to slow I went into a crouch to scoop the lass up in my arms, which caused me to stumble, and by the time I had her wee body secured within my grasp I found myself in a bit of a heap. No sooner had this occurred than it felt as though the very earth shook with the nearby impact of more forceful insertions of lead into the ground. This time it wasn't simply *one-two-three*, rather it was an ongoing release of rapid fire coming from the tower of the school and may very well have reached the twenties or thirties in number of rounds fired. Finding myself lying cross-wise in an exposed position, with Teeny wrapped up in my arms, I began to forcefully roll my long body back towards where we had been playing ball so peaceably just a few seconds before. All the while as I rolled, the lass screamed at the top of her lungs as the ground was torn away behind us and a trail of shredded wildflowers was ripped up by hot lead.

It felt as though another eternity passed as I rolled us away, those few seconds passing interminably as I expected my body to erupt with the impact of a bullet wound at any instant, but then, finally, I found we were at Rebekah's feet and miraculously neither myself nor Teeny were harmed, only very, very dizzy. The firing had stopped and we were again at least out of the direct line of sight of the tower between the dwellings.

Teeny was still screaming as I handed her over to her sister who was looking blankly at me as if even more uncertain of what had just happened than I was. I had yet to get off the ground when I grabbed a hold of Rebekah's wrists and sharply said, 'Take her hame, noo! Get on the floor and lay flat with her! Understand me?'

The lass nodded and began to drag her little sister away. Teeny seemed to come somewhat to her senses then and the last I saw of them was as they ran hand in hand and foot for foot into the rear canvas flap of a dwelling. I didn't know what else to tell them to do, but in realising that I was the only real target to be had, I figured the only threat for them would be a stray bullet and wanted them out of the direct line of fire.

I stood in a crouch and backed up towards the canvas-covered dwelling behind me so that it blocked my view from the tower. I had no idea what I was going to do next. The answer of what my most immediate action should be came when the canvas itself ripped about me as bullets tore through it. I hit the sand, nearly realising too late that the soft covering of the building would do nothing to protect me. It seemed that the shooter was taking pot shots, attempting to strike at my last known position, so I began to crawl then, moving away on my belly down the length of the structure in hopes that a better situation might be found just around the corner.

The fire from the tower had ceased as soon as I hit the ground, so when I reached the rear of that building I stood and began to make my way around the corner only to find myself surrounded. Five lads with guns, all wearing what seemed to be the male uniform of matching sarks and trousers, stood staring at me. I looked in their faces in hopes of recognising one or more of them, but they were all fully unfamiliar. They were loosely grouped at a distance of about fifteen feet. Instinctively, I put my hands up as the oldest one, perhaps about twenty years of age, came walking right up to me with a dark revolver having a very long barrel in his hand and a sneer on his face. His mouth curled up a little to reveal misshapen teeth and I recall thinking how queer it seemed that the attitude he presented suggested that he viewed my presence as being some sort of personal affront.

At first, despite already having just been shot at, I foolishly presumed that my capture without harm was again the intention, but then those words of Alexandra flashed through my mind: *You'll be given a chance, one chance to see if they can trust you.* I understood then that my one chance had come and gone, and so I prepared myself to do something, anything, for I could see that this unco lad possessed both the means and the intention to put an end to me right then. Only I wouldn't have the opportunity to act.

While he approached, the lad was grinning at me as he found himself about to be the recipient of a certain visceral, primitive pleasure, that of sticking a gun against my head and pulling the trigger. It was a sickly twisted look of glee, and even in what I thought might be my last moment, I wondered at how a person could be so detached and cold to walk up to a stranger and do such great harm when they stood defenceless. But then, suddenly, my contemplations ended as he lost his head, quite literally.

A rose of blood bloomed from his hair as a bullet exited through his temple. No sooner did I hear the first gunshot than a second of the lads went down in a heap in response to a second bullet while the remaining three scattered, temporarily cowed until they could find the source of the gunfire.

A beautiful sight came running for me then from behind the next dwelling. A bonnie young lass in a brown serge dress, her white teeth flashing at me with an unco, heavenly brightness in the grey morning twilight, came at me carrying a revolver in her hand and said, '*Buenas, Señor* Fisher. We are going somewhere?'

Gunshots then. The three lads had taken positions, one behind a tree near the edge of the woods, and the other two on opposing sides of us, partly concealed by dwellings, and they were not hesitant in pulling their triggers. The canvas had already proved a poor substitute for a concrete wall when bullets were coming at me, but feeling that it was better to be concealed than simply stand out in the open, I grasped Ana's arm and pulled her inside the tent flap behind us.

On account of the dim brought on by the low-hanging clouds outside, the inside of the tent-house was nearly fully dark. I was aware only of the most basic furnishings as it seemed that the space was meant for sleeping and little else. Beneath the wooden frame and the canvas, there wasn't much more than three small cots inside, and I didn't wonder that they were usually occupied by several bairns at night based upon their size and the fact that the cot nearest us had one of those unfortunate *golliwog* rag dolls sitting atop it with little more than his great, white grin visible in the gloom.

In a whisper I speired Ana, 'What do we do the noo?'

I could still just barely make out the brilliance of her teeth as she said with a smile, 'I am only the shooter. It es up to the planner to make the decisions.'

'Wha is the planner?'

'Hannah.'

'And waur is she?'

'*No se, señor,*' she said with a shrug. 'Now you are the planner, no?'

'Ach. Weel what do ye do?'

Ana laid a single, slender finger on my arm as if to silence me so that she could demonstrate. I was looking to her face when a sudden gunshot erupted from the end of her other arm and she calmly said, 'Oh, no...' There was a wet sort of *thwack* outside as I realised she had just shot another one of the lads through the canvas. And then she aimed again about ten feet over, seemingly at nothing, and said, '*¡Por favor!*' only to again pull the trigger and hit another mark.

'Now you are to tell me, there es how many more *hombres* out there?'

I was beginning to understand how this worked. As Hannah had said, usually if she were to get involved in something like this where there was a lot of 'hardware' about, she would have a full crew, and obviously each member of that crew would have her own function. In Hannah's absence it was up to me to fill some part of the void for Ana. So I shut my eyes and tried to feel out the presence of nearby bodies, only that was easier said than done as those on the outside were trying to kill us, and Ana was right next to me shooting people concealed by no more than a thick piece of canvas.

I began to be able to feel within my mind what my eyes could not see when I was suddenly drug back to that dim little room where we knelt behind a cot by the sound of Ana saying, 'Oh, this will not hurt a bit!' And then she fired at the canvas and another body hit the ground.

I shut my eyes again and tried somewhat desperately to sense out if there were more lads in our vicinity and was not reassured by the impending feeling of half a dozen approaching bodies pressing upon me. I was just beginning to be able to resolve them into specific targets when Ana said, '*Uno mas*,' and quickly turned to fire once more directly behind us. Apparently her aim wasn't quite so perfect in that one instance, for the sound of the bullet striking something solid through the tent was followed by a pained gargling. Ana turned to me and I

185

could just barely make out her grimace as she said, '¡*Uy!*' She lowered the weapon then said, 'And now we are going?'

My lugs were ringing and gunsmoke was thick in the air as I said, 'There's muir on their way. Hoo lang can ye hold them aff?'

She held up her smoking revolver and said, 'With this *Schofield*, no more. It es a six-shooter, no?'

'Ye mean ye dinna have any muir bullets?'

'No, Hannah has the bag. I was not meant to do any shooting here.'

It occurred to me that there was likely plenty of weapons and ammunition laying about outside on the ground at that point, and so I said, 'Let's gae afore muir laddies arrive. We'll see what we can find laying aboot.'

'I think they were boys, not ladies.'

'Aye, that is what I meant. Only ye sud know what they do to them.' I pointed towards the front of my trousers and said, 'They cut aff what they have so they are no' men.'

Ana's face twisted painfully at that. 'Why they do that?'

'That Reverend Lotson is the faither of all the cheeldren ye see here. He makes certain nane else gets the chance once the boys start to get aulder.'

'How many years they have when they do it?'

'Thirteen or sae, I am thinking. But never mind that noo. Let's gae.'

I don't know why, but I instinctively took Ana's free hand in mine and she warmly squeezed my fingers as I pulled her the few feet towards the tent flap.

I only just exposed my face to see the lad who so recently had intended to put the barrel of his gun against my head lying on the ground. His dark, long-barrelled revolver lay just beyond his open hand, partly concealed by scrub grass. I felt as though I were making a wonderful target of myself as I did so, but I set foot outside of the tent flap so as to get a hold of the weapon, and then stepped back in and held it before Ana. Thinking on its size, I speired, 'Do ye think ye can handle it?'

Ana smiled and said, '*Sí, señor.* It is the Colt .45 with the single-action made for the cavalry. Four years ago they stop buying for army and they all get sold to the people.'

She set her own revolver aside and barely had the new gun in her fingers when she made a tsking sound and said, 'Needs oil. I do not know how well cared for it es. Or if it will fire.'

I felt the absolute certainty earlier when it was being levelled at my head that it would fire if the trigger was pulled. As I heard Ana open the cylinder to make sure it was loaded I said, 'It's what we have, the noo. If we can safely do so, we'll gae oot on the side waur ye hit the other three and see what else we can grab.'

'*Sí, señor,*' she said as she cocked the revolver's hammer with her thumb.

Before we made our egress, I sincerely said: 'And Ana. *Gracias.*'

She said nothing but I could see her smile as she gently laid her free hand on my shoulder and squeezed for one tick before taking the revolver in both hands.

Again I looked outside, then I set both feet out and Ana had just enough time to expose her weapon before firing at the tree line. Something exploded directly behind us as a bullet ricocheted off of the wooden frame of the dwelling at the same instant that Ana pulled her trigger. For one tick my ken tried to resolve the notion that she had just fired above and behind us, but then my mind made sense of the fact that someone was shooting at us from the trees. This was the first time I had ever found myself in such a firefight, and my mind kept having issues in reconciling individual events as they occurred. Ana only fired the one round and then I had her by the hand and instinctively began pulling her around to the east side of the dwelling.

We came about and ducked down above the body of the single lad she had shot on that side of the structure. The first thing I noticed was that his throat appeared to have exploded from the inside, but I quickly cast my eyes aside to look for a weapon. Seeing it, I went to my knees just in time for Ana to fire another round just over my head in the general direction of the school house. As I picked up the revolver I found that its wooden grips were somewhat rotted and the dark metal had rust spots on it. I had never thought on it before, but in the back of my mind I had always possessed the bairnish notion of a gun being some sort of charmed object that required no maintenance and if only loaded with cartridges would always be ready to fire at the pull of the trigger. I was then learning, at the exact worst time in which to be schooled in such matters, that my preconceived notions regarding the operation of firearms were little more than a phantasy. Just as the men of my home country in centuries past spent a great deal of time between battles jumping up and down on the blades of their broadswords simply to bend the inferior bog-iron back into a recognisable shape, revolvers needed constant care and attention, especially after being fired, and especially in the tropical moisture of this land I had come to call home. Case in point, this weapon had in no sense been well maintained, and Ana's earlier concerns about the revolver she now possessed came to mind only to be interrupted by the sound of her sweet voice.

'Where are we going, *señor?*' she called out to me.

We were back to back and then I turned to look over her shoulder just in time for her to lift her revolver and point it into the trees. '*¿Si o no?*' she gently speired while cocking the hammer and then pulled the trigger. There was a sudden plume of red mist ejected into the air, and then a body partly concealed by the fronds of a fantail palm fell to earth.

I said, 'I kenna what we can do. There are too many of them.'

She casually replied, 'Get me more bullets and I can shoot all day.' As she held up the long-barrelled Colt she said, 'Need the .45 for this one.'

'I kenna hoo!' I could hear the despair in my own voice as I said, 'The tower's behind us and there's muir bodies coming up alang the tree line!'

Without looking at me, while again cocking the hammer with her thumb, Ana said, 'Have faith, *señor. Dios existe.*' Then with scarcely a look as to where she was aiming, she pulled the trigger and said, 'We go on until we are really finished, no?'

'Aye, of course,' I said as I tried to open the cylinder on the weapon I held. The metal was so rusty that I had to force it open with my finger-ends, but then there were six fresh rounds available that I ejected into the loof of my hand. 'Will these work?'

'*Sí.*'

I handed the ammunition over to Ana and said, 'Stay here.'

'*Uno momento*,' she said and then fired once more towards the trees, seemingly at nothing. She then opened the Colt's cylinder and ejected the spent ammunition before quickly reloading.

She turned her attention back to me and said, 'Okay. *Ten cuidado, señor,*'

I had no desire whatsoever to expose myself to the treeline where hidden shooters might wait to snipe at me, but I had even less interest in making a target of myself before the school house tower, so I went around the back of the dwelling in hopes of finding something useful on the bodies of the three lads Ana had so recently felled. I dropped and crawled on my hands and knees and as I passed the tent flap, Ana let loose a sudden volley of four rounds, as I supposed in order to create a diversion while I was in the open. On the far side, I found the three lads, all having suffered from headshots that I hoped had brought a more or less instantaneous end to their lives.

Upon crawling up to the first one, I did my best to ignore the fact that he appeared to be no more than fifteen years old. Despite the divot in the side of his head, I recognised his serene face as having belonged to one of the lads who so recently had me trapped only a few feet away.

I still remember seeing his youthful countenance as the older lad was walking up to put his gun against my head and as I turned him over to search for his gun beneath him, my mind registered the uncertainty in the lad's eyes as he had watched the drama of my near demise unfold directly before him. There, beneath his young body, laid a small, silver revolver without a spot of tarnish upon it. I retrieved it and then gently laid his body back down. Behind me, I heard another shot fired from just around the corner and reasoned that Ana was running low on ammunition again, so without another thought on the morality of what was happening, I stepped forward to search the next body just in time for another fusillade of gunshots to tear through the canvas.

For one tick my heart froze as I feared for Ana, and then she came running about the corner while another bullet smacked off the frame of the dwelling and sailed away to parts unknown.

Ana knelt next to me and I saw blood streaming from her hair.

'Oh, God, ye've been shot!' I said as another round flew over our heads.

'No, no! Just a splinter,' she said as she set aside the long-barrelled Colt. 'Now what you have for me?'

I handed her the silver revolver and she said, '*Muy pequeño.*' But then as she gently worked the trigger and hammer she excitedly said: 'Oh, but double-action!' Then she backed up against me as I moved forward to see what else I could find.

In another few ticks, I found two more serviceable revolvers, and handed one over to Ana while retaining the larger for my own big hand. Ana turned to me and said, 'If this es all, then we had best be going, *pronto.*'

'Aye,' I replied and looked around, trying to feel out what our best route would be. I felt myself to be in a swither as I cast my eyes to the west, for it felt as though my body was being pulled back in that direction, and I had no desire to draw fire any where near the dwelling in which I knew Rebekah and Teeny to be hiding. Alternatively, we could not go to the north where we would be exposed to fire from the tower, and it seemed that despite Ana's best efforts there were at least a few bodies still concealed in the wooded area to the south. So that left us the choice of staying put or heading to the east, which felt physically wrong to me, even to the extent that I felt an ache in my bones upon contemplating it.

Ana fired two rounds from the small, silver revolver with ease and said, 'Well, we are going?'

I pointed to the west and said, 'I feel that is richt, but...'

'You have what Hannah says is the skill. You decide; we go!' she said with a determined smile.

I wanted to run in that direction, felt that it was the right thing to do, but I said, 'We canna. There's innocent lassies over there with naething but a tent to protect them.' As I pointed, I licked my lips then forced myself to say: 'We're gang this way.'

Ana turned her head so that she could look directly in my eyes for one tick. The blood from the splinter, as she had called it, was oozing from somewhere within her dark hair and running down her temple. Most of it continued down her cheek, but some of it was running into the corner of her left eye. I noted this, but largely ignored it for her dark eyes were too full of something I didn't wish to see then, or ever, for that matter. She doubted me. Ana had been determined to follow me, but then she had heard the self-doubt in my own voice when I hesitantly, purposefully misdirected us, and even then I had to wonder if in her prior dealings with 'planners' she had never before heard such indecision. Taking Hannah as an example, she was certainly decisive, if nothing else.

But we didn't have Hannah to feel out or plan for the situation. We had me. I had made my statement, and like some sort of good soldier, Ana obeyed my command, even though she had never officially been conscripted into my army. Up until the very moment that I had presented my doubt to her, she was ready to follow me like some great leader of history, some Bruce, some Wallace, some Knox, for whom the biographies suggest that despite many setbacks, there seemed to be no ultimate obstacle to glory other than death, and then I stated aloud precisely what I knew to be wrong, and she heard it in my voice, and saw it in my eyes. I failed that young woman right then and there, and I don't know what is more terrible. That I was willing to lead her astray in that simple matter, or that she continued to follow me.

VIII

She continued to walk unsteadily forward.

'Ellie?' the woman in green was saying.

She kept walking until she found herself in the trees. The vines grew so thick it was difficult to see even a few feet in front of her, but as she slowly advanced she kept thinking within the silence of her mind: 'Good, good.'

The sky had turned grey and the air was thick. The woman became fearful and her voice threw angles in the air.

'Ellie! Oh, please, Ellie!'

She kept stopping every so often to let the woman see her. A flash of her white dress here, a brief sight of her smile. The woman kept coming.

And then she became frightened.

Something terrible, a violent, painful sound erupted behind them.

She saw the woman stop for one instant and look behind her. Then she ran forward in her bare feet.

'Ellie, this is no time for games!' the woman shouted fearfully.

'Please, Ellie!'

She let herself be seen.

The woman was crying. When the woman picked her up, her tears fell like hot rain upon her head.

She felt her tender kiss.

'You can not go running off like that again, Ellie. Please.'

And then there was movement in the trees.

She understood that they were looking for her.

The woman in green crouched down, holding her against her soft bosom. A man came walking through the trees. He had a big knife and kept hacking at the vines. Then he stopped only a few feet away.

The woman grew fearful. The woman's heart hammered within her bosom. She could feel it beating against her cheek.

It was frightening, and yet she grew calm and let peace reign within the silence of her mind.

The man had the knife in one hand, and a gun in the other. For one long instant he stopped and looked directly at them. The woman held her breath as he squinted and stared, trying hard to focus his eyes. Then he moved on as if they weren't there, as if he couldn't see them.

Time passed. There were more frightening sounds behind them, outside of the wilderness. Pain. Shouting. Angles in the air.

'Ellie?'

She silently kicked her feet about in a little exercise that felt good.

'What just happened, Ellie?'

She let her feet dangle and looked at the peaceful trees.

The woman in green was worried. 'Do not worry, dear. Mary will find us. And then we shall go home. Would you like to go away from this place? Would you like to go home with us to a place that is always green?'

She turned her cheek to the soft bosom and sighed.

Monday, 20 April 1896, 7:20 AM

We were running.

How can I properly describe the beauty of Ana-María de la Paz Rodríguez Morataya? Is it really enough to say that her skin was unblemished and was possessed of a hue like the richest coffee with only a wee drip of the purest cream in it? Is it enough to say that her hair was soft and dark like some angel's silken raiment, cast down from a starry heaven while the earth was shrouded in night? Is it enough to say that she bore an utterly feline aspect of form, not only in her ability to slink gracefully about, but in her every movement, her every charmed glance, her every shift of countenance?

No.

Because ultimately what brought about Ana's return to my side, and her subsequent capture, had nothing to do with her physical being. Rather it was on account of her soul wherein resided her belief in the righteousness of my statement regarding our need to assist the bairns of this isolated township called Bela. Ana had wanted to obey Hannah's order and leave me behind, but in her heart she knew she was turning her back on more than just me and Abigail. She had seen the children, seen the deranged manner in which they were kept and sent to a place called heaven, and knew they needed help. When Hannah would not even consider the idea of lending her assistance, Ana, being a natural follower, looked for a new leader. Dear God, why did she have to choose me?

The simple answer to that question is because I was at hand.

So Ana returned to find me, and I am eternally grateful that she did. Unfortunately I wasn't ready to lead. I wasn't ready to plan. I wasn't ready to play my part.

What I had yet to understand was that in order to lead in that particular capacity I also had to be ready to follow, and though it seemed that a certain spirit was available to show me the way, I still thought I knew best.

And so I lead Ana in the exact wrong direction.

I wouldn't know it for some time, but just to the west, visibly hidden from me, stood Abigail and Ellie in the trees. We could have gone to them if only I had followed the very urging of my bones. But I chose to run in the exact opposite direction for what I thought to be the best possible reason at the time.

It felt like we were running forever.

At intervals the tower came into view and bullets were randomly striking all about us. Then there were more laddies up ahead.

Ana put on an amazing display as she stood and fired with a revolver in each hand, not in any sort of combat pose, but as if she was simply target shooting for pleasure. I held my revolver and occasionally pointed it in the general direction of any body I thought to be a threat but felt reluctant to pull the trigger both because half the laddies ran at the sight of Ana's awesome demonstration and because I was well aware of the shortage of ammunition and felt that I would likely be wasteful of it. In the end, I handed over my revolver to Ana without having fired a shot.

Random bullets kept flying all about us as we came up against a more permanent structure composed fully of wood. Ana fired behind us twice, and then once into the woods and speired, 'And now where, *señor?*'

I was looking around, trying to feel out our surroundings despite the constant distraction of leaden balls ricocheting all about us. Even then, some hundred and fifty feet from the dwelling of Teeny and her sister, I still felt the tidal pull of a force wanting me to go back the way in which we had come. Behind us to the north was an open field leading to the school house and the danger of the tower. To the south was the woods which wound up to the east of us. We had effectively reached the end of the dwellings, and it seemed, our own dead end.

Ana fired one last time. She lowered her revolver and didn't hold her hand out for another. She knew I had no more to offer.

One more bullet flew over our heads. And then there was shouting.

'Stop! Stop shooting!'

I recognised the voice.

Ana turned her head to look quizzically at me over her shoulder.

'It's Ben,' I said. 'Let us hear what he has to say.'

She whispered, 'That is well, because we are out of bullets.'

A moment of silence passed and then I saw two hands extend out from behind the canvas of the next structure to our west.

I shouted, 'All richt, Ben, we see ye. What do ye want?'

His hands withdrew and then I saw just half of his face as he put one eye around the end of the canvas to look at us. 'I want no more shooting. I have orders from Esther that she wants you brought in safely. To talk.' He hesitated then before letting out a squeaky: 'Please?'

I swallowed hard and said, 'I kenna if we sud trust him...'

Ana turned her face to me again and said, 'It es no good to fight now.' She threw her revolver on the ground. 'There es a time for all things. A time for war and a time for *paz*.'

I looked her in the eye and again said, 'Thank ye for coming back for me.'

She smiled gently, sadly, but held her wheesht.

* * *

I would say we were surrounded but there were only four lads, including Ben, still available at that time to aim their weapons at us. At least that was enough for each point of the compass.

Ben picked up the revolver Ana had dropped and put it in the waistband of his trousers. Then they began to lead us two lassies, who marched steadily forward ahead of the business ends of their guns, a bit to the north in the general direction of the school. Then we detoured a bit towards the treeline to the east where another concrete cube was sunk in the sandy ground.

We walked down an oaken, timber staircase to an open door followed by the four lads, and were ushered inside the concrete to discover a series of cages composed of iron bars built with the general dimensions of four feet by four feet by four feet. Finding that we had three revolvers and a scatter-gun pointed at us, it seemed reasonable to acquiesce to our captors' demands that we be manacled and housed within the cages. The cages were then padlocked with the turning of a couple of keys which were handed over to Ben.

Once inside and so trapped with our hands secured behind our backs where they were tightly shackled at the wrists, I looked around the dim interior to see that this cube was not so sunken as the one I had briefly been imprisoned in earlier that morning. The roof stood at least two feet above the level of the ground, and this structure, which seemed to be nothing but one generously sized room, had winnocks all about near the ground level allowing the dim early morning light to filter in. Additionally, there was a large dish of various odds and ends of candles burning on a table to provide some added light. Looking to the floor, I noted that unlike the concrete of the other building, this one had a mixed surface of dirt, sand, and rotting pine needles with palmetto beetles and earwigs scurrying about. Otherwise, there was very little of interest to report on our surroundings.

Ana and I were housed in two cages sitting next to each other. On either side of us sat two more toom of occupants. For several minutes following the locking of our gaols, the four lads stood about goggling their eyes at us, and it was hard to tell who they inspected closer, me or Ana.

As for the lads, the oldest one was Ben with his scattergun, then there were two more around twenty years who both wore the same uniform sarks and trousers, and then there was one lad who I thought to be about thirteen and whose trousers were cut off at the knees. The three older lads looked with curiosity upon me, but the youngest one kept casting his eyes at Ana, and then away, as if fearful that she should catch him looking upon her. This continued for some minutes until the entry of another body.

The four lads stood straight as if suddenly coming to attention when Esther came walking down the timber steps. She set foot inside the door and looked about to see that everything was in order according to her desire. Then she walked forward and looked directly down at me. I cast my eyes up at her and in the dim light saw those big, ropy veins on the side of her head thrumming away with the pulsing of her heart. She looked angry and incredulous at once.

Several ticks of the clock passed and Esther said to Ben, 'Get out and try to find that cretinous baby. She shouldn't be that difficult to locate, but even if she is, that woman Mrs Fisher ought to be with her and unless you're blind you can't miss her. All of you except Lucas, get out there and find her!' she ordered with her finger pointing at the stairway beyond the open door.

Ben turned to the young lad in the cut off trousers and held out his scattergun. 'Let's trade, Lucas,' he said as innocuously as if they were passing cards in a game. The young lad handed over his revolver and then held the long arm close to his chest. I watched as Ben also handed over the keys to our various locks, then withdrew the revolver with the spent ammunition from his trousers and laid it on the table next to the dish of candles. As the other lads left, Lucas turned his attention back on Ana until she looked at him and smiled. He quickly averted his eyes as if frightened by the radiant glare of her braw smile.

Esther was staring at us until the three lads left. Then she went to the door and shut it. She turned back to us and said, 'That was some interesting work you did this morning.'

'*Gracias*,' Ana pleasantly replied.

Esther glowered at her and said, 'Shut your mouth you dego maid.'

Ana turned her eyes back to Lucas and displayed her teeth again. The lad looked away.

Esther was looking directly at me for a spell and then she speired, 'Why did you come here?'

I earnestly replied, 'We foond Ellie and thocht she belonged here.'

'No,' she stoutly said. '*Why* did you come here?'

I couldn't help but roll my eyes and said, 'I juist told ye...'

'No!' Esther stepped forward and squinted at me with a pained look on her face. 'This has nothing to do with some hideous cretin-child. This has to do with me and my father. Alexandra warned us that this would happen someday, that you would come for us. She warned us to be careful about who we let in here, and if you came, she told us what to do, how to effectively deal with your kind.' She was looking at me with a sneer, and as she hovered in her speech her lip curled up a bit. Then she said, 'I should have known. I saw you and thought you were the ugliest man I had ever seen, but there was something more than that. Something so inherently *wrong* about you.' She sadly shook her head. 'Truly these must be the last days if monsters like you roam the earth, killing my children.'

Ana said, 'Actually, Missy Esther, that was me what did the killing when they try to shoot us.'

Esther looked angrily over at Ana and said, 'Shut up, shut up!' She went to Ana's cage and kicked it which resulted in a single, dull clang. Then she stepped back and looked to me again. 'The only reason you're not dead is because your wife is out there in the woods and you're going to get her back for me.'

'Why, sae ye can kill her, too?'

She did her best to bare her teeth in a friendly smile. 'No, of course not. We wouldn't hurt her, or you, if only she would come back. That shooting earlier, that was just some of the boys getting over-excited. You know how boys can be with guns,' she said as her grin widened. 'We only want what's best for you and your wife. Why, if only she would come back, you could both live right here.'

My hair stood on end when I heard that statement, but it was unnecessary. Of course I knew she was lying. And I would never want to live in that hell-hole anyway.

'You see, our only concern is that she might tell about our angel and the miracles she performs, and we can't have that kind of attention.'

'Ach. I winna help ye, bitch.'

Her face hardened again and she said, 'You can help us find her, or sooner or later we'll find her on our own. Now is the time to demonstrate whose side you are on. You can be on the side of God or the devil, and in the end, God will win.'

I nodded and said, 'In that much, I feel certain ye are correct.'

Esther's eyes narrowed somewhat and she nodded at me. 'You can't fool me. On the final day, even the devil will be forced to admit so much.' Then she turned and went to the door, pulled it open, walked out and clashed it shut behind her. The last I heard of her, she was stomping up the timber stairs.

I turned my attention back to Ana just in time to see her wink at Lucas. He turned somewhat red in the face and looked away.

I sighed, then said, 'Ana, I'm sorry I led ye into this. This is all my fault.'

She turned to me and smiled gently before saying, 'No, *señor*, I was aware of the danger. I should have done right and followed Hannah. But I want to come back. It es my decision.'

I did my best to smile reassuringly but I felt there was little I could do by means of encouragement given the fact that I was locked in a cage with my hands shackled behind my back.

Ana said, 'Do not worry. We are not finished yet. Remember what I say. Have faith. *Dios existe.*'

I nodded and said, 'I'm glad ye are so confident, Ana.'

'*Por supuesto.* I learn it all from *mi Abuelita*, my granny. Faith until the last moment, the last you breathe.'

I looked askance to Lucas and saw that he was taking his chance as Ana was talking to me to look upon her. He seemed quite intrigued by her, not only her overall beauty, but by what to him was no doubt an earthy exoticism he had never before encountered in this isolated place, something both foreign and pleasant born of her *mestiza* blood. I certainly couldn't blame Lucas for his interest.

Something unvoiced between Ana and myself suggested that it was time for a distraction, so picking up on her last statement I said, 'What exactly did ye learn from yer grand-mither?'

Ana had her back facing away from Lucas, and as she began to tell me some about her family, her hands started to move against the fabric of her serge dress where they were manacled behind her. She said, '*Mi Abuelita*, mother of my father, was of the Wixáritari people of the north of Jalisco. They are the natives of my homeland who live there for many thousand years before *Cristóbal Colón* thought he ran the *Santa María* to ground in Asia. She marry *mi Abuelo*, who was mostly a *Negro*, and they very happy together. My mother was born to *peninsulares* from *España*, and when she es enamoured of my father her parents try to have him killed because they want to keep the blood pure. But my mother run away with him and they live with his parents, *mi Abuelo y Abuelita*.'

Ana paused for a tick and shifted her eyes back to Lucas who immediately looked towards the ceiling. I was watching Ana's finger-ends move against the fabric of her dress alongside the big buttons that ran its length. Then she continued, '*Mi Abuelita* never give in. She tell me always about two gods in this world, our good father the sun, and the one who opposes him, Nacawé, the goddess of rain. But also she tell me about *Jesús y María*. And *balero*.'

206

She hovered in her speech long enough for me to speir: 'Wha is *balero*?'

Ana looked to me and smiled. She said, '*Balero* es not a person, only *un juego para niños*.'

When she failed to continue, Lucas gently cleared his throat and speired, 'What is that?'

I supplied: 'A game for cheeldren.'

'Yes,' Ana said. 'A cup and ball, both attached with string for you to catch the ball in the cup. Only *mi Abuelita* still play it when she very old. That was how she met her husband. They play together when very young. She challenge him, you know? And she win. He was a good prize, I think, so she keep playing with all the children until she die.'

Ana kept fidgeting around with the fabric of her dress as she said, 'Every year, *Abuelita* walk north into mountains to join her people, her Wixáritari, for ceremony of corn, blue deer and *águilas*. There, they have the cactus *mescalito* and many visions. It is long journey, and yet she always go, for she say as long as she have faith, she must walk.' Ana shook her head gently. 'She go last time by her self but never arrive. My parents go and find her in the desert, still with her *balero*. Legs no longer work, but she say "I can still play. I can still work." She was very serious and worked hard all her life. But she never gave up the faith of a child, you know?' Ana's fingers shifted to the buttons of her dress as she looked to me and I nodded. 'And so, neither do I until we are finished. *Mi Abuelita* had many children and grand-children and grand-grand children.'

'Great grand-cheeldren,' I supplied.

'*Sí*. We all love her very much. That is what I want. That is what I have faith that I will have some day. I will be old and have many children.' She had already begun to pluck loose the buttons of her dress. Then she turned her dark eyes on the lad with the scattergun and speired, 'And what about you, Lucas?'

Lucas's eyes darted between the two of us and then settled on a point somewhere in between. 'What do you mean?'

'I mean, will you be an old man like Reverend Lotson someday with all these children about? Like me? That will be me someday when I find a man, you know?'

Lucas didn't look at her. His countenance twisted queerly as he said, 'I-I don't know.'

'You do not know?' Ana speired with affected concern.

'I mean. No. I guess. The end will be here before then, so it doesn't matter.'

'What end?' I speired.

Lucas's eyes shifted to mine. 'You know. The end. Of everything.'

I shook my head. 'Enlichten me.'

His brows knit together and he said, 'Is this a trick?' I shook my head. 'You know. The big fight.'

'Ooooh. The *Armagedón* of the *Apocalipsis*,' Ana said.

Lucas nearly met her eyes with his own as he said, 'Yeah.'

'And you will fight then?'

Lucas held the scattergun a little more erectly and quietly said, 'That's right. I'm ready to be a soldier of God.'

'Yes, and until then? Will you be a man? Will you be like me and have many children?'

Lucas perfunctorily stated, 'There's more to bein' a man than that. I don't want children.'

Ana's fingers were still moving so far as her manacled wrists would allow. She had several buttons undone on the back of her dress as she earnestly speired, 'Lucas? Will they truly take away your father parts that are in your *pantalones*?'

The lad looked sick at that but recited, 'If your own right eye offends you, you had best pluck it out.' With an obvious tone of uncertainty he said, 'It is for my own good if it keeps me from sinning.'

Ana shimmied her shoulders about and pulled at the fabric of her dress until it fell away to reveal that she was wearing a rather chaste *sostén* beneath. 'But Lucas, if they take those away, then you will not want this. You will never have this,' she gently said as a great expanse of her coffee skin was exposed to the light.

Lucas's eyes grew huge and he stuttered out: 'Uh-ah-uh.' Then he snapped his mouth shut and fully turned away from us.

For a few ticks the lad was in a swither of indecision as to what he should do. Then Ana said, 'Lucas. Turn to me. Look to me.'

The lad didn't. He awkwardly walked towards the door, opened it, and then quickly made his way up the stairs and out of our sight, which was fine with me except for the fact that he had the keys.

Ana began fidgeting at the fabric of her dress again and I saw what she was doing. As she began to extract two metal pins hidden in the weave she said, '*Jesús* forgive me. I do not feel well for the trying to make that boy enamoured of me.' Then with the pins secure between her fingers, she drew up her legs and carefully brought her hands underneath and then in front of her. I rolled about in my cage and mirrored that action myself as she said, 'Please, *señor*, fix my *botones* now.' She pushed her long back up against the bars of the cage and I carefully worked my manacled hands through the gaps with my eyes fixed on the little ridges of her spine that were visible just below the nape of her neck. Coming near to her, I found that she smelled like a mixture of gunsmoke and flowers, as if she had worn a light perfume or washed her hair with some sort of scented soap.

I didn't know exactly how Lucas felt about Ana's display of flesh, but I can honestly say that my own finger-ends shook somewhat as I pulled her dress back into place and re-buttoned it. While doing so I speired, 'Jalisco is in Mexico, aye?'

'Yes. We have a saying. *Jalisco es Mexico.*'

'Aye, and betimes it seems that the Highlands are juist aboot all Scotland is known for.'

Ana turned in her cage to face me and said, '*Dame los manos.*'

Again I squeezed my hands in between the bars of my cage and she began to work on the lock of my manacles with one of the pins, carefully twisting it back and forth until it seemed to stick in place. As she began to work the other one about, I speired, 'What is that *ametralladora* in the school house tower?'

'The battery gun of Doctor Gatling. They crank like the coffee grinder, you know? Hundred or hundred and fifty shots a minute. They use in the war here thirty years ago, but now there are better machines. Like many guns I see here, they were sold to the people after the army wanted them no more. When the people here do not buy, then the old guns go to my country.'

She had continued moving the second pin about while she spoke and in a moment's time my hands were free.

'The cage, now,' Ana said.

The lock on my cage was facing away from Ana. I said, 'Maybe ye sud give me the pins and I could try?'

'Have you ever pinned a lock before?'

'Nae, never.'

'No time for the learning. You will move the cage.'

At first I didn't know what she meant, but I quickly found that with my wrists free I could grasp the bars on either side with my hands and force my big clog-feet through the bottom and with a great deal of effort actually lift the cage and move it about. Punctuated with several pained grunts, I brought the cage up on my back and turned it around so that the lock was facing Ana. When I dropped it again, I collapsed and sat gasping air while she lifted her bound hands and began to work at the padlock with the pins.

'Rest now. This will take *uno momento*. Then you must go,' she said as she kept slowly inserting one of the pins and sweeping it around.

While she worked, I speired, 'Hoo is it that ye're sae guid at the shooting?'

She was looking at her long, tapered, feminine fingers as she said, 'Really for me it is about how to hold the gun. Any gun that is made correctly, and fits your hand correctly, you only have to hold correctly and then you point.' She stopped working the pins and held up her first finger. 'If you are holding the gun correctly, only think you are pointing your finger and you know where the bullet go without looking at the sights.' She resumed working and said, 'Other than that, there is the gravity and the curve of the earth. With practice you will know. And you can guess how quickly the bullet will drop depending on what kind of gun and the barrel of the gun. The length. Other than that, it is only skill you are born with.'

I nodded and watched her continue to work, then said, 'Once ye get me free, ye're neist.'

She didn't falter in her efforts as she said, 'No, it will take too long.'

'I'm no' leaving ye.'

'Yes, you will.' She withdrew the one pin then placed it in her mouth and began to chew on it. Around the metal she said, 'It will take much longer for me to open my own locks.' She withdrew the pin and shoved it back in the lock until it seemed to stick. Then she began working the other pin around as she said, 'The direction I must come at them es very bad. You will get out first and I will work on my own and join you.'

'Na, na, I dinna like that,' I said despite feeling it would be a prudent choice on my part. It also felt cowardly to be abandoning the lass who so recently had saved my life.

'You must remember Ellie, and Percy, and all the others. And your wife. I am safe in my cage, now,' she said and smiled at me as my lock came open.

I reached through the bars and pulled it loose and cast it to the ground. I forced the door open and as I stepped out I said, 'Ana, please let me help ye first.'

'No.' She pulled back within her cage, the pins concealed in the loof of her hand. '*No disputa.* I will not start to free myself until you are gone.' She was looking at me sullenly and I felt my paunch twist as I started to walk towards the door.

Once I had one foot on the stairs, I turned to see that Ana had a pin in her teeth and had lifted her manacled hands up so that she could work it around in the lock. She briefly removed the pin from her mouth with her fingers and said, '*Vaya con Dios, Señor Fisher.*' She smiled radiantly at me.

I nodded and said, '*Gracias*, Ana. *Hasta la vista.*' And then I stepped upwards from the gloom and turned my face towards the light.

* * *

The remaining lads, excepting Lucas, I supposed, were out in the woods searching for Ellie and Abigail. That much I knew.

Looking about from the top of the steps I tried to get a bearing on my location within the township of Bela. Two lines of trees ran to meet together creating a corner nearby, and I was aware that I was in the southeast of the cleared area. To the west was a long line of tent-house dwellings including the one in which Teeny and her sister lived and the one which earlier had its canvas effectively shredded by bullets fired both from within and without, both at the far western end.

I could see no one just then, but I could sense them out there concealed in the trees and feared exposing myself to their eyes. On the other hand, behind me to the north was the tower and I didn't want to wager that the cease-fire was still in place.

My senses still felt somewhat dulled, but I was aware that the fifty or so bodies remained cruived in the school house. Other than that, I could sense a few random souls spread about the dwellings and could only hope that they were more bairns like Teeny and Rebekah, simply hiding on their own until the storm blew over.

My first move was to get away from the concrete building, the roof of which only stood a few feet above the ground level. I wanted to get away to somewhere in which I would have adequate cover, and it occurred to me that I might simply want to head for the trees. After crawling up the timber stairs onto the ground and beginning to rise into a crouch, just as I began to move forward I heard a hacking coming from beyond the treeline, the sound of someone attacking the vines for the purpose of creating a path. I hesitated only one tick and then turned and ran the opposite direction.

For one instant I caught sight of the tower out of the corner of my right eye and then it was concealed from my view as I went to my knees behind the first dwelling to the west. I wasn't paying attention to my immediate surroundings and jumped up to sprint to the next structure when a lad walked directly in front of me from around the corner and I ran him down. For a moment, we were nothing but a mass of tangled limbs, and then my left hand felt as though it were swelling with the need to dang him about some until I got a look at his face. His visage presented a mixed bag of surprise and fear as he looked tremblingly upon me. Then I saw the gun. He had dropped a revolver when I ran into him, and I quickly went for it expecting him to do the same, only he didn't move. He simply sat and bemusedly watched as I picked up his weapon.

I stepped back with the gun in my hand and looked at the lad who was probably no older than I was. He was still on the ground, looking up at me with astonished, dark eyes and his mouth hanging open in a pant to reveal his misshapen teeth. I was standing with the gun in my left hand, usually a certain death sentence for my enemies, only upon getting a good look at him, I didn't feel even the slightest urge to do harm to this lad. Instead, with the revolver hanging loosely at my side, I held out my right hand and the lad grasped it. I gave a gentle tug and he was on his feet.

'Hoo many muir of ye are oot here?' I speired him.

His eyes grew big and then he furrowed his brow before trying to speak. 'Nyung nyuh nyuh, nyung,' was about as much as I heard. Looking to his mouth as he spoke I saw that his tongue appeared fully malformed.

I smiled as pleasantly as I could at him and said, 'All richt, gae on, noo. Gae and hide somewaur until all this shooting is over.'

'Nyuh nyuh nyung?'

I made a motion with my right hand and harshly whispered, 'Gae on, laddie!'

'Nyuh nyuh nyung? Nyuh-nooh!'

I lifted the revolver and pointed it in the air as I said, 'Gae. Noo!'

I began to wave the gun about menacingly until the lad seemed to comprehend that I wanted him to leave, only he still remained standing and staring at me, so I lowered the gun and pointed it at his feet and said, 'Gae noo or I start shooting!'

His eyes got big and he turned and began to run towards the trees. He started to make a hideous, moaning cry as he ran, and I said, 'Wheesht! Wheesht!' as he went, though he only got louder the closer he came to the treeline.

'Dammit,' I said under my breath.

I had just enough time to turn my attention back in the other direction when gunfire erupted from within the trees behind me.

'Shyte,' I said as a bullet ricocheted off of the wooden frame of the dwelling I was standing against.

I turned my eyes towards the trees and was aware that multiple shooters were firing at me. I lifted the revolver to return fire in their general direction in hopes of forcing them to take cover while I ran, only when I pulled the trigger on the gun I found that the action was so corroded that it wouldn't cough up any bullets. I certainly was no expert on weapons, but I was schooled enough to know that if the revolving part of a revolver doesn't revolve, then the gun is fairly well useless.

As I ran in the rear tent flap of the dwelling I very nearly threw the gun from me but had presence of mind to realise that the ammunition might be needed at some future moment if the cylinder could be pried open, so instead I dropped the weapon in the pocket of my trousers.

I entered the dwelling to find it unoccupied, and like the other I had seen it contained several cots and little else. No sooner did I register these facts than another fusillade was unleashed in my general direction. Bullets ripped the canvas and splintered the wood frame, and then suddenly the entire structure began to fall in as one of the wooden supports broke in two. Without thinking I instinctively made my way to the opposite side of the tent and jumped out and into the dim light only to see the tower looming in the mist a hundred feet ahead of me.

Apparently the operators of the machine weapon were already well aware of my location due to the efforts of the lads in the woods on the opposite side of the dwelling I had just exited, for no sooner had I stepped out and set my eyes upon the tower than the weapon unleashed on me. *One-two-three* and I saw the hot streaks like fireflies shooting through the air around my head, number one by my left lug, number two by my right, and number three just above the level of my hair. I felt so certain of my impending doom just then that when the weapon ceased at only three shots, and silence suddenly reigned, I somehow thought myself to already be dead.

Then there was the sudden sound of a small arm being fired, and for a tick I thought it was the lads in the woods heartily keeping up their efforts behind me, but then I realised the sound was coming from the tower.

First I saw one body fall forward to land with a soft thud in the sand at the base of the tower, and then a second went flying out into the air with a rope in his hands. The lad let out a high-pitched shriek to rival that of the night time owls as he fell away from his perch, holding on to the rope until it reached its terminal length at which time a bell was heard to forcefully ring. The pull of gravity on his body was too strong for the lad to hold on and no sooner had the bell erupted with that one loud clang than the rope became taut and was ripped from his grasp. He fell the final few feet to the ground unimpeded and lay still.

So dumbfounded was I by this very sight that I didn't know what to do. Everything had suddenly become so perfectly silent and still that I simply stood blinking up at the tower until the lads in the woods decided to start up again. Bullets were again flying randomly about as the half of the uncollapsed canvas behind me still provided some cover. And then the machine weapon started up again and I thought I was still to be gunned down, only as I hit the ground I realised that it was being wildly fired high above my head into the treeline a hundred feet behind me.

The operator was clearly having a great deal of trouble in controlling the weapon, not only in the sense that it was being aimed somewhat haphazardly, but also because the earlier, quickly repeated pulse of gunshots was now dilatory at best. Nonetheless, it had its intended effect as the lads apparently gave up their shooting for the sake of taking cover.

Then all grew silent again. As I lifted my head to look at the tower, my first thought was of Ana, that she somehow had managed to escape her cage the instant I left

218

her and had made a beeline to the tower. But then I caught a flash of a particular colour, though it was dulled and obscured in the mist. Blue. It was that silly, frilly dress of Hannah's, and I smiled just a bit to myself to realise that she had come back.

Figuring that there was no time like the present to cross the big open space to the school, I jumped up and sprinted to where I had seen the two bodies fall. The lads out in the woods were apparently still cowed enough not to fire upon me, so I safely made the passage in only a few ticks.

When I arrived at the base of the tower, I found that the one lad was a bloody mess where apparently he had been shot at least twice before falling. The other, the one who had grabbed at the bell pull, laid rather serenely, though somewhat awkwardly, in the sand, with what looked like a smile on his face. I barely had time to note that he was breathing heavily, yet steadily, when Hannah walked up behind me, somewhat out of breath.

I turned to her and earnestly said, 'Thank ye for coming back, Hannah.'

I don't know why, probably it was on a mixed account of the fact that since leaving Ana behind I was feeling low and lonely and that I had nearly just been shot several times, but I put my right arm out and about Hannah as if to hug the lass.

Hannah looked displeased and violently reacted to my affection, shoving me away from her with both of her hands. 'Get the fuck off me! I didn't come back for you, I came back for Rodríguez.'

Still I smiled down at her and she frowned up at me. She turned away and went to one knee next to the bodies and started searching. While her hands roved through pockets she said, 'I can't go back without her and she knows it. She didn't even bother to try to give me the slip because she knows if I wanted I could track her down in a heartbeat. Nope.' She came away from the lad empty handed and began to search the other, the one who was still breathing. She continued: 'Instead she waits until we get a little ways out then turns and runs off on those long legs of hers without so much as an *Adios.* My one chance would have been to shoot low and hope I hobbled her.'

Hannah withdrew her hand to show me that the lad's pockets were stuffed with what looked like yellowed, worn, loose pages from an old Bible. She dropped them on the ground and said, 'Nothing of use for the present situation.'

Then she turned her attention to the gun in my hand and speired, 'Loaded?'

I looked at it and said, 'Aye, probably, but it winna fire.' I pushed at the cylinder and got it open and ejected the ammunition, then held the bullets in the loof of my hand for Hannah's inspection.

'Those are no good for me,' Hannah said as she rummaged about in her handbag.

'Hoo can ye tell?'

She withdrew a tiny, nickel-plated revolver and said, 'I've got a Model 1. Needs special .22 shorts, and those are .45s.' After withdrawing a small box on which I read the name *Winchester,* she dropped her handbag on the ground and flipped the barrel of her revolver up so as to have access to the cylinder. She quickly extracted seven cartridges from the box and nimbly reloaded and reassembled the weapon before picking her bag up again. Then in reference to the bullets I still held, she said, 'Throw them in. We might need them later.'

I dropped them in her bag as she said, 'Now, before the shooting starts up again, where is Rodríguez?'

I pointed in the general direction of where the sunken concrete building was located and said, 'Ye canna see it because it is in the ground and so dark oot, but she's over there. When I left there was nane watching her.'

We began to move around the base of the school and Hannah casually said, 'This building is full of people.'

'Aye, they're hiding until the shooting's over.'

'Good for them. Now what is the situation? I presume you didn't just leave Rodríguez behind because you grew weary of her charm.'

'She was in a cage. So was I. She was able to free me and sent me oot because it would have taken a while for her to get herself free.'

We were at the corner of the school and looking about. From that point forward there was no good cover to be seen all the way to where I thought the concrete building to be. I felt Hannah grab a hold of the front of my sark and she said, 'What the hell is your problem?'

I looked down into her angry, clear blue eyes and said, 'What do ye mean?'

'You just left her there?'

'Weel, aye, she told me to. She wisnae even gang to work on her locks until I left her...'

I felt a bit of panic as Hannah pointed her wee revolver at me. She didn't seem to be consciously making a target of me, rather she was using it like a natural, though metallic, digital extension of her hand as she poked me and said, 'You never, ever let them tell you what to do. She was wrong to do that, just as wrong as running off on me, and it'll probably get her killed.' Again she poked at my bosom with her wee revolver and said, 'If you ever allow them even one decision, they'll want it forevermore and then you have chaos. We have to always maintain control over them at all times.'

Hannah withdrew the revolver and turned her attention away. She was scanning her eyes about as I said, 'But she wouldna do what I said. And I have nae authority over her, anyway.'

Hannah looked in my eyes again and said, 'Yes, you do. You're just too ignorant to know it. Come on,' she said and we began to run forward.

As we ran through a patch of pole beans on our way to the sunken concrete cube, I contemplated Hannah's words, and considered Ana's earlier actions and the way she so wilfully obeyed my commands, even when she thought me to be wrong. It seemed that Hannah was trying to tell me something I didn't know about myself, something I could scarcely believe just then, about being a leader. I nearly wanted to accept that she had seen something within me of which I was unaware, but I wasn't ready to make that leap of faith. Instead I shook my head as if I could dislodge the very notion from my ken, and quietly said, 'Ach,' under my breath.

We arrived at the building in peace and found the steps descending into the darkness. Hannah lifted her revolver to point down the stairs then immediately dropped it to her side again. She voiced what I already knew to be true. 'There's nobody down there.'

I started to turn away but Hannah quickly disappeared down the timbers. I followed her to find the room in a surprising state of disarray. Not that it was particularly orderly before, but clearly some sort of disagreement of a physical nature had occurred during my absence.

The most obvious sign of disorder was in the overturning of the table with the dish of candles. A few still had burning wicks as they lay scattered about on the floor, but most had been extinguished on account of the upset. The plate itself was smashed on the floor. Looking across the room, Ana's cage door was standing open, and turning my eyes down I found that there was an obvious trail made among the sand and dead pine needles where it appeared someone had been dragged while flailing their appendages about some. I nearly missed it in the dim light but I also noticed that there was some small amount of blood present.

'Oh, God,' I gently intoned.

Hannah turned to me and speired, 'Where is she?'

I shrugged my shoulders and said, 'Hoo sud I ken?'

The lass turned on me then and stretched her arm up to dang me sharply, violently in the side of the head.

'Think, dammit!' she shouted with a touch of genuine rage in her voice.

I realised then what she was getting at and I started to say, 'I still feel so dull in my senses...'

'Nevermind that. Do what you do to see where she's gotten off to. Hurry before someone else shows up.'

Hannah was looking angrily up at me but I did my best to set her annoyance aside in order to focus on my breathing. In and out, and slowly the world fell away until I began to feel something, and as I thought about her, it was as if I could sense Ana's recent departure. It was obvious that she was taken out the door and up the stairs, but I was having difficulty in sensing anything beyond that. And then, suddenly, I felt Hannah's fingers on my arm, and fear welled up within me as I thought she was trying to get my attention and worried that someone had come looking for us.

I just barely had time to open my eyes when Hannah calmly said, 'No, remain calm. Focus, Fisher. Let me help you.'

Hannah had placed her fingers near my elbow, but then I gently felt them walk their way down my sleeve until she reached the exposed skin of my wrist. I felt her hand close around my flesh, almost like she were a nurse taking my pulse. I immediately felt magnified in my focus, and suddenly a path was clearly laid out before me.

I opened my eyes to see a track of pristine white, as dazzling in the grey, morning gloom as Ana's beautiful smile.

Hannah released her hold on me and gently speired, 'Well?'

I pointed up the stairs and said, 'I have it. But there's one muir thing.'

I walked to the overturned table and looked about. Its steel was dark, but I could still barely make it out in the gloom. I picked it up and said, 'We got this aff of one of the lads. Ana was using it until she ran oot of bullets.'

Hannah set her revolver aside and held out her hand and I gave her the weapon. She opened the cylinder, used the rod to eject the spent brass onto the floor, then began to rummage about in her bag. She withdrew the .45s I had given her and handed them to me. Then she dry fired the revolver and said, 'It's serviceable and it's double-action. Do you know what that means?'

I shook my head.

'No need to cock the hammer, just pull the trigger.'

'Juist point and click, then,' I said as she began taking the bullets from my hand and loading it.

'More like point and bang, I hope. If it only clicks, you've run out of bullets.'

She gently pushed the cylinder closed and handed me the weapon, then without saying another word we went running up the timbers to find the air had further thickened into drizzle.

* * *

In the thick, humid air that morning, my clothes and my skin had already surpassed the simple adjective *damp*. Now in the drizzle I soon moved on to *drenched* as I quickly found myself saturated and sodden.

While this did little to improve my comfort level, as the precipitation fell it provided another layer of visual cover for our movements.

The path I was following stood out in the purest white and moved quite directly towards the trees where it suddenly came to a stop about ten feet from the natural fence line.

I pointed at a squat fantail palm sitting atop a sandy promontory surrounded by weeds and scrub grass. 'They took her there.'

Hannah narrowed her eyes and squinted at me, then finding that I was in earnest, she approached the wee palm tree and knelt. She began to reach about the base of the mound and pick out some weeds and I joined her. Within a few ticks of the clock, we had found a metal grating in the sand which we were able to get our fingers under. Hannah may have helped a bit, but mostly it was my own strength that pulled the grate, with the palm sitting firmly atop it, aside to reveal the gloom below.

I was panting from the effort as I said, 'That's it. They took her doun there.'

It was a tight space and looked something like a cement sewer. It was perhaps no more than three feet wide and immediately descended some ten feet before curving up and levelled out somewhere below the treeline.

Hannah quietly swore under her breath then picked up her revolver and said, 'Grab the back of my dress. I'll lean in and look, and if there's trouble, pull me back out.'

'Aye,' I said and grabbed a hold of her as she knelt and bent forward into the hole.

For a few ticks she said nothing, then I heard: 'Okay.' She pushed up with her free hand and I helped pull her up onto the sand.

'I can't see anything more than a few feet ahead,' she said. 'There's probably a foot of standing water in the bottom, and near to the entry where there's some light I can see it's been splashed about on the cement as if someone just walked through it.'

'Is it a sewer?'

'It doesn't smell like a sewer. At least not the kind you're thinking of. It's more like a tunnel,' she said. 'A convenient way to get through the trees to whatever's on the other side by going beneath them, only it wasn't designed to withstand the rainy season here, apparently.'

'What do we do?'

Hannah pinched the bridge of her nose as if pained and said, 'I don't want to go trudging through that, but I have a feeling it would be the quickest way to our destination.'

I turned and looked behind us. The drizzle had turned to rain and I could see nothing beyond about twenty feet, but I felt certain that Abigail and Ellie were in that direction.

As if reading my thoughts, Hannah said, 'They're fine, for now. Rodríguez is the one we know is in trouble. Let's go get her.'

She began to warily look back in the hole as I said, 'I want to see Ana safe, but why sud I risk myself working with ye? Abigail may be fine for the noo, but for hoo lang? Besides, as soon as we find Ana ye'll juist leave me again.'

Hannah sighed and ruefully said, 'No. I won't.'

I looked down into her eyes and considered them for a tick. They were blue, but possessed nothing of the richness of Alexandra's. Of course, ultimately, appearances meant little if anything, as I had so recently as that very morning been reminded. Hannah's eyes were nearly clear and I felt as if in that moment I could see directly to her soul. She seemed to be waiting for me to acknowledge the fact that she was telling me the truth, and after a spell of study I said, 'All richt. We gae for Ana. And then we all find Abigail and Ellie and get oot of here.'

She nodded and said, 'And then once we're all on the outside, we can decide what to do about this place.'

I held out my hand and Hannah looked to it for a tick before extending her own and we cracked loofs like gentlemen. After all the fash she had given me before, and the way she had simply walked away with Ana in tow to leave me and Abigail and Ellie to our own fates, I didn't exactly want to ally myself to the bitch. Yet I felt the honesty of her intentions in that one moment as we shook hands, and felt the blessing of whatever spirit it was who seemed to want to lead me forward.

It was a queer thing, but it seemed neither one of us wanted to release the other's grip first. Even after a few up and down pumpings we simply held hands while staring in each other's eyes. I felt a queer urge then within myself to stare the lass down, or better yet, to squeeze her wee hand until the pain was too much for her to bear. But then I remembered Abigail, and knowing that time was of the essence, and that we needed to proceed forward to find Ana in order to get back to the search for my lass, I wilfully released Hannah's grip and let my hand drop. Before looking away from her face, I saw the corner of Hannah's mouth twitch ever so slightly as if she were pleased with herself for winning some trivial prize. It was a trial for me, but I forced my pride down and turned my attention back to the hole.

* * *

Since my final days as a lass in Scotland, I had worn my father's old tackety-boots for the two reasons that, firstly, they were available, and secondly, because they fit my oversized clog-feet. Pre-fitted lassie's shoon did not come in my titanic size, so for some years I had discarded the notion of procuring such footwear for myself. Besides, I frankly didn't care for such feminine styles. They didn't match my ensemble.

Hannah, on the other hand, had dressed for this investigation in the style of a rich young woman, wearing a frilly dress and matching headgear to effectively play her part, and, unfortunately, her shoon matched in that they were high in price but short in quality when it came to wading through the elements.

Before we descended into the dark, she removed her wee button-booties to reveal her stocking feet. Then she threw her shoon and her wee handbag in the skirt of her dress among the blue ribbons festooning the hem and rolled them up along with the skirt and her silken, blue petticoat. This revealed a good deal of her legs, which despite both being thin like the rest of her, demonstrated an impressive amount of development of the muscle of the calf, but I made no comment. Certainly this was one of those situations in which I was glad to wear trousers.

At first I thought that Hannah might wish to lead, but clearly she was reticent to drop into the hole. 'You first, Fisher,' she said.

I looked down into the gloom and speired, 'Do ye have a match at least in yer bag?'

She shook her head. 'It may not smell, but let's not take a chance on there being any trapped gasses down there. Believe me, I would love a light, but an open flame might be deadly.'

I nodded and let that sink into my ken for future reference.

I put my feet in first, but before letting them drop to the cement where it curved down and out of sight, I considered that I might ought to argue my position that I shouldn't go first. Then I looked up to Hannah's face and observed her displeasure at this entire endeavour. She seemed distressed, to say the least, and so I decided to go ahead.

Upon putting my boots down, I quickly discovered that although the surface of the cement above the water line appeared to be for the most part dry, it was incredibly slick. I had wanted to try and keep my boots up above the water by pressing them against the sides of the tunnel but that was impossible. I was soon sludging through the muck, and then I turned to look up towards the light.

'All richt, Hannah,' I said.

She was standing up there with her skirt and petticoat kilted up in one hand nearly so far as to reveal her garters, with her revolver gently clutched in her other hand. Then she took a deep breath and threw her gun in with the rest of her possessions and sat at the edge of the hole and let her feet dangle. I reached up and helped her down, only when her feet hit the curve of the cement, she slipped and her hinder nearly went all the way down and into the water. After letting out a wee gasp she icily said, 'Pull that grate back across so no one knows we came this way.'

It was difficult to manoeuvre around her, but I managed to reach up and put my fingers through the grating and drag it more or less back into place. Then there was nothing but darkness.

'You first, Fisher,' she quietly said again, her voice echoing away into nothingness.

I cautiously made my way around Hannah and began to move forward through the still waters. Then I felt her hand placed gently on my back. I didn't say anything, but made certain to move slowly forward as I heard her feet sloshing in the water behind me.

We proceeded along in this manner for perhaps twenty feet. I was carefully feeling out the bottom with each step, happy that, as yet, the water had not come over the top of my boots. And then something occurred to me and I stopped.

Hannah speired, 'Fisher, what is it?'

'Life,' I said as I raised my revolver up with my left hand and pointed it ahead of me in the dark.

It was so quiet in that confined space that I could hear her swallow. Then she said, 'It's not human. What is it?'

I shut my eyes, feeling foolish for doing so in the perfect darkness, then left them shut anyway and tried to feel out what it was.

After a few ticks, I started to say, 'I think it...' but then it moved and with a sudden surge of fright I felt forced into action.

There was a terrible thrashing in the water just ahead of me and suddenly Hannah screamed right up into my lug, which was deafening enough in and of itself, but then I levelled my revolver at a forty-five degree angle downwards and pulled the trigger. I saw his ridged, reptilian back just once in the flash of the muzzle.

The sound of the gunshot ricocheting in that compact, cement enclosure once it had passed through the beast's body was immediately deafening. And yet I could still hear Hannah screaming behind me. And then she got a hold of herself and suddenly held her wheesht.

There was more thrashing in the water ahead of me, but we collectively decided to back up without speaking on the subject first.

I was well aware that Hannah was shaking a little as she tremulously speired, 'Wha-a-a-at the *fuck* was that?'

I was breathing hard myself as I said, 'Alligator.'

'What?' she said incredulously. '*What the fuck?* Where did it come from?'

She was standing apart from me and I could sense her distress wirelessly telegraphed to me through the air at the same time that I could feel the water sloshing against my boots, the end result of her stocking feet shaking in the same medium only a short distance away from me.

I didn't feel good about what I had just done. I wasn't a vegetarian because I thought it was healthy. I didn't eat meat because I had a policy of not bringing unnecessary harm to the beasties, and in my gut reaction to shoot and kill even a simple animal such as an alligator, I felt physically ill. And yet I felt so little dismay on my own behalf versus the discord I felt wafting off of Hannah that I gave no thought to myself, rather I focussed on my companion. Hannah was hardheaded and tough in the light of day, but, quite clearly, she was afraid of the dark.

I almost feel ashamed of myself now for my unseen smile. But regardless of right or wrong, the fact of the matter is that I did smile, or at least, I grinned a little. Hannah Beardsley had been such a bitch to me that past day, and in some way had acted as if she felt herself somehow better than me, that I felt a wee bit of triumph in discovering that she had weaknesses and faults like any other person. But I didn't smile long. I felt wicked about my own feelings of being superior to her in any way, and decided to do what I could to help her instead of standing about acting like an airse.

With the revolver clutched in my left hand, I took one step towards Hannah and held out my right arm. When my finger-ends made contact with the fabric of the bodice of her dress, she flinched away from me. I let my hand simply hang there, and felt her shoulder as she moved forward a few seconds later and came back to my touch. Gently, I put my arm around her and felt her body trembling for a few ticks. Then she began to calm, and then there was more thrashing again in the water ahead of us.

She started to shake and pull away from me as I said, 'Calm doun, Hannah. He's dead, I feel. It's probably juist reflexes the noo.'

She still shook a little before breathlessly saying, 'Are you sure?'

'Weel, I'll make certain. Stay behind me for juist a tick.'

I stepped forward and set my boot down atop the body, pinning it to the cement beneath the water. I reached back and grabbed Hannah and pulled her around my leg as I said, 'This way.'

Once she was past me, she began to splash ahead through the water, then suddenly stopped, waiting for me.

I pivoted atop the body held beneath my foot which even through my boot I could feel to still be flexing and moving about. Then I stepped forward and put my arm about Hannah again and we proceeded forward.

We made it only a few steps, and then I nearly stumbled to the side as my boot discovered a juncture to our right. I thought to myself *Probably that's waur that 'gator was hiding when they came through with Ana afore us.* I looked about me in the darkness and found that the white path remained ahead of our position. 'Straicht ahead,' I said, and we continued forward.

Another twenty feet ahead without further incident and the cement began to curve upwards again. I handed Hannah my revolver as I put both my hands up to feel around and found another grating with roots growing wildly about it. I found a couple of handholds and gently pushed up and slid it aside just far enough to admit some light.

'Just open it enough to let me stick my head out,' Hannah said next to me.

I stepped back and looked down to see her face in the light. There were tears on her cheeks which she fully ignored as she handed to me the contents of her skirt and then began to position herself to look out the hole with only her revolver in her hand.

She hovered with the crown of her head just below the grate for a few ticks, then silently pushed herself upwards and looked about. Then she ducked her head back down to me and said, 'Looks like a whole new world. Give me a boost.'

I did my best to push her wet stocking feet up with my hands and she disappeared into the light, then I threw her bag and booties up and she helped me slide the grate further aside for me to crawl out.

Once I found myself on the relatively dry, sandy ground above, I took a look about while Hannah put her booties back on. The drizzle had come to a stop but the air was still thick with moisture and mist, obscuring my view at a distance. Yet as Hannah had said, I could already see this place was much different compared to the township of wood and canvas dwellings we had just left behind.

Behind us, to the west, was the seemingly impenetrable woods through which we could see nothing. It ran north to south for as far as the eye could see, but just like on the opposite side of the cement sewer, it came to an abrupt stop where man had delineated its end. In our immediate area on this side we found ourselves surrounded by orderly rows of what I easily identified as blueberry bushes. Beyond that, neatly ordered lines of date palms seemed to define the perimeter of some property that we could not yet properly identify.

Hannah stood with her gun in hand and said, 'There're people that way. A few.'

I nodded and said, 'Aye, two.' I looked about me and pointed towards the southeast as I said, 'The path to Ana leads in that direction.'

I looked to her to see a tear remained clinging to each of her cheeks. Hannah forced her mouth into a pout and curled her bottom lip up and quickly blew once to each side, sending the tears flying. Then she said, 'Let's have a quick look from the treeline first.'

We began slowly walking along the edge of the trees towards the south in hope of getting a better look at our surroundings before exposing ourselves. The mist still obscured physical forms at a distance of more than twenty feet, so finding no immediate threat, we stepped forward and walked in between the blueberry bushes.

When we came to the end of those, we stepped out and put ourselves against the thatched trunks of a couple of palms and keeked around them to see a large, dark building looming just before us in the mist.

Hannah was leaning around her trunk to inspect the structure, then she pulled her body back around and looked to me and held up two fingers. I still felt only the two bodies within so I nodded, but then I held up my hand to show her its loof to indicate she shouldn't move. I mouthed at her, 'Horses,' but I don't think she understood. Then it was only a few ticks more and she heard them herself.

Their clop-clopping approach sounded muffled in the thick air, the way horses' hooves would sound in the street when hay has been strewn on the cobblestones by a family in mourning to dampen the sharp sound of iron striking stone in front of their home. As Hannah crouched down and peered into the mist, that is what I was thinking on. A funeral. Or maybe several. Then suddenly she began to move forward in a crouch towards the next tree. I dropped to the ground and followed her.

We could smell smoke, and then we saw two braziers, just like the two which had stood in front of the kirk building. They were burning brightly, their very heat seeming to dissolve the mist about them, and revealing the warm, welcoming façade of what looked like a traditional plantation style home. Only this was a compact version lacking in the size and depth of the real thing, though it still maintained a certain amount of upper-level respect as if it wished to present itself as being the natural product of cotton and forced labour. It was possessed of a grand front porch which stretched the entire length of the building, with rocking chairs and intricately carved railings. Over the front double-door entry was a wooden sign, much like the signs ordering the traveller to repent that Abigail and I had seen the previous evening, only this one was emblazoned with the words: *Arcadia House* at the top and *Welcome to Heaven* at the bottom.

To the front of the house stood a grand roadway stretching up from the southeast, and it was from that direction that we could hear the approaching horses, though as yet, they were visibly concealed from us due to the climate. I turned my attention back to the front of the house just in time to see the two occupants we had earlier felt exit the doors to stand on the porch. They were clearly waiting to welcome the approaching riders, whomever they might be.

Sago palms ringed the front of the building, and we had found a particularly squat one to hide behind. Hannah was next to me and I set my hand on her shoulder and then pointed to the porch. She turned her eyes from the sound of the approaching horses to look.

For one tick as I first saw them, my mind tried to resolve the vision of the one woman into someone recognisable. I thought I was looking upon Esther, but a more careful inspection revealed that this was another woman altogether. She had stepped out of the doors with a lass that I could suppose to be about sixteen years of age. The lass's appearance, however, was fully incongruous for two reasons that I supposed were to make her look more like a wean than a woman approaching adulthood. Her hair was teased out to each side of her head in pigs' tails and dangling from her hand, as if unaware that it was in her possession, she carelessly carried a limp rag doll, featuring yarn hair garishly dyed red and a thin smile sewed upon its face.

If there had been any doubt that this grand place was related to the decrepit township of Bela on the other side of the trees, that doubt was effectively dispelled by the way they were both clothed in the same plain, white cotton dresses as all of the females of the kirk. And then there was one other thing. Although not nearly so fanciful as Alexandra's, the lass wore similar, though much less complex, wings on her back, again composed decorously of white bird's feathers.

The older woman, whom I supposed to be near to fifty years of age, bore a similar sharpness as Esther had, with big, ropy veins visible at her temples even from a distance of twenty-five feet, only she wasn't quite so trig. She stood erect as if happily anticipating the arrival of the horses and their riders, while the lass stood with her shoulders in a slump, the weight of her wings seeming to create in her back a premature hump, and her eyes cast down, staring at nothing in particular. Then the woman turned her attention on the lass and sharply said, 'Do you think men want to see you with that sulky look upon your face? They want it to be clear by your smile and your posture that you desire their attentions. Now, stand straight!' The lass obeyed, standing at her full height and with a smile painted upon her face just as thread-thin as the rag doll's, but her eyes remained vacant, distant, altogether toom.

Hannah whispered to me: 'Rodríguez was never in that house.'

'Nae, she wisnae.' I looked to the ground where the roadway was beaten out and saw her white trail pass down it to the south and east. 'They took her that way,' I said as I pointed.

'All right. As soon as those horses get here and everyone goes in the house, we'll go around.'

I was looking at the lass with the wings for a few quiet ticks. I observed her dark, empty eyes then said: 'Nae.'

Hannah turned her clear, blue gaze up to mine and said, 'We have a particular goal in mind.'

I nodded and said, 'We do. And this is juist a stop alang the way.'

Hannah's forehead creased and I believe she was going to say something harsh to me, only I noticed from the corner of my eye that the horses had become visible as they emerged from the rolling banks of fog, and I directed her attention towards them.

The wee cavalcade consisted of four horses and four horsemen, and given some of my recent discussions with Ana and Lucas I couldn't help but think of the Four Horsemen of the Apocalypse, only I would come to discover that these men brought with them a wholly different kind of plague than those which St John the Divine reported in Revelation.

We waited and observed. The four men rode up to an ornately carved hitching post set out a ways from the front of the house. After dismounting, removing their riding gear and dusting themselves somewhat, they began to approach the porch with an expectant air about them of some coming transaction to be completed.

As they walked in between the two braziers, I got a good look at them. Three of the men were relatively young, white and non-descript. The fourth was somewhat stout and dark-complexioned and looked to have been without a shave for several days. He was wearing a leather gunbelt lined all around with bullets gleaming feebly in the dim, grey light, and with one revolver hanging in a covered holster at his side. The rest had on light coats that I reasonably believed to conceal weapons. The four of them looked like the same men you constantly, casually encounter throughout Florida. They could have been any body's brother, father or son.

As they came up to the porch, they stopped at the bottom of the stairs and the woman addressed two of them familiarly by name. One was Mr Smith, and the swarthy fellow she named as Mr Guzman. Then as she waved her hand at the lass standing next to her, the woman said, 'The both of you remember our little angel Gabriella, of course.'

Mr Guzman let out a guttural chuckle as he pointed down at the wooden floor boards and said, 'Oh, yez. Floor model.'

The other men laughed with him as Mr Smith turned to the body next to him and said, 'Well, what you think, Rick? Cute as the dickens, eh?'

The man, Rick, stepped forward and looked at the lass, at the cotton-covered trunk of her body but not her dark, toom eyes, and said, 'Yeah, yeah.' He swallowed hard before shyly saying: 'Looks a bit like my little girl did before she got the mumps.' Rick appeared to be about twenty-five and I certainly didn't expect that he ever had a daughter of Gabriella's age.

Rick was clearly nervous and the other men all laughed at him as he turned a bit red in the cheeks. Guzman said, 'Well, *hombre*, I think we let you go for a try first.'

Rick quietly said, 'Well, fellas, you know...'

Mr Smith said, 'Don't worry about it. We'll send you to the bedroom. Nice and private.'

The woman smiled and said, 'Yes, that can be arranged immediately. Now, gentlemen, why don't you come in for some breakfast? We have some tea, coffee, or something stronger if you like.'

As the men began to walk in, Rick looked about as if still doubtful of proceeding with this venture and nervously said, 'Yeah, I might need something stiff, you know?'

'Of course,' the woman said over her shoulder as she pushed the angel-winged girl in front of her and walked in the door. 'Welcome to heaven,' she casually said and then they all disappeared inside.

'What the hell was that?' Hannah whispered.

'I think there's gang to be an adoption,' I said. 'Or at least that was their plan.'

Hannah turned her head and looked up to me for a few ticks without saying anything. I looked in her eyes and there seemed to be a certain level of agreement there. She said, 'Okay, but first let's have a look around and plan this out. It seems a little odd to me that for four men who were clearly expected there's only the one Gabriella. And no other men about, none of the boys, as it were.'

I said, 'Maybe they're all distracted in looking for me and Abigail and Ellie. I kenna why, but it disnae matter the noo. We'll take oor opportunity as it is presented. Let's gae.'

Hannah looked at the house and then silently pointed in a motion to indicate we should go around the east side of the structure. She looked to me and I nodded agreement. Then we began to move.

We crossed over the beaten road and stopped behind the horses. I could see no movement, could hear nothing from the house. Then we continued around to the north until we were on the east side of the house, with our backs to the wooden panelling where massive snails, with shells the size of overgrown walnuts, were making random tracks of gour in every direction.

Most of the winnocks on the ground floor were extremely high. Even at my great length my head only barely reached their sills. The one exception was towards the front where a nook was built into the wall featuring multiple panes of glass facing in various directions. The walls of the nook extended out some several feet from the flush face of the rest of the wall, and as we crawled beneath its winnocks, Hannah pointed up with her free hand and then held up four fingers. I nodded. That left two bodies somewhere else in the house.

We continued forward to find that the thick, overgrown trees ended at a large shed, but we didn't go that far. Sensing the presence of two bodies nearby, I stopped and looked at the winnock that was just above my head and thought for a few ticks. Hannah was looking curiously up at me and then she said, 'Do you want to boost me up there?'

I shook my head. 'Nae. It'll be easier if I juist look myself.'

The winnock-sills were made of stone, and I reached up, put my finger-ends on the hard surface and gently, quietly pulled myself up until my eyes were at a level that I could see in. For one instant I saw the two bodies, and then the trembling of my muscles caused me to lose my balance and I fell. Hannah helped break my fall so that I didn't land in a heap. Then we looked in each other's eyes again and she simply nodded.

'You don't need to tell me,' she said.

'Aye.'

Teeny's words from just after dawn that morning flashed through my mind. We were so bairnishly playing ball as she said *I've seen heaven. It ain't that great, anyway. I don't like all that pink and gold. I don't want to go there.*

I didn't want her to go there either.

The sign out front read *Welcome to Heaven*, and the room I had just seen looked to be decorated like a lassie's dream. It wasn't the spare, rustic, bare-bones arrangement of the tent-house dwellings of Bela, it was a real room with real furniture and a canopied bed just the size for a ten year-old lass. Of course, the two bodies inside were far too large for that wee bed-space, and so it appeared that they hadn't bothered to go more than one step past the door-sole, for that is where I saw the man named Rick standing with Gabriella kneeling before him. I will say nothing particular about the act itself except to note that in performing such an intimacy, the winged lassie's body was contorted in such a way so as to pull herself as distant from the man as possible with the necessary exception of her mouth. There was no mistaking her displeasure in the act, and if Rick had even the slightest amount of conscience, then it was no wonder he needed a stiff drink to conquer his reservations and quickly go so far with Gabriella as he had.

When Hannah had helped me to make a soft landing, she had dropped her revolver and put her hands on me. She left her right hand on my left arm for a few ticks and felt me trembling. I had been prepared ever since Alexandra's speech earlier that morning for the distinct possibility that something terrible was happening to these bairns, something even more horrific than the simple fact of being part of such a twisted family, but upon having the sight received by my eyes and filtered into my ken of the debasement of Gabriella whom they dressed to look even younger than her years, I instantly began to shake. With each tremor of my body, it felt as though my left hand began to swell, and I felt that growing need yet again.

Hannah seemed to feel my bodily response as well, for she let her fingers fall to my left wrist before saying, 'Don't go off all half-cocked, Fisher. We need to plan.'

'*Fuck planning*,' I said between my teeth as I began to walk further along the length of the house to the north.

She was plucking at me, trying to grab the belt and waist of my trousers in an attempt to slow me down as she said, 'God dammit, Fisher! What do you think you're doing?'

I didn't know what I was going to do but I felt the certainty of what was coming for those men oozing from the marrow deep in my very bones. I stopped and turned to Hannah and leaned down so that I was nearly at her level. With her wide eyes only an inch from mine I growled out, 'Those men need to be dead for a while. I'm gang to gae take care of that, the noo.'

I pivoted on my heel and walked away, leaving her standing by her lane. As I turned the rear corner of the building, I looked back once to see Hannah sombrely staring at me. Most of her long, blonde hair had come loose from where she had it pinned in the back the previous night, and several braids fell forward over her shoulders while a few wisps of hair fanned out around her face. A bit of light caught her from behind but the golden halo around her head didn't make her look like an angel to me. Rather, the dampened, random plaits of her hair somehow reminded me of the arms of a flaxen octopus settling himself atop her head. Then she was out of my view and I felt ready for my left hand to lead me with my revolver in its grip.

The back porch wasn't so fancy as the front. It was more utilitarian and somewhat dirty looking. The railing wasn't ornately carved nor were there any rocking chairs. There was a single door set in the centre of the rear wall and it was standing open, likely for the sake of air flow. A hinged, wooden frame with mosquito netting tacked across it covered the opening and I stood outside it for just a tick and looked inside. I saw the man Rick walk out into a wide hallan with the winged Gabriella following meekly behind him. He didn't even give her the courtesy of his attention now that her service to him was completed. She looked sullen and moved slowly as they approached the front of the house to the south where my big lugs could hear voices. With my right hand, I reached up and opened the screen door and stepped inside, gently pulling it closed behind me.

I began to walk forward down the hallan and stopped just outside the room that Rick and Gabriella had so recently occupied. Inside it was pink and gold. Outside were two small, wooden placards. One had carved in it the words *Try Before You Buy* and the other said *All Sales Final.* My left hand surged with more blood as my heart began to beat rapidly in my chest.

I slowly, silently stepped forward through the gloom of the hallan. I could hear them talking. They were having a good time.

The woman was saying: 'I'm sorry we weren't ready for you this morning, only something came up on the ranch and Esther took all the boys to deal with it.' My hair began to stand on end at the sound of her lie. Something had come up, but it wasn't on the ranch. It was in Bela, and the boys, or at least most of them, seemed to be searching the surrounding areas for several people including myself. The woman continued, 'In a few minutes we'll get some girls over here and you can see if you want to adopt some.'

I heard Rick's bashful voice then, 'Well, Miss Edith, if they're anything like this angel here, I definitely want one. You know, just... well.'

Edith said, 'Just what? We're all friends here. Have another drink?'

I heard the men laughing as I presumed Rick to drink and then he said, 'I just mean I want one... younger. You know.'

'I have one in particular in mind for you. One of Gabriella's younger sisters. How does seven years old sound? Then you can raise her up as you see fit. Someday she'll be the exact kind of woman you want.'

'Yeah,' Rick said. 'Yeah, that's good.'

'And what about you Mr Guzman? Are you going to take another half-dozen off my hands again?' Edith speired with a friendly laugh, like the consummate hostess who could bring cheer to any situation.

The man chuckled in return. 'Oh, yez. If chu got them, I want them.'

'Hey, Paco,' one of the other men said, probably Mr Smith. 'How do you manage so many of them at one time?'

Guzman laughed again and said, 'Well, I get them out the country. Get down to Caribbean where no one

247

knows what they say. They can yell all the *Inglés* they want! Help help! Ow ow! It hurts! Go ahead, leedle girl! No one know what chu saying!'

They all laughed at this and it seemed that my left hand was as engorged with desire for death as it was going to become. Like some wound up automaton my legs propelled me forward then until the six of them were in my view.

The four men and Edith were all sitting about a mahogany, octagonal breakfast table which featured a cream pot, a brown bottle, some tinned biscuits and assorted mugs and cups set about a glowing oil lamp. The entire nook was concealed partly from the hallan and the large parlour at the front of the house by two wooden partitions that created a sort of alcove. When I stepped around into the aperture, Gabriella was the only one standing. She had a coffee pot in hand and was filling Guzman's mug. In the light of the lamp I saw that Mr Smith was staring at her with something resembling lust while Rick was looking at her from the corner of his eye with something like embarrassment on his face, as if he still wasn't fully comfortable with the lassie's recent performance.

The woman, Edith, sat in a chair between Smith and Guzman who were on the far side of the table from me with the grey winnocks behind their heads. The other two men were on the near side of the table, sitting so that I could see both of their faces only in profile.

The men all seemed somewhat distracted as I stepped into view, and because of the relative darkness of the hallan versus their lamp and winnock lit nook, they didn't seem to even notice me at first. It was Edith who looked directly at me and as her bemused face speired a question I spoke.

'Is this a private party or can any body join?'

Everyone's face turned towards mine including Gabriella's. There was a moment of silence then as she kept pouring until the coffee ran over the side of the mug, and then she levelled the pot but continued to hold it aloft.

I had walked in with my left hand, and the revolver it held, concealed partly to my side. Everyone remained frozen as Edith began to answer me except no sooner had she a word out of her mouth than Guzman's hand dropped to his belt. I jerked my left hand up to point my revolver at him, and as I cocked the hammer for show, I said, 'Nae. No' like that, Paco.' I made the slightest motion with the barrel of my gun and he understood to put his hands on the table.

Edith cleared her throat and with a welcoming smile said, 'What is your name, sir?'

I dropped my revolver so that it pointed somewhere close to the centre of the table, near the lamp, and said, 'I am Mr Fisher. I'm interested in lassies.'

Edith was nervous but she still smiled pleasantly, ready to play the hostess, as she said, 'You mean girls.' She motioned at Gabriella.

I nodded. 'Aye. I want her. And I want young ones.'

Edith's dark eyes flicked once to my revolver and I could see her throat convulse as she swallowed. Then she said, 'Of course, we have many girls here, Mr Fisher.'

'All richt, then. I'll make ye a deal fair and true. I'll buy every last one ye have,' I earnestly said as I lowered the revolver further.

Edith smiled and lightly said, 'Well, Mr Fisher, I don't think you have that much money. There are a lot of girls.' Then her face painfully reposed somewhat. Her eyes looked past me and I could feel the hope in her that some of the lads would show right about now. But I could feel the honest truth of the matter. There was no one else out there. Except Hannah.

I said, 'I dinna care hoo many girls ye have. I'll take them all. And I'll pay ye for them.'

The men were all looking at me. They seemed curious as to where this talk of business was going, and sat calmly, somewhat detachedly watching as if they were observing some courtroom drama from the public gallery, but they were wary. In fact, all eyes were on me then except for Gabriella's who seemed to have retreated to somewhere within herself so distant from that house that she might as well have been on another continent.

I didn't care to be the centre of attention, though my actions that morning of course demanded that I do so. The more they looked at me, the more they stared and contemplated my apparent queerness at presenting myself before them, the more jittery I became. I had walked myself into this mess, but it seemed that the longer it drug out, the worse things became for me in an emotional sense as I seemed to be losing control of myself. So I decided to cut to the chase.

As I felt the blood surging all the way from my heart into the trigger finger of my left hand, my right hand went in my trouser pocket and withdrew a single note. I flicked it on the table and said, 'There's my payment. I want all of them. Noo.'

Edith looked down at the one dollar U. S. note and with a bewildered visage, sharply speired, 'Is this some sort of joke?'

'Nae. This is deadly serious. Life or death.'

And then I jumped to my left so that I was partly hidden behind the wooden partition and drew my revolver up and fired once at the big form of Paco Guzman. The swarthy man had already dropped his hand towards his holster during my final words regarding death, which neatly acted as the catalyst to my sudden movement, and I easily shot him once in the gut. He didn't go theatrically flying back, rather he simply gasped and went falling to his side on the floor after his fattened body had shaken violently as it absorbed the force of the bullet's entry. No sooner had this happened than Rick stood while kicking his chair back, and then put his left hand under his coat. He had just enough time to extract a revolver before I fired three shots at him in quick succession, aiming low at his most central mass. The revolver was kicking more than I had expected, and so the three shots were fairly widely spaced, vertically. The first shot hit him somewhere near the waist, the second in the chest, and the third made a red, clotted mess of his left eye while bits of skin and hair exploded onto the wall behind him.

Rick had yet to hit the ground before I went rolling away and broke straight through the first door on the left of the hallan. I quickly turned myself around and looked towards the breakfast nook with my gun at the ready.

Six-shooter I thought to myself. *And I already fired once when I brocht an end to that alligator in the cement sewer.*

I could hear Edith screaming, and I could see Guzman on the ground writhing about. He was doing his best to shout out a diatribe in Spanish which he punctuated with, '*Vaya a la mierda, gringo!*'

He kept on groaning and moaning and Mr Smith shouted, 'Shut up, Paco!' When the big man continued emitting various painful moans, Smith shouted, '*Shut the fuck up!*'

I was watching. I couldn't see Gabriella just then and was worried about the possibility of her being hurt. And then I saw Edith. She was on her hands and knees trying to crawl out of the alcove when I saw a pair of arms come about her waist and grab her, pulling her back behind the partition. She screamed once, 'Let me go!' and then suddenly became silent.

The fourth man shouted, 'I don't know what the fuck this is about but I'm coming out and I've got Edith with me!'

The next thing I knew, the man was walking out, side-stepping towards the front door with Edith held in front of him and his revolver pointed in my general direction over her shoulder. It seemed the queerest thing to me that he thought I wouldn't shoot with her in the way. I didn't even think about it. Instead I thought about what Ana had said, that I only had to aim as if pointing with my finger. With my left hand I aimed and fired one round at Edith's bosom, as near to her heart as I could point. The bullet passed directly through her and hit its mark in the man's chest before continuing straight through one of the winnocks in the nook behind him, shattering the glass. The man's entire body seemed to spasm when the bullet passed through him, and his arm holding the revolver rose up to fling it onto the floor only a few feet away from me. Then their two bodies, his and Edith's, fell in opposite directions, he to the right, she to the left, and both were still when they hit the floor of the hallan.

This precipitated a vile torrent of blasphemy from Mr Smith which did not improve my opinion of the man. As for Mr Guzman, he continued groaning and rolling about on the floor.

I was still laying on the door-sole with the revolver in my hand as I thought to myself, *Shyte, that's five here and one for the 'gator.* The weapon was now useless, but fortunately Mr Smith didn't know that. I laid it aside and set my eyes upon the revolver that had just been flung a few feet before me into the hallan. *Double-action, I hope.*

I was thinking of crawling out to grab a hold of the revolver, but although my left hand still throbbed with immediate need, I waited patiently until Mr Smith got a hold of himself and ended his hateful diatribe for fear of exposing myself to him. From where I lay, he was concealed behind the wooden partition on the left and I looked to the oil lamp still sitting undisturbed on the centre of the table as he spoke to me.

'Okay, now! Fisher is it?'

A few ticks of silence passed. I could hear Gabriella sobbing. She was with him.

I said, 'Aye. Fisher.'

'Okay, Mr Fisher, listen. We're both gentlemen and we can sort this out like gentlemen. You said you want girls? There's plenty to go around. Honest. I been here before. They keep 'em close by, out in the woods.' He was quiet for a few ticks then said, 'We'll just not say anything about what happened here. They can find out later about Edith. After you're gone.'

Guzman began growling out something unintelligible in Spanish and we let his mutterings fill the void for a few ticks. Then Mr Smith said, 'God dammit, I told you to shut up, Paco!'

'Rrrrr-ugh. Fucking gringo shot me!'

'Shut up!' Then when things were quiet again, Mr Smith said, 'What d'ya say, Mr Fisher? I can tell you where they're at. I won't interfere.'

'Is that it? Ye came to buy. Hoo much money do ye have on ye?'

He grunted something under his breath then said, 'This ain't fair! We came here like gentlemen!' He was getting annoyed and as his ire rose I could hear Gabriella greeting with greater intensity. I could picture him holding on to her and the very thought of her having to be in contact with that man made me ill. But I held on, waiting for him to make a move. And then I saw something curious through the broken winnock.

What looked like a large tin with ragged edges around its top suddenly rose up in the grey light of the winnock that had been shattered by my last shot. It was a copper and brass cube that bore the appearance of having been hacked in half. Then, as it rose higher, I saw two small hands holding it aloft from beneath and I knew it was

Hannah up to some sort of trick. Fortunately I realised what she was doing before she acted, and so I was already on my way forward into the hallan before she made her move.

Hannah carefully positioned the can in the shattered winnock as I made my way past the two bodies of Edith and the fourth man, reaching down to scoop up the dropped revolver in the process. At the same time that I did so, Hannah gave the can a liberal shove into the breakfast nook and having some of the contents randomly slosh on to him, Mr Smith shouted: 'What the fuck?' And then, as I continued to move forward, I saw him.

He was on the ground, in the corner, trying to make as small a target of himself as possible while holding the greeting Gabriella in front of him, with her false wings crushed between their two bodies.

Although the man was suddenly in my line of sight, I didn't even consider firing directly upon him for fear of hitting his hostage. Instead I took the lesser of two evil paths and with my right hand fired the revolver I had just scooped up twice at the burning lamp, shattering it with the second shot. Flaming oil exploded across the table top and flames suddenly licked at both Mr Smith and Gabriella. They were hardly in any immediate mortal danger on account of the small amount of petrol which had actually reached them from the winnock, but that didn't matter. What was of account was the surprise and fear of suddenly finding themselves ignited. Gabriella immediately screamed and began to crawl away. Mr Smith swore and jumped up, and that was all the impetus I needed for bringing him to an end.

He was in front of the broken winnock with flames climbing the sleeve of his coat and burning his hair. He looked at me and aimed with a dark object in his hand but didn't have time to pull the trigger. I quickly fired three rounds at the man without making much of an effort at aiming. Only one of three bullets struck the man in the shoulder at which time he tottered backwards and fell into the winnock and on to the shards of glass. He screamed and flailed about some but seemed pinned in that position so I let my attention fall on Gabriella instead.

The lass was in flames the same as Mr Smith, and after crawling beneath the table and out of the alcove she stood and ran past me with the feathers of her left wing burning brightly. As she ran out the door I shouted, 'Stop running! Stop running! Get on the ground!'

As I ran after her I heard a single gunshot behind me but didn't think about it. I kept running after the lass and, after passing between the two flaming braziers, I finally tackled her about forty feet from the porch near to the horses who stared down at us in alarm. First I grabbed the wings and ripped them off of her, then I began patting at the flames on her gown with the loofs of my hands while she rolled about in the wet sand. All the while she kept screaming at the top of her lungs and trying to wriggle out from beneath me. Finally, she managed to halfway turn over about the time I got most of the flames dampened down, and then her wee left fist swung out of nowhere and slammed me in the jaw.

'Ach! Stop it! Stop it!' I said as she fought with me, and then she began scrabbling at my face with her finger-ends, I could swear with the intent of gouging out my eyes, and before I could get off of her, she gave me a wicked scratch across the cheek.

She was on her feet and running a moment later. I watched her as she went, just happy to see the flames out, as she disappeared down the road into the mist, still screaming at the top of her lungs.

I was still on my knees in the roadway when I heard the whistling of a jaunty tune behind me. I turned to look and see Hannah walking about the corner from the side of the house with another petrol can in her hands and her frilly handbag dangling by its strap from her arm. She casually walked up the steps while continuing to nonchalantly whistle *Dixie* as if she were out for a casual stroll.

Inside, just making his way into view through the open front doors, was Paco Guzman. He was trying to escape the flames behind him by pulling himself forward by hand while also pushing with his feet and grunting painfully with the effort. Seeing Hannah step before him, his hand went down to his side and after fumbling about he withdrew his gun while she dropped the petrol can and stepped up to him and simply wrested the weapon from his grasp. Then as he ferociously groaned in pain and feebly tried to grasp Hannah's wrists and push her arms away, she managed to get under his paunch and unbuckle his gunbelt, and pull it off of him. Then she returned, picked up the can and began to dowse the man with it as nonchalantly as if she were watering a patch of posies.

I sat and watched this entire curious display from outside without moving. Guzman was shouting again then, telling Hannah exactly what he thought of her with several words such as *bruja, perra, puta* and *gringa* all punctuated with the generic feminine adjective *blanca.*

Hannah casually said, 'What's that? I don't speak Spanish. You can scream all you want and I wouldn't understand a word. Well, except for one,' she said as she levelled the man's gun at his head. '*Adios.*' And then she pulled the trigger and he finally held his wheesht. Then Hannah went to digging in her handbag, and after stepping back a few feet towards the porch, she lifted one foot and struck a match on the heel of her bootie. She flicked it at the body and simply walked away as the dead man and the carpet he was laying upon were both engulfed in flames.

She walked out into the light, down the porch steps, between the two braziers, and approached me holding her handbag and the gunbelt, then sat in the sandy mud next to me.

We looked each other quite directly in the eyes and she said, 'All right, that's done with. Rodríguez next.'

I spit a stream of blood from the side of my mouth where Gabriella had danged me with her wee fist and said, 'Aye, and then Abigail.'

'And Ellie.'

'Then the rest of the bairns.'

We held up our hands in unison and again cracked loofs. Then I stood and helped Hannah to her feet, and we prepared to move forward to discover what was next.

IX

The horrible sounds had ceased.

They had been hiding in the wilderness for some time and the woman in green would not let her out of her arms. She kept thinking, 'Good, good.' And then she remembered her mother. And the man with the sword and the red jewel. Then she thought, 'Bad, bad.'

She began to moan and wriggle about.

'Shh, shh,' the woman in green said soothingly. 'It is all right, Ellie.'

Then she put her hand down between her legs and pushed.

'Oh, do you need to go?' The woman looked around. 'All right, dear, we shall find a place.'

She moaned some more and the woman said, 'Do not be embarrassed, Ellie. I need to go, also.'

The woman helped her to go, and then she began to position herself. It was difficult for the woman, having only one hand, but she carefully squatted only a few feet away to do her business.

And then there was peace within her mind and she began to walk.

'Ellie? Ellie!' The woman was frightened.

She stopped once among the trees, the peace dissolved briefly by the angles in the air, and the woman saw her.

'Ellie, stay there!'

Then there was peace again and she kept walking.

'Ellie! Oh no, please do not do this, dear! Stay there! Ellie!'

Again, there were angles in the air. The woman's pain hurt her, made her stomach roll, but she knew what she had to do.

'Ellie?'

The woman was behind her. She let the woman see her ever so briefly.

'Ellie, stay there!' she harshly said.

And then she toddled forward. Every so often she let the woman in green see her.

'Ellie, please!'

The woman was following her.

'Good, good,' she thought to herself.

Monday, 20 April 1896, 8:45 AM

Before the *Arcadia House* filled with smoke, I had retrieved the available weapons and ammunition from in and around the breakfast nook. We walked away with what seemed to be the best hardware and left the rest behind.

At first we were walking in silence along the side of the road, but something about the quiet was bothering me, especially after the sounds of the gunfire, and all of the shouting.

Within my ken, thoughts of what I had just done, the deaths brought to so many people as a direct result of my actions, began to crowd out my good feelings regarding the righteousness of my efforts. I easily reasoned with myself that every one of the dead got exactly what they deserved, but it didn't seem to matter. This wasn't the first time I had killed, and I was beginning to understand that there was a certain pattern to be followed. When I was certain that a man, or woman for that matter, needed to have their life brought to a close, it seemed that there was nothing that could stand in my way. There is a feeling of righteous certainty that I associate with those moments, and it feels good, not only because it feels just, but because it feels absolute, and in performing the desire of my left-hand at such times I feel to be lacking in doubt, both of myself and my actions. But afterwards, that feeling quickly fades, and after the flames burn down I'm left feeling cold with only the ashes of my remorse to warm me.

So feeling the need to occupy myself with conversation, and hoping Hannah felt the same urge, I said, 'I heard a gunshot. It was after I chased Gabriella oot the door and started to beat the flames dead on her.'

'Sic semper Smith and all of his kind,' Hannah casually said. 'He was wiggling about on the window sill where he was stuck in the glass. I probably could have just left him there to bleed instead of wasting a good .22 slug. But that was a pretty thick leather coat he was wearing and I didn't want to think he might come to and try to settle the score with us.'

We were walking through the trees on the north side of what seemed to be a major roadway curving up from the south side of the *Arcadia House* towards the north east. Ana's path ran on the road itself which was wide enough to feature two sets of wagon ruts, though as yet in the early morning there wasn't any vehicular traffic. Yet it seemed odd to have such a grand thoroughfare so near to Bela, even if the wee township was surrounded by dense woods.

There was a quiet between us again, and I thought on Hannah, how she had so coolly walked up to that man and doused him in petrol and then put his own gun against his temple. I felt as though I wanted to share with her my uncertainty, the tangible pangs of remorse that tickled my conscience, but then I thought: *she disnae feel the same way.* But, on the other hand, I realised how easily I had walked in and killed three people, all of whom I had never even set my eyes upon fifteen minutes earlier, and I tried to tell myself that it was the same for Hannah. Like me, she probably had her own doubts now, her own thoughts about the fact that they were horrid, disgusting people. And yet they were, after all, *people*, and like most people they probably had families, other people who in some sense cared about them, and might not ever have the courtesy of knowing what had become of them. I studied the profile of Hannah's face, but it was a closed book, one of those wee diaries that lassie's sometimes have that require a key to open. So far as I could tell, Hannah had the key hidden somewhere deep within her heart, and she wasn't about to hand it over to me.

Still, feeling the nervous need to fill the silence, I lightly speired, 'Is *adios* really the only Spanish word ye ken?'

Hannah laughed a little under her breath and said, 'No, I know plenty. *Taco, burrito, enchilada...*'

Oddly relieved at the sound of her mirth, I laughed along with her, then said, 'It's amazing hoo those are always the first words to be learned. The food.'

'Yup,' Hannah agreed. 'Yet I don't know a single Scottish food, I don't think. Except for the *Scotch Egg*.'

I looked to her and she smiled a little at me, a pleasant tugging at the corners of her mouth, but then she looked away. I said, 'I kenna even waur ye are from.'

'Does it matter?' she speired with a sudden, sharp edge to her voice.

'Weel, betimes ye can learn a lot aboot a person simply by kenning waur they were born. I certainly learned a lot aboot Ana in the short time we had thegither by learning about Jalisco. But even if she hadna told me aboot that particular state, juist saying she was frae Mexico would have been a guid start.'

I had hoped this might lead to a further dialogue, maybe a little bit of opening up about ourselves, for I found myself wanting to get to know Hannah a little better, especially in that moment in which I was looking for a friend to commiserate with. As it was, I knew only the barest facts of the circumstances relating to the past three years of her life, and nothing before that. Unfortunately, her book remained closed; she wasn't about to offer up any new details for my consumption.

She clearly wanted to change the subject as she said, 'Listen, Fisher, I'm sorry about not jumping at the chance to help you before. And especially about not helping you find your lass, as you call her.'

I looked away and said, 'Aye. I understand.'

'No,' she said and stopped walking. She grabbed a hold of my arm and as I came to a halt she said, 'I didn't mean to be so cold. You know. About her and everything else.' She ran her tongue about her lips then said, 'I know how you feel about her, and...'

'Do ye?' I speired sharply.

She let go of my arm and I stared down at her for a few ticks until she said, 'I was married once.'

I felt it was a start, a good sign, so to speak, that she at least equated my relationship with Abigail with the sort of feelings traditionally attached to marriage. But then I said, 'I believe ye told me that yer husband was murdered. And that ye were tried for his death.' It was the only major detail of the lass's life that I knew.

She was still looking up at me, her clear blue eyes searching mine plaintively as she said, 'Yup. That's right. And I didn't beat those charges.' She hovered a blink before saying, 'People complain that the judicial system doesn't work. In my case it did. They had it right when they convicted me.'

I swallowed hard and said, 'Yer husband was a bad man.'

She nodded. 'I didn't know when we got together. I was stupid, and I married him because he was handsome and rich and in my little world he was the big man. I mean, he was gorgeous. And look at me. I'm no great beauty. Could I pass up marrying an Adonis?'

'I think ye're quite fair on the een, actually.'

Hannah snorted and said, 'Well, *you* would think that, wouldn't you? You really are a serious dog, Fisher.'

'Ach, I kenna what that is supposed to mean. Believe me, I have nae interest in ye if that is what ills ye.' I tried to offer an honest compliment when I said, 'Ye've a braw look, is all I meant.'

'Well, regardless, he was out of my class in looks and family. I should have known something was fishy.' She shook her head then said, 'Of course, thanks to him I found out that it doesn't matter how big you are, how much money you have, or how handsome you are.' She held up her hand and made a squeezing motion. 'You can have everything in this life, every advantage, and it can all be taken away in an instant. By anyone who has the mind to do it. Just as easy as point and bang.'

Hannah looked away and sighed. 'But, hey, that's life. Easy come, easy go. I should be helping you and me both to hang on to what's good instead of being a tool for my boss. And what's good in our lives are some people we know... Ana and Gail, for example.'

We started walking again and I said, 'Wha's yer boss? Ye mean yer chief? Was it that Amy Jackson bitch I met with ye doun at Doctor Lamb's?'

'Yup. At least she knows what she's doing. Mostly.'

I thought about the taciturn, red-headed woman then said, 'Sae what's her special skill?'

Hannah didn't hesitate in saying, 'Mostly she's a really good liar.'

* * *

It was odd the way we were casually walking along as if on a pleasant morning constitutional, since despite our nice conversation I had a revolver in each hand. Hannah had Guzman's gun in her right, his gunbelt with all of its shiny bullets slung over her shoulder, and her frilly handbag hanging from her left wrist.

It was difficult to see, and yet I could feel them out there, cloaked in the thick morning fog. But before I could see them, there was a distinct smell of the bovine in the air mixed with smoke, and it wasn't the smoke of the smouldering house fire we had left behind us. It reminded me of the smell of a small power plant I had recently encountered out on the gulf which had been built primarily for the purpose of producing ice to pack fresh fish in. I thought on the electric lights stringing the hallan of the underground concrete cube, as well as the fancy visual effects of the angel's entrance into the kirk, and the fact that petrol was being stored on the property, and reasoned that it was a distinct possibility that there was a small generator system on the ranch. After all, Teeny had stated that in her stravaigerings she had been in the meat factory where there are lots of machines and it was icy and cold. There was nothing naturally icy or cold in the area, and so I surmised that the process of harvesting the cattle had likely been electrified.

We came upon a fence line composed of rustic, oaken wood shortly thereafter and I directed Hannah to turn left and walk along it towards the north.

'The further away from Bela we get, the sharper my senses are becoming,' I said.

'Yup. I feel it, too. It's that so-called angel they have working for them.'

'Esther said the angel had warned them aboot oor kind. Hoo does she keep the feeling of all the bodies oot here hidden from us?'

Hannah said, 'It takes some effort to get started, but then after that she's probably been working it in the back of her mind all these years. It's like a shield in the shape of an umbrella pulled down over their little town. If we were passing by one of the roads either on the west or that one to the south that we just saw, we'd never know anyone was hidden in there in the woods. That's the real miracle that angel is working. Now we're moving out from beneath her influence the farther east we go.'

I stopped for a tick and closed my eyes. 'Aye. I can feel Ana directly the noo, no' juist her path.' I pointed into the fog and said, 'She's that way.' My heart was thudding sickeningly in my bosom as I added: 'And she's frichted.'

'And I don't blame her,' Hannah said as she started walking again.

It was horribly quiet for another moment as we walked, and then we heard mooing. The kyne were calling to each other. Once one started, the rest began in a chorus. There were dozens nearby.

Finally we arrived at our turnoff. A tall post stood next to the fence line with electrical lines stretching from it to the east where we were heading, and to the west, back in the general direction of Bela. The fog was so thick ten feet over our heads and the lines so loose that they appeared to stretch off into infinity like a couple of thin arms being lifted in a shrug.

All I had to do was look and I felt a pull. I said, 'Let's follow the lines.'

We climbed over the wooden fence and moved towards the east, post by post, stopping behind each one to look about, sensing nothing but kyne.

Then about the time we reached the fourth post I felt something shoot through my ken with the force of a knife twisting through my grey matter.

For a tick I didn't know what happened. I had dropped both of my revolvers and fallen to my knees. Hannah was in front of me with her face just before mine saying something. I looked to her and took a few deep breaths then said, 'I kenna what happened. It was as if my mind juist exploded.'

She had a worried look on her face as she nodded. Then she helped me back up and knelt down to retrieve the two weapons and put them in my hands.

We continued on to the next post and it happened again. The pain came in a flash, but no sooner did I register it within my mind than I felt the first finger of my left hand to be in flames. I dropped the guns again and looked to my hand to see that my finger had become fully invisible before my eyes. Hannah tried to stifle me as I cried out a bit at the sight of my missing digit, but then I grasped a hold of the finger with my other hand and realised it was still there. I looked again and it was visible.

I was on my knees and Hannah was before me. She said, 'Listen to me, Fisher. They know we're coming and they're playing tricks on us.'

'Wha-a-at?' I said as I shuddered.

'Like you said, the angel warned them what to do about our kind. They're using Rodríguez against us. You have to stop thinking about her. Right now.'

'But hoo can...' and then I crumpled up and groaned out in pain again.

Hannah fell to the ground with me and set her hands on my back as if to comfort me. She calmly said, 'Forget tracking her, you have to let her go. You have to shut off that part of your mind that can feel her. You have to do it now.'

I was shaking and feeling of my fingers. In that second instance, it had seemed that the first finger of my right hand had momentarily vanished in a jolt of pain. As I lay on the ground reassuring myself that all my fingers were present and accounted for, a roiling nausea threatened me and my stomach heaved a few times.

Hannah said, 'Get her out of your mind. You have to.'

One thing I was not well versed in then was shutting off the influences of the outside world. I had already had the experience of being assaulted with random emotions in the past, but this seemed to be directed clearly at me for the purpose of debilitating me. And it was working.

Hannah said, 'Shut it out, Fisher. If you have to, visualise something distinct to represent your casting off of Rodríguez. I know that may sound cruel, but that is exactly what you need to do.'

I nodded and started to say something when again I felt one of my fingers screwed off of my hand.

I was curling up into an ever-tighter foetal ball and Hannah was leaning just over my head to whisper in my lug. I could feel her long, loose hair brushing about my cheeks as she said, 'Have you ever turned an electrical light switch on and off?'

I had my lips clamped shut to keep from screaming and couldn't speak. I simply shook my head.

She laid the loofs of her little hands gently on my bumpy head and said, 'All right, let's use an example that you've had a lot of recent experience with. Forget everything but what I am saying. Listen to me.' She was speaking calmly, soothingly as she said, 'Your mind is a revolver. Don't only picture the weapon in your hand, but actually feel it in your hand, with the cylinder open, all chambers unloaded. This is your mind. In your other hand you hold a bullet. Look at the bullet in the palm of your hand and see that it's Ana Rodríguez herself. Take her bullet and load the weapon. You close the cylinder. You aim it towards the sky. Feel your finger on the trigger. Feel yourself pulling the trigger. Feel the gun kicking in your hand. In a definitive flash, she's gone. Her bullet has sailed up into the sky, into infinity, to no one knows where.

Your connection is severed, just as distant as that bullet is from your mind, the gun.'

For a few ticks, Hannah gently ran her finger-ends through my short hair as if feeling for the fissures in the ossified plates of my skull, then she slowly withdrew her hands from me and I sat up. I lifted my own hands to look at my fingers. 'Ana's in trouble,' I said.

She nodded at me and said, 'Yup. We already knew that.'

'I can still feel her a wee bit.'

'All that matters is that you can function without falling on the ground and writhing about.'

I looked towards the east into the mist and said, 'Aye.'

Hannah retrieved her revolver and handbag from where she had dropped them. I picked up mine as well and stood.

'All richt,' I said. 'We're gang to find a building over there,' I said as I pointed. 'And she's somewaur inside.'

'They know we're coming, so expect a trap,' Hannah said. 'Come on.'

* * *

We met one soul along the way. A steer stood next to one of the electrical posts calmly chewing grass. He looked up as we passed and then returned to his breakfast.

We passed two more posts and then the electrical lines arced sharply up into the air. A few feet more, and we saw the brick façade of a two storey building before us. It featured winnocks that had been fully blackened with lead.

Hannah quietly said, 'There's no one in there.'

I said, 'Nae, but there's several a ways back.'

We were standing behind the final electrical post as we considered what to do. The posts were thin and provided little cover for us should someone have decided to take a shot at us.

Hannah said, 'Maybe we should go around.'

I shook my head, 'Nae, let's see what this building is, first.' I didn't like standing about in that exposed position, and my desire to move helped me decide to proceed more than anything.

There were two grand, wooden double-doors at the end of the building, big enough to allow entrance of a vehicle. Next to them was a single man-door. We approached it and found it unlocked, and entered.

It was nearly completely dark inside, the leaded winnocks admitting only a small amount of light. The first sensation to be felt was one of cold which felt more extreme by comparison to the heat and humidity outside. And then a certain smell wafted out. It was the distinct smell of blood, and it was so strong that simply inhaling the air was enough to taste its metallic qualities on my tongue.

I began to draw back immediately when the sense that bodies were approaching about the outside of the building from both directions fluttered through my ken. 'They're coming. Get inside.'

'I warned you of a trap...' she started to say.

'Nae time, gae!' I whispered harshly and shoved Hannah in the door. I quickly followed and quietly pulled it shut behind me.

'Great, I can barely see a thing,' Hannah groused.

We stepped forward into the cool air and something huge loomed just before us, its indistinct silhouette swinging side to side, directly in our path. We paused one tick to try and discover what it was when the entire building was suddenly filled with electric light.

I very nearly screamed at what I saw revealed in vivid detail in front of me. An entire beef carcass, sans head, legs and tail, was hanging from a meat hook, dripping a massive puddle of blood which ran along the uneven cement beneath our feet to join a thick river of red which was gurgling down a large drain in the centre of the floor.

Hannah grabbed me and pulled me around it and I looked to see that there were a dozen such bodies suspended from the ceiling twenty feet above by chains between which ran several rows of electric lights. Ringing the room were numerous long tables with chunks of melting ice of various dimensions.

Hannah was pushing me, 'Come on, come on! They're coming. They probably hoped we'd come in here.'

We made it to the other side of the building, which was comprised of one grand room, and found that there was no exit to be had. There was only the one man-door and the two grand double-doors.

'Fuck, Fisher. We're like fish in a barrel. Get ready to shoot.'

I casually stated, 'These lads are no' vera bricht.'

'So?'

'They only seem to think in twa dimensions.' I looked up. Hannah followed my eyes.

She sighed and said, 'Hurry up, give me a boost.'

273

After helping Hannah up to the high grounds, I dropped my revolvers in my trouser pockets and, after grinding my teeth together a bit in anticipation of being disgusted, I jumped onto the driest looking beef body I could find and began to climb. My stomach was altogether toom, but again my paunch twisted and threatened to heave its nothingness as I climbed up and came to a stop.

Then the door opened.

I could just barely see Hannah's eyes from over the rump of my carcass. She held up her hand with four fingers extended and I nodded. Then we turned our eyes forward and watched.

I had left the one revolver in my pocket and held the supporting chain with my right hand while I tracked the approaching bodies with the second weapon in my left hand. Three of them seemed to be running about fully at random among the bodies and I watched as two of them caught sight of each other, aimed, and nearly succumbed to friendly fire.

I recognised two of the four. One was Ben. He remained near the entry door with the scattergun in his hands. Then the other one met up with one of his colleagues just below my feet and I heard him say, 'Nyuh nyuh nyuh, nyung.'

The fellow with him casually scratched his head with the gunsight on the end of the barrel of his revolver and said, 'Beats me.'

Then they both started walking back towards Ben.

There was a brief discussion at the door. And then they started to exit. Only Ben remained for a few ticks more. He was at a distance of about fifty feet from me, and it was difficult for me to see his eyes, but at one point I could have sworn he looked right at me, or at least directly at what little of me wasn't concealed by the carcass I was straddling. Then he turned, exited and shut the door behind him. A moment later, the lights shut off.

I slid down some and then dropped to the ground and found Hannah in the dark, then helped her down. I ran my right hand over my sark and found that thanks to being cautious in my climbing I hadn't become too terribly soiled. Hannah, however, was a bit of a greasy mess.

We silently walked towards the west end entry of the building and then waited for a few ticks, trying to sense the presence of bodies outside. Instead, I could feel them all behind us, on the other side of the far wall.

'There maun be another building over there,' I whispered as I opened the door just a crack to let some light in.

'Yup,' Hannah said as she rubbed what looked like a clump of matted hair from the front of her dress. 'I just can't wait to find out what's in it.'

* * *

We made our way around the south side of the building and found a small cattle pen with fattened kyne cruived in tightly together. They were all mooing distressedly at each other, and I had to shrug off the emotions wafting out of them, perfuming the air with their discomfort.

Where the cattle pen began, there was a change in the exact hue of the bricks of the wall and it was obvious that the area we had just come from had been a more recent structural addition. It was still foggy out, and scanning our eyes as far as we could, it appeared that there was a shut gate on the pen which led to a fenced-in path just wide enough for the kyne to move single file towards the building. Following that with my eyes I thought I could just make out an entry to the building.

It irked me to do so, but having no better way to traverse the dense field of kyne which ran right up against the building, we ended up walking across their backs to the sounds of their surprise. It felt to me like a further insult to the beasties who had been corralled for the purpose of their murder, but I couldn't see any other way to reach our destination without circling the entire building and chancing finding another entry.

We soon made it to the gate and jumped in the open area on the other side to look upon a single sliding door set in the side of the building before us.

I said, 'There's six bodies in there, including Ana.'

Hannah said nothing, simply nodded. We looked up and scanned the brick work. There was a row of clear, thin winnocks on what would be the second level of the building, likely for the purpose of admitting light for the work performed inside. Somewhere on the roof, though we couldn't see it from that angle, there apparently was one or more chimneys belching up large amounts of smoke which in the still, heavy, humid air was being drug back down to ground level instead of drifting away into the atmosphere. My nose and lungs were burning and Hannah had to stifle a few coughs.

'We need to find if there's another entry. Obviously this is the meatworks where they do the butchering and there's got to be some convenient way to transfer the beef slabs over to the cold room where they were getting bled,' Hannah said.

I shook my head. 'Nae, let's gae in.'

Hannah said, 'Listen to me. This is a big building. We have no idea what the internal configuration is. We know there's about five people with guns in there who want to shoot us. We know they've got Rodríguez, and are most likely using her to lure us in. If we simply open the door and both walk in, they can start shooting at the big open square of light and it's a good chance they'll hit one or the both of us.'

'Aye,' I said. 'So when the door opens, we winna walk in.'

'Wait for the reload?' She shook her head, 'I doubt these boys are good for synchronised shooting. There likely won't be a time in which they're all empty at once.'

I looked behind us and said, 'We winna gae in. No' at first.' I sighed and said, 'It fashes me to even think on it, but given the situation, I think we micht axe for some help.'

Hannah followed my gaze to the kyne.

I said, 'We'll open the gate and get them on the move afore opening the sliding door. Then let them crowd in the building and in the confusion we make oor entrance.'

Hannah warily speired, 'Have you ever dealt with cattle before?'

'Only once,' I replied. 'And they kept me from getting shot then, too.'

* * *

Apparently, prior to the problems of dealing with the appearance on the property of us lassies, the plan had been to do some butchering that Monday morning. The kyne had been gathered into the pen with that anticipation and were so tightly packed that when Hannah opened the gate leading to the fenced-in path, the beasts immediately squeezed into the open area single file and begun hoofing it towards the big sliding door. With Hannah encouraging their swift progress forward from the gate, I slid the door open just in time for the first cow to keep running right in the door. Gunshots immediately rang out from the dim interior of the building and my heart nearly stopped in my chest as the steer in the lead bellowed out in pain, though he didn't falter in his forward momentum. Then, suddenly, I saw Hannah crawling up along the fence line on the other side of the stream of bodies to stand at the opposite side of the door, and as the kyne continued to push in and the gunshots ceased on account of the confusion warranted by their appearance, we entered the building ourselves.

That lead steer was bleeding but apparently was none too terribly injured as he continued to run up a canvas-covered ramp lined with metal railings which led up towards the second level with a steady line of kyne behind him. At the same time, Hannah and I squeezed in between the wood of the fencing and forced our way between two cows. Once inside the abattoir and on the ramp, Hannah slipped herself through the metal railing to the left and dropped below the ramp, somewhere on to the ground beneath it. My first inclination was to do the same, only my much bigger body didn't want to fit through the available opening so I ended up maintaining my course with the kyne, squeezed between the head of one and the hinder of another.

At the top of the ramp, the beasts began to congregate again atop a large, metal platform with various grates built into it. Obviously I had found my way to the killing floor, and for only one tick I marvelled at its sophistication, for in the back of my mind since discovering the cold bleeding room, I had expected the Oglethorpe slaughterhouse to be something like an old-fashioned shambles, lacking in any modern organisation. Then that brief contemplation was quickly erased by the overwhelming revulsion I felt on account of the physical presentation of the place. The entire area smelled terrible, like a disgusting, salty mix of fear-filled perspiration, excrement and blood. It would be another ten years before President Roosevelt would commission an investigation leading to the Meat Inspection Act, and casting my eyes about it was no great surprise that I saw piles of filth all over. I would have fain gone anywhere else to escape that repugnant location, only it was at that instant that I heard a familiar voice hoarsely cry out from the distance as if strangled with pain: '¡Ayudame, por favor!'

Then, ever so gently, I could hear the echo of her sobs from somewhere ahead and below of my present location. I wanted so badly to call out to Ana, to tell her we had come for her, but I feared giving away my position, so I held my wheesht. Then there were gunshots.

From somewhere behind and below me came the sound of multiple small arms firing and I felt certain Hannah was involved, either in doing the shooting or being shot at, or both. The fact that she didn't scream out in pain indicated that they hadn't gotten her yet, and since it seemed she was providing a ready distraction for me, I took a tick to think and look around. And then I moved.

There were a few electric lights around in the building, and one smouldering fire some distance ahead of me on a level below the killing floor, but most of the light was provided by the high winnocks, and that was dull and grey. In the dim gloaming of the bovine chamber of horrors I found myself in, I noted that the various grates on the platform had levers next to them and so surmised that was how they were operated. I squeezed around the cattle and scrabbled forward on my hands and knees to look through the meshed metal and see that, when opened, the various grates led to chutes in which the flesh of the butchered beasts might be directed in various directions below with the aid of gravity. I searched until I found a grate which seemed to lead in Ana's direction. After shoving one revolver in my trouser pocket, I laid atop the metal shelf like I was certain many a butchered beast had done before, and pulled the lever next to me.

I fell below and was turned toward the north side of the building by the curving metal of the chute. I landed roughly on a length of canvas that was apparently part of an automated electrical system, currently not running. I had only a tick to get my bearings when I heard more gunshots towards where we had entered the building followed by the sound of bullets ricocheting about. Only a few feet behind me, a high-pitched scream suddenly erupted, and after ducking down behind the filthy conveyor, I turned to see a lad walking along with a limp. He was still carrying a revolver which he casually threw away from him before he fell down in a heap. I observed him briefly as he began to rummage about in his pocket, and I pulled the second revolver out of my trousers as I thought he was going for another weapon. Instead he withdrew the loose pages of a book and held them at angles in the light until he could read them. It seemed the lad was done fighting the instant he was winged, and so I left him sitting there with his lips moving silently as his eyes scanned over the words on the page before him.

The gunfire continued behind me as I moved farther towards the fire on the north side of the building, and then there was a blast as if from a scattergun, somewhere above and behind me. I turned to look up towards the killing floor, but could not directly see anyone.

I turned back around and made my way in the dark among various wheeled carts. There was a partition of wood ahead, and I could indirectly see the flickering flames of the fire burning behind it. In front of the partition, a wooden staircase led up to a metal walkway which then ran directly back towards the killing floor. I looked about, and neither seeing nor sensing any body nearby except for the lass I had come for, I took to my feet and ran into the room behind the partition.

There were two large wooden doors apparently leading to the outside, as I could see the dimmest, natural grey light coming through the cracks in their planks. There was a large stone fire pit in the centre of the room with a small fire burning within it. On the ground next to it sat what looked like a blackened branding iron. Ana sat hunched over next to it, facing away from me. She wasn't bound in any way, simply sitting unattended next to the flames and the iron. I ran to her then and held one of the revolvers over her shoulder and directly in front of her face and, with a smile in my voice, said, 'We've come for ye. Time to help us get back oot of here.'

I expected her to take a hold of the revolver and resume her earlier display of marksmanship, but instead, upon seeing the weapon floating before her eyes, she simply cried out: '*¡Jesús!*

I stepped about her to look down and saw that she had her arms crossed over her bosom and her hands worked up into her oxters. The blood running from her hairline had dried and some of it had flaked away, but there was still a mass of it next to her left eye. I followed her gaze to see that she was looking down at something on the sandy floor between her feet.

I felt sick. 'Ana?'

I looked down into her face. She leaned back ever so gently and let me see her countenance. Her dark, greeting eyes looked painfully up to mine as she withdrew her hands to show me. Then I looked down to see what was between her feet.

Four fingers.

I don't know why I should have expected to simply run up and find Ana unharmed, ready to resume the fight with us, but up until that instant I had expected everything to somehow turn out right in the end. For one brief second, a thousand thoughts shot through my mind, images of miraculous healings and my own abilities in such matters and the possibility that I could somehow fix this. But then when nothing came to me, no right-handed urge

282

to correct this horrible injustice which was presented before my very face as Ana lifted her hands, both missing first and middle fingers, I felt my mind loosen its grip on the situation as the very fabric of reality briefly became unravelled within my ken.

I dropped both the revolvers and went to my knees. Like some sort of idiot I picked up two of the fingers and held them up to the burned stumps on her hands as if I could simply screw them back on. Ana was greeting so hard and she began to shake as I did this. And then she began to convulse as sickness threatened to take over her.

I dropped the fingers next to the two guns and looked about. Then I understood. What I had earlier felt was Ana's pain. Her terror had shot out to me through the very air as the tool laying on the ground next to me had been used to remove her fingers. I understood then that it was a cast-iron castrator, designed for use in transforming a cow into a steer, but most likely also used for the gelding of many a lad.

Ana was still sobbing and retching as she tremulously said, 'I-i-i-it was E-E-E-Esther.' She took a shuttering breath. 'She e-e-e-es near.'

'I'm sae sorry,' was all I could say.

Tears were on her cheeks as she shook her head at me, casting them away. Then she said, 'I am not finished. I can still play and I can still work.'

I was sitting and staring at the shaken lass and then she turned her eyes upon me and strongly said, 'We have to go.' She shoved her fists back in her oxters and said,

'Pick up the guns, señor. You remember what I told you. Just point your finger.'

'Aye,' I drily said. Then I helped Ana to her feet and picked up the guns.

Random gunshots continued behind us, and so I decided it would be best if we could avoid having to go back into the interior of the building. I ran directly to the big wooden doors and rammed them where they met with my shoulder but they didn't open, simply creaked with the effort as they were in some manner locked from the outside. I thought for a moment that I could possibly break them down as the wood of their construction was obviously old, but then a bullet ricocheted off the brick only a few feet from my head and Ana let out a gasp of surprise. I ran back to her and we both took cover behind the partition as the gun battle seemed to be coming closer.

She was shivering and moved right up against my body as if freezing. She was a long lass, though not nearly so long as me, and with her huddled against me I found my chin just over the top of her head. 'Ye sud get ahint me I said,' I said, but she didn't move.

'No,' she firmly said. 'You must listen to me.'

My hands were full but I tried to twist her around me. 'No!' she stoutly said and looked up at me.

I extended my arms around her head with my elbows resting on her shoulders and the two revolvers pointing towards the opening into the abattoir. I didn't know what else to say, so I plainly began, 'I'm sorry. I'm sorry ye came back. I'm sorry this happened. I'm sae stupid! Ye sud have never listened to me...'

284

'Stop!' she commanded. Then she took a deep breath and after tilting her braw face up to mine, she gently said in a whisper, 'I do not know why you think so little of yourself. I heard what you said, and I wanted to follow you, wanted to come back, for the children here. And for Gail, and Edna, and Ellie and Percy. And for you.'

I had been looking over her head, awaiting the appearance of some target from the dark as the shooting seemed to be moving closer again, but then she used the remaining fingers of her hands to tug at my sark and I looked down into her dark eyes to see her earnest concern. 'This was not your fault, Mary,' she gently said. 'Even if it was, you were correct in what you saw as a problem. These people are very bad. We must make the sacrifice sometimes, no?'

I nodded at her. 'Aye.'

She smiled ever so gently and said, 'Thank you for letting me help you, Mary. And thank you for leading me.' She started to say, 'I hope we will do so again...' when I suddenly squeezed my elbows around her lugs and slung her about behind me.

Ana hit the ground and I dropped in front of her, firing into the opening where I saw one of the lads who was walking down a conveyor lift a small arm to point at us. I was firing without aiming from my right hand and the bullets flew by him to ricochet against the metal of the killing floor above his head. He turned and immediately dropped between the belts, and I could hear him shuffling away into the dark.

I turned back to Ana and said, 'All richt, let's gae afore they all heid in this direction.'

285

The lass had a pained look on her face as if she were fighting back nausea again. She simply replied, '*Sí, señor*,' as she got to her feet to follow me.

Ana was just behind me, making a loop of her pirlie finger and thumb of one hand to grip my belt so as not to lose me in the dark. I led her towards the wheeled carts and we crouched in between them for a few ticks. Three shots rang out ahead of us in the dark, the flash of the muzzle barely visible in the gloom.

Ana quietly said, 'Hannah, I think,' then swallowed hard as if trying to contain her roiling stomach.

She retched just once as her whole body seemed to convulse. I whispered, 'Wheesht, some body is near.'

Ana tried to contain herself by wrapping her arms around her waist and gritting her teeth, but when the force of her convulsions became too much, she started to crawl away from me in preparation to vomit. I dropped the revolvers and reached out for her but her long legs kicked loose from my grasp. Then there was a sudden blast from the darkness followed by the ricochet of a hundred wee, leaden balls all about me, a few of which bit me in my scalp. After snatching up one of the guns in my left hand, I threw myself on top of Ana and aimed towards the muzzle flash and unloaded five rounds.

Ana was squirming beneath me and I said, 'Dinna move!' while I strained my eyes in hopes of seeing a bodily shape in the dark.

The gunfire ceased. The entire building had suddenly become quiet except for the wee voice I heard from the lass upon whom I was laying. '*Jesús, sálvame.*'

I dropped my gun next to her knees and crawled up the rest of her body.

'Ana?'

She said nothing.

I turned her over and put my hand upon her bosom, just over her barely beating heart, to feel the bodice of her dress covered in blood.

'Oh, God,' I said in a wee voice.

It was so dim in that terrible place, and yet everything within my vision was turning red.

'Ana, please!' I said as if it was up to her whether she stayed or left me.

My vision was closing in like a tunnel. More and more, all I could see was the scarlet of freshly spilled blood.

With my right hand still lying gently upon her heart, one final time she said, '*Dios existe.*'

As her last breath rattled from deep within her bosom, my left hand swelled and the tunnel of my vision caved in. As I slowly rose to my feet, I found myself blinded with bloodlust, and with my hand, engorged with blood and desiring death, leading the way, I stumbled forward with no other thought than to locate the person who had fired the fatal blast at a wretched, wounded lass lying prostrate on the filthy ground for the purpose of being ill. In the flash of the muzzle I had seen a white dress, and a sharp, angular face crowned with grey hair, and knew it was Esther who had been holding the scattergun. My left hand wanted her, and so did I.

I was on my feet blindly moving towards where I had just seen her. My hand strained for her, but not finding the hideous woman, my feet propelled me forward and I began to walk beneath the killing floor among the various chutes designed to shuttle the dead about. Then, suddenly, there was a body before me, and though I couldn't see him for all the red that had curtained the winnocks to my soul, I could palpably feel his unco fear at seeing me. I reached out and grabbed the lad with my left hand, only finding that he was not the prey for which I was seeking, I flung him away from me and heard his shriek echo in my lugs as he went flying through the air and then landed in a heap.

I continued forward like some mindless thrawnie and felt the heat of the kyne massed at the front entry of the building. I paused for one tick, took a deep breath, and as if inhaling the putrid stench of that woman I felt her path laid out before me and moved outside into the thick air.

'Fisher!'

For one tick I felt small hands upon me, snatching at my arm. Then I snarled and pulled myself free from Hannah's grasp.

'Where is she?' she speired.

I was running then. The beasts parted fearfully before me and I jumped over the fence.

'Wait! Fisher!'

She was behind me yelling as she panted with the labour of her efforts to keep up with me. My legs were so much longer, and she had to work hard to keep me in sight.

Then I smelled smoke. It was the smoke of a wooden house burning. I was distantly aware that the *Arcadia House* was slowly consuming itself from within as if its heart had rightfully succumbed to the fires of hell.

My big nose drew in air and I could smell Esther's path ahead of me. She was running, quickly heading west. I passed near the house and continued on.

I found the open end of the tunnel. She had been here. She had crossed back over to Bela.

One final time I heard my name screamed from behind me. Then I dropped into the hole.

I was sloshing through the water, not caring if my feet were wet or dry, my boots filling with liquid. I stepped on something. A dead beast.

There were echoes all about, reverberations of my movements through the water, of my hard breathing, of Hannah just behind me, shouting at me.

And then I was at the far end, and I was climbing back up, returning to the stagnant air above when something slammed into my head.

I screamed and forced my way up anyway. Then came another blow. And another. I fell back into the water, landing in a heap on top of Hannah, then gasped once before everything red turned to black.

X

The woman in green was afraid. Her voice kept casting sharp angles into the air. And yet she kept thinking to herself, 'Good, good.'

Every so often she would stop and wait in the swirling fog. The woman would see her and come running in her bare feet, then she would walk away before the woman could reach her and let the peace fill her mind again.

'Ellie!'

The woman kept following her, looking for her in the mist, desperately trying to find her.

'Please, Ellie, stop!'

She was leading the woman.

She would sometimes think of the mean man with the sword and the red jewel and think, 'Bad.' But mostly she thought of Mama and thought, 'Good.'

Finally, they left the trees. They were in the open with the fog hanging thickly in the air.

'Ellie, stay there!'

There was no one around.

She kept walking.

The woman in green kept following her.

One Little Word

She saw the stairs and thought, 'Bad, bad.'
She descended into the dark.

Monday, 20 April 1896, 9:50 AM

Throbbing pain.

My eyes slowly opened to reveal a thickly woven Persian carpet. At first I thought its ends were frayed into thrums, but then I realised that I was seeing double, maybe even triple. It might have been that I saw extra for each time I had been struck in the head by the stock of a scattergun.

My blood-drunk search for Esther was over, and now I felt myself gripped by a cold sort of sobriety tinged with the painful, dizzying efterins expected of such an emotional binge.

I moved my arms and legs about to discover what my situation was. It was not good. I felt weighted at both wrists and both ankles.

I was weak with the exception of my left hand. It still felt engorged with blood and strong with purpose. It began to swell again, pulsing with need in rhythm to the pounding in my skull, and I could feel its binding growing tight.

I was laying on the ground. I began to lift my head. I saw the walls. I thought the room I was in to be within the sunken concrete cube where Ana and I had been caged. Then I looked up. The concrete ceiling featured winnocks with grey clouds beyond them. Through the glass panes I could see plants growing in wild clumps. They stood perfectly still in the stagnant air.

Across the room from me was an opening covered by a white veil that had grown dingy and spotted with black mould due to the damp, underground atmosphere. Standing before it was the woman I had so recently sought.

Esther stood looking down at me with her lip curled up as if disgusted by my very presence. She looked very worn, tired and covered in filth, especially around the bottom third of her white dress. She still held the scattergun in her hands. The same with which she had shot Ana, the same with which she had danged me in the head when I came up out of the tunnel.

At first, the only other person I was aware of was the thirteen year-old lad named Lucas. He was standing only a few feet away, looking down upon me with the wooden grips of a revolver sticking out of his waistband. I first became aware that another body was present in the room because Lucas kept furtively looking past me towards something, someone else.

My left hand crawled towards Esther, inched forward by its fingers, and then began to strain towards her. I realised then that it was tethered by a chain, the same as my other three appendages. Esther was looking warily down at me, at my hand, which had fully taken on a mind of its own. I ignored it to follow Lucas's occasional glances and find who else joined us. Lucas stood to my left, and in looking to my right at first I didn't understand exactly what I was seeing in my blurry field of vision. I saw two feet extended into the air over the arm of a sofa about ten feet away from me, and if I hadn't recognised the filthy button booties, I wouldn't have immediately known it was Hannah.

I slowly got to my knees. Then I knelt for a spell until the worst of my dizziness ceased, and then I rose to my full height.

Upon gaining my feet, I first stared a challenge at Esther until she blinked. Then I turned my dry eyes to Lucas. He wouldn't look at me, or directly at anyone else, rather his eyes kept quickly darting about, occasionally setting upon Esther, and then shifting for a tick to Hannah. I turned and looked to her. She was lying face down upon a short sofa with her legs hanging over the wooden arm at its end. She had been tightly bound with rope, hog-tied as I have heard said, and a thick piece of cloth was wrapped around her neck and over her mouth, but her eyes were free to look at me, and she had her head turned to the side so that I could see her face, where I could see a sharp gash weeping blood upon her cheek. She was fully clothed, still wearing her stockings and booties, but with her airse upended, the skirt of her dress and her silken petticoat had gotten tangled and pulled up above her waist to quite ignominiously expose the lace of her undergarments made somewhat dingy no doubt by her falling into the water of the sewer when I had landed unconsciously atop her. With her legs twisted ever so slightly where the rope had been carelessly looped and tightened around her body, a particularly intimate portion of her nether regions was exposed to the air with only a thin layer of cambric covering it, and I understood that location, as well as the thin spaces of pale thigh visible above and below her garters, was acting like a magnet to Lucas's attentions.

Hannah's eyes looked to mine and for some reason I expected reproach for my insane actions following

Ana's death, or some form of anger or even outright fear, but instead I saw a sort of grim determination. I sometimes think back on that instant of our eyes meeting and realise that if Hannah had been a weak person, I might very well have fallen into despair. But I saw her clear, blue eyes, remembered the hard-headed strength she possessed, and then my ken immediately jumped to Abigail. And Ana. And my own older sister who raised me when we had no one else. And then a certain resolve fuelled by the strength of the lassies in my life filled my heart, my bones, my very soul. I turned back to stare at Esther again.

After all the earlier gunplay, the silence was deafening. I decided to speak.

'I shot yer sister, bitch,' I plainly stated. 'Richt through the heart. Edith's dead and gane to hell, already, I uphold.'

Her dark eyes grew big and she actually took one step back as if fearful I might reach out and grab her. After tightening her grip on the scattergun, she said, 'You burned our house down, didn't you?'

'Aye, bitch. Hoo could ye do that to little girls?'

Her eyes flicked to Lucas's as his turned up to my face and darkly speired a question.

I was going to continue but Esther shouted, 'You murderous man. How dare you! The only reason you're alive is so you can help us get that wife of yours down here.'

I ignored her. Instead I turned to the lad and said, 'Lucas, do ye know what has been happening oot at the Arcadia House all this time? Sacrificing little girls to the depraved lusts of men.'

'Lies!' Esther shouted pre-emptively.

And so it became obvious to me that at least Lucas didn't know if she would want to deny the truth before him.

Esther said, 'The Arcadia House is my sister's business, not mine!'

'*Was* the dead bitch's business,' I corrected her.

For a tick, I thought to follow up on that track about what had been taking place in that house, but something, some spirit, you might say, told me to move in another direction.

I somehow knew that I didn't need to say much to convince Lucas that this woman was an evil person. After looking at the lad for a tick, I turned my face back to Esther and simply stated, 'Ye murdered Ana.'

This had Lucas's attention. He looked directly at me again, as if searching my face for the truth.

Esther said, 'It was necessary. I killed her. So what?'

I held my wheesht. This seemed to be a family matter and I decided to let the family work it out amongst themselves.

Lucas said, 'You killed her?'

He was looking directly at Esther. His own grandmother.

She looked to him and said, 'Lucas, she was a dago maid, a Catholic, idol-worshiping whore!'

She stared at him expectantly, as if awaiting his affirmation that she had done the correct thing.

Finally, she said, 'We have been through this before. You know when an outsider comes in, we mustn't let them pollute what is holy. It is up to us to determine who is evil and then *smite them!* So, what is your problem, Lucas?'

He started to shake. Their eyes locked, and then he looked away and quietly said, 'I liked her.'

A certain resolve formed on Esther's face as she thought she saw him cowed. '*Oh,*' she said with emphasis. 'I see how it is. She tempted you with her dark ways.' She shook her head and continued: 'This is exactly why you can't be trusted with the parts of a man!' She looked away, rolled her eyes and said to no one, 'We need to lower the gelding age. It should be eleven, not thirteen. I have said so before, but then Edith always said we had to let them go a few more years so they would properly grow, at least half-way. But clearly I was correct!'

She turned her eyes back towards Lucas, who was staring at her with a countenance twisted in disbelief. Considering that her entire discourse centred on the life-long maiming of the lad, her soliloquy felt utterly surreal.

She said to him, 'This is why only the reverend can make these decisions! Don't you see! If you had your way you'd be mixing your seed with that disgusting, filthy whore, with her Indian blood, and her slave blood! You could tell just by looking at her that she was diseased! All of those pharisaical people are! Everything they do is *wrong.*'

Lucas was trembling as he speired, 'And is what you do with your own father not wrong?'

'How dare you! Father's read the Bible to you in church, and you *know* it is sanctioned! Besides, there is no one else righteous in this whole world, not one.' Esther bugged her eyes out at the lad as she said: 'Clearly not you!'

Lucas couldn't stand still as he pointed to me and said, 'And is what he said true? Sacrificing girls? My own sisters? Where's the justification in that?'

'Jepthah!' Esther shouted.

'And gelding the boys? I suppose that's for our own good?'

'Lucas, even the Ethiopian Eunuch was saved!'

There was one final pause in which the woman and the lad stared at each other.

Esther was wiggling her fingers on the stock of the scattergun as she sharply said to Lucas: 'See what that woman did to you? Why you can't be trusted?' Then her eyes narrowed and she speired, 'Did she touch you? *Did you touch yourself?* Nevermind! I don't want to hear about your disgusting onanism! We're having you fixed tomorrow!'

Those were the final words the woman ever spoke.

I watched as Lucas casually set his hand on the butt of his revolver and withdrew it from the waistband of his trousers. As he began to bring it up to point at that horrid woman, her eyes grew big and she lowered her weapon at the lad, cocking both hammers with her thumbs as she did so. Esther was one fraction of a step ahead of him as she aimed and pulled the trigger. Click. She had fired two blasts in the abattoir, and she had never re-loaded.

Lucas casually said, 'Thou shalt not suffer a witch to live,' then shot her once in the middle of her body, around her thinnest point, and she dropped the scattergun and stumbled backward. She was looking at him bemusedly as if she couldn't believe this turn of events was actually occurring. And then Lucas screamed at her as he fired repeatedly in a tight grouping around her heart. Esther fell back against the wall and slowly fell into a slump, leaving a scarlet trail on the concrete behind her, her grey hair mopping its way down through the blood until it settled atop her head like a crimson crown of death.

The lad stared at the stilled form of his grandmother. I could feel his natural distress. It was like something sharp in the very air.

'Lucas,' I calmly said.

He was shaking, barely keeping his hold on the revolver.

'Lucas, listen to me.'

And then he raised the gun and put it against his head.

'Lucas, nae!' I screamed.

He pulled the trigger. Nothing.

The hammer clicked repeatedly as the lad greeted and tried futilely to end himself.

I spoke as gently as I could. 'Lucas, stop.'

He let his arm fall to his side and dropped the gun.

'Lucas, I know this may be hard to believe, but I know something of hoo ye feel. I know everything is twisted up terribly richt noo and seems hopeless, but this does no' have to be the end of ye. It can be a beginning...'

He was greeting, his little frame wracked with sobs, but through the turmoil he was also listening to me.

'Ye can get past this, past the despair and confusion...' I was saying only to be interrupted. From behind the veil came the evil man himself.

I held my wheesht as I saw how things were going to play out. Lotson stepped into my view with Edna

Kibblewhit before him. He had one arm around her neck, holding her between himself and Lucas like a shield, and in his other hand he casually held what looked like an antique muzzle-loaded pistol pointed over her shoulder at me. The woman was blindfolded and gagged, but her hands and legs were unbound. The cream of her clothing had turned dingy with what looked like soot, and the suede of her shoon appeared ruined with the moisture of that dank place. One of her silk stockings, the left, was still in place, but the other had fallen the full length of her leg to wad about her ankle with its suspender trailing behind to become tangled in the fibres of the Persian rug, giving her an uncertain gait as it was randomly caught up and released in the fabric of the carpet. Despite having her limbs free, the woman's fear and confusion were such that she may as well have been bound. Lotson walked her forward into the centre of the room, the scimitar with the red-jewelled hilt still hanging at his side.

The man stared at me for several ticks and I felt a repeated need swelling within my left wrist. My hand lifted and strained at the man, and then there was sudden surprise in his eyes as the manacle binding it snapped from the pressure and I was able to reach a few more inches towards him across the several feet between us.

Seeing that the rest of my bindings still held, the man relaxed and he laughed. 'I was warned,' he said. 'Alexander told me that this would happen someday, that he could feel those like you, possessed of devils, wandering about, wanting to get in to our sanctuary and destroy us. I should have known. The instant I saw your ugly face, I should have known that one like you could only find inspiration in the devil.'

'Lucas, ye see this man is hopeless. He cares naething for ye. Probably hates ye as much as every other body in his life.'

Lotson's eyes turned down to the lad and he said, 'Boy, believe me, I do not hate you.' He barely cast his eyes back towards the bloody heap of his daughter Esther, then said, 'And I don't blame you for that. You did me a favour in killing her. She was useless as a woman, dried up years ago. The only thing she could do for me anymore was procure handmaids to take her place.' At this statement, his eyes ticked across the room to where Hannah remained bound atop the sofa.

She was staring venom at him as she took slow, steady breaths. Then as Lotson turned back to Lucas, my eyes met Hannah's briefly. Again I felt that stultifying influence in the air as I had returned to Bela and greater proximity with the angel. Yet through that mask, I could feel something, like a distant song echoing down the corridors, and knew that my lass was coming closer to me. She wasn't alone, and in looking to Hannah's eyes, I saw that she felt it, too. A growing pressure of need electrified the very air, a feeling that seemed to dwarf my own throbbing, bodily sense that my left hand would explode if it didn't have its deadly way.

I turned back to look upon Lotson as he casually hung over the trembling Edna Kibblewhit. Upon finding that Lucas was unarmed, he had relaxed his hold upon the woman, but she remained shaking in her place as Lotson continued speaking down to Lucas. 'Listen to me, boy. In hearing Esther speak, I realised that she was wrong. Maybe you don't need to be gelded at all. You just need proper instruction.' He motioned over towards Hannah with his pistol and said, 'Just think, Lucas. A few snips of fabric, a few thrusts of your hips, and you would be a man, with all of the attendant pleasures and powers.'

I turned my attention back to Hannah for one tick. In a moment like that, seeing someone bound in such a way and sported over so casually, you tend to realise your true emotions. After her having been such a reluctant bitch, I hadn't yet fully settled how I felt about her until that moment, but without having to think about it, I knew then that I truly cared for her. In realising to what ends I would be willing to go for her, I felt a certain swelling of affection in my soul much like what I felt for my own sister.

All of that feeling, the basic foetal growth of what would some day truly become a familial relation between Hannah and myself, formed inside of me within that single tick of the clock. And then I turned my gaze back to Lucas. I witness in his face an ugly thing, but truthfully there was the slightest flicker of interest in the proposition laid before him, the recommendation of pleasure and power offered to him by the man who had just lost his primary co-conspirators with the deaths of his two daughters and was looking for someone new to lead down the broad path of destruction.

It is my experience in this life that there is rarely an evil man so self-assured that he doesn't actively seek at all times for at least one soul to lead astray for the simple sake of assuaging his own guilt as it relates to evil-doing, since so long as he can find one person to go along with him, he can, at least within his own mind, share some of the burden of his sin. Surely, Lotson had spent a lifetime perverting his daughters with his corruption until they thought nothing of conspiring in his evil plans, and with them gone, he apparently would waste no time in finding another *protégé*. But despite the fact that Lucas's countenance lit with the slightest hint of desire for one instant, his entire face quickly turned down before he stared incredulously up at Lotson as his disgust at the very notion of the man's suggestion became evident. It was clear from the look in the lad's eyes that there was about to be further ugly words on the subject exchanged between them, only a certain distraction presented itself in a wee, tottering form.

In other circumstances, the sudden appearance of Ellie from the darkened concrete corridor might have been surprising, even comic, but the queerness of the many incongruous events of that morning resulted in a certain suspension of disbelief on everyone's part. I watched as the wee lassie unsteadily stepped into the room, staring at the red jewel at the hilt of Lotson's sword as if transfixed by its glow. All eyes, except the blindfolded Edna Kibblewhit's, were on Ellie. For several silent ticks of the clock, no one spoke. Then Lotson lowly said, 'What is that cretinous child doing here?'

His voice seemed to awaken something within Ellie, for she slowly tilted her flat, wispy-haired head back to stare up at the man with her grey eyes. Then she lifted her left hand, and with her stubby first finger extended, she pointed at the hilt of his scimitar.

'Idiot! Stop pointing!' he shouted down at her.

Ellie didn't so much as flinch. She continued to point.

Lotson seemed insulted by her presence and angered by her recalcitrance.

He leaned over Mrs Kibblewhit's shoulder and glared at the bairn and said, 'No, you may not touch it.' With a scolding voice, as if he was simply warning her away from ruining her appetite with sweets, he said, 'I told you before to keep your hands off.'

Still she kept pointing. And then a curious thing. The scimitar began to rise from his side.

Lotson looked genuinely rankled as he focussed his attentions on Ellie. The scold in his voice was replaced by actual ire as he said, 'Any child who is too stupid to behave is too stupid to live.' Then I felt my blood chill as he began to level his pistol at Ellie.

There he was, Adoniram Lotson, a big man with a cowering, greeting woman in his arms, taking a moment away from instructing his great-grandson on the finer points of becoming a man through the raping of a bound lass, bringing a pistol to bear on a gentle seven year-old bairn simply because she liked a shiny object that he possessed.

As he was lowering the weapon to Ellie's level, he was fully ignorant of the fact that his own scimitar had levitated into the air and gracefully turned itself about so that the jewel upon its hilt aligned itself perfectly with the wee lassie's extended finger at a distance of about five feet. And then as she shifted her finger to the man with the gun who towered above her, Ellie finally spoke. It was only one syllable, but it was perfectly distinct, and it reverberated throughout the concrete walls of the room despite the softness of her voice. Her lips moved, and she summed up the entirety of her opinion of Lotson as she uttered the one little word: 'Bad.'

I observed all of this directly, Ellie being my particular focus, but with Lucas in the corner of my eye. In one instant, he was merely a lad waiting in the wings of the theatre, little more than a scenery-stooge, someone never to be seen by the audience, and then he saw his sudden chance to take centre-stage. Standing only a few feet away from Lotson, Lucas was in the perfect position to grasp the hilt of the floating scimitar. The lad took it in hand but didn't bother to consider what he was doing. I believe that, prior to the dawning of that day, Lucas had already decided what kind of man Lotson was, and exactly how he felt about him, but in seeing the old man's petty disregard for human life so clearly displayed in the fact that he would even contemplate pointing a loaded firearm at such an innocent as Ellie drove the point home, and there was no need for further consideration on his part. As Lotson, clearly possessed of intent, cocked the hammer of his pistol, Lucas swung.

The first strike was little more than a gentle bludgeon as the blade danged Lotson in the side of the face, for Lucas hadn't wasted time in drawing the weapon back to give it more room to gain speed with a wider swing, but that was enough. Lotson's entire body jerked back at the blow, and his arm pulled up just enough to accidently fire over Ellie's head as the wee lass remained stoically standing in the same position, with her finger still pointing up at the bad man.

As the sound of the bullet ricocheting about in the corridor filled my lugs, Edna Kibblewhit and I both fell to the floor in heaps, in her case on behalf of a swoon brought on by the proximity of the blast, and in my case on behalf of Ellie. I was on my knees, straining for her, calling to her as Lucas followed through with the scimitar, and again glanced a blow off the man's head as he struck Lotson a second time with the flat of the blade.

'Ellie, come here,' I said as I stretched my finger-ends for her. I was just able to get a hold of her dress and pull at her when Lotson began screaming.

'What are you doing?' he cried out.

I managed to get Ellie in my arms and bring her face to my bosom. I gently covered her lugs with my hands and turned her eyes away. But not my own eyes. I watched. It was terrible and terrific all at once, something as horribly, inevitably bloody as two passenger trains heading towards each other at full steam on the same track.

Lotson was on the ground, dazed. The first blood was spilled when he held up his hand as if he could simply ward off the coming blows and Lucas neatly sliced his fingers off. Lotson screamed and fell back. He looked up to Lucas just in time to see the blade coming for him again.

'No!' he cried out, and with another hack, blood sprayed into the air.

Lotson was backing up, trying to get away, and ended up right next to Esther. He looked up to Lucas who bore the bloodied face of a maniac possessed of a legion of devils, and with a final gushing forth of venom, Lotson shouted, 'Damn you to hell!'

Lucas paused just long enough to say, 'No, God damn you. Those who live by the sword, perish by the sword!' And then he raised the scimitar and made a final end of the man.

Lucas dropped the sword and it clattered numbly against the Persian rug, the ruby on its hilt having grown dark.

I was gently rocking Ellie with as much give as my chains would allow. Other than their gentle rattling, for a few ticks, the only sound to be heard was the sobs of Mrs Kibblewhit. Then she said, 'Oh, God. Oh, God!' This seemed to awaken Lucas from his reverie as he stood dazedly staring down at the hacked remains of his grandmother and great-grandfather. He went to his knee then and began to search among the blood. He stood back up and casually walked to me with the look of a lad who had recently dispensed of some terrible burden, and after a few turns of a key, I was freed.

'Thank ye, Lucas,' I said.

His eyes were dazed, but I could still see the flicker of his soul within.

'Please release Hannah, noo.'

He went to her, and before beginning to work on her bindings, he reached between the rope wrapped around her and pulled the skirt of her dress back down to at least cover her hinder. This was the last thing I saw before I walked out of the room with Ellie in my arms, leaving Mrs Kibblewhit on the floor, still blindfolded and moaning to her Maker.

I walked down the darkened corridor and I found the corner with the metal door where I had met with

Alexandra early that morning. I turned by it into the connecting hallan already knowing who I was going to find.

For one tick Abigail looked terrified yet oddly resolved at the same time to fight single-handed whoever she might encounter. And then she saw it was me, and that I was holding Ellie, and she ran to us with her bare feet padding softly upon the damp, concrete floor.

'Oh, Mary, oh my God!' she said as the three of us came together.

I transferred Ellie to her care then, and the lassie happily laid her face against Abigail's bosom and casually kicked her feet about as if altogether undisturbed by recent events.

Abigail was greeting as I began to lead her back down the corridor to the metal door. I didn't want her to see what I had just left behind, so I opened the door to the false, yet pleasant domestic scene and allowed her entry. I looked about on the wall outside and found the switch. I flicked it and the electric light snapped on.

'Sit doun and rest yerself, lass,' I said. 'I'll be back in a few minutes.'

Abigail looked alarmed at the thought of us parting again and I took a moment to calm her. The tears were glistening in her green eyes as we kissed over Ellie's flat head.

As I pulled back from her she said, 'Mary, your face!'

Ellie was comfortable in her lap as Abigail reached up and put her finger-ends to my cheek.

'I know, lass. I micht be scarred and bit up somewhat, but I'm fine.'

A look of serenity came over Abigail's countenance as she observed my eyes. Then she said, 'Mary, are you going to leave me again?'

I swallowed hard and said, 'I have one muir issue to resolve, Abigail.'

Her braw eyes darted back and forth as she studied me. She said, 'Do not forget that I am hard by. If you need me...'

'This is something I need to handle on my oon.'

'Mary. Do not rush things. You are smart, and if you stop and think things through, and do not rush to judgement, I am sure you will come to the correct conclusion. The correct path. Remember that what you do in one moment may come back to haunt you for years.'

Again I swallowed hard as I nodded and said, 'Of course, Abigail. Stay here. Ye'll be safe.'

I turned from her, exited the room and shut the door with the feel of her worried eyes on my back, then I hurried down the corridor and re-entered the room to find that the white veil had been pulled down and thrown over the remains of Esther and Lotson. Blood was seeping through the white fabric in patches among the black mould.

Hannah was on the Persian rug with her arm around Edna Kibblewhit. The woman was speaking loudly so as to be able to hear herself after the deafening blast that had been fired just next to her lug. 'Percy! Where is Percy?' she was saying.

Hannah shouted at her, 'I'm sure he's fine! We'll find him in a minute!'

She looked up to me and I speired, 'Waur's Lucas?'

Hannah motioned towards the dark space behind where the veil had hung, and then the lad stepped out. He had a sick look on his face which I at first thought was due to his earlier hack work, but I was to discover that he had found something else to be disturbed about. I began to step towards him but then stopped when two lassies of about fifteen years, both nearly identical in appearance, and both very pregnant, stepped into view, holding hands.

Lucas looked to them and said, 'These are my cousins, Ruth and Leah.' I set my eyes upon them and observed their emaciated frames and sullen, distant eyes. Their long hair was ratty and tangled and their dingy white gowns were filthy. Lucas said, 'Edith told us they went to heaven and were adopted months ago.' He swallowed hard and said, 'I found them in a cage back there.' He shook his head and said, 'Ellie's mother is back there, too.' He looked to me and said, 'I can't... I just...'

He held up a ring of keys and I took them from his fingers. Then he extended his arm and gently grasped one of his cousin's hands and began to slowly lead them away. Before he left the room, I speired, 'Lucas, what is this place?'

He stopped and replied, 'Lotson called it his Holy of Holies. I only ever saw it from the hallway. I never knew what was behind the *parochet*,' he said in reference to the veil.

Then he walked out with the two lassies in tow with Hannah leading Edna by the hand close behind. Before she disappeared into the dark corridor, Hannah looked over her shoulder at me once. Then she was gone, and I felt a terrible void in her absence, but steeled myself to proceed on my own.

I walked back to find what the veil had concealed. What I discovered there was something akin to a mediaeval dungeon. There were iron bars set in the concrete for the explicit purpose of caging people in. There were manacles set into the walls, and more sofas like the one Hannah had been so recently constrained upon. The entire place smelled rank and in its way reminded me of the killing floor of the abattoir. All of the standard scents of human fear and pain filled the air, along with the thick stench of excrement.

I found Ellie's mother, blindfolded, gagged and bound, lying on the floor behind locked bars. I randomly stuck keys in the padlock until I found the right one and then stepped inside and knelt next to her quivering form. There was no doubt of the relation of the woman to Ellie when I saw her face. She was shaking as I removed her blindfold and gag, and as I untied her, I said, 'My name is Mr Fisher. That man wha imprisoned ye is dead. Can ye tell me yer name?'

She looked frightened of me, but upon seeing that I was releasing her, she said, 'Debra.' Then: 'Where's my daughter? Have you seen my Ellie?'

Once I had her free and on her feet, I directed her around the veil-covered remains of Lotson and Esther and out to the corridor where I pointed down its length towards the metal door. She ran from me as I turned back to the so-called Holy of Holies, and as I re-entered the dungeon, I quietly said aloud to myself, 'Time to locate the Mercy Seat.'

One more remained inside; I sensed her presence. My left hand, finding its earlier desire unfulfilled, had finally returned to its normal state, only to suddenly begin its surging need again. I felt ready to answer a specific question, and settle a certain problem, in the way that only death can resolve with finality.

I walked in among the barred enclosures to find a wooden panel about four feet wide set in between two cement walls. It stood out so perfectly in that it was the only wooden surface to be seen in that place, and I remained before it and stared for a few ticks, not wondering too hard why it might be there. Then I lifted my foot and with one sharp kick put my boot through it.

There was a surprised scream on the other side. Alexandra had been sitting on a stool in the wee space between the two concrete walls, not expecting me to so suddenly come for her. She quickly jumped up and backed away, but I stepped in and grabbed a hold of her head. As I drug her out by her long hair, I saw that behind her was a stairway leading up to a door with a wee winnock in it through which the mid-morning sun was visible. I drug her flailing body out of that bit of light and into the darkness of Lotson's dungeon, then continued on into the room where his body laid.

Alexandra kept fighting me, alternating between pushing at me and attempting to strike at my face, but I fully ignored her feeble efforts. After having been scratched, punched, struck repeatedly in the head with the stock of a scattergun and having had my skin pierced with several buckshot balls that morning, it seemed there was really nothing she could do to deter me.

Once we made it back to the bodies of Esther and Lotson, I went down to my knees and pulled her with me. I lifted the veil from off the hacked bodily remains and said, 'There's yer keeper, bitch. That's wha ye've been protecting all this while!'

She wouldn't look at what remained of him, a hacked heap of viscera. She kept turning away from the bloody mess, so I dropped the veil and stood up, pulling her to her feet. She was still wearing all of her jewellery, and I quickly ripped the rings off her fingers and flung them about the room as I said, 'Is this why ye're really here? Gold and jewels?' Then I grabbed the thick necklace from where it hung over her bosom and whipped it away. Some of her hair caught in it and she shrieked as it came out at the roots.

'No, no, please!' she began pleading as I drug her over to the sofa where Hannah had earlier been bound and threw her upon it.

'Ye've been working for him so that he could rape lassies all these years? And what of his dochters? Sell them aff for men to do what evil they please?' I was thinking about the two pregnant lassies that Lucas had just introduced to me as I leaned in over Alexandra's cowering form, and quoted as cleanly as I could: 'Behold noo, I have twa dochters which have no' known man; let me, I pray ye, bring them oot unto ye, and do ye to them as is guid in yer eyes. Are those the words of a richteous man? Is that hoo it is?'

'What? No, no!' she said again, but I didn't want to hear it.

I was dizzy with pulsing need as my left hand flew to her throat and the squeezing began. It seemed that her death was inevitable, that there was no force in the universe that could stop me from bringing an end to Alexandra right then and there. I was pushing her down onto the sofa, and as I climbed atop her trembling body her eyes bulged, and I looked into their deep blue depths, feeling nothing but revulsion now while tiny striations of red appeared throughout the whites as capillaries burst from the intense pressure. She was gasping while trying to fight with me, her fingers prying weakly at my hand as I throttled the life out of her. Her legs were flailing about beneath me and as I put my weight upon her writhing body to hold her still, I could feel the nervous excitement within her, pulsing up at me, re-doubling the intensity of my own consuming need in accomplishing her death. Again everything within my sight began to turn to red as the tunnel of my vision collapsed. All I could see was Alexandra's fear-filled blue eyes, all I could feel was my own shaking desire. And then, suddenly, a force stronger than my need to kill presented itself as a true angel intervened on Alexandra's behalf.

When a hand laid gently on my arm with the tranquillity of one at peace with the world, I looked aside to see the verdant green emeralds of my lass. She was looking into my face, speiring a question with her eyes.

'No, Mary,' she gently said. I barely heard her sweet voice over the pulsing thrush of my own blood in my lugs.

I slowly released my hold on Alexandra. She writhed about beneath me, greedily gasping at the air. Abigail and I ignored her as I climbed off of her prostrate body and stood on my own two feet. Then my lass calmly took my hand in hers, and together we walked away.

We stopped just outside in the corridor and Abigail put her hand up on my highest point and pulled me down. I knelt then in front of my lass, and let my head fall against her bosom. For a few ticks she gently stroked my hair as I took deep breaths, doing my best to calm myself. Then her arms fell about me and she held me near. She was treating me so tenderly in light of the state in which she had just found me that I couldn't help it. The tears came.

As I shuddered in her arms, she quietly said, 'Shh, shh... It is all right, Mary.'

I trembled as I speired, 'Hoo can ye love me?'

She gently ran her finger-ends through my short hair as she said, 'Because I know you, Mary. You are not a monster. You are the same as any other person. You get tempted to do something, and sometimes, in the heat of that moment you might make a mistake. But that is where I step in. It is because I love you that I make certain that you shall not do something that you will later come to regret.' My tears were beginning to dry as she continued: 'I know how it is, dear. Sometimes the desire to vent my spleen is simply too much, and I do not always properly govern myself. In those cases you also help me to remain mistress of myself when I feel tried.'

I still shuddered some as I speired, 'Hoo did ye ken that I was in trouble, Abigail?'

'Your eyes, Mary. I only had to look into them to see that your soul was troubled. But all of that... It does not signify, now.'

She gently laid her hand on my shoulder and pulled. I came back up to my proper height and, after drying my cheeks on my sleeve, I put my arms about her. 'Thank ye, Abigail,' I said. 'Ye are richt. I sud think afore I act. And when I dinna, I'm glad ye're aboot to keep me straicht.'

She smiled at me, then took my hand and we began to walk away.

On our way past the metal door, I quietly speired, 'Waur's Ellie?'

'Her mother has her,' Abigail sedately replied.

I squeezed her fingers but held my wheesht.

Inside the door at the bottom of the steps leading up to the ground stood Hannah with Edna leaning on her. Hannah warned, 'They're out there. That Benjamin and some of the others, including the one farm-boy who roped me like a calf at Esther's insistence.'

I was still feeling somewhat unsteady as my tachycardic heart fell back into its normal resting rhythm. I took a deep breath, then said, 'I dinna think his name is Benjamin. Maybe muir like Ben-Ammi.'

Hannah didn't comment. She simply speired, 'Want me to go up in case there's trouble?'

I took a deep breath through my nose, as if I could somehow discern Ben's feelings with my olfactory senses. 'Nae,' I replied. 'There will be nae trouble, the noo. I'll gae by my lane.'

'No, you will not,' Abigail said. 'From now on, we do everything of import together, Mr Fisher.'

I looked into her eyes and saw the love they held for me. It wasn't far from my understanding that she felt the need to watch over me, and given the circumstance in which she had just found me, choking the very life out of someone, I agreed that I needed her steadying influence.

I might have been able to justify Alexandra's death in dozens of different ways, but I was ready to honestly admit to myself that part of that terminal interaction that so nearly took place between us had to do with the very real, very physical carnal pleasure that I would have enjoyed in succumbing to my left-handed desires. I didn't understand then, but I most certainly know the truth now. Alexandra had tempted me the once that morning, and it was a gross fault of mine that I very nearly gave in to a different kind of desire in the heat of that one moment when we found ourselves on the sofa together.

My lass had seen this act nearly come to fruition, but armed with both the maturity of one who could stand on the outside and see exactly what was transpiring, and the perfect love of one who had decided to take me as I was, in every degree of my queerness, both good and evil, she had turned me away from doing a mortal wrong with nothing more than a look from her beautiful eyes and the weight of her fingers upon my arm.

Knowing that I needed her in order to stay steady on my course, I nodded to Abigail and then we walked through the door. We stepped up the stairs and entered the light together, walking hand in hand and foot for foot.

The fog had evaporated and the sun had finally broken through the clouds to reveal five lads and two lassies awaiting us, four of the lads holding guns.

Lucas was one of the five lads. He stood with his two pregnant cousins. Next to them was Ben who still clutched a revolver.

A few ticks of silence passed and then Ben addressed me. 'Is it true what Lucas told me?'

I nodded and said, 'Aye. Lotson and Esther are doun there. Only Alexandra's still alive.'

Ben nodded. He looked over to Lucas, and then to Abigail, and then back to me. He said, 'I saw the Arcadia House. Tell me why'd you burn it down, Mr Fisher?'

'It was a bad place, Ben. Do ye no' know what happened oot there?'

He tiredly said, 'Adoptions. That's what we were always told. Esther couldn't stand children, never dealt with them. She first suggested sending some of the children away years ago. When I was little. But the actual adoptions were all Edith's doing. That's what Edith arranged.'

I felt the truth of his statement, the fact that he had been unaware of the final disposition of those sent to heaven. I said, 'This is a cruel world, Ben, with evil men in it.'

'Lucas told me what was in the Holy of Holies.' He nodded gently and said, 'And we found Gabriella. She was kneeling in front of the burned up house just crying. At first I thought she was sad that it was gone. It was the most beautiful place any of us had ever seen, after all. But then she told us what happened. And told us about Edith, and those men, and that she was glad they were dead. She told us why she's been living out there the past few years, and what Edith always said were the consequences if she talked. Apparently something bad has been going on there for a while. Even longer than a few years. I had a little sister. Nearly my age. We grew up together until she was adopted. That was bad.' He paused and looked around. 'This whole place is bad.'

I ran my tongue across the backs of my teeth then stated: 'Edith, the younger daughter, was yer mither.'

'Yes.'

He seemed to become aware of the weight of the weapon in his hand then. He lifted his gun and looked at it for a tick. Then he tossed it away. He speired, 'And now what do we do?'

I said, 'That's up to ye, Ben. Great evil has taken place here, but it is over, the noo. Yer faither, yer mither, everyone wha ever told ye what to do all these years is dead. Noo ye have the choice to make things better.'

There was a long silence, then Abigail speired, 'How old are you, Ben?'

Ben swallowed hard and answered, 'Twenty-seven.'

'Are you the oldest?'

He nodded. 'Yeah.'

Abigail motioned towards Lucas, Ruth and Leah. She said, 'These are little more than children. And how many more are there? I saw dozens and dozens last night. Now what you do, Ben, is you care for them. They need you.'

He looked at her for a few ticks, studying her eyes, then nodded.

Hannah had come dragging Edna up the stairs behind us. In the direct sunlight, Hannah's unruly mass of blonde hair looked washed out, bleached nearly clear like her eyes. She added, 'And we'll help you, Ben. You won't have to take charge of things alone.'

He looked to her, then scanned his eyes about to everyone present. I saw the lad with the malformed tongue standing behind him. He still held a revolver in his hand, but now cast it aside. The other two lads dropped theirs.

The decision had been made, but as yet, no one knew exactly what would be required to follow through on it.

* * *

Ben took us to the school house. The doors weren't locked, simply latched on the outside. He opened them to reveal the bairns cruived within. They looked tired, hungry, and frightened, scared by the sounds they had heard from outside.

I stepped in with Abigail to find more than forty children, including Percy Kibblewhit, staring numbly up at us. And then I saw the one adult, the one man present.

I went walking up to where he sat atop what looked like an old piano bench backed up against the wall with the two wee lassies, Janie and Alice, sitting on his lap, reclining upon him with their faces pressed to his chest. He had his arms around them, and as I approached, his white eyes went to darting about, doing their best to search out my form. Until the moment I spoke I believe he still didn't know who was going to be walking into the school once the doors were re-opened. I suppose he expected either me, or Lotson, and he seemed only slightly surprised when he heard my voice.

I stood looking down at him and said, 'Sir, I think it's time ye and I had a wee talk.'

The two lassies gripped protectively at the old man, but he said, 'Girls, everything is all right. I'm goin' go talk to this man.' Then the mob of cruived bairns separated before him like a sea of white bodies, and he stood and led Janie and Alice out by their hands, and the rest of the crowd began to follow into the sunshine.

Before finding a private place to interview Moses, Abigail reminded Ben that the first order of business was to get the hungry children fed since they had been locked up all morning without any breakfast. The lads went to tend to that duty while Abigail and I had a long talk with the old man.

* * *

I had absolutely no reason to trust Alexandra. I had little more reason to have faith in Moses. And yet during the course of the interrogation, which consisted of speirings both from me and Abigail, I came to realise that Moses was actually ignorant of every queer happening in Bela other than the incestuous relationships that had proceeded for decades. He still thought it to be just as perfectly moral in the modern day as it had been in the time of Abraham. Whether they simply kept the full truth from him, or whether he wilfully turned a blind eye, I have no idea. I wanted to believe his seemingly earnest statements that he didn't know anything about the *Arcadia House* or occasional imprisonment of persons in the so-called Holy of Holies, yet it was hard for me to believe that someone, anyone could live in that isolated place and be truly ignorant of what was going on so close by.

If anything decided his fate that day, it was the bairns themselves, for having had their fill of luncheon, they came searching Moses out with genuine affection in order that he might join in their games. After a certain fashion that is how I came to look upon him. As a big bairn who never wanted anything more in life than to find a place to belong.

The only problem with that was that in hindsight I could see Lotson as being little different at the core of his being. His interaction with Ellie in the last moments of his life, when he so selfishly refused to let her play with his shiny, bejewelled scimitar, made me see him in something of the same light. A child who simply refused to grow up, and who simply could not fathom the very notion of sharing his toys. The great difference, of course, was that while Lotson was willing to do any sort of injury or violence in order to live out his phantasy where he was some sort of harem-keeping sultan, Moses was nothing but a benign old man possessing a few altruistic tendencies. After all, he did try to help Abigail and myself escape that wretched place with Ellie, even if it was with the requirement that we ignore the worst of what was happening there in exchange for our freedom.

* * *

Abigail quickly became involved with the bairns then, doing exactly what came naturally to her in performing any little deed she could to care for them. The lads, led by Ben, went to searching out the bodies of their fallen brothers, and the process of burial began. While they did so, and Abigail was occupied with the wiping of noses and changing of diapers, Hannah and I crossed back through the tunnel and made our way to the abattoir.

We found tools in the shed near the remains of the *Arcadia House* and brought them with us. Then we found Ana.

I wrapped her up in a clean sheet and carried her out a ways with Hannah bringing a shovel in each hand, her frilly handbag hanging from its strap on her arm. While I held Ana's body close to me, I noted that the smell of gunpowder was gone. Only the gentle scent of flowers remained.

We both dug. I laid her down. I had cleaned up her face, wiping the blood away from her hair and where it had dried next to her left eye, as well as the fresher spots around her mouth that she had expelled with her final words. I had left her body wrapped in the sheet when I placed her in the grave. Only her head and shoulders were exposed.

We looked down at her beautiful, serene face for a few ticks. Then we prayed. It seemed as though one thing Ana never lacked was faith, so it seemed somehow spurious and unnecessary, but we made the effort.

I only looked once to Hannah's face to see the tears hanging from her eye-lashers while we silently, reverentially covered her over. I nearly commented, but it felt somehow intrusive to do so. Hannah was purposefully shutting me out of her mind, withholding her emotions from me, and I decided that despite the fact we had grown somewhat closer that morning through our shared experiences, I still felt I didn't have the right to force myself upon her as a friend. I would wait for Hannah to open up to me if she chose to, though I found the thought of her staying distant from me painful. It's a queer thing to think on now, but I found myself truly yearning for her friendship.

For a few ticks we sat quietly next to the mound. Then Hannah dug about in her handbag and pulled out a couple of long, slim corona cigars. She handed me one and then dried the heel of one of her booties on her blue dress which had turned dingy with a mix of blood and dirt, and then struck a match on the sole. For a time we let the smoke flow from our mouths. The air remained still and Hannah blew thick, generous rings with her pursed lips that seemed to fly out into infinity among the vines clinging to the oaks and pines.

Finally, she said, 'Don't you have a boat to catch?'

'Aye, but nae. We're staying until this gets sorted oot.'

Hannah shook her head and said, 'This'll get sorted out as soon as the law gets involved. In other words, as soon as the sheriff is notified.'

'Ach.'

'Do you know the sheriff?'

'Nae. But I fear he micht ken me by reputation.'

Hannah nodded. 'I think maybe you ought to go and see if you can catch that boat.' Then she held up her hand and rubbed her fingers together. *Money.* 'I know the local sheriff. Not a bad man. But things go a lot smoother with him if cash is involved.'

I sighed and said, 'It seems that's the way of the world.'

Hannah nodded and said, 'I bet there's enough money in this place already to see every child here properly cared for. The problem is the state. Hand over fifty children and fifty million dollars and if you don't keep an eye on the people in charge it'll never be enough cash. Every hand the money passes through will peel a couple of bills off. Fortunately, I know some people I can get on board with this. We'll make sure things turn out right for the children.'

'The Network?'

She shook her head. 'This isn't Network business. Ana and I should already be out of here and in contact with the boss. Guess I'll be late getting back to the office.'

'I'm sorry ye lost another one,' I casually said, wondering what she might have to say in response.

I looked to her, observed her clear, blue eyes as they stared off into the distance. She swallowed hard and simply said, 'I'm sorry I lost Ana.'

* * *

We were walking back when I speired, 'What aboot Alexandra?'

Hannah had left her locked up in one of the cells in the so-called Holy of Holies. She had taken care of that problem herself because I didn't feel as though I was ready to be trusted around Alexandra yet.

Hannah said, 'She's dangerous for the simple reason that she doesn't care. She knew too much about what was going on here to turn a blind eye. With her abilities, she might be the one bit of real Network business in this place.'

'Ye'll take her with ye?'

'Most likely. I need to get in contact with Jackson and see what I am to do with her.' Hannah rubbed at her eyes with her fingers then said, 'I'm not looking forward to that.'

'Hannah, listen, aboot Jackson...'

I paused and she said, 'What?'

'When I was staying with Doctor Lamb and he was trying to help me understand wha I am, and waur I fit in the grand scheme of things, he said something in the sense that if yer boss, as ye call Jackson, were to find oot wha I was, what sort of wight I am, she would be over sorry for no' taking tent with me when she had the chance.' I ground my teeth together a bit and speired, 'Do ye think that is true?'

We kept walking for a bit, then Hannah said, 'Yup. I know what Doctor Lamb meant. You came here in all innocence, seemingly by random chance, but you just couldn't help yourself, could you?'

She turned her eyes up to mine and I looked away. 'Aye,' I said. 'It all juist sort of happened...'

'Well, if Jackson knew about the specifics of the way things happened here, the way you just walked in to the Arcadia House and started shooting, she'd want to recruit you.'

'Weel, then maybe I could do some guid in this world.'

Hannah grabbed a hold of my sark and pulled me to a halt. Again she looked up into my eyes and said, 'The Network doesn't work that way. You understand that, right?'

I looked at her and held my wheesht.

'If you ever get involved with us, sometime way in the future, then you'll find it's a rare day that anything works out for the better.' She let go of my sark and started walking slowly again.

I said, 'Sae ye're saying no' to get my hopes up that the Network is something guid?'

She shook her head. 'The real truth is that you should never get your hopes up about anything in this world.' She pushed her lips together for a few moments of quiet thought then said, 'Except it seems that you've got something special in Gail. Go home, Fisher. Take her with you. If where she's from is as great as you make it sound, you should do everything you can to get her there immediately and stay there forever. And be happy.'

'Are ye sure we sud juist leave ye here?'

'Yup. You've made a nice mess here and I'll clean it up. This time. First one's on me,' she said with a generous, toothy smile.

'I do need to get Abigail oot of here and back to her hame. I promised her, and promised her family. But when we do work thegither again, and we will, I'll do my part.'

Hannah grabbed at my arm again to stop me. I looked down at her and she said, 'Fisher, let me be clear: there won't be a next time. I was just contemplating things, contemplating you, and it's not just me thinking you should go home and be happy, or even that the Network isn't for you. The fact is, you're too undisciplined. Too dangerous.'

I nodded in earnest agreement, but I said, 'I'll get better. I'll learn to control myself and listen to others.'

Hannah didn't say anything. She released her hold on me and we walked back to Bela in silence.

* * *

'You have such beautiful hair, Teeny,' Abigail said.

She had retrieved our carpetbag which contained her hairbrush. She was using it to carefully make order of Teeny's hair which was naturally wild on account of her bumpy head.

The wee lass smiled widely to reveal several missing teeth. 'Thank you, Gail. You are very pretty. I have never had anyone make my hair look so nice. What with my knotty head, and all.'

Abigail laughed and said, 'Well, I have had a lot of experience with knotty heads, as you call them. Mr Fisher's head is as gnarly as an old, hurricane-twisted oak.'

They were being pleasant with each other and I hated to interrupt, but I made eyes at Abigail until she stepped aside to hear what I had to say.

I put my arms around her and said, 'We're leaving, Abigail.'

She looked up into my eyes and I thought for one tick she was going to speir that we stay on the bairns' behalf, but then she laid her face against my bosom and said, 'I feel as though I could do some good here. But I need to go home.' She turned her eyes up towards mine and said, 'I have been away from my family for so long, and I know that not only do they need me, but so do the children of Greenhaven.'

'Aye. They're every body ye've ever kent.'

She nodded gently. 'Do you believe things will be properly resolved here if we leave?'

328

'Aye. I hate to say it but if we stay we may only make muir problems.'

'It does seem we have been involved in nothing but trouble since we left Greenhaven and came to the mainland.'

'Aye, and sooner or later that is likely to lead to legal trouble, if ye understand my meaning.'

Abigail was quiet for a while as she looked to Teeny. The lass was playing ball with her sister Rebekah and several other bairns. Watching them toss the rubber lump about while laughing and chattering in the sun, seemingly without a care in the world, made me want to believe that things were only going to get better for them from that moment forward. Yet at the same time I felt a nagging doubt clawing at my paunch from within. That worry was sourced in my growing understanding that when left unchecked, a few men and women could turn the efforts of their minds and hearts to evil, and lead masses of innocents down the darkest paths. Ben and his brothers had actively tried to kill us so long as Esther and Lotson were there to direct them, but just as easily they threw their weapons aside when they discovered that their evil masters were dead. Everyone was at peace in Bela just then, but I worried already at what might lead these bairns towards trouble in the future.

As if intuiting my thoughts, Abigail said, 'If you could, how long would you stay here and watch over these children? Days? Weeks? Months? Years? Would you try to control them, to make sure they did not find themselves led astray?'

I looked into her eyes and said, 'I juist feel like we're gang too fast.'

'Mary,' she quietly said. 'When I began to grow into a woman, I was worried that there were certain aspects of my life, of my very being, that were going to be so different from anything Mama had ever experienced that we were going to find ourselves at odds.' She shook her head. 'I learned something important from her. Just because I am her daughter, she never thought that she owned me, or could absolutely control me. That is the way her mother treated her, as if Mama was her personal property. Despite my having very different ideas about how to conduct myself, Mama never once thought to govern my every moment, my every movement.'

'Aye, but bairns need some guidance...'

'And according to what you have told me, they shall have it. Can you trust Hannah?'

'Aye. As much as any body, I uphold.'

'Then you must believe that they are in good hands,' she said.

I let her words regarding my desire to possess these bairns swage in my ken for a few ticks more. Then I said, 'All richt. We're gang, and we'll make guid time. I ken waur we can get some horses, and I think we'll be able to catch oor boat hame even after all of these delays.'

* * *

Abigail had our carpetbag, and I went back to my temporary lodge of the previous night for my cocoanut leaf hat and greatcoat. After slipping my arms in the sleeves and setting the hat upon my head, I could feel someone standing behind me. In the absence of the angel's

330

interference, I could clearly feel the confusion, and the natural remorse, of the lad behind me. I said, 'I'm glad ye came to see me, Lucas.' Then I turned and looked upon his face.

He said nothing. He seemed to be waiting for me to act, for me to somehow lead him, for me to tell him everything was going to be all right. I did my best to feel him out, then I said, 'I know that ye are conflicted over what has happened. Any body would be. But ye did richt.'

He lowered his eyes and gently shook his head. 'I'm not sorry for killing Esther and... him. I'm sorry that I followed them for so long.'

He began to dig about in the pocket of his short trousers and withdrew a handful of loose pages from a book. He held them up and I stepped forward to take them in my hands.

I was looking down upon them as I said, 'This reminds me of hoo I learned to read, Lucas. The loose sheaves of random books. Only I see this is nane too random.'

He nodded and said, 'The Bible. We aren't allowed to read it.' Then he corrected, 'Weren't allowed. At least not on our own.'

I was studying the loose pages and speired, 'Waur did ye get these?'

'Moses. He got that Bible from a travelling preacher way back before I was born. He learned to read right alongside the older boys in the schoolhouse. Then he went blind and tore his Bible up because he thought we'd learn something from it. He spread the most important parts around Bela. Us boys have been secretly passing them around for years. You know... inspiration.'

'Aye. One way or another.'

The pages I was looking at were from the twenty-sixth chapter of Matthew. One verse in particular was circled in pencil. I read aloud, 'For all they that take the sword shall perish with the sword.'

Lucas cleared his throat and said, 'I read that verse so many times, and then when the actual moment came, I misquoted it.'

I swallowed hard and again said, 'But ye did richt, Lucas.'

He seemed uncertain. Then he said, 'I'm glad they're dead. But.'

'Aye, but what?'

He looked at me and there were tears in his dark eyes. 'I can't face her again.'

'Wha?'

'Your friend that's staying.'

'Hannah Beardsley?'

He looked down and nodded. 'I hated that man so much, and wanted him out of my life no matter what I had to do just as much as I wanted Esther gone, and then, when it came right down to it, I hesitated because he suggested something... wrong.'

'He wanted ye to do as he did... to follow his ways.'

He nodded again and said, 'And for one second something inside me, some part of my body, wanted that. Wanted to be the same.' He made fists of his hands and struck his thighs. 'What kind of man can I ever be? No better than... *him*.'

I didn't know if I should, but I laid a hand, my right hand, upon the lad's shoulder and earnestly said, 'I saw yer face, Lucas. For one tick, that is, for one single instant, something inside of ye agreed. Ye were tempted.' He lifted his head and looked at me. As two tears were ejected onto his cheeks, I said, 'That, temptation, is part of being a man. It is something every man faces again and again.'

He searched my eyes for the truth. 'Really?'

I nodded. 'I'm still learning that myself, Lucas.'

'You seem to be... I mean. You're married.'

I nodded and said, 'Aye, I have my Abigail. I sud be a responsible, mature adult. But still I get tempted.'

'But that temptation. You don't understand. In that moment, the things that I thought I could do, to that woman, because I think these things, sometimes, wicked thoughts, and then for that one instant I...' and then he snapped his mouth shut and pulled away from me.

My arm stretched but my hand was still on his shoulder. I squeezed, leaned in toward him and said, 'I absolutely understand.'

He turned his face back towards me with speiring eyes.

'It's a terrible truth, Lucas, but we all, man and woman alike, are subject to temptation. And sometimes that temptation may be a terrible, twisted thing, and yet something within us tries to convince us it is all richt and justify oor actions. But juist as ye did this morning, we maun use oor intellect, and oor heart, to decide it is wrong. For one instant something came to ye and told ye to do the wrong thing, but ye triumphed over it. The same thing happens to us all. The important thing is that ye did the richt thing in the end, and recognised the evil within yerself, and ignored the temptation.'

'Sometimes it is hard. I don't understand. But.' He looked to me, made contact with my eyes, then quickly looked away. 'That woman.'

'Ana,' I said.

He shut his eyes tightly then nodded. 'I don't understand. I didn't even know her. But I liked... Ana.'

'That's hoo it often is. We meet people in this life, and with naething muir than a look in their eyes, we decide that we love them.'

He opened his eyes and looked back to me. 'Love them?'

I nodded. 'Aye. It's all part of being a man, Lucas. What ye need to know is that it's normal. Ye're normal. It is confusing, and I micht be aulder than ye, but I'm still learning as I gae.'

'That feeling of being around her. Of hearing her speak. Of seeing her... skin. It nearly hurt like the blade of a sword in me. How do I deal with that?'

I smiled and said, 'The only thing I can say is that sometimes it helps to beat oor swords into ploughshares.'

The lad looked to me for a few ticks and then smiled. Then I laughed, and he joined me.

He looked away again, out the door and towards the dwellings in the distance where groups of bairns were playing. After a silent spell, he said, 'Thanks for talking to me. I don't feel quite so wicked as I did.' Then he speired: 'So, what's the deal with Ellie? And why did the sword float up in the air when she pointed at it? Was that God who did that?'

'Ach,' I said. 'That I canna tell ye. I think ye know as much aboot it as I do.'

* * *

After Lucas left me, I sat in the front of the wooden dwelling and let the distant sounds of playing bairns wend their way to my lugs. Then Hannah came along a few minutes later with her handbag bulging. She walked up to me and opened it. Looking inside, I could see it had been stuffed with a motley assortment of paper bills in a number of denominations. Sitting atop the giant ball of cash was Hannah's wee *Smith & Wesson* model 1 revolver in a holster. She wormed her fingers around it and withdrew a single bill. She held it in the loof of her hand and I saw that it was the five-hundred dollar U. S. note I had used to buy my way into the kirk service the night before. I silently took it and slipped it into my coat pocket.

'All this evil was rooted in the love of money, it seems,' I said casually. 'What was the money for?'

'I talked to Ben and he showed me. Weapons, primarily. He said Lotson was ready for the end of the world which they expected to come just about any day now. All of the old firearms created for the army during the war are getting sold off to the citizens as new models are introduced. From what I've heard, those in the know say it looks like there's going to be a fight with Spain and the government is buying the new and selling the old in preparation.' Hannah pointed over her shoulder with her thumb and said, 'Over there, there are thousands of old guns and swords and cavalry sabres down in another concrete vault underground without any drainage. A bad idea in Florida.' She shook her head, 'Much of the hardware bought with the money made from donations to the church, the selling of children, and running the old Oglethorpe ranch, is sitting in a hole growing rust and mould, rotting away. Useless.'

I felt a chill of melancholy in my bones as we were silent for a few ticks.

'What aboot Ellie?' I speired.

'I'm going to make sure Ellie and her mother, as well as the Kibblewhits, get safely home in the coming days. Then when I get out of here I believe it might be prudent to pay Mrs Oglethorpe a visit and,' she said with gravity, 'sort her out.' Hannah gritted her teeth a bit then continued: 'She has several grown sons, the older brothers of Alexandra, living it up on the proceeds from the ranch that Lotson's boys have been running for years, and at some point their doings might need to be looked in to. More mysteries, but they can wait. I have no reason to suspect them as being directly involved, only their mother.' She hovered a blink before continuing: 'As to the child, I don't know what to think about Ellie except that obviously she's one of us. It was rather surprising that she should have such an amazing level of influence over that sword after only having touched it once that I know of.'

I nodded in agreement. 'It's quite a task ye've set yerself to, taking care of this situation, Ellie and all these other bairns. I thocht ye didna like cheeldren?'

Hannah's eyes were clearer, icier than usual as, with the gravity of one taking a hand-on-the-Bible oath, she solemnly stated, 'Actually I like children. That doesn't mean I'm any good with them. If there weren't plenty of older people around to help, to make sure I wasn't doing something to foul the little ones up, then I wouldn't have offered myself like I have.'

She stared hard at me, perhaps directly through me, and in hopes of thawing her gaze with a change of subject I speired, 'What aboot Ellie's ability? Will ye report on her to the Network?'

Hannah's eyes seemed to focus again. She looked steadily at me and said, 'No more than I'll report on you. Life's difficult enough when you don't have people like my boss breathing down your neck. Let's not make trouble where there needn't be any. Not just yet, anyway.'

'I've thocht some on what ye said, and maybe ye're richt. I micht ocht to simply gae hame with my lass and keep quiet. It's no' far to Greenhaven and...'

Hannah abruptly said, 'I don't want to hear about it. Where it is. I don't need that information.'

I felt oddly saddened at her saying that, for it was on the tip of my tongue to state that I could see Abigail safely home and then return to help Hannah make certain that everything was properly worked out for the bairns in Bela. But sensing that she wanted nothing more than to be done with me and for me to go, I nodded, swallowed hard, and said, 'Weel, thank ye, Hannah, for everything.'

'Yu-up,' she slowly, simply said.

She silently stood and looked me directly in the eye and we had a final moment of feeling each other out. Then without another word, Hannah turned and walked away.

I watched her as she moved away from me. She had pulled the braiding out of her hair and let its usually straight length fall in an unruly, wavy mass over her shoulders. In the bright afternoon sun it looked lighter than ever, and just as her eyes appeared to be two washed out orbs that might have once held a dimension of blue as deep as the Gulf is wide, her hair bore the look of the modern day bottle-blonde, though I knew that she was naturally flaxen.

As she slowly wended her way between the canvas dwellings, I felt a dull thud in my bosom as I considered Hannah and what little I knew of her. Seeing her in the plain light of day, she looked like a ghost, and I wondered what the bleached shell of her body had once contained. Regardless of her circumstance, I found that I cared for her. I didn't yet know it, but the experiences of that morning had provided the solid foundation for more than just a mutual respect between us, for in time, in our many years together in the future, our relationship would grow into something akin to familial love. That potential outcome was far from my mind that morning in Bela. Instead, though I left the thought unvoiced, it occurred to me that rather than trying to follow Hannah away from Greenhaven, I might ought to have offered to take her home along with us.

* * *

Before we left Bela, there was a painful moment. I almost think Abigail was avoiding Ellie, but of course it was only fair to say a proper goodbye.

Debra tightly held her daughter in her arms as if fearful of letting her go. Abigail smiled as pleasantly as she could, but I was well aware of how attached she had become to the lassie in the past day, and it was painful for her to see Ellie in another woman's arms, even if it was her mother.

Ellie sat up in Debra's arms and kicked her feet. She looked to Abigail and held out her hand. Abigail took it and gave her a gentle squeeze before letting her go. Ellie held up her arm and gave that sort of bairnish salute that is more a flexing of the fingers and thumb than an actual wave. Abigail returned the favour. Then to Debra she said, 'Keep a sharp eye on her. I could swear she vanished before my very eyes a few times.'

Debra smiled and said, 'I know. That's how I lost her in the church yesterday morning.'

Then Abigail turned and we began to walk away. From behind us, Ellie quietly said, 'Good.'

We looked back to her, but she had laid her face against her mother's bosom and shut her eyes.

* * *

We didn't have to cross back over via the underground tunnel. A path had been hastily cleared through the trees by the lads as it seemed the days of hiding the queerness of Bela from the world were quickly coming to an end.

On the other side, we passed the smouldering remains of the *Arcadia House* without comment. Abigail barely cast her eyes aside at the rubble with its pirling reek seemingly ascending all the way to heaven in the still air.

We had our choice of horses.

I could tell that Abigail's mind was distant for one of the beasts was a beautiful Palomino and she neglected to comment upon his golden coat and white mane. Rather, she remained silent as I helped her mount side-saddle and then climbed atop my own beast. We got the horses running at a comfortable, light trot on the road leading southwest from the remains of the *Arcadia House.*

After some quiet distance was passed, I looked once to my lassie's face to see tears on her cheeks, though, despite having left a bit of her heart behind in Bela, she never did look back. I understood the truth that for a brief time she had entertained the hope that some unfortunate circumstance might have resulted in the orphaning of Ellie, and that she might have played mother to the bairn for more than just one very long night and morning. But, of course, it was best that I had found Debra unharmed to claim her daughter.

During the past twenty-four hours, it seemed that Debra had come to realise that Alexandra was correct about one thing. Ellie was perfect, and she was blessed to have her for a daughter. I found myself praying that she would never once forget it for the rest of her life.

After a few miles, the road re-joined the original path we had been following the previous night and we continued south towards Venice. The trees began to crowd in on us again and created a canopy over our heads. Storms brewed somewhere beyond their covering branches. There were a few flashes of lightning barely visible through the close-knit leaves and thunder brattled our bones, but for all the atmospheric fash it never did rain upon us.

Mary and Abigail return in

Yet the Sea is Not Full

Their baggage ready, their tickets bought, Mary and Abigail are mere steps from boarding the ship that will sail them home to safety and a peaceful life in Greenhaven when a man seeking vengeance for the death of his brother at Mary's hand ensnares Abigail and uses her as bait to lure the longest lass into a trap from which she may never escape. Evading a posse of crazed lawmen seeking the enormous bounty placed on her head by a mysterious businessman, Mary races to discover her lover's hidden location while Abigail must put her heart on the line in order to navigate through the emotional tempests conjured forth by a madwoman whose secret past contains the key to survival in a house where insanity rules. As her enemies become ever more desperately violent in their attempt to capture her, Mary reluctantly turns to the one left-handed skill she possesses with which she is certain to win the day. In the end, the rivers may run red, yet the sea is not full...